Dark Pleasures &

Enchanting Pains

From the Life of

K. K. Foster

Dedicated to my LGBT+

First Edition

ISBN: 978-1-69-232912-9

Chapter One

-Dominion tastes for a one-eyed Cowgirl

Storming through the front door with his blanket flowing in the air behind him, Noah listened to the sound of their home in the buff. He could only hear the sound of the blanket gently resting to the floor behind him. Jordan stood outside the door peeking in to watch her man at work, and protect his back.

Quickly, he took through the foyer, up the split stairs, and tore into the bedroom ready to fight. Jordan waved for Samira to drive away before coming in cautiously, behind him.

Noah ran to the broken clock on the wall, stuck at 3AM, and got to the small safe behind it. Punching in the number, he drew his mean, Walther, 9mm PPX handgun, and grabbed Julian's small but, mighty Walther, PPS M2, 9mm sub-compact handgun. Grabbing the preloaded magazines, he loaded both of them with the clips, when the hall floor creaked. Instantly, he scrambled to the end of the bureau, and got on his knees facing the door, and sighted his 9mm pistol on the doorway...waiting. With her pistol, he pointed it to the wall next to the door, only lower. Both guns led the sound as it approached.

As the creaking vanished and returned closer, his breathing got smooth, and was going to cap this rapists blonde Stick-Bitch once and for all. A long flow of black hair was tossed in front of the doorway, and he waivered with relief it was his Texas bride. She tossed her hair in front of the doorway again, and he came rushing to her, and handed his thick, hourglass, and very short Cowgirl, her gun.

Instantly, his now armed bride re-took command of him, her Alibis, and her secrets.

"Noah, sweep upper levels, I will take the main floor, and meet me at the basement steps. Boots on. Understand?" She asked after her orders, and Noah nodded. He was intent, but I think Jordan had less mercy in the moment.

Quickly, they scattered going separate ways. Jordan crept through the kitchen and into the dining room listening for any leads. If Rachael or anyone working for Rachael, was in the house, they would find them. She checked the family room and heard Noah upstairs searching rooms. Immediately, she rounded the interior, opening all the closets quietly, and looked out the kitchen window to make sure the backyard was safe. She heard the sound of the door to the garage open in the dining room, and she dashed over to the room at the ready, and got on one knee with her one eye not behind her eyepatch, looking down the sights, at the door. Her voluptuous Texas rear, pulled the back of Samira's stretch jeans down again, to bubble out. As her finger warmed up the trigger, with her good-eye looking long down the barrel into the dark garage, she picked up movement. Noah was quickly dashing through the garage, searching. Jordan exhaled her tension and looked around for signs of disturbance as she removed her finger from the trigger, and exhaled her nerves. She knew Rachael had been there because she asked her to bring her things from the house. She opened the fridge to see Noah's chalice for her, sitting there, full of male seed and

4

undisturbed, and their two missing cell phones on each side of it.

Her eyes looked up into the distance, as she watched Rachael pour seed into her vagina at the hospital, claiming it was from Noah. "AH SHIT!" She whispered in her raspy, trying-to-heal voice whisper, and stomping the ground with her right boot to release her quick anger and fear. Noah came rushing out of the dining room into the kitchen, and without telling him what she discovered, they stormed the basement; guns at the ready. She was really going to shoot Rachael, now. Jordan hoped Rachael was letting Noah jerk off for her at the hospital, and bringing the seed to her. She really hoped that was the case.

Walking back up the stairs, Jordan slapped nude Noah on the ass with her gun, and he rushed to get away from her chuckling. Jordan took chase, and ran through the living room behind him, laughing. As he dashed back around the kitchen, Jordan stopped in the living room, and pulled her scrub top off, exposing her smashed breasts to him, and waited. She held her gun, perched between her beautiful, sagging breasts, and exposed her large, scared nipples to the world inside their home, without reservations this time. She kicked her big round hips to one side with her other hand on it and waited.

Noah peaked around the corner, and all he saw was what he had not been allowed to see, enjoy, without guilt, for their entire marriage Accord. His smile dropped along with his arms, and love started to erect his monument, and his smile. His eyes were wide open to the beauty of those big, dark saucer-size areola, with a light-colored, scar line down the center of each one.

"Jordan, you are sexy! WOW! Thank you, Cowgirl. Can I kiss them?" He started to step into the room anxious to kiss them in the daylight. "You...I don't know what to say...but WOW!" He choked his words to her. Likely a side effect of his erection.

Jordan smiled at his appreciation, and quickly pointed the gun at his face, dropping her smile, and his. She let the silence fill the entire house before she put down her boot...at gunpoint. Jordan was not playing well with others, even if she was half naked.

"Noah, put your weapon on the carpet now. You are under arrest for raping Julian. NOW!" She whispered in a raspy pitch, and jammed her gun at his face, ten feet away. Noah's eyes drew wider and having been shot once before by his loving wife Julian, he reached out and dropped his gun to the carpet, and placed his hands up in shock and fear.

"What is happening here, Jordan?" He said in a higher pitch voice, not to upset the arresting officer. His erecting monument changed its little mind, too.

"New rules, Noah James. There will be no more IDentifY in this house. Understand? No more sex under IDentifY-EVER AGAIN! IDentifY Personalities of SANICS's Dissociative Identify Disorder Covers Program, will be destroyed as soon as possible."

With the familiar growl in her voice, and more forceful, she demanded of him, "Did you think you and your Alibi could rape Julian, and get away with it, and wait for the next time? My tits have enough scars from the last rapist, and remind me every day of my life of rape." When Noah started to answer her, he knew something was terribly wrong, and raced to remember everything Rachael had warned

6

him about the fragmenting and zombie brain. His head slowly shook, in fear from confusion, and the only other time she pointed a gun at him, she shot him.

"Pick up that IDentifY mirror off the ledge next to you. NOW!" Her Texas voice tried to bark but, it was held back by sore cords, so she articulated her words in their raspy whisper and gun pointing, "AND...USE...IT! He was pinned down again, just like with Rachael. Only one had raped him, and he had raped raped on-this one, and the victim was armed this time. "Goodbye, Jon." She said, as he got the mirror.

His voice was shaking, "I can't IDentifY. It didn't work at the hospital, remember?"

"IDentifY, Noah NOW!" She growled at him jamming the gun forward. Tipping the toe of her right boot into the carpet, and pulling it back slowly, she carefully planned her attack. His time to cooperate, was running short.

In a rush of anxiety, "IDentifY, Noah," he said to the mirror.

She adjusted herself for more support by spreading her legs a little, and re-gripping the gun with both hands to fire. Brashly she said, "Turn a little, and let me see your face when you IDentifY."

Noah held the mirror up, and did it again for her. "What is going on Jordan? Are you going to arrest me now? Come nearer me and put your gun down, Baby. I love you." He pleaded for her.

"NOW!" He held the mirror back up to his face, and tilted so she could see his eyes during IDentifY.

"IDentifY, Noah," and looked to see tears building up in her one seen eye.

"Now toss that mirror on the couch closest to me, Cowboy. I don't know what you have been doing with Rachael for days, or what she told you. WE! Are not taking any chances." Jordan's tone was every bit the Personality who stood over him weekly with her arms crossed, and forced him to masturbate as she stared at him, emasculating him for Julian's control. It was a ritual of her OCD; needed to feel balance in the bedroom, since Julian was a submissive Southern Woman at all times. He knew Jordan's tone real well, and she waited, staring him in his pretty, brown eyes. She rustled with just getting this over with but, she was too nervous, too wet, and too happy to shoot. Just like the last time she shot him, years ago.

Jordan stepped over to the couch watching him closely, and grabbed the mirror with her left hand and looking into it, "IDentifY, Julian," she said into the mirror. She tossed the mirror back on the couch, and stared at him with her eight hollow-point bullets pointed at his face. She did not speak, a she decided his life...again.

Outside the birds were singing, and traffic traveled down the streets of suburbia America. And she still didn't speak.

"Do you want to rape me again, Noah?" Her softer, raspy whisper carried through her pierced lips, and her body began to shake. Before he could answer, she grabbed her hair and placed some across her lips, and made sure her eye patch looked good. True signs of Julian. Her nipples began to tighten in the changing affect her mind was making.

Noah shook his head at her with his hands still up above his shoulders. He was very worried she was crashing and IDentifY was not working.

8

Tilting her head, "Why not, Noah?" She whispered seductively, keeping him at distance with the threat of a very loud bang. Or worse, a bang, bang. But, he detected a twang in her voice. It was the familiar Texas accent, only Julian had. He didn't know how to answer her. She waited him out and he just kept slowly shaking his head to tell her not to shoot as his limbs got colder, and he curled his fingers into a fist to get warm. She picked up his physical effects of fear, instantly.

Still a seductive whisper, she tugged at him for an answer. "Because I be havin' a gun, Noah? That what be stoppin' you from puttin' that dick in me, again. That fuckin' NOT TEXAS Wyomin' dick, Noah? 'That you shoved up my ass, and be rippin' my va-jay-jay apart with? The pain forced me into IDentifY Covers that you were not supposed to know about, to escape the brutal pain of yer' beatin' me. You brutalized me and my Alibis, Noah-ALL OF THEM! That was secret material, Noah James. You fragmented some thangs I am goin' to have to repair quietly-WITHOUT ANDREA AND RACHAEL AND THE AGENCY, and I need you to make sure it happens. Every one of my Alibis got to see and feel you beatin' me, Noah James. Alibis you didn't know about. Alibis that felt you ravishin' my body." She spoke softly as her emotions pushed the tears from her eye, "Ravishing my soul. I had no choice, but to fragment, and let them out to deal with the pain. I never meant for the Rape Therapy to be so brutal. Why? What happened to you? Why so brutal, Noah? Do you hate me?" She paused for an answer, and he could only shake his head, and feel the pain in his heart from the guilt, he could never escape.

"I don't know why you turned into rage on me. You raped me, Noah." Her gun shook at him,

9

and her eye leaked her tears, as a small smile began to emerge behind her gun. This was the sign that a decision had just been made.

"And you cured me of Simon, Noah. I love you so much," as her tears raced down her cheek.

He stared back. Noah was guilty by proxy. He knew it. His crashed Alibi would have known it. Now, he knew, her Alibis knew it, and worse, he could not remember most of her Rape Therapy.

Noah and her fragmented Alibis, watched her toss the gun onto the couch, and she looked back at him through her tears and as she cried, she curtsied to him. And in a whisper she made another new rule, "You can rape me as much as you want, Baby. I love you my Angel. I'm so sorry. Thank you for rapin' me, Noey." She ran to him as he stepped to take her into his arms crying, without hesitation. She immediately kissed him panting her love, as her boots hung off the floor, one knee bent, as their chemistry reunited completely this time.

Crying as she absorbed his emotions into her heart, she poured out hers, with a promise. "Rachael tried to destroy us, and I couldn't let that happen, Noey. God knows how much I be needin' your love. I be needin' yer' punishments."

"I love you more than anything, Cowgirl. I will kiss your ass forever, Baby."

Between her many wet kisses, and each other's tears sticking to each other cheeks, she told him, "Thank you for lovin' me."

"Thank you Julian Michelle, for being my wife and my Angel." Her reservations broke, and the room echoed her acceptance of his soft passion, that meant as much to her as his abusive passions...that were really her passions.

His reservations broke as her emotional reflection filled him, and cried with her as his chest shook from him trying to control himself in the moment. With her arms around his neck, and her sobbing buried into his neck, he held her off the floor with one hand on each bare cheek of her round Texas rear, Samira's pants just couldn't keep her rear covered completely. They put themselves back into each other's hearts, where they belonged...and without a wedge named, Rachael.

"I will never let you go, Noey. You cured me of Simon, Baby. You done took away my rape fears of his DNA living in my mind. You really are an Angel, Noey. My Angel. My Killer Angel. I promise Baby, I will submit to your will again...right now and forever. I will worship you as I worship God, Baby. I swear. I love you so much Noeyyy. 1 Corinthians 14:34." She embraced him harder after each time she spoke. Happy to be back into his arms without feeling the weaponized guilt, Rachael had worked into her subconscious. Both her knees bent as her hair dangled between them and below them.

She collapsed into her own bawling cry as it hit her again, that her fear of Simon was cured. He had haunted her for ten years, and handicapped her marriage, and her life, leaving her with guilt over both.

Though her outbursts of emotions handicapped her for the moment, she managed to whisper to him, "Mark 10:8 and 9, Noeyyy!"

Nodding to her, "I love you so much, Julian. You are my beautiful, brilliant Southern Woman. I love you so much. I will never leave you, Tomboy. I am by your side, ALWAYS!" He said between his almost-choking sobs over her shoulder. Gently, he grabbed some of her hair and placed it in his own lips, and reclaimed the love of his life, after the long, ten-year Accord, infected with Rachael. This was a new beginning for both of them.

He stepped into the living room carrying her, "Psalm 37:26, King James" she whispered with her tears, "My King Noah James is merciful and yer' seed is blessed. Thank you for rapin' me, Noey. I love you. Thank you for punishin' me. Thank you, Noey, for understanin' me." Going up the split stairs to the hallway, she kept crying out her emotions and words. "I'm so sorry, Noey, for lettin' Rachael get between us. Genesis 3:16, my Love. My desire is for my husband and he shall rule over me."

Turning into the bedroom, Julian reached for the digital radio on the sink counter and carried it, as he carried her. Noah gently laid her onto their bed, and when he tried to get up, she would not let go, as her whispering tears continued. He picked her up again smiling, and stepped onto the bed so they could lay together in the middle. She had to give her whispers to the man who had never questioned her disorders, quirks, religion, and became the rock to her and her children. He held her, streaming his tears into her hair and face. He would make her happy again, since sexual pain was always her best cure.

Chapter 2

-Hostage of Essence feels the pain

She started singing to a love song from Beyonce, and felt him tugging at her boots. Appreciating him taking her right away, to refuse something she so wanted, he rescued her from the mondegreens she sang, with rewarding comeuppance.

She scooted away as he got up to take them off of her. She rolled Samira's pants down in the front, since the back was already well below her big butt, and she smiled at him with the humiliation of fact, and glowing in anticipation.

He tugged at her stretchy pants, and she arched her back to help in any way. Snapping her fingers at him, she pointed to the rolled up waistband stuck behind her exceptionally fat Mountain of Venus, her favorite humiliation fact, and he jerked them off her huge bump, and whisked them into the wall behind him. She immediately spread her legs for him, and rubbed herself sore Venus mountain, as he worked her boots back on.

"She's hairy. I'm sorry, Noey. I won't let it happen again. My mound is like a C-cup size. That's why you shave her every morning." He crawled between her legs, and kissed her thigh all the way down to her sore, still purple and blue, C-cup size mound with Texas labia, and gently kissed them from the bottom up. Sucking up her stream from her Mountain, she seeped for him from her precious pocket, and onto the bed below. He rubbed her bruised thickness against his tongue, lips, and beard to carry her precious scent to her mouth, and climbed up on her, as she instinctively covered her breasts with one arm. His well-cut, naturally tanned, eight-pack abs, leaned into her flat, pale-White stomach.

Noah noticed it, and as he got over her breasts, she slowly pulled her arm away puffing short breaths of anxiety, and laid both hands into her hair, and down to her side to tug the inadequacy fears nibbling at her. She felt the guilt of denying him her breasts for so many years, yet, felt the strength of her devotion pushing her to give access to this last personal quirk, left by Simon. He smiled at her warmly, and finally, he glowed to the breasts that had only been ghosts in their marriage. She tingled with fear and excitement, as she read him admiring her motherly breasts.

"They really are beautiful, Julz. I have wished for this day since our first date. I snuck peeks every time you breast fed." She chuckled at him embarrassed. *It feels like first date,* she thought, *AND I'm puttin' out.* She smiled at herself, remembering the joke-rule she always told Rachael; 'Big girls have to put out on the first date, because they are big girls.' But, Julian never said it was because they wanted to.

"They sag a little. I have breast fed two babies...and pumped a lot for YOU!" She was begging for compliments. "I breasts fed Ally for four years."

"Yes, but you only let me suck them in the dark a couple times. The kids saw them more than me." He smiled as he softly kissed her left nipple.

Her tone picked up at him as he teased her nipple stimulation, "I'M SORRRRRY! I'm sorry for my irrational fears of Simon, and maybe been takin' it

14

out on you a little," abashing from the honesty. "I be promisin' Noey, I will never deny them or anythang to you again...anythang. I want you to own me, and all of me. I need you to own all of me. Not just my hair, body, and conjugal. I really want to feeeeel owned by you. Our Rape Therapy made me feeeeel owned...and ohhhhh how I felt owned afterwards. It would have been even better had I woken' up to you holdin' me...but Rachael fucked that up on us. Like she has for so long while still pretendin' to be my friend." He kissed her with a smile for her reassurance.

"I really be needin' you to keep me in my place...for us...and our kids-my Angels. For God. Ephesians 5:24, Noey, I will submit in everythang to you, as I do the Lord. Songs of Solomon 7:12 Noey James, my 'pomegranates are in bloom, there I will give you my loves.' Let you and our children, forever drink from my pomegranates, Noey. Punish me with love and pain, to keep me in my place." She really was anxious to finally, be able to show herself to him, in every way, like she did Rachael. Maybe showing her breasts so freely will remove a few other fears.

Noah slowly rubbed his short beard on her nipples, tickling one of them, and the other tickled, just not as much. His manhood was throbbing to the new rules and her nipples reached for his attention. Tasting them, he licked across her large areola and curling it from the cool blow, following. She felt the tease warm her entire vulva. He noticed the teeth marks from someone recent, yet he licked her wounds as he always had, and hoped it would all work out.

Quickly, she offered, "Rachael bit me in an argument. I swear," and he kissed them softly as

15

she put her hands on his back, and tugged on her hair with both of them. This was her quick method of managing rushing anxieties.

"Proverbs 5:19 thy Dominion, let my breasts be satisfin' you at all times, Noey, and ravish you with all my love. May we be exhilarated with the one you'z love and I love you'z. I ask fer' yer' fergiveness as you have given me my Exodus of a rapist named Simon, by raping his rape, of me. Phobia against Phobia, Noey. Disorder against Disorder." He drove her eyes back to the long lost pleasure she once endured, before her tragedy, and left her work Mottos behind.

She tightened her back muscles to push into his mouth, and he swallowed her nipple in acceptance of her pomegranate offering. She felt as if her final gift to him would satisfy them both, and her reward was the teasing pain drifting through her partially, sensitive nipples.

Kitty knew how to respond. Her wetness forded its way through the thick, dark-tipped labia and rushed her nerve endings with exploding warmth. As usual, she leaked from under the Venus mound down the center of her swollen glands, and into her precious Texas entrance, to where it was enjoyed the most. Julian sang softly with the music, and silently begged for his return, to the Heart of Texas. Her Southern upbringing required euphemisms for sexual parts. Her Heart of Texas was the special spot inside her love canal that his eight-inches of manhood, could suffice.

She whispered to his strong desires, since she was not allowed to ask for pleasure, only punishments for pleasure. "Song of Solomon 1:13 Noey, my well-beloved unto me a bundle of myrrh which lies all night betwixt my breasts.' He shan't be

16

denied forever more, my Cowboy." Her religious tongues, always lit her own fire.

"Drink from my breasts, not from the cup, so Dominion. Furthermore shall my milk enchant our love, never spoil, and grace thee with my seed. Should you seed me. HINT! HINT!" Noah slid his right hand down into her wet ring of fire, and soaked them. Her instant moans promised him wonderful things from Texas.

His seed-soaked fingers from Texas, moistened her large, dark areola and he spread her wetness over her remaining bruises, given by his hand. She grinned at the embarrassment, though, the more he spread her wetness on her, the sexier she felt. His left hand embraced the left nipple, and pinched it harshly as she moaned in pain and need. He knew what she was offering, and he was taking his time to burn her fire, and kiss all the bruises, before he gave her more of them. Julian reached down to feel her clitoris touch her fingers, and he slapped her hand away in recent ownership of her conjugal. She didn't have her gun now, and gifted he was, with her ownership desires.

"Are my boobs handsome enough, Noey?" she asked him enjoying the chemical triggers that were reoccurring inside her body. He moaned his approval and stretched her sore nipple out causing her the right kind of pain. Even though she winced and held her breath a moment, her moans told him the pain was appreciated.

Noah, immediately looked up at her, stretching nipples with Rachael's teeth marks, and she felt his doubt. She was quick to answer his non-verbal question. "We got into a fight at the hospital. She bit me." She started her growl as she raised her whisper, DO NOT LET HER STEAL THIS MOMENT!

17

She was always good at stealing moments." She stared at him, and let him feel her jerk her hair twice.

"During sex?" He inquired, while not doing to her what she wanted done to her, at the time she wanted it done to her, by him.

"NOEYYYYYYY PLEASE-"

"NO WAIT! That is how she got the black eye?" Noah said it with encouragement; tilting his already tilted head, more, as the puzzle pieces fit together.

"She has a black eye?" Julian asked surprised and cheerful.

"Oh yeah, Girl! Shiner like...well, like yours Babe. I'm sorry." Julian's look of concern returned to the smile in her eye, and she immediately remembered her eye patch, and pulled it off into her hair, to display her reading material to him, completely.

"Do not apologize for punishin' me ever again. I will never cover my body again...UNLESS...you command me, Noey. NEVER! Don't apologize because it weakin's my feelin's of bein' owned and...desired." Wanting the ego boost back, she returned to the fight to brag, not recognizing, Rachael was the topic during the love making, thus, stealing the moment, again.

"I roundhouse kicked her in the face for threatenin' my Alibis." She had to tell him the exciting part at least. After all, he taught her hand-to-hand combat, after sleeping with him on the first date in college.

He manhandled two fingers into her wet, sensation center, and rolled her eyes back as the signals reached her reward center, attached to her vineyard. *That will shut her up,* he learned. He

18

immediately tasted her and bunged her again, letting her sip the wine off his two-finger chalice. In her mouth, she pushed her thick wine to her palate, and slowly let it string down on the back of her tongue with lusting tingles. Her finish was perfect, and she would not swallow yet, as the essence lifted into her other senses. Noah got up, and made his way down to her Fat Kitty, inhaling her bouquet as she watched him bury his face between her thick thighs, licking her excess wetness, and tasting from the enology flow whence her Venus Mountain. Julian savored her palate finish, as he tasted from her vineyard. Her fingers found their way into her wetness deep under her big mound-mountain, and dabbed it behind her ears, and rubbed it on her nipples before licking it off her fingers. She looked down at his eyes hiding behind her mound, and pleasing her. *Who owns who, Cowboy,* she thought.

"I love my fat Texas mound, Noey. It really does flow like the Rio Grande, instead of a Snail Creek, back'ome." She heard him sucking in her juice from the bottom, and delicately up her crack to the Mountain crest, and the sound tingled her loins with burn.

"Please give me some more?" She whispered so no one would hear her dirty request, a power taken from her in the Bible, and enforced in her Southern Life. He continued to inhale her fresh wine until his mouth was full and his palate satisfied. She could feel who owned who, in this wet moment. "Song of Solomon 4:16 Awake, O north wind, and come, thou south, blow upon my garden, that the spices thereof may flow out. Let my beloved come into his garden and eat its pleasant fruits." Her raspy whisper carried to him the words of God, permitting her dirty desires to be fulfilled, without her feeling guilt.

Mounting her, stirred her inhibitions, and her chest rose as her skin tingled over her entire body. Keeping her hair in her hands, he pushed just the warm head of his penis into her aching Kitty, and using his arms to push her bent knees back into her breasts. Her heart fluttered when she felt its warmth of being trapped. He would not waste his leaking seed, and leaned his tall, tan, muscular body over her, and flexing his pecks for her, he leaned in to kiss her, ripping her hair from her hands, and smothering her body with his. Fears rushed her, and she panted at their stimulation.

She opened her mouth just inches below his and he let her seed slowly pour into it. Kitty started spraying like a fire hose at a fire, as the flutter interrupted her breathing.

"Notre amour livrera nos circonstances ensemble," he whispered to her.

Julian reached for her four feet of long black hair, and slid some of it into her wet centerfolds below. She guided him back in taking small panting breaths, and keeping his leaking inside her, before he knocked on her Heart of Texas. He knew her lovemaking necessities after so many years of being inside her with her. He felt himself leak, and teased his meatus in her wet warmth, as his cock pushed her long hair slowly deeper into the Heart of Texas. She twisted a rope of hair and put it into his mouth, and kept her blackened, blue eyes swimming in bloody white, on his brown eyes, as she roped the last of it for her.

"Notre amour livrera nos circonstances ensemble," she whispered back to him with subtle tears in her eyes. Please be gentle, Noey? I have stitches inside there. Let's just take it easy, and take from me what you need. I promise my husband; your seed shan't be wasted. 1 Corinthians 7:4, submission to your will..."Genesis 1:27." She kept her eyes to his and he knew it was time to please his bruised owner. Without having to look, she looped her hair and slid it into her mouth as a pacifier, before he kissed her.

Gently her labia pulled on his thick shaft, and he slowly forced its leaking head through her warm, burning need, and her eyes rolled back, until he hit her healing cervix.

"AAAAHHHHHH NOEY! STOP! Oh Jesus. Baby. I'm so sorry, Noey." She began to cry through her pleads and covered her face in shame as he thrusted and finally stopped.

"I'm so sorry, Baby. I can't take it. It will tear my stitchins' and not heal properly. I must remain fertile, Baby. My uterus was crushed and my cervix torn, Baby." Noah pulled out of her and kissed her to silence her cries, and instinctively, she started pulling on her hair, and made sure it did not exit her vagina.

He spoke up, "We are fine, Baby. I will just fuck you in the ass." He whispered, knowing his wife would never let that happen because he didn't like it.

"What?" She said, no longer crying. Looking at him with excitement in her mind, she saw his smile, and felt the tease of his humor burn inside her yearning rear. *Of all the timing for him to FINALLY offer to do me in the ass, he picks a time when I have to say no,* she thought.

"Tomorrow. Please?" she offered, hoping he would think she was serious. "I have stitches there too, but you can if you have to. I won't say no. I'm

21

not allowed to say no. I don't want to say no, Noey." She reached down and took his manhood, and put it back inside her fat Kitty, and nodded at him taking a deep breath to fight the destruction. Noah, slowly pushed his way into the Heart of Texas, and she whimpered and clenched her teeth, nodding. She kept her rope of hair inside her cheek to pacify herself, as she began thrusting into him, and he slowly worked up the pace. Knowing her well, her pulled her hands to her sides, and held her against her will.

Noah felt the rush of her pleasurable gift, and his sack slapped into the familiar, and wonderful sound of the wetness. It drove up his pace, further. He was actually pretty close to seeding her already. When he looked back up at her, she was crying silently with a terrible cringe on her battered face, as she let him have what he needed. He pushed it deep and held it to give her more pain, as she held her breath. Finally, he pulled out, denying her his seed, which she had rights to, by the Bible.

Exhaling relief, she let her cry loose, and he rolled off of her, and slapped her pussy extremely hard. She hushed instantly, and smiled from his mild abuse. He slapped her fat labia again, and she screamed the best she could, showing her love for it, and he slapped it again leaving his fingers marks all over her wet, bruises. She opened her legs up more inviting him, and he slapped her again. Staying shut, her eyes never rolled forward.

Waiting for more, she encouraged his sexual abuse in whisper, "Let thy husband render unto his wife due benevolence: and likewise also the wife unto the husband."

Shoving her legs together, he rolled back on top her and fingered her fat Venus Mountain

22

upward, and slammed his impatient cock up under her mound and sunk it in four or five inches. Julian moaned in pain and shook as his wet dick slid deep under her bruised Mountain jamming her, and sliding his warm girth along her puffed clitoris. She wailed in wonderful pain as he fucked her, and kept her legs together under his. He was taking what he needed, from the Woman who wanted to be owned.

She immediately tried to slide her wrist under his hands as the pain rushed in each thrust, and he trapped both of them to the sheet. Her moans encouraged him as he stirred her Hostage Fetish within. With each pounding, she jerked cringing and screamed, as her mountain bulged upward, separating from her pelvic bone. He fucked her so fast, her screams never finished as he slid along her pulsating, seed-covered clit. It hurt so wonderfully, as the pain started to blend with important signals; flexed her cervix for more pain signals. He stared at her breasts as they shook off the sides of her chest, and sucked her hair into his mouth. This was ownership. Her fetish teased her mind, as she struggled to get her arms loose, of the man who had raped her a week ago. With each pull, he watched her mouth briefly smile over and over as it stimulating the fear. He knew what she was doing.

His thrust winced her over and over as she heard and felt the burn of constant lubrication pour out her canals, and a cock separating her fat mound. When he fucked her Venus Mountain, it was one long, painful orgasm that never stopped, or let her breath. She roughed through her Proverbs under her weak breaths to fight the terrible thrusts stretching her skin from the bone, "Proverbs 31:12, the Wife does the Husband good at all. Wife does

23

good to Husband at all times. PLEASE GOD IT HURTS!"

Finally, she ripped into louder gasps and begged him with her crying. He did not have to stop fucking his hostage. He owned her; her body; her pleasure; her heart. He pounded her harder and harder to give her more pain, as her bruised Venus Mountain jerked and shook, high above her flat stomach. The long orgasm was in effect and her pussy drowned with wonderful, wet sounds. She screamed and gasped and screamed and gasped turning her head away from him, and finally, had to tell him. "I'm gonna' get sick!"

He didn't stop, as her gag reflexes held back her heaves for the moment. Her chest jerked as she noticeably held her mouth shut. The pain was just too long and stimulating. Not a second too late, he let out his scream and jammed it into her pussy below, as she put his chest to her chest. She jerked screaming and tried pulling her arms away, as her larynx sent sharp pains through her voice, and silenced her to a closed mouth, high pitched moan of ownership. He seeded the Heart of Texas, and gave her the reward. She squeezed him to hold him in longer, and cried as she needed, in more ways than one. He just held it in there, and didn't thrust her as the pulsating cock filled her desires with hot, sweet seed that she owned. His screams grew louder as his man-machine lubed her parts, and shook his entire body.

He kept squirting into her as he jerked into a twist of his body sucking on her hair, and finally, she let out her exhale of exhaustion from her long, pain driven orgasm, now sticky from being his wonderful feeling cock, being forced into her body.

Thankfully, his drained penis began shrinking inside her, and she felt instant relief, in her lower stomach.

Still fighting back the feeling of opiates, and dizziness, she whispered her devotion to him. "I'm your Southern Woman, Noey. Thank you Texas and Wyomins' for your gift." The burning pain felt wonderful down there.

He slowly pulled out of her, and rolled off of her to the side, and she got up fast, burying her face in the fresh, wet stain on the sheet. Both their seeds had leaked out, and she panicked. Noah got up, and she got on her knees to stick her ginormous Texas ass in the air for attention as she licked up his seed. He knew his other job, and slid his three fingers under her mound and parted the heavy, dark curtains, and scooped up her seed with his as she pushed it out of her used pussy. She slowly immediately turned around, and licked his fingers clean, as he smiled at her dirty obsession.

After her organic snack, she slid down on the bed, and rolled over on her back, and fingered herself for any loose semen. Finding a quantity of hers and his blended essence, she rubbed it on her face and mouth, before licking her fingers. Noah smiled at her warmly, as he felt the devotion. Her Fetishes were everything he was used to, and loved about his wife.

"Next time, you are lickin' me clean, Noey James." She declared. "You promised to snowball with me every day. I'd be lovin' you to snowball with me from now on, My Love. Please?"

He climbed up on her, stroking the last bit of his seed out, and she gladly accepted it into her mouth. After sucking down his shaft to clean it, and rubbing his balls with her hand, she gladly reminded them both, "Genesis 38:10, thy wife shan't waste any seed, and lives to have more. Thank you fer' lovin' me." She winked with a grin.

Noah finally spoke up, "I need to brush your hair, Baby, I have really missed or morning routines." She smiled warmly at him, and got to the floor quickly, and leaned back against the bed. The warm taste of his cum still lingered in her mouth, and she hoped it would last. Julian felt at home again, and finally exhaled completely.

Chapter Three

-Painful Converses with Creaking Doors

Fussing with her cold phone, she hit send with bravura, and felt her anxiety level fall, only to drift into the next thought, to bring her anxiety in from another direction.

Text from Jordan to Rachael: You are fired from SANICS, effective immediately. Report to field office Columbus-Drew Vances, Field Director. I have notified him of the situation and your conduct. BACK OFF BITCH! Do not contact me or my family or you will be ARRESTED!

Nibbling on protein bars and sipping on near-frozen Lone Star beer, Jay wagged her new Junk Gypsy, 'She Who Is Brave,' tall Honey western boots in the air, as she laid on her stomach in bed him, nude. Needing a chug of her finest Texas beer, she laid on her right side giddy as her Momma's Jaybird, as Noah finished off his beer, and she chased it. Noah reached for another Lone Star, smiling at her with appreciation, for letting him, love her.

After rinsing her palate, the back of her head came down to rest next to his chest on the bed, as she scooted her feet to the side of the bed, and rested on her back. Noah had put his Cowboy boots on that Samira had rescued from the hospital, and shifted on his left side facing her with smiles and spills. Momma Julian liked to hear those spurs rattle, because it meant he would rattle her.

"Rape Therapy? Who be knowin'
like...that...that...that it could be like that, and work
on me. I have no fear whatsoever, Baby. It is like
you...you...cured me of a disease or took my
virginity, AGAIN!" She chuckled, as did he. "I can't
wait to write this paper, and my diary."

"The first couple-three days was rough
though. I admit but, my heart feels pure again. My
soul feels like it's been bleached of Simon's stain
and shines your watermark. I really do feel his DNA
in my brain facing to a lame horse. You are my
hero, Baby. As always, Noey." She smiled and
tapped her beer with his.

Noah, was staring at her nipples. There is no
other way to describe it. Frustrating years of only
getting to touch them, or feel them in the dark had
taken his toll, and he was taking in as much as he
could...while he could...in case she relapsed or
changed her mind. He was making the dirty plans of
sucking, fucking, making them sticky with his seed,
and finally, milking them straight to his mouth.

"I love the curves of your breasts. Your
nipples are huge, Julian. As he reached over and
measured them with his thumb and finger, and her
saucers were still bigger.

"My nipples be the pointy brown thang in the
middle you liked to pull, and that part around it, be
called the areola. It helps Baby Angels feed...and
husbands with milk fetishes." She looked down at
his measuring courageously. They both had shared
her milk during pregnancy, but only Julian and the
kids got to drink it from the tap, in the light. He
wanted her pregnant, and today was not fast
enough. He was already planning to seed her again,
and again, and again.

28

"What do you thank? Noah?" His eyes were mesmerized by the size of the dark, brown area. "Noeyyy? Hello Noeyyy?" She shook her beer at him spilling it across his chin, and he looked up at her. She was smiling, still with a waning apprehension about them. "They love you too, Cowboy-All yours. Never will I hide them again, my Angel. Please feel free to well...make me scream yer' name, Baby. You WILL drink from'em after I'm pregnant, Noey. I promise. Nine months and I promise. Drink all day, and punish me all night." She was getting a little red under her black eyes but, she got the point across.

Noah kissed his thumb, and reached over and touched Julian under her bruised left eye, then kissed it for the other eye. Gently, he spread the kiss out massaging the swelling, and blood buildup underneath. She closed her eyes, and enjoyed his touch and manly smell. She was home. In her bed. No longer fearing her enemy, and realizing how much she missed him by sharing her devotion with Andrea.

"I am loving that eye patch, Julzie. I want you to wear it from now on when I make love to you." He whispered.

"Really? Every time, Noey?"

"Well...most of the time. I think you rock it. I am actually shocked I think you look hot being a Pirate."

Giggling, she asked, "Well, why don't we get one for you durin' love makin'?" She suggested it with love and hoping to get his light bulb to come on. But, you know men.

"I like that idea, Julz. Whenever I wear it, you have to wear it, and whenever you wear it, I have to wear it." He said with a glowing smile and watching her boobs shimmy, from her giggles. If

29

she could have rolled just the hidden eye, she would have, unfortunately, both rolled, and he saw it. Then, he removed her eye patch for battle.

"Noey Baby, I was rodeo'in a lot in the hospital to exercise Kitty. I need to rodeo three times a day, and we need to put Cowboy into Fat Kitty every day to see how she feels. I need to get all my toys workin' on her."

"I'm not sure-" She cut him off with an outburst.

"NO TEXAS PETE! That shit burns." She immediately back peddled, "Maybe a few times when she is better." She looked up at him to make sure he heard her confession, and he was waiting to finish his sentence.

"I can't be able to be here for all three-four-ten times a day you want to rodeo, Babe. How about Samira?" he asked.

"Thank you for lettin' Rachael Witness in the hospital. I would not be so heal-." Noah held his hand up slightly to stop her.

"I never gave you permission to have Witness in the hospital?" He said with a curious look on his face.

She got a little more urgent to prove him wrong, "You sent me a text sayin'-" He stopped her again.

"I didn't have my phone, Tomboy." He raised both eyebrows to her, and waited for another confession.

Her face lit up as her light bulb came on, "Rachael did it. Rachael had your phone. Gosh dang her," She said with a scowl expression. "She was playin' me...again. She was answerin' yer' text, Noey. Don't you see? Ohhhhh I get it now." She pierced her lips in admiration to her ex-lover. "She

30

was pretendin' to be you, sayin' 'leave Noah for Rachael,' 'Take the kids and go with Rachael'." Julian stopped to look up and think. "One kick was not enough-Bitch pulled my hair the wrong way. If that is possible? And Noey, I'm so sorry. This is all my fault." She put a finger to her chest plate, "My Fault. I saw Rachael taking over Andrea. I saw it, and should have done somethang about it. I designed our DIDCs with Andy. I love Andy. I need my Andy. She needs to crash Rachael into an Envelope. Bitch tryin' to be my Master."

Noah waited for her moment to finish, as she avoided referring to Andrea as her, Cuckquean. He had no clue, as he had not reviewed his phone yet. Julian let out a mighty exhale, and got up to go to their small bathroom off the bedroom. He could hear her filling up the cup with water, and then the water running changing sound, and without him seeing her, she took her medications, and other things.

Julian nodded in the mirror as mid-swallow of the first batch, she remembered his question, and spoke to him. "Samira, I be thankin' she might be an Angel, too. I got a moment with her in the hospital, and her soul was very pure. I got to look close into her windows. I have to wait to see her dimples, and...purge."

"You said that about Rachael." He reminded her. "What does 'Purge' mean, again?"

Purposefully skipping that sexual question, she led him away. "Noey, What all did Rachael and Andrea say to you when you were cuffed to the bed...were you there all three days. Food and water?" She needed to know some things in case she had to 'fix' some things.

With her still in the bathroom, he yelled it to her, "Julian, I'm grantin' you permissions to penetrate Fat Kitty when you need to. You know...to help her heal. I need her healed so you can make our baby Angel. I would like you to be fat, and barefoot by Christmas." He smiled at her warmly, expecting a big thank you. "Ten days only, Cowgirl. No longer."

She was shocked, and her expression was easy to read, as she retreated into deep thought and began jerking her hair immediately to the anxiety he was pushing. "Really, Noah? Really?" He nodded and sipped his beer as she peaked around the entrance at him from the bathroom doorway.

"I have never put anythang in Kitty since I was like...twelve. Just the sponge." She thought about it, and put her boot down. "No. I don't like this at all, Noah James. No. That is your duty, as the Dominion. Do not give me that power, and frustratin' choice. Please. I'm not." She leaned on the counter as her OCD fears bit her in the ass, hard and her hair got the abuse. "NOOOOO! She belongs to you. I don't want the choices. MY OCD CAN'T DO THAT!" She scoffed at him, as she came back to the bed. He ignored her resistant body language, because his word didn't need to put a boot down. He had the Bible to do it.

After his last guzzle, he laid the empty beer bottle on the bed, and packed his Copenhagen Long Cut Straight tobacco snuff. When he took out a pinch, Julian watched him put it in his lip, and she wanted it, but told herself, she was quitting. He pinched more, and began to answer her question.

"Stick-Bitch Rachael was naked the entire time. Every day, she came in and got naked, and played with herself in front of me tryin' to talk to me about you and IDentifY, and said you were crashin', and she was going to crash me, and..." He stopped short of his honesty.

"She said a lot of things and used IDentifY as different people...like Jenna. I am honestly having a hard time rememberin' everything she asked or told me Julz. She might have given me something to fuck up my memory." He looked down, and concentrated. "My memory is a fuzzy blend of it all."

Both hands wrapped her hair around them, for the long journey her nerves were getting ready to ask him for. She gently jerked on them simultaneously, and moved on the bed, to avoid him reading her body language and eyes. "Well Baby, did she talk about her and I, at all?" Finally, the word Jenna made it to Julian's brain that was more ready to lead the conversation than listen. We Woman have secrets that must be protected at all costs.

Blurting out for control of the conversation, "She claimed to be Jenna? WTF? Jenna was Med School IDentifY material...basic stuff we attempted for se........x." Julian's left side of her mouth lowered as one of them there secrets slipped out. She was not looking at him by the time she finished the word 'sex.' Slowly, she looked back at him, and he was still in thought. *Close one,* she thought, and not to her Alibis. Then, she quickly distracted using a classic verbal linked to male DNA programming-a sexual response elicits the penis brain to think, slowing the male mind down-DRAMATICALLY!

"My pussy feels really good after you fucked me like a Ho. Made me so wet, Noey. My pussy feels good, Baby. Thank you. My pussy is wet for your big dick. You be knowin' that, right?" She pondered as the signals went through the many regions of his

33

brain, and she slowly counted in her mind, *two, three, four, five, look,* and Noah looked up as she expected. He was none the wiser to the secret, to her slipped-secret. Take notes, Sisters. He heard the dirty words, and his penis brain prioritized them.

"I can rub her some more, Baby. Maybe kiss her a bit. I saw she still had bruising. I am sorry and I will never do that beatin' again." He said with guilty love and affections.

"Wellllll, let's not go that far. I want my Venus bruised regularly. I enjoy that. The big fat mound? I still want you beatin' that part." She responded, keeping the option on her side, "I was glad you took care of it. It was worth it, and judgin' by what you did to my Venus mound earlier, I thank you know why I love it abused and always sore. Now be rubbin' some coconut oil on yer' Tomboy, Cowboy-in your spurs, please." She leaned in and kissed him on the lips really fast, and smelled her essence on his beard and mustache.

She got up and rolled onto her chest, and waited for his caresses. She still had control of the conversation, and tossed her hair across the bed beside her, intentionally. He had her hair fetish too, and this was a good, minor distraction that could be used, if necessary.

"You know you can always just give me anal until I heal." She bravely offered. This was just a tactic of bogging down his thinking, and some truth by desire. "I never liked it but, I will let you have what you need."

His spurs rattled as he climbed over the back of her thick thighs, and dangled his penis and balls between them. He could look right down at her big, round ass cheeks and see her thick, dark labia smashed four or five inches down the inside of her thighs, and bulging out the backside. He spit tobacco juice on them, and laid his face dead center on her big Texas ass.

"Hey! Did you spit on her again, Noey? Why do you do that?" She asked somewhat playful, faking her disgust.

"Take me, please? Yer' my Dominion, Noey." She begged in her little girl voice, and he ignored her request. "I'm so stressed, I need..." She almost said it...another secret.

With his right cheek laying across her butt crack, he slid his legs down, and his spurred boots slide past hers. He was fourteen inches taller than her short five foot, and nothing height.

"Baby, if you lose this big ass. I am gone. I was never an ass man until the day you walked into my class, and I slammed you to the mat. You had on them yoga shorts and cowgirl boots, and when you hit the mat, you jiggled and made me an ass man, instantly." He snuggled her big round hips and salivated, letting the juice run out of his mouth into the crack of her ass, and down to her labia where it would burn a little excitement into her. She shook it from side to side, smiling from knowing she owned his desires.

Laying with her face on her right cheek at the head of the bed, she talked with half her face buried and her long, black hair lying over the right side of the bed, and hanging off the side. "Don't spit on my...your pussy again. Unless-" She stopped herself for her best loving, innocent wife voice, "You can nibble my fat cheeks back there Cowboy, and make Momma's big ass feel some love." She knew he would not resist his favorite foreplay torture.

He palmed both her cheeks roughly, and began kissing each bruise, and licking them.

Working toward the center, he licked all the way up her crack, and all the way back down, making her head rear back in intense Womanly sensations, as her mind instantly forgot to breath. He could see the muscles in her pale, blue skin back, just below her neck, flinch. He smiled at her response, and winked at her Longhorn Steer Tramp-Stamp, watching him.

Who has the power now? He thought. As he buried his mouth over her anus, and licked his Angel's dark desire. She squirmed, and shorted her moans to take the tantalizing sensations that made her flow instantly from her desire center, every time. Only humiliation could give her as much instant stimulation.

When he stopped, she dropped her exhausted face into the pillow exhaling her tension. He knew it, and she couldn't resist it. Inches from the Heart of Texas, she loved having her ass licked for all the right reasons, and maybe a few wrong ones. IF, there are wrong reasons for a man to kiss a Woman's ass.

"Rachael or Andrea-" he was quickly interrupted by the one getting her ass kissed at the moment.

"Rachael, not Andrea, is givin' me a headache with her shit." She blurted out between his licks, and realized, she couldn't think enough with his licks, to chat. "Go on Baby, sorry. Keep lickin' yer' Ark, please." She quickly exhaled as he worked her, and she worked him.

"Rachael said, you were life-flighted to Cleveland?" He asked improperly.

"No. I was...well, I don't be rememberin' that part. I woke up, I thank at, DoctorLands the next mornin', I thank. No. I don't thank I was life-flighted, Noey. She is lyin'...again. I am goin' to

36

have to train you better, Noah. No wait, if I do, you will know when I am lyin'. Scratch that idea. LICK ME, NOEYYYYY!" she said with her demands. "Lick every bruise and dent and...everythang back there. You know it relaxes me. Kiss my fat ass."

"I know Baby. I see the wet spot on the mattress under your Kitty, already. You don't have any cellulite. It's smooth and round, Tomboy." She worked her thick right arm under her body, fighting the squished boobs that got in the way, and rubbed her very sore mound.

"Because you spit on her. You know she gets wet from it."

♫ *Text Alert on Julian's Phone*

He bit her right ass cheek in different places making sure it hurt, and she busted out laughing and wailing as it rushed invigorating tingles up her spine. In an instant, the Man, was back in control of kissing Her ass.

As she shook it with laughter he went on, Rachael said-"

"Noah, please do not begin every sentence with 'Rachael said'. This is goin' to be a long day if you do. Okay?"

She pulled her elbows up to take pressure off her D-cups, and peered back at him over her shoulder to make sure she wasn't too harsh. She saw in his eyes she hurt his feelings a little.

"Yes-um." He uttered quietly and kissed her Venusian dimples to apologize. Julian laid back down and redirected him and looked at her phone alert.

37

Text from Anonymous Number: I have done everything for you. FAT BITCH! FIRED ME! HE IS GOING DOWN! HE RAPED ME TOO!

Julian dropped her face into her pillow growling, and pushed the phone to the side.

"Please kiss my ass, Noeyyyy, and tell me what the Cunt said. Lick me. You know what I need. I'm stressed, Baby."

Noah laid his cheek back down on her ass, and snuggled it with his gruff beard. Softly, he did what he was told.

"How come you never told me Rachael was really Jenna from your childhood?" His tongue barely worked its way into her sexy crack before she burst back up on her elbows, and stretching her neck to see him.

"WHAT?" He wasn't looking. "She ain't Jenna, Noah. That was a game we used to play in Med School. She is...was just screwin' with you. NOT MED SCHOOL! College. YES! It was in college we tried IDentifY games. 'Cunt wishes she was Jenna."

He kissed her Ark tattoo, and she rushed to cover her mistake. "I would know if she was Jenna. I dated Jenna until college, then I met Rach freshman year. Jenna has a barbed wire scar just above her va-jay-jay. Rachael doesn't." *Damn it*, she thought, *I did it again.*

"Am I really Noah or am I from Florida, and Noah is another IDentifY cover I can't get out-" she cut him off again.

"WHAT? What did you say?" She was aggressive in her Tomboy form, looking at him kiss her butt. She wiped her forehead to remove the anxiety squeezing it. Leaked stories about her past, true or false, and getting questioned by the man

38

one hides true stories from, can be stressful. Noah was her masterful interrogator but, if you dodged long enough, he got bored. *I have to be cautions, instead of aggressive,* she thought.

"Am I really Noah or is that a Dissociative Identity Disorder Cover and I don't know it?" He uttered it, keeping cover behind her naked cheeks, and licking at her labia bulging up between her thighs. He could feel the jiggle of her physical expressions to the answers.

"OMG! She was screwin' with you, Noey. You are my husband by Accord. Not some IDentifY cover. You are smarter than that. What is wrong with you?" She rolled over, and jerked him away from his dessert he was using for protection.

Confronted, he back-stepped his strategy. "Julian, I don't remember her giving me anything but, my memory is just blank from...I don't know what from. I remember her coming in and playing with her nipples and talking, but I can't really remember the timeline as it happened. She stared at him silently, searching for lies, for tale-tale signs of deception, and she felt safe that he was being honest about his fuzzy memory, and laid back down for him to worship her. Being less rough, he settled down on her rear again, as Julian wondered if Rachael drugged him.

"Did she give you any medication, Noey?" He shook his head not really remembering.

♫ Text Alert on Julian's Phone

"No. How long has the affair with Rachael really been going on...since College? Quickly turning back toward the headboard to avoid eye contact, she exhaled and knew she needed to be honest,

39

since Rachael likely told him everything to destroy their marriage, and he would likely remember it in pieces. Back on her elbows, she rubbed the stress from her face again, or the lies, and gave her best answer.

"It started in college Noey, and we died down after you and me was Accorded, and before Zachary was born, I pushed for it to end, and I..." She exhaled for a moment, "...I kept givin' in to her advances...sometimes. It is not her fault, Noey. It is mine. Sometimes, I just woke up in bed with her, and we did NOT violate the Bible...well we...DAMN IT!" She rubbed her face again, and worked her fingers through her hair on top of her head and jerked it. "We did. I let her inside my va-jay-jay, and that is when I started pushin' for it to end. I knew it was wrong. I let her help me in the hospital for us, and she turned on me...she turned on you...she turned on us."

Text to Julian from Anonymous Number: YOU LIE TO EVERYONE ABOUT YOUR DISORDER! I'M REPORTING YOU!

Julian through her phone off the bed growling at it, so she could not reach it, and buried her face in her pillow. "Julz, she showed me nude photos of you in the hospital...and other pictures and videos of you confessing to loving anal sex with Strangers." He stayed humble when he asked her. He needed to know the truth. Her hands and boots jerked into the air over her, and slammed back down on the bed. He softly kissed her ass, and let his tongue enjoy her pale skin on her voluptuous cheek. He purposely avoided the sensitive area, to see her response.

40

Both of them knew it was to keep them connected and communicating with their mutual interest at hand. She was giving and he was taking, and she was accepting and he was offering. This worked for them to get through the pain of honesty. Of course, kissing his favorite sexual feature of her, was her idea during their first argument.

She reached for the comfort of a fist full of hair, and pulled extra hard to the side, even though her face was still in the pillow. After five or six good jerks of it, she got up on her elbows facing the headboard, and not him, to formulate her sentence, and he reminded her.

"You have always denied me naked pictures of you." He rubbed his hairy chin down her spine and followed the outline of her Longhorn steer, and she blurted out her answer.

"WHAT DO YOU WANT ME TO SAY? I FUCKED UP! I FUCKED UP NOAH!" She grunted, and buried her face again in shame to speak. It was muffled by the pillow. "I will pray. I need to pray. MY GOD! I AM DYIN' INSIDE!" She shook her head as the skeletons kicked and beat on her closet door. Her biggest fear was if Emily, opened it. The thought of Emily made her raise her head to speak, but after she pushed her ass into his face to make sure, she was offering him, she wanted to continue holding each other for the answer.   "Noey, please believe me. I let her have those pictures to send to you before I knew she was turnin' on us. I asked her to take them, and send them to you. I was tryin' to lurer...luror...lurer...however the FUCK THESE CITY DWELLIN' PEOPLE SAY IT! LURE! FUCKIN' DYSARTHRIA!" She took a short breath and searched for calm.

41

"I can suck a big dick but, I can't be sayin' simple freakin' words." She exhaled her anger and took another calming breath and tone, as she looked back over her shoulder to see him out of the corner of her eye, "I don't know what to say. I...I was feelin' brave after our night. But know this, I will never say no to you now, because of my Simon fear bein' gone...I...Noah, I promise you, you can...I will never say no to you again. My slutty fat ass was showin' everyone in the hospital my tits. My-Not just Rachael. I really felt free. Please take nude photos of me. As many as you want. I have been wrong to deny you those privileges and I'm sorry. My fear cursed us...then and I will show you how much braver I am. Thank you, Noey for savin' me." She buried her face again, and spoke through her palms filled with more hair, and begging for it to all be over.

"Go on, Noey. FUCKIN' BITCH! I HATE HER!" Silence held the moment as he just laid his cheek to her tramp-stamp, and hugged her hips as he rubbed them. Finally, he felt her deep, silent inhale.

"Just tell me what you be rememberin', Baby. You ain't guilty of anythang, Noey. Please. I need to know everythang she done said. Every word." Her whisper tone was desperate, and turned to encouragement, as she struggled with not knowing what was discussed about her.

"Are you sleeping with anyone else other than her, Julian?" He asked, fearing how she would respond, and read her every physiological response.

But her answer was whispered with care and affection to him. "No Noah. No Baby. I was only seein' her, and it was not what you thank it was. I was wrong but, it was more like just occasionally-little thangs would happen and often out of stress. I stopped years ago when you and I agreed it should end. Just little thangs. Nothin' for us to argue about. It is over with her, and that be the best thang for us. I never let her penetrate me. Well, sometimes. You won't fist me and sometimes...a girl needs-I fired her from SANICS, didn't I?" She finally looked back over her shoulder to make eye contact, but he was snuggled up on her rear as his pillow.

"Noah, I love you, but you seem...how do I say this Baby? More emotional than usual. Did somethin' happen you are not tellin' me, about? I...I thank I'm readin' guilt signals from you. Did you have an affair you want to tell me about? Now would certainly be the time."

"No Julzie, I have always been faithful to you, except for the Angel you asked me to seed. But, I saw a picture of you layin' in the grass nude with men jerking off on you, Julian." Her entire body felt like a building crashed down on her as she fought to keep from trembling. She buried her face in the pillow and screamed what little scream she could give. The extremities were starting to freeze solid.

She didn't move. Didn't express. Didn't dictate. Didn't want to be alive that very moment. Noah, read her clearly, and listened closely. He appreciated that she had a conscience.

"She said you drugged me to rape you, and that you have been keepin' me on drugs, and she has been helping and keepin' you on prescription drugs, too." She felt his grip get tighter on her hips, and she directed her anger away from him.

"FUCKIN" BITCH is out of her blonde mind. Some of the shit she did to me was temptin' for...for...FUCK! FOR entertainment!" Her growling exhaled, spoke volumes to him. He could feel her rhythmic jerking of her hair, as it began to shimmy her ass.

"She loves to poke people. YOU! All men. She knew I would battle her. You be all Braun, Noey, and I love you for it but, mind games were Jon's strength, not yers'. She be lyin' to you. Please understand that. She was gettin' control of yer' thoughts. Plantin' ideas…gettin' between us. I will not….OH I HATE HER MORE NOW! Fucking with yer' mind." Julian slammed her face into the pillow to whisper below the bottom. "Fuckin' with my man like that shit. OMG NOAH! Please Baby, get up and rub your dick against my ass or somethang-before I EXPLODE! I AM GETTIN' PISSED! GET THE COCONUT OIL!" She found her redirect, and held her power as her nerves boiled over into closet doors creeking.

In a late thought, she rolled over to watch him get up, and stare into his brown eyes.

"NOEYYYY! Did she touch you?" She blurted at him with severe concern on her face. He fumbled with the jar too long for her experience. "Noah James?" He just fumbled with the open jar lid, not looking at her, and he waited for her to turn back around on her chest. But she didn't. Her head slowly turned, but her eyes kept on him, keenly to confirm her readings.

She pinched her hair between her lip and bottom teeth, to think and monitor. "She touched you, Noah. I can see it on YOUR GOD DAMN FACE!"

Noah shook his head, looking at the open jar. That was a distraction he could control, and avoid. He listened to her exhales, and subtle growls nervously. Julian turned back around on her chest in deep thought. If it wasn't medication, she toyed with his reward system and planted ideas. *Positive*

Reinforcement Baitin' and Reward trainin'-like a dog. Rach stimulated his reward system- penis stroke, stopped, leashed him with information, stroked reward-fuckin' Bitch used my own papers against me.

Aggravated, she repeated it out loud with her back to him, daring him to contest her, "Noah James, you had sex with Rachael." She pulled her hair with both fists as hard as she could, growling to help regulate, and waited for his answer. He watched from behind and studied her every movement. He did not know, she already had an idea of what happened. Neither one remembered him mentioning it, when he was rescued.

Chapter 4

-Conscience or Conscious, Skeletons Dance

He sat across her thick thighs, and spread a thick coat of coconut oil on her proud Longhorn tramp-stamp to melt, and watched it puddle in her profound Venusian dimples. While she wiped away her silent tears and mascara, from her bruised face.

"I comprenda, Noah. All those times she asked about how to manipulate an Alibi. I knew she was up to somethang. I KNEW IT! That Bitch-OOH...that feels good, Noey." His palms raced up along her spine on each side hitting her tense, sore thick muscles, and his flaccid cock, teased into her rear crevice. As her tension released from his palm, his poking around, just tensed it again, only it was a rewarding tense. "Noah, did you use an Alibi to protect our Accord, when you didn't have sex with her?"

She heard his lips smack and exhale with reservation, before he spoke. "I think so. I was cuffed to the bed, and I remember both hands being cuffed. She said you and her, as teenagers, had sex with animals and drank animal semen-" He didn't get to continue.

"OMG! NOAH JAMES! Don't tell me you believe that? And I have a gun right here, Noah. Remember that. I WON'T BE TOO ANGRY IF...IF...you used an Alibi when you slept with her. I need to know you protected our Accord, Noah James. IF you did, I will only shoot you once."

"Julz, I am just remembering things here and there and telling you what I can remember she said." He kept working her backside as his cock teased her unknowingly. "I would IDentifY as Jon as instinct, if I could have. I'm not nearer to rememberin' right now. And I can't IDentifY, Jon at all now. I can't figure it. And what's the difference, she is an Angel."

Julian rolled her eyes. That was her excuse, not his. "Noah Baby, just the important stuff...leave out her sick animal fantasies. Okay? She has bestiality fantasies, not me." She changed her inflection to be more loving, "I need to relax Baby, and you're my Love, so you get to enjoy relaxin' with me before we go to Momma's to get the kids."

"You never told me you and Jenna were lovers, Julzie. I thought you were just best friends." Noah said, and honestly already felt he knew the truth.

"I have told you we were lovers, Noah. She was my first love. My first love. Okay, so maybe I didn't just toss the sex acts at yer' ears. YES! Jenna and I were lovers, and I don't feel like I intentionally misled you. I have moaned her name at you while doin' a rodeo." She actually rolled her eyes at the wall. This was no secret, and he knew Jenna was her first love. She pulled her hair over to her, and roped the entire length, and put it in her mouth to calm her anxious nerves.

"She said I was going to jail. That she had evidence. DNA evidence, Forensics, and was going to plant it with unsolved cases to make sure I got life and she got you." He said rubbing his hands together with oil to work her lower back.

"WHATEVER BITCH!" She said in her loudest raspy whisper to Rachael in the world. "Not goin' to happen. I will be callin' tomorrow mornin' to see if you have warrants. I bet you do not. I did not do a rape kit, and snuck into the shower and washed away everythang...even inside me...where your DNA would be found by default. Thus, Reasonable Doubt."

Putting her rope back in her mouth, she pulled it right back out. "Noah?" And the long exhale told him it was a truth she was about to get off her mind. "I did slip you somethang that night and I'm sorry. You remember the blue water? My anger over Rachael is distractin' me from your questions. I did slip you a drug in the blue water with breath mints. It was Sildenafil, you know-erection pills, and I thank you understand why." She let out a big exhale before putting her hair back in her mouth, and buried her face in the pillow to hide her shame. It would show up in any blood test Rachael may have taken, and used as evidence. She remembered writing her Momma the prescription, and getting it filled the next day.

"Emily told me that." He said, hoping to get to the bottom of her closet.

♫ *Text Alert on Noah's phone.*

She jerked her head up fast, but did not look back at him. "WHAT DID YOU SAY? Did you say Emily? DID SHE TALK ABOUT EMILY?" Urgent were her anxieties as the flushed her face of what little color she had, and she glanced back to read his eyes to read the amount of damage Rachael had done, and he denied her any cue. Immediately, she slammed both palms to her forehead as she looked forward again. Frustration burned inside her, as she dragged her hands down her face, and rolled them around, and back up. "This is so FUCKED UP!" She screamed in her raspy whisper, as he checked his phone.

Text to Noah from Anonymous Number:
ARRESTING YOU SOON! YOU RAPED ME! CHARGES
FILED! EMILY HAS BEEN FUCKING ME BEHIND YOUR
BACK!

Julian responded to the pressure. "That does it. FUCKIN' RACHAEL STOP TEXTIN' US!" Twisting around to get her point across, she exhaled at his phone with a dirty look, and finally got eye contact with him, and growled. "That is what is happenin', Noah James. Andrea is not supposed to have more than one Alibi, and now Alibis know about each other." She shook her head and expressed her real concern, "This is fucked. She is crashin'-fragmentin'. Those others were crashed. OMG Noah! I thank she is crashin' in pieces, only she is tryin' to crash Andrea, and maintain as Rachael. This is seriously bad. If she crashes Andrea, then Rachael will never be stabilized, and without boundaries. She will lose her conscious, and thrive on sub-conscious levels, and that is violent to herself. She will just self-destruct herself like a freakin' real life zombie brain. We have got to sedate her, and crash her Noah, before she really does produce any evidence." Still staring at her, he was nodding, and she felt his fear of losing everything with Rachael using his DNA.

"We will be fine, Noey." She assured him, and laid back on her chest as he got back on her.

Palming her lower back, and working his way out from her spine, she moaned her approval and asked. "Did you hear me?"

"Yes, Baby. Thank you." He said, softly.

49

"Jay, would you have left me for her? Did you marry her?" He asked while getting back to his normal, not so emotional state. He intentionally thrusted his hips to make his dangling penis rub her where her nether regions come together.

Lowering her head to reach her muscles, she told him what she had didn't want anyone to know, so she said it slowly. "We had a mutual agreement marriage, Noah. It was with an IDentifY and not me. It lasted like...six months, nothin' on paper. Just an agreement. I'm not leavin' my Angel, Noah...not even for another Angel. She is really PISSIN' ME OFF!"

Now, with reassurance in her voice after her burst of anger, "I would not leave you for her, and that is what she is mad about. You won. That bitch, I SWEAR!" She rubbed her rope of hair on her face, and with a lasso of it, pushed it into her cheek. He reached for his tobacco spit bottle, and she punched the bed, and turned to throw her anxieties at him. She couldn't hold this much fear inside, and hide it.

"GOD DAMN HER TELLIN' YOU ABOUT EMILY! GOD DAMN HER!" Julian punched the bed again and looked at him fiercely, though it was really desperation. "NOAH, I SWEAR! DO NOT BELIEVE ANYTHANG SHE SAYS ABOUT EMILY! WHAT DID SHE TELL YOU? I WANT TO KNOW NOW!" When he didn't respond as fast as she had liked, she blew her top.

"FINE! EMILY WAS HER FREAKY SEX IDENTIFY IN COLLEGE! OKAY? PLEASE BELIEVE ME! EMILY IS NOT REAL! NEVER BELIEVE ANYTHANG ABOUT EMILY SHE SAYS, NOAH! MY GOD WHAT DID SHE TELL YOU?" Her hands covered her face as she fought back crying, and when it didn't work, she burst out with anger again.

"I AM GONNA' TO HAVE TO CALL MOMMA! I NEED HER DIDDY MEDS TOO, FOR TELLIN' YOU WHAT SHE DID!" She barely took a breath to get it out. "SHE...SHE WOULD IDENTIFY AS EMILY AND GET FUCKED BY STRANGERS WITH A TOWEL ON HER HEAD SO SHE WOULD NOT KNOW WHO IT WAS RAPIN' HER SICK MIND! I'M NOT EMILY! PLEASE BELIEVE ME! I DON'T KNOW WHO EMILY IS! JUST ONE OF HER IDENTIFY SHE TOYED WITH!" When she was done yelling, she punched the bed and slammed her face into the pillow crying in despair and hiding from all of it. Her tears absorbed into the pillow, hiding her secrets as she cried. Her husband stayed quiet in his now, submissive role, as she heard the skeletons waltz across the bed chanting 'Emily. Emily. Emily.'

Talking into the pillow, she somewhat reassured herself and him. "God will not permit us to separate, Noah." She lifted her face all the way up, and echoed her whisper off headboard. "I am for us bein' together for a lifetime. Please don't..." she buried her face in the pillow again, and finished, "...leave me." He melted another handful of oil, and softly placed the cured coconut oil between her ass cheeks to melt slowly, and spread it with is fingers. Kitty woke up and Julian floundered with the rush of over stimulation blending with her anger defense, propped up by anxiety, and overwhelmed with needing this delicate topic of conversation, about something she couldn't, wouldn't, shouldn't talk about, but was. Noah tossed his bride a lifeline, by giving her a simple question and a warm touch.

"She also said your Pastor raped you and her, and some of your family members. I don't believe that story." He noted to her.

51

She looked up in front of her, disgusted by Rachael's lies, and spoke without looking back, "You and Simon-! She paused. "I'm sorry, Noey, I am not being the respectful wife to you as I should. I will accept your punishments and pray, after we are done talkin'. Please. I am sorry, Noey. Simon is the only person ever to rape me. I did not mean to say your name and his name together. I'm sorry, and of my terrible frustrations, I am not bein' myself for you. I am not bein'...myself for you. I hate how I feel. Please. Please. PLEASE continue to wear my panties." She looked back at him with her begging eyes, and he glanced, but did not offer any cues.

He pulled the bottle out and sat it aside, and spit his warm Copenhagen juice on her ass, and rubbed it in with coconut oil. "You...you dirty, dirty man." She smiled at the warm offer, instantly releasing some of her tension, and he flipped the tobacco can to her. Humiliation was offered only with love.

"Why not just spit on my pussy-" He did, and it took her breath away. "Thank you, Noey. I love you, too." She said it, knowing what punishment he was wanting to give her. She never wanted or had to say it but, spitting on her nudity was an instant wetness she refused to admit, even to herself. Being it a seed, just made her tingle but, being it seed with Cowboy tobacco juice, nearly made the humiliation of it, stain her pale skin for others to know. And that stimulating her brilliant mind, even more. To be bruised by her lover, gave her the same affect. She wanted men and women to notice, and judge her for appearing used, thus tingling her humiliation desires. Even her Alibis signed a secrecy agreement for this disgusting but, instant 'humiliate me and fuck me' fetish.

He worked the brown juice and oil, all over her cheeks with his palms and fingers, and occasionally slid over her back door teasing her pleasing. She shook a little each time from the immense rush up her spine as she pinched some of the tobacco, and put it in her lip. He noticed her quiver and occasionally slid down her long crack toy with her stimulation rushes.

"How many people did you witness for in college, Julzie?" She immediately perked up, holding her lips to keep the tobacco in. As he caught her off-guard with that question, she was thankful he could not see her face. Up went the blood pressure, tense went her neck muscles, and both hands prepared to shovel, as her subconscious fought her shaking-head answer.

He worked the oil into her thick thighs and spit on her backside, waiting-glancing-reading the moment. She was going to use his spitting as an escape but, felt it was too obvious. She struggled with what to do, because being spit on, touched her yes-to-sex button, and she didn't want to move as he pushed it over and over again.

"Noah, please believe me. I don't know anything about Emily. And my Bible study groups were...well...not many-a few. Some. Uh...Mostly women lookin' for guilt-free release and some...religious...friends we would read and study. Uh...Some-a few gay friends-Soy-boys-types. It...uh...was before you and I met, so I was allowed to help them........study. I didn't drink any seed if that is what you are really accusin' me-maybe one or two-ONLY!" She clenched her teeth after the final word delicately came out loud. It looked like she was trying to add a closing point. She still held fast to hear any kind of response to her dodge, as her mouth curled downward and both hands stopped shoveling the crap.

"OH MY GOD! I AM GONNA KILL HER! I didn't swallow seed until we started datin', Noah. EVER! NOT EVER! I mean a few. I had to learn it. I knew you were the one for me. You are my only real Angel." She said with kinder inflection. Her neck muscles were killing her. More important, he didn't ask anything about her swallowing semen.

"High school?" Julian buried her face in her pillow again, and didn't respond.

"She bragged that you were secretly on birth control and having abortions."

"I DON'T KILL BABIES NOAH JAMES TAYLOR! I AM AN ANGEL OF GOD! I WOULD BE SUBJG...SUBDIG...SUBJECTGATED! FUUUUUCK! I WOULD GO TO HELL WITH YOU IF I DID! AND MY ONLY BIRTH CONTROL IS SWALLOWING AND I LIKE IT!" She exhaled her stiff shoulders, and went on with a calmer tone. "Menses is unclean per our Bible, and the perfect time for intimate birth control but, I swallow for you during menses so it is not wasted." She actually chuckled at her little valid statement at the end of her answer, and went back to feeling his touch. So she could calm down.

He kept rubbing her bruised ass cheeks deeply, and finally started working his fist into them in circles, to work the old blood out, and get fresh blood with healing oxygen, into them. Her back arched from the pain, and the intense rush of pleasure. He didn't say a word as he grew more powerful, with his touch and unnerving questions.

"Black guys at the Holiday Inn?" He asked or said. It was so neutral, even Julian had to roll over and look at him. When she did, her eye met both his strong-willed ones. The room was silent, and hands

54

and feet began to chill on his Cowgirl, again. She detected he would wait her out. Bones rattled in the background louder and louder, as her dancing skeletons grew their grins wider and wider. She was dying to glance their way but, she had to maintain her stare.

On her elbows, displaying her entire nude front to him with her knees together and bend, she looked at him worried but, hiding her fears, and hoped he could read her unspoken words. Her hair tried to finish falling off the side of the bed. It was a witness to everything in her past, present, and future. Their eyes still read into each other, one another trying to protect their souls, as she refused to answer him...verbally. This was a big bone to deal with, as he grew impatient with the skeletons.

He leaned down still looking at her drawing his fist back, she slowly opened her knees to him without looking away, and he punched her with his fist on her Venus mound...hard. She jerked with her eyes rolling back, and curled into a reactive fetal position. She quickly looked at him again, and sat back up, and put her knees apart again, as he spit Copenhagen juice on her large, sagging breasts. Keeping her stare and asking for punishments, she spit tobacco juice on her own chest, and stomach, thus confessing by non-verbal agreement with his humiliating actions. Neither would look away but now, for different reasons. Lure and reward was now at a stand-off at lure.

"You are makin' me wetter than the rivers of heaven, Noah. Beat her and make me explain." Her eyes meant it, as she begged for his reward, first. Noah jerked his knee back, and shoved her legs apart as she watched him. The burn of her lubrication preparation started immediately. He reached down, and painfully smacked her across the pussy to spank her. It was not gentle, and she appreciated that.

Slowly, she began to tell him, as her neck muscles tightened, and the corner of her mouth lowered as she stayed on her elbows, and presented herself for abuse. She wiggled both hands as she fought her subconscious, and spoke her first word, she held up one finger either to say one time or hold on. The words of her story would have intent, and she wanted to get the wording correct. He was growing impatient at her stalling. I hint of creating a memory, instead of retrieving, he knew.

"In Med School, Andrea had some guys she slept with. Yes, you know she loves Black men. If they got a room there, she had sex with them. Every guy in school got a room there just fer' her sex. I would go with her, and watch her have sex, and record it on her phone. She did not feel-"

He slapped her pussy harder, and she felt her skin burn on her shimmering vulva. The scowl left her face, and her expressions fell silent, thus bland.

"Andy needed me there to make sure she was safe." He drew his hand back, "I DID NOT SLEEP WITH ANY OF THEM!" He slapped her mound again leaving marks, and again, as her eyes rolled back, her painful reward dripped into her brain increasing her propensity for honesty, by chemically reducing her fear of consequences.

They still stared at each other's windows for reading material. Silent, she opened her legs for him, and let him have her way. He slapped her again for not being completely honest, and she waited in anticipation for her masochist humiliation. He spit in her face, and it dribbled down her cheeks and nose. As it curled around the base of her nose, the brown seed slowly fell to the corner of her mouth, and staring back at him, her tongue reached for it.

"She shared the semen with me." She gave him an intense stare, as she killed one of the skeletons. "I watched her about...regularly each...a couple times a week...regularly...as two or three men fucked her. I did a rodeo. I DID NOT FUCK THEM! I ate her out afterwards. My Black guy was in college, and he was sweet...turned out to be too sweet when he brought guys to my dorm and Bottom'ed for them." She paused, begging for him to spank her pussy again but, he held off her punishment or reward.

"I liked watchin' them and her. Is that wrong? I like hearin' people have sex. Okay? I'M ACCOUSTICOPHILIC! I need it. I like hearin' you scream in pain, too." She reminded him, and then her tongue searched her lips for more of his spit.

Noah slapped her vulva again, and again, and again, and again, until she looked down. And again. Rolling her head forward, breathless as her mouth dangled open, she nodded to him for more, and he slapped her pussy so hard, the juice landed in her face. In her confessing whisper, she acknowledged the transaction of love and pain. "Thank you. We were married and I didn't ask." He slapped her pussy again, and splattered her tits, and face with her river of seed. She did not look up at him. "Thank you for spankin' me, Noey. I'm sorry. It be all my fault."

He pulled her legs back together, and spit up her body again, and she spit down her body in agreement, waiting for her Dominion.

Slowly, he leaned down over her, and kissed her softly on the lips, and laid his head between her breasts, and pushed her legs together between his. She felt the warmth of the brown seed between them, making her pussy deluge its own vintage.

Chapter Five

-Skeletons Hide Fetishes for Skeletons

She quietly began to cry but, told him more of the bigger picture as he laid on her body. "Andrea's preaching father raped her for more than ten years, Noah. She has been treated, medicated, counseled, used, abused, and lied to. I thank she wishes it had happened to me too, so she wouldn't feel alone. It did not. I love you, Baby, with all my heart. Andrea needs someone who shares her trauma. She never had a mother to bond with. My rape by Simon filled her need, and I made her feel safe. She made me feel safe. She hates her body so much because she blames her body and stuck with its memory. I was really beginnin' to feel that way, until you cleansed my soul with the Rape Therapy." The room fell silent as the bones stopped rattling for the moment.

He mumbled from her chest, "Andy has severe mother issues with her, and sexual issues and-" Julian cut him off.

"I know, Baby. I have tried NOT to provide any more maternal intimacy to her over the last few years, and I feel guilty, because in the hospital, I let it happen again to gain favor to influence the investigation of you. My DIDC Cover Casey, used to role play as her mother for her. Role playing Andy from birth, Andy would what us Psychiatrist call 'Infantile' and Casey breast fed and coddled her." She gestured with her hand, "it is Buildin' trust and bondin' in a way a mother and daughter must bond, to build individual core in the child. She was denied that by her mother's passin' away from givin' birth.

That itself is guilt ridin' in her. She seemed to reach a point, where it was about sex. That was dangerous, and I ended the sessions. She even had made, a Mother Cowgirl Doll named Julian she could Infantile with at home."

"I think-" She interrupted him, and petted his hair as he roped some of hers, and sucked on it to listen.

"I kept Dakota a secret from Rach because I didn't want her involved with motherin' her sexually. Dakota is for your Momma Issues and I like you and Momma Dakota havin' those special moments. It really seems to help you work out your feelin's. Casey played with fire and they both got burned."

"I don't know who Casey is, Julzie." Noah said looking for clarification. "Another Alibi?"

Julian kept rubbing his hair with her thumb, and he focused on listened to her choice of words. "Yes my Angel, she is an Alibi for Sex Counseling. You have not met her. She is very Progressive and a good fit for Andrea's personality and needs. A very Liberal woman, and super smart. I like her a lot. Dakota is more conservative and native to your regional characteristics and religious faculties."

Text to Julian from Anonymous Number:
SECRETS MEDS GOING IN MY REPORT! YOU KNOW YOU WILL LOSE YOUR CAREER! I WILL NOT LIE FOR YOUR REAL DISORDER ANYMORE! YOU DID ME WRONG FAT BITCH!

Julian didn't bother to get up to get her phone off the floor. "Noah, please understand, Casey didn't seek out sexual intimacy. We saw the lack of her maternal bondin' that pent up without a mother's fulfillment, and it became us much of the time durin' crisis, and with Andrea, every day was a crisis. I really have been good over the past several years about endin' thangs and denyin' her. I pushed for her to find others to fulfill my sexual roles and Casey's position with her, and she would only find band aids and not allow growth beyond superficial needs. It is my fault and I am so sorry all this went on behind your back. Me endin' all my relationships with her, is probably the best for all of us." She paused to make sure he heard her next reminder.

"I am allowed to enjoy my lesbian desires, per the Bible, and to behold you as my husband. I was wrong, and should be punished severely for this intentional betrayal. Mother bondin' went on since about our last year of college and stopped only when Ally and Zachary were gettin' my bondin'. I swear. It was worse back then when Rach learned she could not have kids, and begged me to let her a boyfriend-ANY boyfriend impregnate me, and have her baby. Pull my hair, Baby. Please. My OCD is itching on those crooked boots."

"Emily, Julian Michelle?" He timed it so she was on topic of Alibis, and mildly jerked her hair.

"DON'T SAY THAT NAME EVER AGAIN, NOAH!" She exhaled her frustration in small amounts, enough to talk in a normal whispered tone but, she waited a few seconds for him to feel her anger.

"Honestly, a pregnancy would have been more damagin' to her psychological needs, and I could never do this. It's called Paraphilic Infantilism with erotic stimulation for her. Little girls will form their first sense of self and rely on a mother completin' her identification process as a girl. That never happened for Andrea, Noah, and side effects show up in her relationships, such as child cuddlin', pettin', sucklin', eye gazin' her partner, etc... If not,

Girls fail a necessary, secure attachment to develop a constitution. I was her female model by accident or incidents or proxy. What we are seein' now with Andrea is separation anxiety and anger over expectations of relationship failures. These development failures breed deep self-hatred and rejectin' her own feminine identity. This is her disturbed process of gender identification. And, needs to be careful of Transference with the next woman." Emily, was successfully dodged.

"Thank you, Casey." Julian blurted sarcastically. Noah noticed her answer was genuine, and a situation that she had already analyzed and solved with Casey. Julian smiled, and actually felt a little bonding herself, now that she was being so honest about some things. He did not get tripped up by the big words, titles, diagnoses, redirect, sexual imaging, fear-casting, responsibilities, etc...she put it all in that long dodge.

"Rachael was designed to protect Andrea, and now, Rachael is feedin' her men who treat her without respect and use her hard...just like her Father." She whispered to him. "Recognize Noah, I need yer' love WITH punishment. That is why I did not sleep with her men. I don't want JUST PUNISHMENT or JUST REWARD like Andrea, and Emily is her secret IDentifY, Noah. There I told you."

"She says she has a video of me raping you, Julian. Security camera. I don't know." He offered from the bosom to which brought them a new happiness.

"If I am arrested-"

"STOP! If you are arrested, I will never testify against you. That is a spouses right. I will never do it." She insisted, while petting him and his fear.

"This is Ohio, not Texas, there is no Accord

here. No common law marriage. You do not have that right, Julzie."

"I be havin' the right to refuse to testify. End of charges...hopefully."

They laid there holding each other wondering how ugly it was really going to get with Rachael, and in court. And more importantly, how it would affect their children, and their happiness.

"Who is Emma?" He asked while listening to her heart nestled to his ear. She knew it too, and stepped up her long, quiet breaths that sounded like a tornado in her chest. She had to admit it to him, since he was listening to her nerve center inside.

"My first baby girl. She talks to Angels. You hear me play that song about her and I, on the piano, for her. I got pregnant in College. She was my baby girl. I named her Emma. I lost her goin' into my seventh month. God was punishin' me for my sins or...I guess her father was not an Angel." She said it while fighting back the sad memories, and doing a decent job. He knew his smacks would give her enough endorphins to numb her enough for this question. She taught him that chemical mind trick.

"Why am I just hearin' this now as your heart tries to run a marathon, my beautiful Texas Rodeo Queen?" Letting her know it was okay by putting his pet name in there, made her lose the fight not to shed the tears for her lost baby. His understanding, devotion, and love that has no judgement for her past, gave him the throttle on power. If, he knew all of her past.

"I had lost my faith and was bein' bad. I was on a quest to be punished...instead, I just got used." She exhaled trying to control herself, and just let the tears stream down her face quietly. "I was angry at God for takin' Emma. Born of sin. I began to be Andrea-like. I took too many risks, Noah. Angry at God. I was bein' a bad girl to punish him, and when Emma came to grow inside me, I found my faith again. A sign from God to brang me back home to him. My prayers thanked him daily for his gift. After the miscarriage, I just let go of my faith, and got on my back to have another one. It never came to be, until I met you."

He glared at her nipples scar beside his face and asked, "Simon's baby?"

"NO!" she blurted out spitting accidently on his cheek, then wiping it up with her hair, and embarrassed her Southern elegance was slipping.

"Ally, my child Princess?" She finally shook and quietly cried, purging the overload of emotions, she couldn't speak. She did not see that full skeleton sneak out of the closet. Finally, she nodded her head repeatedly, and wrapped her arms around his shoulders to keep him from leaving her. Her strength, her power, her composure-needed him when Emma's guilt took her.

"Doubts?" He asked softly as she shivered and cried just six inches from his head. She shook her head trying to keep her mouth closed, and held on. She knew it was not a pretty image of her. He looked up at the tears streaming down her grimaced face, and looked at her cathartic eyes.

"Did you abuse drugs back then, Julian?" He kept watching her wet windows for clues. She shamefully shrugged a confession, and he nodded, very gently.

"Abortions back then, Julian Michelle?"

Letting her emotions run wild, she faced him staring at her interrogator, and she shook her tears. That answer did not require a distraction or stall.

"Never say 'No to men' rule?" He asked turning his head to keenly read her. She nodded and whispered, "I only said yes to Angels. Emily said yes to anyone."

"Are you keeping up on your medications now, Julian? She nodded confidently, and kept nodding.

Noah reared up on his knees and hands, and leaned back, and spit juice on her pussy mound while still staring her down. She spit down her chin, chest and stomach in a shameful agreement. Slowly, he laid back down on her in their blended seed, to scare her skeletons away, and read her pain with love, as he watched her face. That punishment was given, received, and agreed.

"Have you had sex with, Samira?" And Julian shook her head then whispered, "No, Baby. She is very sweet, but no."

He stared, waiting for her to run out of tears.

"Did you let groups of men fuck you at the same time?" She shook hard after he asked her, and began to sob. Her hands were curled up near her chin now as if she was in fear for her life, her reputation, her trust, her marriage, and her real secret. Her eyes washed away some of the truths, and much of the shame, but in the end, she was pinned down, and not answering would just be worse for both of them. She feared now, that Rachael really told him everything. She chose to shake her head at him, and beg for punishment.

"Please gag me. Please. I need it now. Beat me. Please." He didn't budge and she begged him. "Fuck my pussy as hard as you can...please. I need it. Choke me for lyin'. Gag me in the watershed until..."

Noah sat up on his knees, and she feared his retreat and, most of all, not knowing what he was thinking. He had out-lasted her, and she knew what he was feeling, and spit on herself again asking for his commitment to her. He did not spit back, and that terrified her. Her pleads for abuse, confessed for her. This was one weakness, she could never overcome.

Julian barely nodded, as the threat of retreat, broke her. "I...I...I...Noey. Please God, don't leave me." She whimpered balling at her past. Noah kneeled over her, having circled back, and found his power position to break down her barriers, to let him in. She loved him for his ability to untie her knots, in every way, except her one big knot she was never allowed to untie or tell him. He was an addiction in himself to her and her needs...not just for his seed.

"Say it wife. Say it to your husband now." He commanded her with his meanest and loudest voice. "TELL ME WHAT YER' NOT TELLING ME, WIFE!"

Her face curled like a hot poker was coming too close, and she whispered in her very shaky, and broken, raspy tone, "I don't know. Emily did it."

"How many different men, wife?"

Sobbing uncontrollably, she shook her head, begging for him to not let her answer. She was emotionally devastated. Peering over her, a giant skeleton rattling Noah's spurs at her, haunted her, and waited. This was the reason for his retreat. She kept shaking her head as more and more skeletons chanted Emily's name, and she tried to hide Emily from herself.

"Did you like it, Wife?"

She curled to the side sobbing, and refused to look at him, when she choked on it. He watched his masterful work in play by looking down his nose at her, as she gave in to her Angel. She didn't want to know what he thought of her, even though God knew.

"We tried to stop them. I tried. I cried. I prayed...I cried for Andy to help me. Emily couldn't-"

"I gave her your Crash Key, Emily." Julian didn't know how to respond, or chose not to respond to more damaging information. She just hid her face from reality, and that name.

"That heart-face branding mark I find drawn on your ass occasionally...she says it is her and her friends after you have orgies with them. Is that true? Her friends?" Julian was freezing in her curled up fear ball, and shook her head because she really didn't know.

Patiently, he put his hand out to help her up, and snapped his fingers to signal her. Before she would face him, she had to know if he would leave her. So she offered her roped hair to him, and he did not take it. He just stared at her, and she started crying and begging.

Her sobs and gasps interrupted her so much, she kept her sentences short. "Please Noey. Punish me. Please God make him do it. Please Husband. Please Noey. Please don't leave me. I need you, Dominion. Punish me and bath me for I hath sinned. Please don't leave me. Please help take Emily away from me. I don't want her." He watched her breasts shake from her panicked sobs, and slowly grabbed her crown and took rule, again.

She watched him get off the bed, and hoped he would not let go of her hair. He kept his stare tight but, not her hair. His look was terrifying to her without knowing she controlled the moment. Barely, she sat up on her elbows, and leaned her head back to tighten the slack of his hair leash, as her gesture of submission.

67

"Thank you. I love you. Thank you. Please help me. Genesis 2:24." He barely nodded once, and she pulled her feet from her boots, and slid off the side of the bed to her little feet. Looking down at the floor, she curtsied everything to him, even her tears.

Noah dragged her by her hair to the shower, and she rushed with him to her salvation. Her pussy began to drip to the floor leaving a trail behind her. As he turned the water on over her head, she anxiously got to her knees in the shower, and waited for it to get warm. The fear rushed her arousal through her. She stared up at him with her swollen blue eyes beaten black, and made sure he didn't get away. Her clit pushed her labia apart as it throbbed with her fast-beating heart.

"I will not punish you for your sins of the past, Julian." In fear, she grabbed him by his cock and pulled him into the shower with worry still on her face. Rushing, she began sucking his cock, and holding his ass cheeks with both hands. She wanted that salvation now. She began to work him up, and as his erection reached firmness in her mouth, she pushed his back to the wall and slapped his hands away from her when he tried to console her.

He reached over, and got the hand mirror hanging in the shower, and waited.

Her swollen blue eyes looked up at his towering shaft, and she offered a final whisper to their love, after pulling his waiting cock out of her mouth, "Psalm 51:1 through 4, I have sinned. Bathe me my husband. I don't want to be Emily. Please don't leave me, Noey. 1 Corinthians 7:3 through 5, your wife will not deprive her husband of his demands." Noah held the mirror so she could see herself with his cock in her mouth. She often liked

68

that, and would sometimes IDentifY as Dakota. What he didn't know was, IDentifY doesn't work on Emily.

Crawling her knees back, she put her hands behind her back, and held her long hair tightly as she tried repeatedly to choke on his cock. Swallowing a man was something that has alluded her, and it brought years of frustration within herself. He hung the mirror back on the bar, and stared down into her eyes as her eyes stayed on his. Her fears triggered softly as she forced his long cock to the back of her throat, walked her knees back farther, and leaned into him with the warm shower pounding his belly, and splashing into her face smothering her further. Noah put his hands on the back of her head, as she began bobbing his cock to stab her in the back of the throat. Her lonely clitoris, felt like it was melting.

Instantly, she gagged and choked herself into another gag and choked it with his thick, hard meat. The Texas Rodeo Queen bobbed harder tormenting her gag reflex to punish herself for her sins, both spoken and unspoken. She would not stop until he gave her his seed again, thus she would feel secure about things she didn't really have control of then, and only part control of now. If anything, she would feel secure for the next ten or so minutes, that he would not leave her.

Chapter 6

-A Woman's Fetish Need is Never Done

When Julian hung up her cell phone, Noah kissed her in celebration as he mildly danced. "There were not any charges filed against you with the District Attorney." They sat next to each other on the couch as they held hands with her hair blended between their fingers, and a rope of her blessed hair between her lips. She had called every day to make sure.

She had a very happy tone in her raspy whisper, "Home a few days and thangs be gettin' back to normal. Ally kept beggin' for a ride to school instead of the bus. Momma got her spoiled last week. Rachael will get reassigned today. I spoke with Renner and Vances this mornin' at the Field Office, she got my message. I still have to get some files from Rachael and some information. I will have to meet with her...hopefully in the Field Office. She said she was transitionin' to male and takin' meds, but her behavior is so not her-too aggressive." Julian twisted him a rope, and put it in his mouth as her phone alerted a message.

She quickly deleted it, and went on like it meant nothing as he rushed to speak.

"She said that...I think. She had her gun in my face when she said it. I remember that now." Noah was excited to remember more details of his kidnapping and violation. "-And I would agree to that. I know we didn't get along-especially with her nudity around you to entice you...I wished you had

70

thought about how I felt watching my wife's ex-lover toss her nude self around our house."

"She was my beard, Noah." Instant pleading by Julian. "I had to have it. Simon would just creep up on me when Jordan wasn't there. I can only fire her from the case as her Lead. Vances is shiftin' her to another SANICS Division."

"I know. I know." He said, keeping her hair in his lips.

"I requested Karen Ritzman. Do you remember her?" She asked him, excited to see an old friend.

"No. Not really." He squeezed her hand. "Ally wore her eye patch to school this morning. Guess she insist on wearing it as long as you wear yours." He leaned his head over, and gently bumped her Momma spirit, as she smiled appreciatively at her mothering skills.

"That's our Cowgirl." She said whole-heartedly. "Now, if we could just get some meat on her bones. Poor girl looks starved."

"I still want us to talk tonight after the kids go to bed about Rachael touchin' you. We have to address this completely, and work out yer' emotional issues, and maybe a Counselor. I can feel my anger. I want you to thank about that today my lovin' Cowboy, and understand, it is not your fault. Let's just talk about it. Counselor to patient." She snuggled at him to reassure herself, and squeezed his hand. She needed to know every detail to judge how she should react.

"Casey, the Sex Therapist?" He asked playfully. "I could do her, and help progress her into multiple orgasms.

71

"NO! ME!" She barked playfully, and pulling back some of her lost power from her breakdown days ago.

"Yes'um." He responded, and noted her attire. "No bra today? White shirt. White jeans. Pink band in your hair. All because I picked your pink boots, today? Everyone can see your big dark nipples areas in that shirt. 'Guess you want someone's attention today." He nudged her with his shoulder.

"Hey. It's not just for her, Cowboy." She was smiling with shameless guilt. "My breasts therapy...my nipples therapy. I will never wear a bra again therapy...I mean it. NEVER! I hate them dang thangs. You were right. And the one's you have hidden from me. Pitch them to the Indians. I mean it."

Noah smiled victory. It had only taken ten years, and she finally gave them up. "Slutty wife, Tomboy. What perfume are you wearing?"

"HEY! I'm not a Slut. I wore them long enough. Don't call me a Slut. I don't like that. Chanel Coco Mademoiselle Eau de Parum to go with my Roper Kids Pink and White Checkered boots."

"You are a Slut, Tomboy-A Slutty Pirate. And you smell wonderful in your pink kids' boots that I picked for you to wear today." He pointed to himself as if picking them today was any different than any other day.

"HEY! Do not call me that today. I don't like it. I don't want Samira thinkin' I am easy. I wish she would get here." Julian began squeezing up under her throat to work out the soreness in her esophagus. Punishment has its after-affects, and they are called trophies by Julian.

"You are my Slut. Slut." He reminded her smiling.

"Well, yeah Noey. I'm YOUR Slut. Genesis 3:16 thy desire shall be to thy husband, thank you." She slid her hand down the front of her pants, and got her finger wet. When she delicately pulled them out, both fingers dabbed her scent behind her ears, and on her neck. She sucked the remainder off and tasted her freshness. When she smiled, Noah knew she felt confident.

"And thy husband shall rule over thee. My favorite part, Slut. You're thy Slut. With thy very fat pussy." He pushed her arousal buttons, smiling.

In her pleading little girl voice, "Stop iiiit. My white jeans will get wet." She squeezed his hands asking for leniency. "You know how easy wet I get, calling me that."

"With a huge, fat Texas pussy that can't fit in panties." He moaned into her ear.

"Dear Lord, you are givin' me a headache. YES. I'm a Slut. YOUR FAT TEXAS SLUT! Okay. If my crotch gets wetter, yer' lickin' me dry, Cowboy. STOP IT! PLEASE! I want to look good for Samira. Onan. Baby."

Chuckling he told her, "Yeah Baby, I see the eyeliner on extra thick with the mascara. Let me remind you Fat Slut, your eyes are black underneath where I kicked your ass."

"You didn't kick it...no wait...you did kick it, and punch it. Shame on you, Cowboy. Now stop makin' me wet about it. Buy some Copenhagen while you are out. I want my own red roll." She said slapping his crotch.

"Really? Your own roll now? Back in Texas already?" He humored her. "Does Samira know you chew? Or any of your fetishes? You can be scary at times. AND..." He held up a finger to hold the moment, "I kissed your ass and licked it, too"

She laid her head on his arm, and he put his arm around her to cuddle. She roped her hair and handed it to him, and he stuck it back between his lips. Offering him a twist of roped hair, and he usually gets the message.

"Did you take your Diddy Meds, Baby?" Julian nodded to him showing her nervous side, and glanced at the door, before holding a boot out to admire its bright pink color.

"I can wear kids' boots with my dinky feet." She said to herself. "Five feet tall, one-hundred and ten pounds, and kids size five boots."

He laughed out loud at her. "Rodeo Queen, your ass is one-hundred and ten pounds." She elbowed him in the ribs to correct his figures. Holding himself in pain, he made a suggestion.

"I can work from home as well, Julz. You put in for Medical Leave, and I should be able to get some, too. Maybe-Keep the kids off your back." He leaned down at her smiling.

"No. I'm goin' to work from home on the cases day-by-day. I don't be wantin' to force any triggers on myself. We need to review any updates to the file, and avoid Rachael. Stiff'em is a big case with Big Fish. We just need to find that link, and brang him down."

"I need to talk to a counselor about some thangs. Maybe." She said, and Noah raised his eyebrows but, she answered him before he could ask. "I'm just makin' sure nothin' is hidden inside that could horse-kick us later. I've had some nightmares. I'm on alert about my feelin's when you speak, and do physical thangs, and I imagine parts of the Rape Therapy all over again, and I'm not seein' any triggers that I should be concerned about. No triggers. I just need another pair of ears

74

to dig. Comprendo, Amigo?" She asked sucking on her pacifier.

"Si, Senora." He said in his very limited Spanish, as the doorbell rang. Julian jumped up excited, and ran to the door ripping her rope from his lips.

"Come in Samira. Come in."

As she stepped into the foyer with her bright, nervous smile, she spoke what she had secretly practiced in the car. "I brought you some flowers, Julian. I hope you like them, my Cowgirl friend." She said as she handed her the very colorful bouquet. Julian was giddy, and almost bobbing up and down in her three inch heeled boots.

"Thank you. Thank you Samira. They are beautiful. You are beautiful." Julian immediately hugged her, enjoying the fact that she was about six inches taller than her, without her heals. Noah was busy watching his wife's tits bounce around freely in an almost see through shirt. Men are all alike.

"Sam, this is my husband, Noahhhh. You remember him from the hospital. OH! Annnnd." Julian showed her the badge she wore on her men's side leather belt, next to her large Cowgirl 'Rodeo Queen' belt buckle. "I know you had doubts so I...you know...Noah show her yours, Baby. Let her know we are not Serial Killers." Her instructions lingered nervously from her whispers.

Rachael finally lowered her binoculars hissing. "Julian got a new friend. Another fat Bitch." Rachael said to herself, and looked over at Theresa sitting next to her in the car, nibbling on a brownie.

75

Noah got to his feet and pulled out his wallet, and flipped her his badge and credentials. Julian was bringing Samira to the couch, and nudging Noah out of the way. The gun on Noah's hip made her uncomfortable.

"Get me a vase with some water, Noey. Please?" Noah quickly walked off, humored by his wife's excitement. He just dumped the fake flowers from the kitchen table into the sink, and filled it with water.

He came back and Julian smelled her flowers, and put them in the vase, and Noah put them next to his side of the couch. When they sat down, Julian insisted she be in the middle. Her Southern Ways felt it would be less imposing if Samira had to sit between them. The Women continued to hold hands as they sat, and Noah eyed them, reading their body language.

"Rachael has been fired from my team so you need not worry about seein' her again." Julian rattled off.

"Oookay." Samira said in her nervous state. As Julian's giddiness boiled over.

In his calm, Texas Ranger type voice he spoke up. "Samira, would you like something to drink. Bottled water? Sweet tea? Coffee?" He was keeping up with the Southern Hospitality since his distracted wife, was not.

"Go away, Noah. Let us Gals talk." Julian said, taking in Samira's obvious beauty, and savoring her attraction of being dressed to impress.

"I'm good, Noah. Th...tha...tha...thank you, for asking me."

He got up to leave, so his wife could get what she needed. "I will be back in a bit, I have some errands to run. Wife needs her snuff." He said

76

respectfully but, wedging. And he waited for his wife as she gazed at Samira.

Samira watched him standing there, staring at Julian, and it made her more nervous. Julian finally picked up on Samira staring at Noah, and quickly stood up and curtsied him before kissing him on her tippy-toes, and her left leg lifted at the knee. "I love you, Noey. Take my truck and put gas in it."

"I love you, too. Have fun. Be a good Witness, Cowgirl. You know the rules." She nodded at him as Samira's questions drew close. Julian sat back down on the edge of the brown leather sofa facing Samira and holding her hand again. Samira waited to hear a door shut, and finally, it did.

She immediately leaned in and the Women began to kiss wonderfully. The yearning, had finally been satisfied. It was still just a momentary aid to a lust that had to be explored to be validated.

Julian sat back emotionally exhausted, and leaned her head on Samira's shoulder so they could talk some more. Samira was already prepping herself.

"How the hell do you get to DATE Women, AND you are married?" What is up, Julian?"

"How old are you?" Samira quickly added.

"I'm thirty-two. You?"

♫ *Text Alert on Julian's Phone*

"I'm twenty-seven." Samira said smiling-glowing at Julian. "Is that too much of an age difference for you. I am fi...fi...fi...fine with it. Even though, your world seems to be more ahead of mine on responsibilities. You know, three kids." Samira said it smiling, and feeling unsure if there were too many burdens for Julian to be shared with her.

"No, it is just two...well, if you count Noah, he can be a third at times...just not because he ain't smart, he ain't analytical all the time. Lacks the bridge size between the brains to connect dots quickly. I've tested him. He is my Braun Hubby." And she chuckled nervously.

"Are you nervous?" Julian asked like a good friend.

"Yes. I have never really just met someone and hit it off, I guess. AND I know I made a promise to you to let you Witness, and I...well at...at...at this time, am very nervous about it." Samira was almost frank.

"You do not have to do anythang', Sam. I want us to be friends and maybe more, and if more be asking much, than friends we will be." Julian rushed on, still over-excited in her speech. "When I looked into your eyes in the bathroom-thank you by the way for stoppin' us. I was feelin' very vulnerable, and I'm sorry if I latched onto you. I needed Noah, and he was gone, and you be haven' the same purity that Noah has. Your eyes told me you were a good person. Not many of them out there on the range, you know." Julian offered her hand again, and Samira accepted it.

"I was looking for clues in your eyes, too. You have amazing blue eyes. Not hazel at all. Near perfect glowing azure. 'And that black hair just throws them at you. Does your religion make you have extra, long hair?" Samira asked.

"Yes...in a way. The longer the hair, the closer to God. It's a Texas thang. Noah nearly killed me when I showed him my rang was missin' AND my hair had lost a foot. He is makin' me grow two feet back just to have extra. 'Givin' me egg and oil treatments daily. He wants it grown back today. It

78

has already grown back about an inch." She said it with a chuck wagon of overwhelming Texas pride.

"I would say, judging by the hor…hor…horse statue and the whiskey barrel, and the wagon wheel on the wall, the Star, you are some Texas folk. That cattle skull on the door…it's to me, a different culture to which I was fed." She was trying to be appreciative of the western art theme.

"It is us. So do you have children? Married? Divorced?" Julian wanted to get to know her and, her responsibilities.

"No. No. And no. I have mostly dated women ver…ver…ver…ver-" Julian reached up in her stutter and pulled Samira's face to her, and kissed her quickly. It worked. "…very quietly, as I would like us to be, if we date. And may I ask you again, as to how Noah lets you date Women. Mind my manners, but is he…not capable?"

Julian rubbed her very sore throat when she answered, "Nooo, he is quite capable. It's certain people. Special people…good people…that my heart suspects…well, it's our religion. Luke 6:38. I am allowed to share love with certain Women, and Lesbianism is not forbidden in the Bible. I can sleep with 'very special' men if they meet our religious requirements, too. I have only done that once, and it was more like a Witness. 'Even be seeded by them if my husband approves. Noah is Blessed by God, so he is allowed to sleep with other…'very special' Women in need. Both require the permission, and validation of each other to share our conjugal, and Noah has the final decision as the husband. I thank you are one of the few 'special' people that my religion approve of."

"Ooookay. So you sleep around a lot? Is it a fetish? Open marriage? Shopping?" Samira asked

79

feeling a bit uncomfortable, and near decision to retreat.

"No. Oh NO! Everyone has fetishes Sam, the stranger the better if it be satisfin' them. Mine just happens to be…" She sat up and placed her hand on Samira's thigh to answer, and Samira guessed for her.

"Black?" And Julian shook her head at her with a very seductive smile.

"Women?" And Julian shook her head at her again, still inviting her with her smiling eyes. Samira raised her hands without another answer.

"Special God's persons. I thank when I looked into your eyes, I saw somethang very familiar. If I be right, you have a blessed soul. I recognized some thangs in there." She said with a smile warmly, and honestly.

Samira smirked but, in a good way. An appreciative, strange way. "Isn't everyone God's person, Julian? And I'm not a Christian."

"Some more than others, Samira. I don't be sleepin' around or go after people. Perhaps one in a few million people tend to meet the criteria we aspire to share with them. I'm sorry, I may be forward but, I am tryin' to just be honest. I'm not some dirty Slut…uh don't let Noah hear me say that. I'm his Bad Girl sometimes." She looked around just in case.

"For us, Noah sets the boundaries of my relationship with you. Should we date, he sets the boundaries as the gifted owner of my crown, my body, and my pleasures. It's not an open marriage. This is in the Bible, and we enjoy the responsibilities of it. That is our religion. Heed, should Noah want to watch or join us, he must be welcomed. NOT-"

80

Julian let go of Samira's hand, and put her finger up to stop her from thinking ahead of the explanation.

"NOT! Noah has the right to share our love, and our love makin'. He has never done this. NOT once did he ask, or demand he get to observe or partake in the intimacy in mine and Rachael's relationship. I was with her for nearly twelve years. He is a very dedicated man to me...yes as degradin' as it sounds, Noah worships me...as he should as his wife. His fetishes are not as mine are. You shouldn't expect him to expect somethang from you other than friendship and honesty but, should he want to be involved, the Bible does not let me say no to him. I have submitted to his will, gracefully and thankful for his control of my desires."

Samira reached out and took Julian's hand with both her soft hands and smiled nervously, nodding. "You two are certainly...different...and intimidating to me. I don't want to sleep with him. I...I...I...can say that now. That will never happen." She tapped her long blue nails that matched Julian's eyes on the back of Julian's hand.

"Noah and the Bible, does not allow me to ever be penetrated without the consent of my husband-My Dominion. Noah, thankfully, never allowed Rachael to penetrate me. Though, I did fail him, and was punished for my sins, thankfully. King James, Psalm 37:26, my husband is merciful, and his seed is blessed." Julian rushed to get a breath and started again.

"I am allowed to share my other Texas gifts with other men without his consent, as the Bible does not restrict Women from doing it. And as you know, my Venus Lacuna, too. I am allowed other penetration in places but, it is not somethang I have done since college because I can't manage it."

Gesturing with a smile, she added, "Can't say I wouldn't mind a certain hubby to try and manage it occasionally." She said it playfully, to hide her true desires.

"Other Texas gift? Say to me what that is?"

"My big Longhorn rear-end. Noah likes to kiss it, but I am allowed to share it with other's if I want...without his permission but, I don't. I'm just explainin' our Religious Boundaries to you, openly."

"I...I...I...I-" Julian kissed her again.

"I will kiss you every time you stutter. Even in public, Sam. I thank it is one of the thangs that makes me attracted to you."

"Oh wow. Ooookay. Like your accent with me. No, I'm sorry, that is nice. I cannot." she said shaking a bit. "I have never...cannot...but I don't usually share affections in pubic. Since mostly wom...wom....wom-" Kiss. Sam smiled appreciatively. "I can get used to this kissing 'thang.' I am not open about my Lesbian activities to my family, or friends, or anyone. And I really do like some men. Said if they...they...they...they-" Kiss. Sam smiled again. "My mother did not approve of a man I brought home once, he was White, and it bothered her old school traditions. Can I tell you...I...I...I...I-" Kiss.

"Thank you." Samira said getting less stiff. "I have only been with one man, and don't really have many experiences with men. I would speak, I'm Bi and should I have a husband, I would hope that I could have that...that...that...th-" Kiss. "Okay, you are turning me on, Julian." She said with a big grin. She kissed her again, and Julian climbed up on her lap and trapped Samira with her thick thighs. Their moment was getting closer.

Chapter Seven

-Angels Desirous Master a Cuckquean

Julian's glowing Roper Pink & White Checkered Boots lit the room up next to her white jeans as they dangled off the couch, and her body captured Samira. Their arms wrapped around each other, and their DNA finally blended together on their anxious wet, tongues. Immediately, Julian appreciated the feeling of kissing the real, full lips of a Black Woman.

Both their hearts chased their senses, and it felt like a first kiss all over again. Julian made sure her breasts were above Samira's this time. That was important to her, since Samira's naturally were higher than hers the first time they touched. A subtle challenge to answer her internal question about her position in the relationship. Julian held Samira's face as she looked down to her for the first time, passionately kissing, and slowly lit themselves on fire inside. Julian's over active glands soaked her panty-less, very bruised Venus, and it continued to spread outward. Though, I'm not sure it was a bad thing at this point.

Sam pulled up on Julian's shirt, and without stopping her wet kiss, Julian jerked it off exposing her breasts. When she pulled on Samira's shirt, she was denied. Julian stopped to look her in the eyes. "Tu ne veux pas que j'embrasse tes seins, Samira?"

"Can we talk some more before I...I...I-" Kiss. Samira smiled, and warmly told her, "I enjoy seeing you naked. I'm just nervous. Is anyone else here?"

83

Samira looked down at Julian breasts as they sagged down to her white thighs. She lifted Julian's left breast, and kissed her wounds on her areola. "I love your breasts. I find them sexy-special, and you are soooo White. I love White Women." Delicately, she lifted it up to her face, and made sure Julian watched her. Samira licked her scar from underneath, and slowly touched her way to the top, as Julian looked down and away. Samira read her insecurity, instantly.

"Do you ha...ha-" Kiss. "...have more scars from Noah?" Julian touched herself on the side of her head with her finger, before understanding Samira was accusing Noah.

"NO! NO! Noah did not do this to me. NO! Noah would not hurt me." She said it feverishly and Samira licked her scar again, all seven or eight inches of it, silencing her. This did not stop Julian's leaking problem down below but, may have given one to Samira.

"Rachael told me it was Noah. Thank you for telling me that. I was very uncomfortable with him and...." She said it appreciatively, and almost as if she wasn't believing Rachael to begin with. She just had to ask to reassure her feelings. Julian kept avoiding eye contact when Samira gave her scars the affection they desired.

Slowly, she licked it again, waiting for her pale-beauty Cowgirl to be brave enough to acknowledge the affection to her handicap, as Julian had done for her. A stand-off of enchanted proportions began. "Tu as enchante ma faiblesse, de peur que je n'enchante la tienne?" Samira whispered to her, romantically.

Julian's nipples flexed again as Samira licked it, and gently blew warm air to it, as she chased

84

Julian's shy eye. Finally, Julian looked over at her as Samira kissed her breasts scar with her full lips. Keeping Julian locked window to windows, she lifted up her other breasts and licked her scar. And licked it again, and smothered it with her saliva seed full of loving, caring, hot passion, and let her seed string to her breast and her tongue. Julian finally smiled a hint and answered her, "Oui s'il vous plait."

Samira gently petted Julian's hair as Julian leaned into it. They were sharing data through their senses, and their eyes, and their pheromones, and their bodies, and their seed as they blended DNA on their tongues. Softly, she brought Julian face towards her, and whispered to her.

"I prefer you without any clothes, Julian." And quickly raised her left eyebrow to command her. Elegantly, Julian stepped off of her without looking away or smiling, and unbuckled her manly leather belt and shook her very round hips as she peeled her wet jeans to the floor. Samira put both her hands up in front of her, and Julian put hers up and touched their palms. Samira took her prisoner by twining their fingers together, and commanded her again. "Never take your boots off when we are together. I like you in them, and nothing else. Like our first time." Julian glowed with anticipating senses, as she watched Samira's eyes, and read her body language.

Noah had finally shaved her smooth, and her huge outer labia bulged like her breasts. Her smooth vulva was nearly black with fresh bruising. Staring at Samira, she presented herself to her nervously, to be judged, like a Longhorn. Samira still held her hands, and nudged her to move back, and display herself to her. Julian stepped back with her heart racing, and Kitty dripping on her carpet.

Samira looked at her breasts, her tight-flat stomach, her bulging swollen black and blue pleasure center, her full round hips, her thick, short thighs, and finally, her dripping pussy. It made Samira smile really big.

"Your bruising should have healed more by now....Julian, does your Cop husband beat you?" Samira glanced down at her vulva again to help her understand.

Julian shook her head slowly, "It's not what you thank. My Mons Pubis-VENUS likes it rough...like...always rough." Julian waited for her approval.

Nervous now, Julian watched her get up, and slowly pull down her yoga pants, and purple thong for her. Julian did not look down until it was expressed. Samira did not seem to be as graceful as Julian.

Samira sat back down, and worked her pants away without losing site of the blue window. Her chest was pounding under her shirt and bra. Slowly, she slid her hips forward and presented herself to her Witness. Julian stood waiting, mouth-watering, heart-racing, lungs paralyzed, as Samira controlled her moves with her eyes.

Putting her right hand up slowly, as her left middle finger spread her wetness all over her chubby black labia, Samira savored being watched for the first time. Julian read her shallow breathing, and sensed her desire as she waited impatiently to see it, and touch it, for her. Snapping her fingers at Julian once and pointed to the floor, she had found some grace in her domination. Keeping her thick thighs together, she got on her knees without a word or a peek, as the fresh aroma of essence drifted to her, and she felt herself burning below.

They read each other's evolving story, as their roles got defined their responses.

"Closer." Samira whispered to her. "Closer, my manly-dressing Princess of Beauty."

Julian walked on her knees, and waited for Samira's brown eyes to speak permissions. Julian came even closer, expecting Samira to put her face onto her glistening lips below. When she got just within an inch of Samira's spread legs, Samira raised her left eyebrow once, and Julian stopped.

"Ferme tes yeux, Julian." Slowly, Julian closed her windows leaving her other senses to the moment. Samira's left middle finger slid through her well lubed, pink labia, and circled her clitoris as it yearned for her submissive, almost Androgynous, cross-dressing, gothy, short Princess with natural beauty. Her wetness leaked onto the leather couch as she relieved her clitoris of its painful swelling. She sped up her twirls and began thrusting her hips. "I'm masturbating to you, Julian. I'm cumming Julian. I want to kiss your breasts for you. I..I..I......I'm cuMMMMING! OH JULIAN!"

She took to a gasp, and jerked her pussy into her finger as it swirly-crushed her pink clit into her bone. It took all her will to not scream as she bit down to stifle herself. Julian's over active loins became a dripping stream, and she reached down, and cupped the flow, and spread it all over her face, and in her mouth without opening her eyes. She quickly had to do it a few more times to save her seed, and rubbed it on her own breasts.

Samira exhaled to her when she could let the release out, and still sound pretty. She soaked two of her fingers, and put them against Julian's lips, causing her heart to flutter with anticipation. Like a good submissive Woman, she waited to enjoy the seed, when Samira pushed into her mouth, allowing her desires to be pleasantly tainted. She affectionately sucked them dry slowly in appreciation, and held Samira's thick essence in her mouth letting her sense of taste, entice her other senses.

Samira fed her again, and again, and again, as she forced Julian to practice submitting to her.

Spreading her labia apart, and rubbing herself harder with all four fingers to taunt her Country Cuckquean, she worked herself hard. The wet schlicking sound got louder and louder as Julian's mind raced to give more prudence to her ears, to imagine what she was sensing. Julian's mouth watered as her lover's aroma blended with the sounds of the wetness, and light moans of stimulation.

Impatient, Julian pushed Samira's pussy juice to the top of her mouth, and spread it everywhere in hopes of feeling it smother her mouth. She kept it safe, allowing her mouth to hold her lovers scent and flavor.

"Inhale my wetness, Julian. It is because of your White curves." With great patience, Julian slowly inhaled through her nose to enhance the sweet wine of her Dark Goddess. Her sense of smell had been dominated by the aroma of her wet scent, and Kitty was purring.

"N'ouvre pas les yeux. Je vous offrirai mon Plaisir aussi longtemps que vos sens voudront le mien. Please don't take me in, and break my heart."

Getting close, Samira abused herself, purposefully making her wetness louder. Julian's vagina did not stop dripping, as her mouth watered to the vagina she could not see, yet taste in her mouth, as she whispered, "Je suis un ange de Dieu et je ne peux qu'aimer. »

"Have you ever been with a Black woman, Julian?" And Julian shook her head. "Listen to what you have done to your Black woman." The sound of her wetness bounced off the leather sofa and landed on her target. "I stopped to admire you in the hospital days before we met. You looked so demure, unassuming, so beautiful, so manly elegant, and manly precepts. I masturbated to you that night, having not spoken a word between us." Samira fed her again with her warm juices. "Open your eyes to my promise."

Julian slowly opened her blue eyes to see the beauty before her with one blue eye.

"Apprécier mon vagin, Julian." Samira whispered to Julian's fourth sense. Black as night, full and swollen, labia glistening with her wetness, thick, shaved, accept for a patch of hair above her mound, and no visible labia minora or thick clitoral hood. Her entire vulva zone was darker than the rest of her skin tone. It was pure Black, unlike her brown body. Julian swallowed again and again to the desire she had never seen before, as Samira watched her pupil get larger and larger.

"You are so beautiful, Muslimah." Julian whispered, and needing to clear her throat.

"Back away from her, and stay on your knees, MY pretty Tomboy."

"Yes, Muslimah." Julian said in kind. Samira's clit tingled from that unexpected, very submissive response. Samira even stopped to acknowledge the rush of arousal. Their dominant and submissive roles in the relationship was clarified with just one verbal response.

Once Julian backed up licking her lips, Samira stood up and removed her shirt and bra, and stood over her. She was now only in her short white socks. She saw the huge wet spot on the green rug below where Julian was, and produced more of her own. She stepped over to Julian, and lifted her head up by her chin, and bent down and kissed her softly, and told her, "You are the most beautiful, submissive Gamine, I have ever seen. A mysterious, woman you are, Julian." Julian stared up between her two large brown breasts with puffy black nipples poking outward. She felt dominated, humiliated, and exhilarated. The near perfect arousal recipe for her mind.

"Thank you, Muslimah." Julian whispered as she offered herself to the new ruler of her pleasure, on the Bi side.

"Woo her, Tomboy." Came a whisper from her new Dark Master, as Julian shared small nods.

Samira, spoke as she forcibly grabbed Julian's hair in her fist behind her head, "Embrasse ma chatte," and shoved Julian's face into her warm and wet, Black-Middle Eastern garden. Immediately, the fresh juices smothered Julian's mouth and chin as she worked her tongue between her labia to her woman's pulsating clitoris. Julian's heart warmed her as it validated what she was hoping for, the desire to serve her and be dominated; to feel safe, by feeling owned. Samira jerked her hair, and kept her wide commanding stance as she began fucking her Bitch's face. She was demanding her pretty Tomboy please her. Samira held the back of her head tightly, and quivered as Julian licked her to full capacity.

Samira's hips came forward giving her everything, and jammed Julian's face as Julian

90

repeatedly moaned her acceptance of her Cuckquean role. The Master found what her desires had searched for. Julian reached around with both hands, and palmed Samira's thick, full ass, and owned her role. "Drink my seed, Doctor. Lick my pussy, Julian. Taste me...me...me...me. I'm cumm...I'M CUMMING FOR YOU PRETTY BOY!"

With both hands behind Julian's head, she fucked her face hard as she exploded on it. Her thick, clear wetness sprayed out of her vagina, and dripped down to the floor from Julian's chin. It began to dangle as her thicker seed began to grool. When Samira stepped back to catch her breath, Julian buried her face into the carpet to suck it up like a good Cuckquean. Julian's fifth sense had finally, been satisfied.

Samira watched passionately until she was done, and walked around her, circling slowly. She grabbed Julian's long black hair, and rubbed it softly on her own face as she slowly stopped behind her and laid down on the floor, and waited for her Pretty Boy. Julian was panting, and rubbing the wetness grool of her chest, and licking it. "Thank you, Muslimah for lettin' me please you." She whispered from her soaked lips.

"May I drink the wine of a beautiful, Pale-White, Texas Woman?" Julian turned and smiled, before speaking again.

"Why, yes you may, Muslimah Ishq." And Julian climbed over her pouring her essence across her beautiful, black breasts, and Samira realized this would be a challenge. Julian started to squat over her face dripping, and Samira realized she was not ready for this yet.

"Hold on." Julian continued to drip. Julian's labia hung down under Samira's chin as she squatted and rested on her bare chest. She constantly flowed from the bottom of her hole onto her beautiful golden skin, sprinkled with darkness, with pale-White Texas labia resting on it. Samira was intimidated by her own fears, and scooted out and sat up to she could breathe again. Julian stood up over her waist, concerned.   "Julian, I want to do this for you. I'm not sure ho...ho...how to do this for you. Respectfully as beautiful as your..."she gestured toward her pussy..."I'm not sure I ca...ca...ca...can or know how because of her thick.... She is beautifully overwhelming to me. Please if I struggle, let me up. I'm somewhat claustrophobic, and...and...and that is the real problem." Samira's eyes told Julian everything. She was showing real fear.

Julian smiled and laid down with her, and they began kissing. Immediately, Cuckquean slid her fingers inside her Princess Master, and listened to Samira's pleasure radiate from her entire body.

"I am too, Muslimah." Purposefully, Julian schlicked the sounds of thick wetness, and circled both fingers around her opening, and watched her brown eyes cross as they faded back into her head. Her fingers were ready to sip, when she pulled her soaking wet hand up to taste her again, and Samira stopped her, and pulled Julian's fingers into her mouth, tasting herself in front of her. Julian felt the rush leaking under her, and placed her hair inside her vagina. Samira watched her stuff about half of it inside her.

"Is that part of your religion? I mean, why you must have long hair? Julian?"

"Yes. I'm...a little of OCD at times."

"Why does Noah let you-" Julian got hold of her lovers clit, and gently fingered her long hair

92

deep into her warm, wet, recess. Noah was not the only one who knows how to shut a woman up. Julian fingered her slow and hard, as she laid next to her, making sure their White and Black breasts stayed connected.

Julian edged her to bliss and stopped. Gently, Julian pulled her wet hair out of Samira's wetness and her own pussy, and tied it into a double knot. She worked it back inside her own pussy, and leaned her head back to make it pull tight, and lined it up her thick, wet labia crease.

When she put her two fingers back inside Samira, and rocked her own head with each thrust up into Samira, this gave them both instant, mutual moans. Julian put her thumb on Samira's clit with two finger curled up inside her, and rubbing the back of her clitoris through the pelvic bone, and rocked harder gliding her thumb and two fingers in sync. Immediately, Samira screamed out her pleasure as her new Cuckqean did her job well. She screamed louder and louder to the neighbors, as Julian peaked into her own orgasmic moans with her. It sounded like a crime scene of passion, as Samira's shyness ran away from her moaning.

Julian's head jerked on her pussy knot as she flexed her cervix, trying to hold it inside her leaking mess of pleasure. The stimulation was sore and wonderful, as Julian's eyes rolled back, and both Women moaned to each other until Samira gave in to the orgasm, and screamed Julian's name to the neighborhood. She tugged Julian by the head, and pulled their faces together to blend during Vulnerability.

Julian's reward burned to near explosion after, hearing Samira's cries, and quivered as it teased on edge. Less demure, she clamored to punch her bruised Venus mound, and squealed from the immense pain, and drove her lingering orgasm over the edge. She rolled back collapsing and rocking, as it gave way to intense bliss, and her new Master rushed her sliding two fingers into her with her thumb on her pulsating clitoris, and dragged her orgasm along. Samira gently put her breasts to Julian's as she got cheek to cheek. Julian's orgasm burned with intense signals from bruising in her soft tissues, and whined to the overload her orgasm was, at the hands of her new Lover.   Shaking and grunting her screams, she bucked, keeping her legs apart in submission, as her Muslimah grinded her over and over and over and over. Jay's badgering attempts at screams were mere sounds of nothing compared to the concentrated look of pain on her face, making Samira smile and wetter.

Finally, she arched slowly, lifting her fat Texas ass off the floor, and jolted back down, holding onto Samira's shoulder for Vulnerability. She was gasping when her Master put her cheek to Julian's chest, and three fingers inside her, and slammed her palm like a fist into Julian's fat mound over and over. The pain signals still chased the pleasure signals, and landed in her mind together.

Watching Julian somewhat lag in physical responses from the brutal please, she laid back down to rescue her and most importantly, embrace her. She glowed through Vulnerability, trying to say 'Thank you, Texas.'

"So huge Sammy. I...I...let me catch my breath." Her Master embraced her, and protected her in her moment. "Thank you Sam. Thank you. Thank you Texas." Samira reached down and kissed her as her while Vulnerability came to an end. Both women were pleased with their first time, and laid

94

back holding one another. Julian laid her cheek on Samira's large breasts, and sucked on her long puffy nipple instead of her hair. Samira was petting her again, and whispered about the beautiful woman she was. It would be easier now to speak about what they wanted from each other, in terms of their relationship, now that the sexual tension was released.

Samira reached for Julian's hair, and worked the huge knot out of her pussy, as Julian moaned to her. It was soaking wet when Julian pulled it up, and hugged the knot to her face. Samira watched as Julian slowly sucked on it. She leaned in and smelled the wonderful and teasing scent of her Woman, and sucked on the other side of the knot to see if it worked. She was hooked.

Wetness didn't stop coming, and Samira fingered herself, and rubbed her seed on Julian's large, dark areola before soaking her nipple in the center. "You really do have wide nipple areas, Cowgirl. It covers the entire front curve of your breasts, and under it. I really like that. It…it…it…it reminds me of Black Women. They are near as dark as mine." Julian smiled and reached down and got her fingers wet, and rubbed them on Samira's puffy, black nipples that were half the real estate of Julian's.

"You have very carnal puffy nipples, Sam. I am jealous of them…especially the color. They are so dark, and your entire areola rises like your nipple, they are sexy black. I would love to have really, really dark areola. Everyone could see them through my shirts. I miss college." As she soaked them one by one. "You will feed children well someday, and I hope you share with me and Noah."

"Noah? Uh...Julian most White Boys don't desire Black Women."

"Huh. You don't know Noah. I thank I am his first White girl."

"Really? Impressive Progressive. Was he married to a Black woman?"

Stammering to her, "He wishes. That is all he watches on the internet. 'All he dated in college-He would cower to your Black sexiness power...like me. He grew up in the backwoods of Wyomin'. He never saw a Black Woman in person until College. Instant attraction. Can I ask a favor...a sexual favor?" Julian asked abruptly.

"Would you mind doin' Witness for Noah a few times? With his Racial Fetishism, I would likely get more seed from him. He gives me a chalice of semen twice a day, and I have to watch each time. Would be nice if you did it, occasionally? I will share it with you if you want."

Samira leaned back away from her as her voice pitched up, "You mean, watch him jerk-off, Julian?" Julian nodded sucking off her juice from every crevice of the knot.

"Are you kidding me?" She paused as Julian looked at her with her one blue eye. SERIOUSLY?" Samira barked, and looked away to actually think about it.

Shaking her head with a quick jerk of it, "UH...Okay...Why not? I have already seen his goods." She looked back to Julian, "I'm not getting naked for him. If he wants to see a Black va-jay-jay he better get on the internet...or look at yours. You have a Black Woman's vagina, Julian. Thick and meaty and needy like a Thick Black BBW." Samira said it taking on the challenge. "Okay then. I like watching men emasculate themselves on the internet jerking off. It's humiliating to them, and I like humiliating men."

"I thought you might. Remember Jordan, from the hospital?"

"Oh yeah, your 'Momma-I'm busting loose' impression." And she chuckled, and poked Julian with her finger to share the laugh.

"Yes. That was Jordan my...Officer on Duty side. She usually humiliates him once a week for his pleasure. She emasculates him makin' him do 'it'." She looked up at Samira, when she said it, and rubbed her chin on her thick, dark nipple. "He has some mommy issues and-"

"Please, all men do. Especially Black men." Samira quickly told her.

"Well, White Boy Noah, had some really deep ones. I counselled him and relieved some of his anger, but I left a few thangs unresolved to use as control...sometimes. 'Kinda keeps our marriage balanced. Be nasty and bossy to him. Humiliate him hard like you caught him in the act, and make him finish while you watch. Comment that you-I will just give you some cards on what to say."

Samira smiled at her, before kissing her again. "Let me get to know him first, and then I will decide if I want to watch him jerking-off. Men can be so disgusting at times."

"Thank you, Girlfriend." Julian said, and Samira rolled over on her and laid on her between her legs so there pussies rubbed mounds. Julian wrapped her arms around her, and kissed her on the chest. She felt wonderfully dominated in that position. They had all day to talk, and explore their confirmed roles.

"I will tell you what to say to him-"

Samira kissed to shut her up about it.

"I have never been with a man, Julian. Not all the way. What do men taste like? Can you feel it inside you?" Julian smiled with guilty pleasures.

"It be a warm, thick, wine that requires worship, and appreciation inside your mouth. It makes you feel devotion, and a sense of power when you feel it squirt inside you. Our bodies desire the two hundred nutrients and bodies and vitamins men give us in their seed...as well as the Angels."

"Will you do me a favor also, Julian?" Samira felt Julian nod her head. "You are so beautiful, you could win a Miss America Contest. You are so elegant. You...you...your." She stopped to gain her words. "It's the manly way you act and dress, and really attracts me. You still look so beautiful as a feminine woman but, act so manly. Can you get some of that tobacco stuff and chew it, now? It is disgusting, but I like seeing you do it." She chuckled at her own embarrassment.

Julian knew someone else who liked to watch her chew snuff. She was married to him.

"Watching your feminine beauty and Southern manners act like a man in the hospital, stimulates me something warm. I honestly haven't figured it out yet. I like seeing you dress like a man. You are just...just...just...." *Kiss.* "Thank you, Girlfriend. You are just as bipolar...butch acting...beauty queen cross-dressing. ANDROGYNOUS! That is the word." Julian giggled, hoping Noah would get home soon with her Hillbilly chew. "Do not kiss me with it, please."

"So you want me to be the man in our relationship outside, but your feminine Girlfriend in the bedroom?" Julian whispered.

"Yes. No public affections, either." I am uncomfortable with such.

98

"Transvestic Fetishism-Autoerotic, Girlfriend. It's your internal stimulation. I like it. Blended with negative triggers of the positive form for Aphenphosmphobia...no Philophobia. Very common. We can work on that for ya." Julian diagnosed and began to plan instantly. "I like cross-dressing, and I'm a Country Girl, so most of us do."

Samira smiled at Julian, as she sat up, and got her phone from the couch.

Text to Julian from Anonymous Number: NEW FRIEND? BITCH! YOU DUMPED ME FOR HER? I WILL ARREST YOU WITH RAPIST HUSBAND! FAT SLUT!

Text to Noah from Julian: Samira Angelic. Rachael following us now. BEWARE! If she messes with Samira I will not be nice.

Chapter 8

-Momma with Wet Issues, Boy

Lying on the bed and brushing her hair across her nude body with her horse brush, Julian told him the Stiff'em case had only minor updates except, another body turned up, two nights ago. Forensics was busy with the crime scene, and struggling do to the recent rains. With her laptop open, and reviewing the forensics as they came, her eyes were not on it, or him. She was staring at the Cowgirl Box she could see hidden in her closet. He never got in her closet, so it was safe there. She just didn't feel comfortable keeping it in the basement anymore, where she could not keep her eyes on her secrets.

Noah, finished polishing her favorite Corral Red Slate, Bone-Embroidered, Cowgirl boots he picked for her day, and started putting her laundry away.

"Zachary was still asleep when I dropped him off at daycare. Ally was so sweet, she carried him in with me, slumped over her shoulder. He was still suckin' on her hair. That girl is learnin' the power of her long hair." She said to him, leading to something.

He was already speaking topics. "I tried bringing our guns home yesterday from lock up, but was denied access. I think there is still an investigation going on behind our back, Cowgirl. They had been checked in as evidence, and the word is, it's linked to just our Little Incident. Your ring and wooden cross were not there, Cowgirl. I'm

100

sorry. We will get your ring. I promise." She looked at her finger with its vacancy, and then to his rear, since he was wearing only her panties, and his boots.

"You don't thank they be suspectin' anythang else about our…extra-curricular activity?" She looked around for prying family ears, and he nodded.

"They won't catch us as long as Rachael doesn't run her mouth about what she knows." He turned and looked at her, "Well, she is one of us, and we know what she has done late at night."

"Rain would not stop me from my Investigative Methodology." She refered to the laptop, Criminal Behavioral Profiling is so much fun." She perked up excited about her boots, "Am I wearing those boots today or my Lucchese Sonya Eyes & Pink that match my eyes?" He turned and looked at her, a little impressed that she didn't let her anxieties win by not being able to pick her own boots. Too many choices begins to be too much, hence the reason he picks her boots.

"Yeah Cowgirl, take the Lucchese Sonyas. And you already maxed the credit card on boots. No MORE this year. You have like…how many pairs do you have now?" They both glanced at the cowgirl boot shelving that covered part of one wall, from floor to ceiling.

She pulled her hair over her face under her eyes, and smiled at him with them. She was guilty.

With her raspy Cowgirl in distress whisper, she pleaded, "I have to order one more pair, Noeyyyyy. Please. I can't have an odd number pair. Pairing means two, and I must have even numbers. I love you, Cowboy."

"Juliaaaaaan." He dragged it out on purpose.

"Thirty-nine pair, and that's why I need one more pair. It hurts Baby. I can't have the odd number. I love you. There is a space for one more pair and it has to be filled."

Noah walked over and picked up one of his three pairs of boots, and marched back to her boot rack, and put them in the empty space, and smiled at her. Sadly, her glowing stopped. She had already picked out the next pair to appease her OCD, only she hadn't bought them...yet.

She reached over to the end table next to the bed and pulled out his wedding ring. "Jordan hid this from you, not me. She is very sorry. Here Baby." He took his wedding ring, and slipped it on with a smile.

"Keep it on that finger Mister, or I will spank your balls with my boot again." She said with a dirty glow in her uncovered eye. The Pirate-look only had one day to go for him to see that look in both. She was sick of the lack of depth perception-even if she wore it very handsomely.

"Jordan hid it, huh?" Noah nudged at her fib, and she deflected it.

With a hint of seduction in her tone, she reminded him. "Well, she is my Alibi, Noeyyy." He could tell, she cherished her excuse. "I want to ask you somethang Noah, and please don't comment about it...just answer me? No other comments? Okay?" He politely looked at her waiting

Julian moved herself a little on the bed to brace herself and be more comfortable in her position. "Noah, would you marry me for real, if I asked you...if we were allowed." He stood there, not shocked, and waited for her to break the stare.

Leaning down on the bed onto his hands to make her feel his love, "I would marry you today,

102

Julian Michelle, IF, we were allowed." She grew a big smile in her eye, face, and heart. It was certainly what every girl wanted to hear.

"Even with my problems?" She was needing to feel the love.

"Even with your issues, Baby." He leaned over and kissed her head.

Satisfied, she was honest. "I need to get back to work. I'm goin' nuts at home." She bolstered to him. "I am enjoyin' more time with Zachary until he goes to Momma's condo. I want to pump my breasts, and see if I can feed him again. I can prescribe myself the hormones. And Momma, we have to get her back to Texas. Every guy in her village is knockin' on her curves. Literarly...Literlary...Litlerary. Oh you know what I be sayin'." She rolled her eyes like it was detrimental. "Would you like to be breasts fed, Noey?" She asked it in a very shy, and coy manner.

"Yes, My Beautiful Cowgirl, laying there naked, brushing her thick, sexy body and...you are a workaholic. Take your time, you have like...fourteen weeks left of play time. Relax. Heal. Rodeo. Rodeo with Samira. Get to a Bible Study, my OCD love of my life, Angel."

"Hang those...ours...my jeans by color, Noey. I like that." As her OCD got some attention. He blew a kiss at her, intentionally mixing the color, and hearing her growl at him. He pulled her blue pair out of the white group, and put them in the blue section...growling back. She checked her secret box to make sure it was safe from his intrusion.

She smiled appreciatively with relief, and brushed her long hair down her body from her chin to her bruised vagina mound.

"Noey, can I grow my bush a little. Samira has a cute one, and I might-." She stopped talking because he was shaking his head.

"Yes, my Dominion." She said accordingly petting her needs. "I read Samira the other day. She has male problems I want you to address. She fears men-emotionally. It's deep too. I don't know if it is Daddy Issues yet but, certainly Man Issues. I want you to let her help herself when she gives you Witness." She spoke in her clinical tone.

Noah looked back at her for more information, and Julian chose to reiterate. After all, Noah is a man. "She is very afraid of men. She will be angry at first, as her defense, brutal likely, but acceptin' of yer' kindness in the end. Help her, please." Noah moved on. This was not the first time Julian had pushed him toward other women, to let them abuse him, for their own therapy.

"Who is the UC now?" Noah asked.

Without a word, she held up the hand mirror to him, and he leaned in. "Before we shower," she said, to feel safer.

"IDentifY, Noah since Jon is no-longer here. Who is the UC?" He asked again.

"Derence Swisher, I don't know him that well. Flamboyant Gay guy-very pretty. Nice butt in jeans." He didn't take a bite of her tease, and just went on. " When Karen Ritzman arrives, she and I will do a surveillance of him with the other team...just to get her into the case. We are scheduled for meetin' next week. I like her. Fun. Straight forward. Not much drama. Her husband, so she has told me, is a crazy Texas Cowboy Marine. She told me, he came back from the Marine Corps with some serious programming issues-very aggressive on the trigger. Divulged of emotions.

Which is not a bad thang in bed-SOMETIMES! He is a Momma's boy like you. FIX MY PINK BOOTS! They are crooked...please."

Still putting laundry away wearing her lavender silk panties, Noah issued his version of the look. You know the look.

"NOT your Momma, Noah. Me! Yer' Momma. And Momma needs her mornin' routine with you. Shower me, brush me, rub me with oil, and pick my boots. Those are all your jobs, Cowboy." He didn't take another bite, he had chores to finish, which she promised to do, but never really did.

"I love your stomach muscles, and how they 'V' into your low panties pointin' to my favorite friend." She was fishing with that comment. It could make her wet, or dry up the Nile really fast. It usually led to a draught when he was doing housework. She reached over and took the IDentifY mirror.

"IDentifY, Yer' Momma Texas." She said playfully.

Noah immediately stopped, and kept his back to her. His head leaned forward, and dropped and bobbed up and down intentionally. He wasn't really in the mood as he did his assigned chores, in her assigned panties. She was being silly but, admiring his very muscular frame and firm, well-cut ass. In the moment, she actually thought she wanted him to get a tattoo of Texas on his rear but, only in the moment. *It would mark my territory, permanently,* she thought.

Noah lowered his head and his shoulders, and she smiled. "Yes'um Madam." Kitty immediately burned behind her warming labia curtains.

Momma tossed the IDentifY mirror across the bed to him, and he slowly picked it up and looked in it.

"IDentifY, Momma Texas's Boy."

"Young'in, get your pretty rear-end in the shower with Madam." 'Snapping her fingers and smiling. *Nothing like a little IDentifY role playin',* she thought. "I got to get clean to run some work errands."

"Yes Madam." He said, slowly walking toward the shower with his shoulders slumped, and his hands hiding his bulging front below. She was elated as her heart raced to get her favorite body parts flowing. It had been a while since she got to be Momma of her Dominion. It was the only time Julian, not Jordan, could be in control of her pleasures with him, and a little shared humiliation on him. He worked his panties down, just the way she liked, as an inexperienced nervous young man, who kept himself covered. She could see his meat from behind him as it dangled, and he seductively bent over for no reason. She loved accidental peeks on men's meat.

Climbing into the shower behind him, she immediately kissed him, and pushed all her saliva into his mouth. He accepted it, and maintained his subtle role of the inexperienced Boy by not resisting, and not doing his best, and doing her favorite trick. He got down on his knees to be shorter than her. She pushed him against the wall, and spit in his mouth and kissed him again to share it.

"I hope your parents don't come home. They would tell my husband about us." She whispered and turned her back to the shower, and got her hair wet, while telling him to grab the hair tube, and put

106

it on her hair. She reached down, and stroked him a few times to motivate his lust.

It was not a far reach for a woman who claims to be five feet tall and one eighth of an inch. Perhaps she was stretching the truth a bit about her height.

"I promise you will like this. This will be good practice for you Prom Night, neighbor Boy."

He put the foot long section of pool noodle next to her hair, and slid all her hair in the long cut down its side, and poured shampoo down the top. She stood with her back to him facing the shower, and stuck her huge round ass at him. She knew that would get his blood flowing in her direction. It magically shook.

"Now stroke Madam's hair like when I strokes your pretty cock, Boy." Noah walked on his knees to the other end of the shower holding her hair out and slid the tube up and down the four feet of hair, and worked it into a huge suds pile taking it all the way to her scalp. She worked the shampoo in at the top of her head.

"Stroke your Madam, Boy. Stroke her like when I catch you stokin' your penis in my window at night." Momma walked back towards him, and felt his erection on the back of her thighs. "That is my good Neighbor Boy," she whispered. "Momma wants you to increase your Zinc. I'm gettin' headaches, and maybe I will let you cum on my face."

"Yes, Madam Texas" He muttered keeping his eyes from making contact with hers.

"YES'UM BOY! Madam Texas will not pleasure you."

"Yes'um Madam Texas. I love your sexy curves Ma'am." He whispered to her admiring her dangling breasts and hips.

"I know you do. Boy. I see you peekin' in my windows." And she bent over for him, and put her big ass in his face. "Wash Madam's ass for her, Boy. You can see my pussy without lookin' in my window. Just give me somethang to get me off."

"Yes'um Madam." Noah squeezed a little body wash onto her lower back as she delicately worked his tongue into her sore spots. The feel told her he could not get to the Heart of Texas, and she reached back and stretch her ass apart so he could wash her good before she demanded he lick her good.

He worked the lather down the crack of her divided round ass cheeks, and thumbed it all around her anus. She immediately let out her approvals.

"That's a good, Boy. Momma Texas like that."

She reached between her legs, and slapped his balls up a few times to make him leak for her. Abruptly, she looked up at the wall in front of her. As she diagnosed what she was feeling inside. It had been years since she played with it, but she felt it. Her ass was wanting him, and not the lather, either. She knew adding magnesium supplements to her daily pills would get her wet inside there, again.

Madam got down on her knees in front of him with her ass offering itself to him, and Noah tossed her hair over her his shoulder, and wrapped it around his neck and tied it. She jerked his hard cock and held the head in her hanging slit as she pinched the bottom of her long, thick, brown labia together for him. The Neighbor Boy knew it was his first time. She held her huge labia together tightly as he shoved his cock through it, and her eyes rolled back

108

as he scraped across her nerve endings, and lonely clitoris.

His cock slid through, and poked out the front passed her fat, mound. She tried slapping his balls with each stroke but, sensations were winning again as she shivered from the clitoris contact. *Forget him,* she thought. It was feeling good on her sore Texas Longhorn pussy, as her entire hand squeezed her labia together.

Having been a Sex Counselor for men, who were sexually abused as Boys, by Women, she enjoyed playing with fire with her own Boy husband. It humiliated him, instead of her, and though he was not into humiliation as much as Julian, he still enjoyed the burn of the fire she played with.

"Say it Boy. SAY IT! Moan it louder. Enjoy what Madam's pussy feels like." Having never allowed him inside her during the Madam humiliation, she chickened out again like the girl would his Prom Night.

Text Alert on Julian's Phone.

"OH MY GOD NOAH STOP! She was jerking forward getting away from him thumping on the Heart of Texas, he had accidently inside. She fell into the corner to get away from him. Hiding behind the running water, and bleeding mascara. "I can't yet Baby. I'm sorry. It's my fault, Noah. I'm so sorry, I can't do my duties yet. I'm workin' her hard for us, Noey. I can't make stitches heal any faster."

She pleaded feeling guilty, and he smiled and pulled her into his arms for a husband hug. Her role playing excited her as well as pain, but this was still unbearable. She got up on her feet using his shoulders to keep him down on his knees, and

109

leaned around him untying her wet hair, and spanking him with it.

"Bad boy Noey. Bad boy with Momma. No pussy for you. Bad Boy!" Noah was giggling, and cringing as it occasional hit his sack. Love was fun. He got up and took command of her, and when she looked up at him, when his hand lifted to her throat, she felt her heart palpitate and her loins burn fast. Gently, his hand slid off the front of her neck, and around to the back. She loved his domineering Dominion style, it was her favorite. Husband gently kissed her behind the steamed up glass.

After kissing her warmly, and petting her breasts, he stepped out of the shower, and her eyes followed him worrying. "Baby, where you goin'? I...I...I..." She stopped herself. She is not allowed to ask for pleasure, only punishments. She stood there, unhappy he ran off with her romance toys.

"At least whip my pussy for me, Noah."

Noah came right back, and placed her secret, orange and white, and intensely rough, un-chewed plastic dog toy, under the shower head to rinse off anything she may have left on it from its last joyous meeting with her. She immediately curtsied to him, and her toy named Venus. The only object she gave curtsy, too...besides her saddle.

"NO! NO! NOAH! SHE IS NOT READY! He smiled at her in his sadistic role that she melted for, and turned her around without a fight.

NO! NO! NO! NOAH! PLEASE DON'T! PLEASE! OH IT HURTS! EASY! EASY BABY! OH GOD YES! EASY! He slowly worked the double-rounded end covered in sensation demanding little studs, into her heavy, labia wetness. She did nothing to stop him, like a good Madam Wife. She whimpered and shook as he rubbed it slow and hard through her thick, dark curtains to her Venus mound entrance. Her knees shook as she held her huge mound up for protection, and the wall in case she fell. The dark pink of the insides of her labia, which had shades of black in it, wrapped around the little studs as he pulled it back through. When her knees knocked, he smiled at her demise.

"OH BABY! Venus is so rough. It hurts Noey...harder. Flip it over. Harder for Kitty!" One end of Venus had four round studded balls, molded together as one, with four rounded corners. The other had two round testicles next to each other on the other end, molded together with four rounded corners, and the shaft changed sex lives forever. It was covered in large smooth studs that made urges break. He gave her the fear. The center shaft of the toy was thick with hard, orange, half inch apart, deep and gapped ridges all the way around, with smooth spikes rounded off on the peaks of the five ridges that covered the six inches long shaft. This was her secret Lover, defeater of all vagina's via deep, intense, unchallenging stimulation.

Her squeals rose higher and higher as she shook and contorted her body, and hugged the wall with her body to rescue herself. Nothing mattered in this battle, not even her precious hair. He chuckled when he peeked around to see her face, she was indeed, slobbering.

The other end made her cry while she screamed her pleasure terrors. She worshipped her doggy-toy, and only allowed Noah to use it on her. This was not for the faint of vagina. This was the Venus big league of toys, and Julian had yet to defeat it completely, and today was not that day. The perfect lover Julian had said, for a girl with religious penetration restrictions...though, such restrictions did not apply to the Husband wielding Venus for her little Fetish.

"FUCK ME VENUS!" She whispered to it. "Please."

"Ohhha! YOUR fat pussy needs punishment, Slutty Woman. Texas needs you to win this one, Cowgirl with Gay pride." Noah yelled to her.

"Fuck my fat pussy, Noey." Panting at the extreme stimulation, she blurted her breath to the wall to humiliate herself.

"Momma's fat pussy, Noey. OH MY GOD!" OH FUCK! MY FAT PUSSY! FUCK ME! FUCK ME VENUS! MOMMA NEEDS MORE PAIN!" Noah felt his penis reach its maximum erection and then some. Her pleading humiliation in submission was his Horny Goat Weed.

"FUCK ME! FUCK ME VENUS!" Juliana's screams echoed in the little shower as she bent over dragging her wet face down the wall. Being her screams just above raspy whispers, Noah had done this so many times to her, he knew what she was saying, even if it wasn't loud. Lucky for them both, the shower echoed her moans really well.

He wasn't even inside her yet, and she was sliding down. Noah grinded the length of the spiked shaft through her labia slowly and smiling at her pain, as he squeezed her hanging labia around it. It was like holding a washcloth around a garden hose in one hand, and pulling it through, with the other.

Her thick juice strung out of her hole, and Noah scooped it up with Venus, and used it as her lube. He liked very messy sex. Julian's face dragged down the wall with each push and pull through her thick sore meat. Moaning and slobbering, her head lowered passed her big, round Texas ass stuck in the air, as her submission to his will continued.

Noah slid the two-ball end back over her seeping vagina, opening her labia wide and sped up. She curled into a look of intense concentration, and he finally heard it. Julian's weeps of terror finally began.

Still squeezing her labia into its shaft and ends, he listened to her moans rise and rise without stopping, and to tease her mind, slid it up between her ass cheeks, and pushed his rounded tip spike into her dark, rear hole. Thick white fluid seeped out, and he rubbed it all over one end. She began to cry pleasures knowing what happened next. The four-ball end needed its turn, and that meant she wasn't near finished being punished for her desires.

Noah slowly introduced the four-studded ball end to Momma, working out his Mommy Issues for her. Slowing a bit, he slid it forward, making sure every stud met her. Her stiff knees and huge round ass shook in terror, as the wall beside her became her best friend. He avoided her clit on purpose as she reached to the floor with both hands for support. He wanted to get it lubed first before the battle. One of his round, studded corners pushed up the center of the labia with its rounded spikes, while two forced her labia apart, and pressing deep into her inner sensitive sides of her rare, Texas steaks, she stopped weeping and held her breath. The Neighbor Boy, spoke to her.

"Yes'um Madam?" he asked smiling in his power, and stroking his sore cock against her sweet, big, full ass.

"Yes'um Daddy," she mustered.

Noah slid it forward quickly as he manhandled her labia around it. Sliding the shaft studs along her drenched entrance, he crashed into her Venus mound dragging her clitoris with it. Instantly, her knees buckled, and her weeps returned, and she collapsed on her knees, cuddling her chest. He worked it up a faster, and her face hugged the wet floor crying her very intense pleasures. Composure for this Woman, no longer mattered. She was so defeated, so fast. He kept his pace, and smiled as his dick got harder, from each knee jerk she had to give.

"FUCKING SLUT WIFE! EATING SAMIRA'S PUSSY! I WILL FUCK YOUR PUSSY UP IF YOU LET HER FINGER YOU AGAIN! THAT'S MY PUSSY!" He grounded it into her harder as her Venus Mountain poured out, and her sweet hole, drenched the pain.

"Yes, Daddy." She tried to say. "Yer' pussy."

When he shifted gears she began to shake with her sobs and he knee stayed in one constant jerking motion. The crinkles on her forehead made mountains, as she worshipped the intense, painful pleasure. Daddy demanded it. Buried into the corner of the shower with her shoulder, and her head pinned between the wall and floor beside it, choking on urges for more pain, she urinated without control or concern again, as he worked it across her bruised pussy with real speed and force, spreading her warm piss all over her. She enjoyed the humiliation of it. It was too stimulating to enjoy, yet too satisfying to stop.   He kept sliding it faster and faster as she cried out her prays to her momentary, Neighbor Boy lover that got her hot, but turned into Daddy when she got defeated. Her mind always turned to Daddy as a safe-space during the most over-stimulating sex. She couldn't try to get away or stop him. She had set the rules of pleasure as she had read them to him, from her Bible.

"I'm a Slutty Cowgirl." She mumbled to him. "I'm a fuckin' Slut. Fat Slut gets used." She whispered, and Noah heard it.

Text Alert on Julian's phone.

Noah watched as her urine washed away into the drain, and pushed harder to give his Slut everything she needed, and get what he needed. She started wiggling to get away from him as she quivered on her sobbing face. He stepped on her head as she nearly flipped over into the wall, and stopped her as she cried in severe pain that made her feel good. He would stop the long, constant orgasm of stimulation he was giving to her if she didn't let him abuse the long, constant orgasm. His rhythm changed when her screams ran out of air.

"FAT BITCH! YOUR FAT TEXAS ASS JULIAN! FAT SLUT! I OWN YOU! FAT ASS SLUT! YOU FAT PUSSY LICKING TEXAS SLUT! EVERYONE KNOWS YOU EAT SAMIRA'S PUSSY!" He watched her crying face nod in appreciation, and everything stopped as he slowed the spikes down rubbing the clitoris, and teased her urge. When she stopped shaking and jerking her knee. He immediately stopped, and stepped back.

Julian was nearly up on her shoulder, with her back to the wall and in the corner, and that big, ripe rear, ready for the taking. He smiled when he saw the slobber still draining out of her mouth onto the floor. She was sexually drained, and near comatose from the stimulation her rapist forced on her. But no Big O.

115

Chapter Nine

-Monster with Wet Issues, Daddy

Daddy shut the water off as fast as he could, with a dirty smile in his beard. Julian needed to hear the echoes of her crying defeat without the 'bang' of a final orgasm. Gently, her small gags faded like her will for more. She had served her male Master well, and he defeated her sexually, rewarding him with a boner his Angel was responsible for.

Noah stepped out of the shower, and came back with his phone taking pictures of his nude wife's, huge, round ass still up in the air. He got behind her and took sweet shots of her swollen dark labia dangling down between her pale, thick thighs, exhausted. Her face buried into the floor and crinkled. He shot her entire ass using the wide angle, and finally, put his thick, warm satisfier on top of the crack of her ass, pushing it up between her Venus dimples, and took his last picture. She was smiling in her chemical bliss as he pumped a few more hits of reward into her brain.

"Fat Texas Slut." He offered to her, and she moaned in agreement with her eyes still closed.

"I know. I love your pain so much, Baby. Thank you for lovin' me."

He chuckled looking at her. She was pathetic. She was still having the shakes and small cramps in her abs, as she kept on her knees in a fetal position. If the house was on fire, she wouldn't be able to get up. Her hair was hiding in the corner with her shoulder, and she thanked her dog-toy. Her eyes slowly opened, and her mouth was smooshed open,

116

and she tried to think. *Nope, not time to move yet,* she thought.

His chuckle became contagious, and she shook more as she started to join him in a very exhausted way.

"Some Angel you are. You fat Texas Slut." He said through his chuckles.

"Yer' fuckin' Monster." She blurted out humorously, with the right side of her face still smashed into the floor, and her mouth scrunched. She was looking for some sympathy here. "Wingin' Angel of Sadistism, you. Fuckin' Monster. 'Can jist die here, Noey. 'Tank you, I' Love. God knew is chit givin' yer' tower over my tleasure. Oh God. I neet to pray. My senses is ravisht. Dat had to be a sin, Noey"

He kept chuckling, and she started again making her wiggle across her hips and breasts, which made Noah laugh more, and his dick hurt more. He walked back out of the shower stroking himself in discomfort, and she prayed with her fat ass up in the air, and her face still smashed into the floor. No ritual, no hair. When Noah came back, she was still on her face and knees, and he fingered her pussy spreading her black-tipped labia majora with two fingers, and with love, slowly rubbed her clit with his middle finger. She didn't give a shit. He owned it.

"I need Copenhagen Noeyyyyyyy-"

When the warmth in her labia began to burn, her expression began to change with concern.

"WHAT THE FUCK NOEY! OH MY GOD YOU TEXAS PETE'D MY PUSSY AGAIN!" She was jerking herself up stumbling, and slid on her belly screaming trying to get up again. Her Angelic duties had been called on. As fast as her big anchor-size

117

ass could spin her around, she grabbed his dick, and sucked on it as fast and hard as she could on her knees. She stroked him like a champ in a race. Time was of the most important burning essence at the moment.

He smiled looking down at her as she moaned louder and louder with his dick as her silencer. He loved the Texas Pete burn as much as she didn't, and she was only allowed to wipe it off with semen. She bobbed as fast as she could to drain him. Her rule, put Texas Pete hot sauce on her clit, and she will blow him faster than a Stallion finding a Mare in heat. The burn tingled her inner most delicate nerves and clitoris, as her fat pussy gave every bit of its wetness, to drain it off.

She gagged herself again, and screamed through his pipe from the pain. Finally, she looked up at him with sad eyes sucking down his pipe, and he snapped a picture. She smiled quickly with cock deep in her mouth, and grabbed his balls as she stoked.

Nervous, her Neighbor Boy fantasy turned Daddy, put his hands up, per her rules. He knew the milking was coming. She sucked his long manhood, as she stroked it, and with her other hand began punching his balls underneath, and quickly gaining power. Her clit was on fire until she could make him squirt his wife-owned juicy of Vitamins.

She skipped a few steps, and just punched his nuts repeatedly, and kept his dick gagging her, as he took to screaming before relieving. Julian punched them hard, and fast making his legs quiver, then his body. His girly-scream made her wetness sooth her clitoris. Her mouth, her other hand, her suction, her tongue just under the head of his throbbing cock all worked to rescue Kitty from

Texas Pete's heat. She punched over and over, and he screamed exploding his warm cum into her mouth. She kept pounding his nuts with a big cock-filled smile as he crippled to the wall girly-screaming her name for mercy. As his seed burst warmly into her throat, she milked him dry to the liquid courage she had received. That dick was not allowed to leave her mouth, no matter how far down he slid, until it was milked dry. Her rules. He loved her rules.

Quickly, she got up, and shoved her tongue and cum into his mouth, and he jerked himself away, and fell out the door spitting his seed out of his mouth, and the flavor of his cock. She was fingering his cum from her chin to her clitoris as fast as she could, as she laughed at him, and chastised him.

"YOU PUSSY Noey. You promised to snowball me from now on when I blow you. Pleeeeeease?"

Noah rolled over gagging, but not from his seed, his nuts were banged up for his pleasure, by their owner. Such are the pleasures of love and sex. She stepped next to him on the floor, as his stomach repeatedly sunk in to drive the pain away, and holding his wife's seed-makers. She loved how much his wet muscled flexed. and glistened when he mildly convulsed. She stood over him, cum on her face, and masturbating for the orgasm Texas Pete and his warm cum, were giving her.

She bent down and wiped his seed off of his face, and chin before it was wasted and tasted it, with a smile.

"I'm cummin' Noah. I'm cumin'. FUCK ME! FUCK ME NOEY!"

"STOP IT NOW!" He yelled at her, and reached up and jerked her hand away from her pussy. And like a Real Woman, her pussy chased her hand.

119

"NO! NO! NO! I WAS CUMMIN' NOEY!" Her other hand found her button and started fingering herself again as he held her arm, and leaning down at him.

"STOP IT NOW!" He reached up and grabbed her other hand, and collapsed back to the floor, still in pain from his nuts getting owned.

"NO ORGASM! NO! BAD COWGIRL! BAD! BAD MOMMA!" She gave him a pouted look, and tried to use it and her orgasm faded into memory, as he held her, and dry heaved his nut pain.

Realizing she had lost her Big O, she jerked away from him, and stood up over him like a Texan on a bad day, and kicked him in the nuts. She reached down and grabbed his phone. She stood over him as it was his turn for the fetal position, and took a photo of him near his own death from pleasure and pain. Then she took a photo of her tits for him, and kicked him in the rear.

"Girl Power, Noah. And I like bein' a fat, pussy lickin', Slut. ESPECIALLY THE PUSSY LICKIN' PART!"

As she shook her big, bare ass walking away giggling, she shared all her dirty sex photos from the shower floor in a text to herself, and then deleted them from his phone.

"AND THE SLUT PART!" she said in her after-thoughts.

When she got to the sink, she rubbed cold water on her still mildly burning clit to get rid of her hot sex partner, Texas Pete. "Thank you Wyomin' for yer' seed. Guess I will have to thank Texas tonight when you come home. Meany Dominion. I never blue ball you, Noey. Now I will have blue pussy."

He moaned out his devotion to her, and it sounded lame. "Baby, I love you." Still holding onto her drained nuts for his life, he rolled over on his right side to face her, and still held the fetal position, heaving occasionally. "You love your pussy black and blue, and now your URGE can be black and blue to match it." He took a breath to let some of the pain out, "Cowgirl, if you need to rodeo, and I'm not here, get Samira to Witness. Ask our neighbor, Steph'an. I think Christina is Bi. Her husband?" He was being sarcastic.

♫ *Text Alert on Julian's Phone*

"I can't Baby, Sammy doesn't get off until late. The kids will be home by then." She gave him a sad face, and reminded him, "My laundry still needs put away." Perhaps her sad, abused look would help, and she pouted her lips, and stood demure. "Christina would tie me up and keep me, and you know Steph'an...though very, very pretty, is gay. Like he would want to watch a Sexy FAT PUSSY LICKER, Rodeo." Now she was being sarcastic.

"Video record your rodeo, and send it to me, and I can Witness it for you. Do not waste your seed, Princess. Chalice me."

Her hopes came back as she got excited. "Really? I can do that, Noey?" She asked glowing in front of the mirror-less sink, and bouncing her nude self, up and down. So much for demure.

Nodding he said, "Just this once. I will Virtual Witness. Angels do it on the Internet all the time."

"What? I can do it on the internet?" She was instantly making plans for the world to see her Texas Kitty shake at her own hands. Quickly, her thoughts got dirtier, and she smiled really big with her eyes. It was his fault after all, then she finally heard, he had said the word, Angels.

121

"I can watch other Angels...GUY ANGELS WITH SEED? Do they swallow it?" Her eyes opened wide to make sure she read everything he was saying. She was feeling the throbbing come back her way.

"NO! YOU MAY NOT TOMBOY! DON'T BE POSTING ONLINE! YOU HERE ME JULZIE!"

In her fake sad voice, she answered, "Yes husband. I am commanded," with a curtsy, and still jumping up and down holding her large boobs. He would be going to work soon.

"Noeyyyy...You made my pussy purple and yellow beatin' her good yesterday...now I have friction-burned pussy." She pouted her sad face after whining to him, and threw demure back into her hourglass pose. He shrugged his shoulders at her smiling big. He had already granted permission to rodeo by video.

"You have to wait for two hours before you can rodeo since you let Samira inside her yesterday. He was all smiles to his disobedient Momma. He was pathetic still holding her jewels in the fetal position, and making demands as she stood short.

"You'z a cruel Angel, Noah. I hope God heard you. Thank you for makin' me wait for my orgasm. It hurts more that way. And thank you for the punishment." She quickly, curtsied to him.

"Three hours, Momma?"

"My Lord, you be givin' me a headache. I need some Hillary Klugg music." She walked away leaving him on the floor. An internet search was just a click away to see a real Angel swallow his own seed.

"NOT Hillary Klugg?" He jested poking her with a laugh. "She is a guy."

Text Alert on Noah's Phone.

She stormed back from the bed stomping in her shaking nudity. "Don't you dare be sayin' one

122

thang about my beautiful Angel! We doesn't like you. She be the most beautiful Angel I have yet scene on this earth. Don't you DARE MAKE FUN OF HER!" She was...kinda serious about her crush on Fiddle player, Hillary Klugg.

"Hillary and Julian sittin' in a tree, L...I...C...K...I...N...G!" he sang at her trying to get back in the fight. "...A rope of from Hillary, a rope of from Julian, third-Julian wants to love an Angel named Hillary." He finally sat up and crossed his legs. His privately owned, meat and potatoes laid on the floor between his legs...milked for every last ounce, and aching.

She stepped over to see Hillary's CD case posted on her bedroom wall. "Kissin' ain't all I would be doin' with this Angel. She is breath-takin' beauty." She looked down at him. "She is one of us Angels, Noah. I believe it. She is aware of it...I can tell. I would love to see her Venusian dimples." She looked back to admire Hillary, letting her pupils suck it all in. Oh how she longed to look into those eyes close up. "She would snowball with me, since my husband WON'T!" She added, poking back at him. "And she would be given me orgasms after punishin' me so hard, instead of makin' me wait hours."

"Would you suck on each other's hair?" He asked, just to get her to admit her crush. She stared at her Blonde Fantasy *thinkin' that Angel would be able to help her have an orgasm, in three hours.* "She looks like Jenna, Noey. The Real Jenna. Sounds just like her. I love her."

"I wouldn't just be suckin' on her hair." She said quietly and smiling with all kinds of lust. Quickly, she kissed the end of her wet hair, and touched Hillary's face on the cover. "I would be a bad girl for her." she confessed under her breath turning away, as she went to turn on her music.

Noah rolled his eyes before getting up and limped to the bed. He was not defeated yet. He walked over to her with Venus, grabbed her by the hair on the back of her head, wrapped it around his fist, and twisted her around tossing her naked fat ass on the bed with real manly aggression. It actually scared her for a quick moment.

He climbed on her and put Venus against her very tender pussy lips, as she started to giggle at him. He looked up to see it was fear that made her giggle, and began working it inside her. She winced tossing her head back, throwing her back at him as she kicked her bare feet. He was ruling his domain. She was going to get her orgasm, finally.

"OH GOD NOEY! OH MY GOD! OH MY GOD! IT HURTS! She said to him, really letting him have his way. He was putting it inside her. "PLEASE! NOAH! OH MY GOD NOEYYYYYYY! FUCKING HURTS! OH MY GOD! NOEYYYYYYY! MY PUSSYYYYY NOEY!" She panted her pain out with a dirty grin, when he stopped.

"All the way in." She was still panting the pain away. "I can't see any orange ridges, so enjoy your orgasm in two hours. You must keep the shaft inside her until your orgasm. Am I being clear, Angel Wife?"

She started giggling and her tits shook to the sides of her chest. "ALRIGHT! ALRIGHT! ALRIGHT! MEANY!" She was giggling too much for it not to be fun. He got up and she put her arms out for help. As he pulled her forward, making sure she scooted on it, she screamed and winced to get off the bed faster, and smiled appreciating the intimate challenge. As he pulled her up, he let go and she smashed onto the bed on her rear, and rolled off as fast as she could, smiling and pointing at his evil grin.

"Okay." She said it softly and seductively, looking at her phone. "I need to clean the kitchen, nude. Right Hubby?" She asked with a lead, putting her wet hair in her lips, and gently twirling her body to feel Venus inside her. She was melting him with her blue eyes. "Brush my hair and rub my coconut oil on before you run off lookin' for places to bury bodies." Noah smiled and nodded as he kissed her softly.

"Yes, Momma."

"Two hours before you can orgasm, you Blue Eyed-Blue Pussy Fat Slut." She smiled at him, thanking him with her eyes. *Her day just got fun,* she thought, imagining herself sliding it in and out of her Fat Kitty while watching a Stranger Angel jerk-off on the internet and taste himself.

"On second thought, Noey. I will brush it and do the oil. You get goin'." She finally looked at her message.

Text to Julian from Samira: I need to touch you, kiss you, hold you, you are beautiful Pale Tomboy. Kisses and Tastes. See you tomorrow Cowgirl. Hugs & Snugs Samira.

Text to Julian from Anonymous Number: FAT COW BITCH! HOW DARE YOU SUPPORT MEN AND NOT WOMEN! FUCK YOUR STUPID BIBLE! I AM SEEING NOAH AGAIN SOON SO HE CAN RAPE ME...AGAIN! JUST LIKE YOU! GET RID OF HIM OR BE CHARGED AS AN ACCESSORY TO RAPE!

Text to Julian from Anonymous: I miss you Emily. Call me so we can get together. I have the men ready for us. Call me now.

Chapter 10

-The Devil & Emily & a Rock

On her knees in the kitchen at the table, she watched the clock, and her fourteenth male Angel, jerking themselves off on the internet, and licking their cum off their fingers. Exhausted from Noah overloading her senses, serving his Biblical ruling with a clock, she waited impatiently for two hours with Venus tugging at her Texas gift, while Angels online, teased her semen fetish, and her Fantasy. The wonderful porn left her forcing her thighs together to hold in her friend who kept sliding out from the severe wetness. The kitchen remained untouched.

The seconds hand rounded the last minute and she squeezed Fat Kitty to make sure she still felt the chastity of her husband, inside and outside her vagina. She ached from the ridges of Venus as she held on to the shaft. Together, they were testing her faith, and her commitment to her change. Both of them knew this, and as a strong Woman, and she would not fail again.

Finally, the waiting was over. She waited until the Angel finished squirting into a chalice, and he sipped it before she turned the porn off of her phone letting her mouth water. When she got up, she pressed play on her digital music player, and pulled her sexy Pirate patch down over her eye, making herself the pretty Pirate again. She would dazzle her man, and show him, he is not the only one doing the chores around the house.

Her Lucchese Sonya Eyes & Pink boots with three-inch heels, clopped as she baby-stepped into the living room and set up her phone to broadcast it live to him. She had her hair twisted into her mouth, and the music was going to move her when it started. Her hubby would get one hell of a show from his slutty wife. Her bruised-pussy needing an orgasm, was all hers now. She had never masturbated without a Witness since meeting Jenna at an early age, and felt a bit nervous. But, she was going to do housework, nude, and not lay down and pretend to do it.

With a long black silk scarf tied over her breasts and the big bow on her back, she danced her way to the living room and waited for the song to begin. Her areola could be seen through it but, it hid her scars.   "Momma is embracing sexy, again," she said. Unsure if he was watching her yet, she smiled at Noah in the phone, just knowing he was anxious. Her feather duster was at the ready. She curtsied to him and pointed to the Venus toy sticking out of her fat, clean shaven, black and blue pussy. She was all dirty smiles, behind her red lipstick, and eye-patch.

The fast piano started her body shaking, and she had to sing for her freedom to rodeo alone. "Hey SINNER MAN WHERE YOU GONNA' RUN TO?" Her size D breasts jiggled, her thick thighs, and her huge butt shifted mountains as she sang the words, and danced her way to the kitchen door. Her ass shook at the camera as she pretended to dust the door and handle. The music was infecting her veins with the stimulation she needed to get funky.

Venus tried to work her way out, and she squeezed her tight and moaned. The wonderful wetness was starting again as she showed herself to the phone. Her hair wiggled side to side like a snake, in front of her back and she worked it for him. This was love. This was passion. This was freedom from the drama Rachael had brought to her life, and tried to take over. This was busting loose her desires that Simon took from her.

She bent over to the Rock, painted with Texas colors and a Star, on the floor holding the kitchen door open, and dusted it. 'THE ROCK BE CRYIN' TO YOU!," she wiggled and sang the best her raspy voice could do for the Rock. But, the Rock would not hide her, and she bent over again with her ass to the camera and argued with it singing the song, "WHAT'S THE MATTER?" Noah was getting the show of a lifetime. She pulled her ass cheeks apart and shared everything for him, and shook so her labia dangled with her toy. Her pale legs enhanced the darkness that was both her sweet spots.

The Rock would not hide her so she, danced her way to the three-tiered, whisky-barrel water fountain to ask it for help, and dusted it with her seductive stance. She wiggled and sang her song to him, as she tried to twirl her hair around with some success.

As the tune changed beat, she wiggled her head with it held back, and did a figure eight pattern with it, to make her hair dance gracefully. Quickly, she reached behind her, and pulled her bow loose letting her big, and somewhat-sagging breasts glow for the camera. Her smile glowed even brighter as she physically bragged about her fears being gone.

To help him see her entire areola, she pulled her breasts up from the top to show the full size of it under the bottom curve. The areola covered the entire tip of her of size D breasts. She grabbed her right breasts above her areola and pulled that one up, and stuck it to the camera smiling like his bad Girl. She cupped the bottom, lifting it, and sucked on her nipple and showed it to Noah. This is why the belt buckle Noah bought her read, 'Rodeo Queen.' *Noah would have to be touching himself now,* she thought. Her hips jiggled and twerked sending her tits and ass in every direction. They held on, but she was whipping it like a woman in season.

So, she ran to the Lord, singing to the family Bible as she got to it. Her breasts flopped in uniform direction as she jumped, and twisted herself while singing at it, and stopped suddenly. Standing innocently with her hands together, as if she was really praying, she thrusted toward Noah and tried to flap her labia at him. The fan lifted her hair up behind her whipping it into the air over and over. "I'm down here prayin'" she said to Noah. The fast beat sent her to the Devil, and she wiggled away to him making sure Noah got the best view of her front and backside, and dared him to seduce her. This Angel could play with fire and get away with it, even if she had to tease the Devil.

The Devil was an eighteen inches tall human skeleton carved of wood. It had been painted with dark, recessed eyes, roped joints, and the color red on his tips. She danced for him, and quickly grabbed the dog toy slipping out. As if she was shunned, she looked back at the camera, embarrassed and covering her mouth with her hand. Quickly, she pulled it out painfully, and showed Noah and the Devil, she was being a bad Angel and licked it seductively, before working it back in her not-so-innocent va-jay-jay. She shook her thick Cowgirl ass at him laughing, and leaned back to work her hair again, and whipped herself with it. All this for the

Devil. She cried out the lyrics for him, "ON JUDGEMENT DAY!"

She bent over, facing her ass to the camera, and reached under her vagina and fucked herself with Venus until she screamed and lost her breath from the intensity of his spikes pulling at her wet, and preciously abused, pussy. She tried singing but, could not keep up the words as Venus stole her thoughts away. Her knees buckled with each jerk and thrust. There was some grace to her movements, thanks to the joy of pain.

She thrusted at him, and pulled each time the chorus played. Juices flowed down her hand as she screamed in pain to please its amazing shaft. Venus had to be one hell of a lover if she could take this.

Her seed began dripping to the carpet below. *Would the drums ever end,* she thought, and begged as she thrusted herself up and down to their solo. When she cried out again to the joy of pain, the drums finally ended. Her senses were exhausted, again. She felt like a new woman in a strange new place and stopped for a second, as if she heard something.

Slowly, she started bobbing her head again, and felt the tune. Arching her back to keep her ass sticking out, she was glowing red on her face, and she fixed her hair and kept Venus deep with her muscles. She made her way back to the camera smiling, and showing her sexy, no-longer shy seductive side. The orgasm from Venus must've jarred her world because her slut wiggle, lost all rhythm. She opened her mouth for the camera, and slid Venus out, and sucked her seed off of her toy as close to the camera as she could.

"Where be the Noah? Be him here? NOAH?" She tried to yell, and grabbed her throat in pain.

131

Looking at the toy like she was confused, she tossed it on the floor, and rubbed her breasts, and her head starting bobbing as she got back into the dance. Grabbing her mound with her hand she jerked at it, and screamed in pain, and grabbed her throat again, in pain.

Off camera, she bent over and pulled on her Venus Mountain again, and realized how sore it was and smiled to herself. Aroused, she starting dancing for him in front of the camera again, and turned around to cascade her hair over and over. She leaped and spun around looking to the left and looking to the right, as she thrusted her hips forward shaking her sore vulva. Instantly, she dropped down to do the splits, and stopped when her labia crushed under her on the floor. A text popped up on the screen, and she stopped to read it.

Text to Julian from an Anonymous Number: I miss you Emily. Call me so we can get together. I have the men ready for us. Call me now. Rachael.

Smiling really big, she quickly raised both eyebrows to the proposition, and the music felt even better. Feeling excited and confident, she started dancing again, and jiggling her way over to the banister to the basement, and tossed her leg over and humped it, with a serious look of pain on her face. She laid down on her chest putting it between her big breasts, and lifting her boots.

Instantly she fell off, snagging her right breasts on the banister, and her ass left him slammed onto the floor with her legs. Shook up, she got smiling at the camera, and shook her finger 'NO' to the song. Her rhythm had gone somewhere else, as she body wiggled making her ass jiggle.

When the clapping started in the song, she ran over to the camera so it could see her slap her mound, and she never missed a beat as she shook her hips and boobs like a free woman. She patted it harder and harder, feeling the internal nerve endings fire for her needs.

She cried out "I WANT YOU TO FUCK ME! FUCK ME LIKE A WHORE! I NEED YOU TO FUCK ME AND BRING A FRIEND OR TWO!"

She danced into the kitchen with the phone, and sat it on the counter to show her. Wiggling with a dirty smile, she grabbed an eight-inch sauce pan, and posed herself in front of the camera feeling the music and barely wiggling. Her head held the beat, and she panted with her pan held up in the air above her head. She stared the camera as the music changed its beat again. She was waiting in serious anticipation to hear the bass drum again. Here it comes she thought glowing erotically. She wanted to get off, NOW!

WHACK! She slammed the bottom of the pan into her big Venus Mountain, and screamed from the pain as it ran deep. Buckled at her knees, she stood back up, and whacked her mound again. She repeated it to each bass drum beat, and screamed out in pain buckling at the knees. She whacked herself again, and again and again, and again to the drums as she cried out "FUCK ME RACHAEL!"

She stumbled with the drum roll speeding up, and beating her labia, and finally collapsed on her back screaming in intense orgasmic pain. As the music stopped, she dropped her arms out to her sides, crashing the pan to the floor, and away from her.

She was crying in burning pain, and burning pleasure, as the tears ran down the sides of her face. Her eye patch held, with her hair spread like a peacock's tail above her, she felt sick and tried to slap her pussy one last time, but her hand was empty. She laid there exhausted, proud, and anxious in Vulnerability, and hoping Noah would bring a friend home for fun.

"God that was wonderful," she said respiring her pain as her mind caught onto something, she reflected the curiosity in her expression. Slowly, she reached into her beaten vagina and dug out her other toy. It was a large sea sponge, for very special occasions. *Noah and a friend, was always a special occasion*, she thought. She palmed her sponge and held it high above her face, and squeezed it with satisfaction. Her seed splashed onto her with her mouth open. Her pussy, managed to tingle one last time as it throbbed from her masochist desires. Her eyes rolled back, and she enjoyed the oxytocin melting her reward system. She felt nearly faint with a headache.

When she heard the back glass screen door open and shut, she paid it no mind. She didn't have the strength to care. She hoped it was Rachael, and a few guys, as her mind went back to the text. When she heard the cowboy boots meet the tile, she knew it was the man she was married to, and he would be smiling from her offering. She blushed to him as he walked in carrying groceries, her new Diddy Meds, and smiling at his nude woman on the kitchen floor. *Nothing new*, he thought, *just odd for the timing.*

He was very sweet in his tone. "My Cowgirl, you look like an Angel laying there. Your hair is spread about as your halo." She smiled, and tapped her teeth with her index finger, and worked to seduce him with her expression and words, nothing else had the energy to seduce. "I went ahead and got five more pregnancy tests for you since you are pretty much testing every other day now." He chuckled with appreciation for her desire to have another Angel.

"Well, I am an Angel, Noah. Wansta' enjoy you some of this fine Angel time?"

He smiled down at her lovingly, "I shall."

"Luckenbach song?" He asked with his warm eyes.

"Sinner man." She whispered back holding her seductive finger in her bottom lip.

"Wow Baby! Verrrry impressive. You must have been struggling to get that orgasm out." He said it enunciating his words to get his approval and admiration out. "I must have blue-pussied you badly." He said, with the dirty grin she loved to see whenever she offered herself to men.

"I could just die right here. Fuck my cunt before I die?" She demanded gleaming at him with lust. Slowly, she pulled her knees up, while still staring this Cowboy down, and in a slutty way, she opened them inviting him to poke.

She read him, waiting for a response, and when Noah flexed his erect penis in his tight jeans, she saw it move for her.

"Did you just ask for pleasure?" He said, with a shocked expression. Kitty opened the damn again, and began pouring her wine down the mountain. Her eyes smiled as big as her mouth, and it was as if she purred at him.

"I want you to fuck me. Are you alone?" She said, then asked.

135

"Welllll, yeah. I went to the store like you asked me to. Are you okay, Julz?"

She stared at his crotch hoping for attention. She was like a teenage Girl in heat, in a passionate moment, on the cold kitchen tile that sweat was sticking her naked back and rear to. This, in his mind, an Angel working of God, but in her mind, it was time to party, and get some older men to play with.

Noah put the groceries on the table next to him and kicked off his boots, and pulled his pants and shirt off, as his mind investigated her behavior. She snapped her fingers at him and pointed to the boots, as he tried to put them back on. She shook her head, and he pulled his foot out. *That was very unusual,* he thought.

"I dig your Bitch panties. I like seeing your big dick in them." She stared at him as he touched himself using his entire hand to lift his cock behind her lime-green, silk panties that forced his member to the front and side.

He grinned at her with concern before stepping over, and she suddenly busted up laughing. When he stepped over her big, round hips and stood above her, he knew what Julian needed. She kept her finger in her bottom lip and commanded the man. "CUM...ON...MY...FACE...FOR ME, BITCH!"

Studying her Window, Noah pulled his long, thick dick out for her panties cautiously, unsure of what was happening in the moment. If there was anything this Angel loves, it is looking up at a huge dick hanging over her. She felt the wetness burn in her wet hole, as the cold tile supported her.

"Eat me out on the floor, first." His eyes widened, and he nodded leaning his head back and staring down to her, reading her demand, instead of a request. Clues were starting to register with him in numbers. "I want you to fuck me like a Stranger, Noah."

His eyes got really big as his brain heard that word, 'Stranger.' Without smiling, he reached over to the table and grabbed an IDentifY mirror, and held it above her, and whispered, "IDentifY," to her and she barely shook her head without a word.

"Who are you?" He asked softly, yet still prepared to seed her. She tapped her fingernail on her front teeth, and barely shook her head again. He was silent, with fear for the moment and his wife. Julian had unspoken truths that only few knew. Julian never programmed an Alibi to deny IDentifY. It was not heard of in his experience having one.

"Did you take your medication today?" He asked.

"Where is Momma?" She asked.

He held the mirror at her again, "Could you identify for me, please?"

Slowly, reached up and too the mirror, and dropped it behind her head, staring at him in wait.

Unsure of what to do, he started stroking himself slowly to her, and stopped to stare her down again and waited nervously. This mysterious woman, stared back, licking her red lips at him impatiently. If Julian was messing with him to arouse him, fear was not a fetish that worked on him. Fear was Julian's fetish, even though he was her safe-space for her heart and love.

With no answer, finally, he asked her, "Emily?"

She tapped her teeth slowly and smiled at him.

"Is Momma here?" She asked again, and the mirror fell from his hand as he barely shook his head or breathed. He couldn't take his eyes off her one eye. He did not feel he recognized her.

"Then jerk your dick on my face, Noah. I am your wife, Dude. I want to watch you jerk your monkey." She said softly, raising her chin for him and putting her hands on her tits, and spreading her legs farther apart under him.

"Got any friends who want to come over? How come you never have friends for us to play with like Rachael?" she asked softly. This was not the graceful Tomboy of his desires. Hoping Julian was messing with him, or even Jordan. Slowly, he began to jerk himself fast and hard for her, and his eyes rolled back. He had never met Emily before-if it was Emily but, Julian was in charge of the IDentifY.

She watched his hand slide up and down the shaft, and the head tilted downward to her when he pulled the foreskin back.

"I like two men to fuck me. And Rachael...we always have fun. She is my wife, you know, so it is okay." He looked down at her quickly, but still stroked himself. "Cum in my face, Noah." She reached down and fingered herself and moaned from the soreness, but still fingered her clitoris to him. "I want you and one of your friends to fuck me like Rachael, and her friends fuck me."

Watching her big, dark nipples shake, Noah instantly blew his load across her face as he bent at his knee but, held himself up. She held her mouth open for him. His cum shot her right on the left cheek below the Pirate patch, and she moaned for him. His second shot landed on her chin, and strung down to her neck. His third shot on her left breasts, then between her chest, and each shot afterward landed somewhere on her flat pale stomach.

He looked down at her for approval as the oxytocin slowly faded, and hoped her role playing was over. He was still cautious about her, as he felt heart palpitations in his chest. She was wiping his cum onto both her nipples covering her large dark areola with his cream. She motioned for him to get down on her, and his dripping seed touched her belly when his penis did. She reached down to his softening penis with her one eye, watching him closely, as he got his breath, she motioned with her cum-covered finger to lean down. When he did, she gently rubbed his seed on his short bearded, chin and put her hand down whispering, "Cum in my ass next time. Our friends cum in my pussy, Noah. But my ass is just for you, and Simon."

Noah stared at her with his eyes widening with fear, not recognizing the person in her windows. She wiped cum off her face, and rubbed her finger clean on the tile beside her.

"Lick the cum off my nipple." She told him with a tone of entitlement.

He stood up staring down on her as she wiggled her way off the sticky floor, and too her feet. Emily, he presumed, walked over and got her phone, and walked away into the hall leading to the bedrooms without a curtsy, leaving Julian's Dominion emasculated.

Stopping at the stairway, she wiped his seed off her nipples, and flicked it at him. "BORING!" and she pounced up the stairs telling him.

"I have a headache. Keep your kids quiet."

Noah just stood there, speechless.

Text to Rachael from Noah: Need to talk. HELP! Met Emily? MAYBE. I think you were right. Headaches? Fragmenting? I can't remember much of what you said.

Chapter Eleven

-Emojis and Pirates Humble to Not

When Jordan walked into the staff room, nearly a dozen people were mingling and having their brunch, lunch, or social media fix. Many of them began applauding her return, and even stood to make sure they were seen and heard. Jordan blushed horribly, with grins of emotions and happiness, as she waved them off. It felt good to be welcomed back to work but, never thought she was loved like this. She honestly felt SANICS was not appreciated. She flipped her hair repeatedly, as she made her blushing way to the table. Awaiting her was Karen Ritzman, Special Agent.

Karen was a bit uncomfortable, not realizing Jordan had become such a celebrity at work. Perhaps a little jealous, Karen's beautiful long blonde hair made it halfway down her back, and she could only judge what she saw.

"Alight, alright now...everyone hold down your voices, please. Let's keep quiet. I can only whisper. STOP IT!" Jordan insisted to her audience, bashfully. "Thank you for the big welcome back. You people are terrible. STOP IT! I was only gone a few weeks. I'm still on medical leave. STOP IT! MY GOSH! You are embarrassing me." The board room was filled with various Lieutenants who ran other departments, as well as Jeff, and a secretary from the Mayor's office who was sent in to record Jeff's minutes.

Hugging Karen with her smile, Karen was taken aback by the winds of applause in Jordan's sail. Embarrassed, Jordan smiled and hugged her, and thanked her for accepting the assignment.

"These people are silly. Ignore them. I have only been gone a few weeks."

Karen spoke up."A great number of fans, seem to have missed that hair, Jordan. It is really great to see you again. How is Mr. Jordan, the King of Your Boots? If I remember that right? The kids? Life? Church? More kids? Family?"

Sitting down finally, to get down to business, Jordan flung her hair around, and placed her scrunchie in her mouth, and started on a crooked ponytail.

"The kids are great. Ally is loving math and music and getting spoiled by her Daddy, and Zachary is mine for the taken. As much as he loves my hair, he will be a Momma's boy. He only let's Momma put him to bed with prayers...holding my hair...just like Noah. Potty training...holding my hair. Noah and I are trying for another one soon. How about you Karen, how is Patrick and the kids, Susie, Louie, and Mary, right?" Jordan quickly waved at Spencer sitting at another table.

♫ *Text Alert on Julian's Phone*

Pat's a little balder, still Marine Corps crazy; runs three marathons a year now, worshiping Chesty Puller. I will stick to the 5K's, Sister. The kids are great. Little Angels. Susie is pushing fifteen going on thirty-something, Louie wants to be a

142

teacher, and hopping around at ten, Mary is a Daddy's girl too. Watch out there! But, how is Jordan? I'm sorry to hear about the accident. I'm glad no one was killed."

"OH! The 'accident' right, uh...well...some...how did you hear about the accident, exactly?

"Well, Rachael Briggs of course. She told me all about it. I know you too were...very close, to say it mildly." Karen smiled respecting Jordan's personal decisions, even if she held a silent moral judgment, to which everyone is entitled.

"What exactly did she say about it? IF, you don't mind me asking. I fired her from my team a few weeks ago." Jordan worked faster to get her hair done, and give her, her full attention.

"Rachael told me you wanted her, to get me, caught up on the case. I was able to read the entire file dated up to fourteen days ago. Your team reports ceased up to that point." Karen was a bit withholding of something in her over-gesturing with both hands.

♫ *Text Alert on Julian's Phone*

"Karen, speak freely. I'm not in charge of your promotion." Jordan said, to break the political correctness barrier.

"I'm sorry. It is none of my business. I would rather we just discuss work. What you and Rachael have is not of my interest or opinion." Karen was delicate, having stirred the cauldron.

Jordan stared at her, with her lips pushed tightly together, as she thought of the damage Rachael may have already done by influencing Karen, prior to today. She was finished with her ponytail, and felt, this had to be resolved for Karen to do her best work under her.

"In a world of politics, passive-aggressive behavior is valued but, pisses me off at work, Karen." Jordan was Jordan. No doubt about that.

"Jordan, I value our friendship, and work relationship-"

"Get to the point, Karen. I have had a headache for over a week now." Jordan reminded her quickly.

♫ *Text Alert on Julian's Phone*

Karen felt the tug of war, and let go of her end, and spoke quickly and more candidly. "I guess you demanded Rachael to marry you, and help you divorce Noah, and he beat you and raped you for saying you wanted a divorce. Now you're having second thoughts, and afraid of Noah, and he made you fire Rachael. And I'm sorry. It made me uncomfortable to which I have now made you uncomfortable and created bias in our work environment. I'm sorry and it is not any business of mine so long as it does not reflect in my work. Live and let live, by God." Karen shuffled up her folders expecting the meeting to take an exit.

Julian's healing eyes rolled so much her head rolled back so she could catch them. With both cheeks puffed up, Jordan exhaled and put her hand over Karen's folders.

"Karen, thank you for being honest with me. I can see this false information was intended to infect our working relationship, and how Rachael knew I called you, is a shock to me. I never told her. BUT! Rachael and I stopped our involvement years ago, and she is struggling with it, personally. I needed to

144

get back to my husband, my children and God, to keep my conscience clear. Noah...my sweet Noah, did not rape me or beat me or threaten anyone. We were in a car accident and not wearing seatbelts. I was tossed, and I landed with the gear shift between my legs, and banged my face into the dash. I had to get stitches in dark places, and care for soft-tissue damage. That is it, Karen. Noah banged his head...which might actually help him thank better." She smiled warmly at Karen, who had gradually began to feel better and physically relax. "I have put Rachael under review for her actions following the incident, when she actually attacked me in the hospital. This is how I came to request you to the case."

"I'm glad you're alright. I didn't expect that behavior from you or Noah. I remember him, he is wrapped around your finger, as always. I have seen his devotion to the children when we all went out, regularly. I expected there were problems when I didn't see your wedding ring. Presumptuous and incorrect. Thank you for your clarity."

"Lost my ring and my Daddy's cross in the accident or hospital. We have yet to locate them...lost a foot of my hair, too. The EMT's had to cut it from the car. It was stuck inside somewhere, as I was unconscious." Jordan smiled really big at her next statement, "The entire Great State of Texas, has yet to forgive me. Texas Supreme Court banned me from enterin' the State until it grows back." Jordan chuckled at her own humor, and Karen felt it, and smiled.

"Well, that is better, Jordan. Get me caught up on this case. My OCD is killing me for more information. Nothing worse than feeling like you don't know everything." Together they laughed, and Jordan got up with a marker.

"Is Noah going to be here, Jay? You still go by Jay, correct?" Jordan nodded as she erased the dry erase board behind them, and the crowd around them chattered, and occasionally, watched them work.

"No. He was doing his chores when I left this mornin'." Karen reached down and took a sip of her hot chocolate smiling, and turned to take in the other officer conversing and playing on their phones.

"His chores? Carrying a whip, are we now?"

Jordan smiled, and answered, "No, I'm just smarter than he is."

Jordan signaled to officers around them, and introduced Karen to everyone, and welcomed her into Officer Briggs position. She grunted here and there like Julian but, her raspy voice couldn't carry. The whole room sat quiet, and waited for her to begin. Jordan felt rushed, and flipped her hair to offer a quick dopamine rush that would stall their impatience.

♫ *Text Alert on Julian's Phone*

Trying to speak her loudest whisper, "Okay everyone, as you know, we have one UC working the street, and have not had any leads that are coming back presumable, or even interesting to say the least. The Forensic Pathologist's report states there has not been any DNA evidence found outside the body, however, one individual, Bryon Taperton, the second victim had a recorded three sets of DNA in his system..." She held up her fingers to help her be clearer, "...two in his stomach-all of which were

146

male DNA. We have collected DNA samples from many prostitutes on the street, and suspicious individuals that we have pulled over on the street trying to solicit prostitution, and we have countless contacts with street walkers all over the city. CODIS has not had any concerning hits, in the DNA DATA system." She gestured toward Spencer, and he smiled without speaking, she was appreciating the intense effort he was doing.

"Our young trainee here..." pointing to Spencer, "...has spent days and nights working the streets and spreading the word, as well as collectin' data, hair samples, and investigating each tiny lead that comes in. Which has not been fruitful to finding the Rapist-Killer? HOWEVER...he is busting his rear in the line of duty, as I expect each of you to do." Jeff rolled his eyes at her, and she ignored him.

♫ *Text Alert on Julian's Phone*

Together, Bodi and Spencer applauded her, while the rest of the room just sort of watched. "I don't thank you ladies and gentlemen heard me, but Spence was collectin' hair samples for DNA comparisons and findings...from women." She paused to see if they would respond with due credit, and they didn't.

Karen put her hands around her mouth to speak, "Hello out there, he had to convince women to give him a hair sample. You know-pluck their hair," and she waited. The crowd just looked at the new team member. She waited, and took a big swallow of her cocoa and felt unwelcomed, quietly.

Jordan stepped up to give big credit where it was due. "Women don't give up their hair easily boys, she playfully whispered and waited, shaking

147

her hair at them in her hand. Finally, she told Spencer he did a great job and moved on.

"There has been no blood evidence or any fibers of any kind on the bodies because they are being dumped into the river."

♫ *Text Alert on Julian's Phone*
♫ *Text Alert on Julian's Phone*

Chapter 12

-Both Buttons Both Fear & Pleasure

Noah opened the door, and standing there was thick, African-American, Muslim woman with bushy black hair brushed passed her shoulders, smiling nervously at him with a rope of hair in her mouth. Her tight stretch jeans on her thick thighs snuggled into her thigh-brows, showing every sensual curve of her thinner-than-Julian, hour-glass figure. Her spiked-heels, short-top boots, were sexy, and her baggy colorful blouse made her stand out, and showed her lack of sexual confidence. She was smiling, blushing really, and posed nervously. Noah admired every single curve he could see, and already planned to have her walk in so he could admire her backside without getting called on it.

"Come on in Samira. Don't be shy. Julian told me to tell you that you are welcome to just walk in. She told me to text you the key code on the door, only, I fell asleep." She was admiring his tight, low baggy shorts with a package she had peaked at once-twice-three times before, and how tight his muscular upper body was, since he was shirtless. As typical, he was wearing his cowboy boots only, and the 'V' muscles pointing toward his crotch, was more interesting than his boots. She liked to call them male-cleavage, just not to anyone.

"I am so nervous, Noah. We haven't really talked, and I promised Julian I would come see you for some...alone time. 'Can't promise you anything.

But we can talk and maybe, try Witness. She has been bugging me for weeks now."

His words came out very kind and concerning. "Samira, relax. I'm not going to just 'do it' either. We are going to talk and then, maybe. It's not like Julian to push me toward another woman, so, she must think we have a connection, and that you are very special."

Smiling and shrugging his left shoulder, "She can be a little compulsive with things. We wouldn't be doing this anyway if my wife didn't insist on a semen vitamins...every day." He chuckled to make her feel better, "Wish they sold the stuff at the health store." He said it, as he watched her thighs, and bulging, athletic ass pass him. He had admirations for her assets.

"Something to drink? Breakfast-well lunch. I didn't get to bed until after the kids got nearer to school. Well, Zachary has daycare at Julian's mother's place. Family latchkey, so the kids are never alone." He rubbed his head and was still trying to wake up, and figure out how to get started with what he needed to do, in a sense of priorities. "Julian always leaves a chore list, so she can claim she did it."

He spoke up, "I have only been a Witness for Julian, and a few...well...Julian's role playing other names...since we have been together." He tried to think if Julian told her about Dissociative Identity Disorder Cover Personalities, and honestly didn't know.

"It's not really...we don't invite people over for this or have people over for this. Even Rachael, in her ugly man-boobs did not Witness for us." He was stretching his arm over his head and scratching his back, and she realized her was not completely awake, yet. She liked the muscles as he stretched, and thought. *Not too many, not too little, and cut just right.* He was not pale like Julian, but more naturally tan, and not too dark and very tall.

"Well, I'm not doing 'it' for you. She said I am to watch you do 'it'. Rachael, Really? She was dating Julian for so long." Samira asked, while waiting to be asked to sit down. Noah was finally waking up as he stumbled around feeling jet-lagged.

"I'm sorry. Sit down. Make yourself at home in our home. I'm still waking up." He gestured toward the couch she put her seed on just a weeks ago, and he spoke up.

"I really need a shower to wake up. Would you mind if we just chatted in the bedroom, and I could use the water-closet to shower, and we can still speak." He stood there still massaging his thin beard.

Samira sat down protecting herself with her huge purse on her lap. She got stiff and smiling and, "Ohhhhh, I don't think so, Noah. Julian would not approve of me in her bedroom with you. I don't think to do that."

"Well, she usually demands the bedroom-Jordan does, for Witness. I am going to get a quick shower, and I will be back in five minutes. Please if you change your mind, last door on the left down the hall."

When Noah walked out of the shower, his towel was slung over his shoulder, and Samira was smiling at him from the bed. He jumped and covered himself with his hand, and grabbed for his towel with the other.

"DO NOT COVER UP, NOAH!" She said to him, bravely. Noah instantly felt unsure of himself, from being caught nude, and, from her stern tone. It

151

made him uncomfortable. Stern female voices shook his Mommy issues to his member, and Jordan used that to play sexual mind-games.

Samira was lying on her back, on the bed, dressed and still wearing her heels as they dangled off the end. "I spent the entire night with Julian, the other...other...other...when I was here. We practiced Dominating you, for you. I am so nervous." She sat up on the bed, "I have never done this before. Julian even wrote down things for me...me...me...to say but, I already know what I need to do to you to make me feel...fee...feel bossed." Her voice was shaky as well as her hands.

Noah, stood there admiring her beauty, and struggling with his attraction to Black Women. "Do not ever look at me Noah, until I tell you." With that, he looked to the floor, and smiled. He was growing nervous and aroused.

"Yes'um Muslimah." He answered softly.

Quickly, she corrected him, "You do not get to call me that. That is Julian's special name for me. Did she tell you to say that?" Noah nodded, and she corrected both of them.

"You will call me Samira. I am attached to Julian, not you, and you will dominate Julian with me, for her pleasure and mine, and I dominate you Noah...in the bedroom." She nervously read the next card to herself before speaking, and was obviously not feeling it.

Samira was very nervous, and adjusted herself, as he snuck glances at her, "I'm looking here." She heard the ceiling fan start, and feeling rushed, she got up stumbling her words and her body.

Thankfully, she thought, he kept his eyes to the floor standing there, and she tried to wing it, as she pulled her shirt off to make it feel like she was making progress. There was nothing graceful about it. She was more afraid of him, than he was of her. She took a big breath, and started down her list.

"So you love to sex Beautiful Black Women? Is this true, Noah?" He nodded and turned around to shut the door. He took her breath away with the view. A tight, muscle flexing rear, and male Dimples of Venus, at the bottom of his back. She had never seen them on a man before.

She sat back down, and was losing faith in her and Julian's choice of words on the cards. "Tell me why, Noah. I am almost naked, and need you to convince me to let you see me nak...nak...nak...nak...naked before I make you jerk off to...to...to...to...me. I know you...uh let me see, I lost my spot...Okay. I know you love to jerk off to Black Women on the internet. I'm here to let you please yourself, if you submit yourself to my Witness."

♫ *Text Alert on Noah's Phone*

He was smiling from the lack of pressure, and answered, "I think women of color are more-"

"I can't do this, Noah." She interrupted him,a nd pulling her arms in front of her bra. "Jordan the Cop Lady, has to do this. Her arms covered her large breasts and he looked up at her.

"Samira, you don't have to do anything. You can just watch me, and we will know you were my Witness. We can just lay in bed, and talk first, and if it doesn't happen, Julian will just have to deal with it, and do it when she gets home. We are not here to hurt each other, or you. She just wanted to try this, and she likes you, and trust you, and I think we have to trust each other, first."

After a deep breath, Samira moved her arms as she sat on the far side of the bed facing him sideways, and slowly exposed her bra to him but, could not look at him. Hearing his breathing change, she felt a rush of arousal, and a little more burn down below. She chuckled and felt her cheeks getting warmer, as she looked away toward the curtained window, assuming he was touching himself. He stepped toward the bed, and laid down on his back, and she glanced over at his pretty, shaved perfectly clean, cock. It was somewhat erect, and she her mouth shook as her lips tried to smile, and her mouth tried to hide it. Taking another breath, she unhooked her bra, and let it fall, and laid down on the bed, near the edge, and let her breasts be completely exposed.

Noah rolled over and began rubbing her left breasts, and talking to her. She was so frozen with fright, not only did she not move but, stopped breathing. "You are a very beautiful woman, Samira. I dated many Black women in college-mostly Black Women in college. Julian was the first White woman I dated in college, as a real adult-I guess you could say.

"Did you sleep with them...all of them?" she asked not looking at him yet.

"Well no. Not all of them, Sam. People enjoy other people's touch. Like you are enjoying my touch now." She finally had to take a deep breath, and worried the entire time he would know she was nervous.

He squeezed her breast softly as her puffy nipple responded to his touch. As his soft hand, warmed her nipple, it slid down the curve of her

154

very, Black breasts to her lighter colored, flat stomach, and nerves began tightening her muscles, all over her body.

If his hand is working his way to my jeans, I am going to stop him. But, he turned and rubbed her stomach with appreciation, and back up to her breasts. "I love how soft your skin is. I love how beautiful the colors be. Your skin has a light or golden undertone, like Julian has a blue undertone, and then you are dark Brown and Black on the surface, as Julian is as white as a sheet on the surface." Only hearing a few words of his compliment, her mind was busy being worried about her wet thong. No man had ever seen her get wet.

He reached over and touched her face, and gently turned her to look at him. "Samira, nothing has to happen for us. I don't know if Julian just feels guilty, or likes to share the love she has and owns. She likes to share happiness and love the world to make it a better place as well as...absorb other people's pain. That is her job in life, as she says, her job as an Angel." He stopped talking, and rested his hand holding one of her breasts.

Samira whispered to him, struggling to control the volume of her whisper, "Does she...really believe she is an Angel?" He got quiet, and kept his fingers touching her puffy nipple as she stared at him.

"She does." He said with heart in his tone.

"Is she?" Samira whispered.

He shrugged his shoulders when he answered. "Who am I to say no? I didn't grow up in a religious family. I just know, she believes it, and I love her." He redirected, "Every time I rub your puffies, your eyes twinkle. Can you orgasm from nipple play, Sam?" Nervously, she answered him in a whisper, and redirected him.

155

"Do you believe you are an Angel? She said you are one, and she confirmed it." She actually took a breath, and didn't worry about it.

He took a few seconds to answer her, but kept rolling her puffy nipples between his finger and thumb.

"No." He whispered it so Julian would not hear him.

Samira instantly felt fear of him, and he started talking again, as her mind chased her fear, and not her unspoken fetish.

"Samira, I don't think you are ready to be a Dominant woman to a man, since you haven't had much experience with us. Julian told me." Samira stared at him and nodded, feeling some shame, and actually thanking him for taken the burden of dominating him for Julian, away from her.

"Why don't we just see how we feel about things? Are you wet?" She turned away immediately, and didn't respond verbally. He saw her shiver, and watched the goosebumps rush across her breasts, tightening her nipples.

Rescuing her from her emotional pain, the Man, who doesn't believe he is an Angel of God, gently turned her face to him, and kissed her full dark lips, and she kissed him back, letting their tongues meet for the very first time. Without thought, they traded seed with DNA, and worked to blend it together, and the rest of their bodies, wanted the same trade. She couldn't breathe.

"Are you wet, Samira?" And she nodded her fear. "You have me turned on but, I need more than sex." He whispered to her, "I need an emotional connection." She nodded, staring into his brown eyes, and feeling his warm, fresh breath, near her lips. Someone moved her leg, and she felt his erection. She didn't realize, her body would betray her, and her clitoris was leading the mutiny.

His voice was very affectionate. "You are turned on, or afraid, or both. Keep looking into my eyes, Samira." She inhaled his warm breath, as her body tasted his White Boy pheromones. "My little Masochists Julian, needs both. She needs turned on...and she needs fear. Do you?"

Already aroused by both, she shook her head, fearing he knew it. Let me read those beautiful brown windows to your soul. I want to see what Julian sees." His hand slid down her curves to her jeans, and he palmed her vagina through them, and her eyes rolled back. Slowly, she opened her legs a little. The mutiny had begun.

"Do you want me to stop?" he asked kindly, and she shook her head with her eyes closed. The sensations were her focus, even though he was trying to read her soul.

Noah slid his hand up, and slowly slid them under her panties, and down to her little black bush. Her chest rose up with her short anticipating breath, but he stopped without passing her mound.

"Are you attracted to me, Sam?" He whispered into her ear letting her hide behind her eyelids. She slowly nodded.

"Are you attracted my Julian, Sam?" She nodded faster, but not fast.

"Do you like to feel a man inside you, Sam?" She froze, and he read her like a picture book.

"Do you want me to stop? I will stop, if you want to. Please, tell me stop if you need me to." Her clitoris shook her head much faster, and forced her shaking full lips to stay shut.

He crept his fingers over her mound, and felt her wetness for the first time. She moaned out subconsciously, and forced her lips to stay closed. Lips don't stop moaning but, when reward systems activate in the brain, the conscious decision are over-ruled by the subconscious, and one's real desires. Right now, Mrs. Clitoris controlled everything.

He was gentle, spreading her wetness all over her shaved, Black pussy lips. He slide his finger just to the tip of her pleasure center, and slowly divided her chubby labia as he drew one finger up from the bottom sinking it between them, and getting deeper and deeper, until he gently bumped into her warm, swollen clitoris. She jerked, and moaned keeping her arms to her side, and pushed them to her hips as tight as possible. Her clit throbbed, and she hoped he didn't feel it. He heard the sound of wetness and soaked his fingers while teasing her mutiny captain. His other hand curled under her neck, and it rested around her, and on her the middle of her chest. Oddly, he spread his fingers out over the middle of her chest, and did not seem to care about her breasts with that hand. It had a purpose, she didn't understand, yet. However, it had powerful arousing effects on her, as she felt imprisoned.

She was already close, when he pulled his wet fingers out, and softly rubbed them on her full lips. She opened them, and let him spread her seed all over them without a second thought. To her, it seemed to feel, natural.

He soaked his fingers again, quietly sucked them clean, close to her cheek. *She was going to die*, she thought. She repeated it in her mind, over and over, knowing she was going to climax, with a man, for the first time.

"When you cum for me, Samira, I want you to say it to me. I know you're nervous but, I want you to say it to me." Still keeping her eyes closed, she nodded fast to get it over with. He gently slid his hand back down, and sucked her right nipple into his mouth, and circled her thick, puffy areola. The fingers on her chest dug in a little, and she felt the fear. Her eyes were well hidden as they rolled back, and enjoyed the hormones her mind offered her, to keep her mating. The Mutiny was winning.

When his finger conquered her clitoris, she cringed into her first orgasm at the touch of a man. She bit her lips between her teeth shielding her moans as she shook, and kept herself from making a sound. When she finally exhaled her rush, the moans escaped, and she accepted it. He knew she would feel better, less nervous, and let them have an emotional connection. As her rebooted mind, woke, she felt his the knuckled on his palm, stabbing into her chest.

"How did...I never...that was...I don't...it was big...I am sorry...He turned her toward him, and kissed her again, and traded DNA without reservations. She reached down, and felt his hard erection, and took hold of it. It was the first dick she ever held in her hand, and it felt right. She felt an unfamiliar sense of ownership from handling it. She stroked him with her inexperienced hand to give back the reward he gave her.

"Open your eyes, Samira." She did, and smiled at him. "You are so beautiful, so lovely in your manners." He seemed to be looking past her eyes, as he looked deep into them. "I am seeing now, in your soul, what I needed to see. I think Julian is right about you."

She changed immediately, "About what? Right about what?" she asked, getting up her nerve now that she had eaten her cake...so to speak.

Unsure of the direction this was taking, he answered her frankly, "That you are one of us." He said frankly, and offered her a kiss, that she refused.

"What does that mean exactly, Noah?" The pleasing him stopped as she jerked her hand away from his cock, and her fear from Vulnerability took hold. Her question, was much louder, than the last one.

Noah stopped everything, and smiled to calm her down, "That you are a special soul, Samira." She wasn't mad, her fear was having her put up a retreat, having just experienced the mutiny of desire. The mutiny by a man who pushed down on her chest, and gave her the fear she didn't know she enjoyed with her pleasure, and something else. She sat up throwing his hand off her chest. She would not be a victim of him. Her feet stomped when she put them to the floor, and turned to him to set things right...or until she could run away and hide.

Sitting up reassured her desperate fear, as he tried to explain himself. "We think you are special in your heart, Samira. What is wrong with that?" He gestured his palms up in front of him.

Getting to her feet with beautiful breasts shaking in anger, "Is that how you picked up all the other Black Women, and used them, Noah? Were they special, too?" She stepped back, and her big, athletic rear, crashed into Julian's boot shelves, knocking over about a dozen of boots, and she rushed away from him in a complete panic.

Her voice began to rise as she tried to find her colorful blouse and bra, "You and Julian are just playing with me...me...me...me for a piece of sex." She found her them, and ran out of the room crying in fear of this Monster. Noah laid back on the bed rubbing his wet hair, and his dick stood high into the air, all alone. He could hear her talking to herself in the hall as she stuttered and shuffled, likely getting dressed.

"SHE IS WHITE AS A GHOST, NOAH! YOU CAN'T HIDE HER BRUISES! I SAW WHAT YOU DID TO HER IN THE HOSPITAL! AND YOU ARE STILL BEATING HER!" He closed his eyes, and laid there knowing Julian would blame him.

"I'M NOT FUCKING AN ABU...ABU...ABU... ABUSIVE...MAN NOAH!" and her stomps led down the short, split stairway, and she slammed the front door on her way out. He could hear the tears in her voice when she screamed her final belief.

"RAPIST!" Before slamming the door closed.

Laying back, and already dealing with the ass-chewing Julian would give him, he rolled over and finally, checked the message.

Text Noah from Anonymous Number:
POLYGRAPH TIME FOR BOTH OF YOU HICKS!
Thanks for the DNA sample yesterday-You spit outside Pharmacy. Emily Report went to Bureau. Crash time for her career and you GO TO JAIL RAPIST!

He rubbed his face, "Geez. Have all women lost their minds? RAPE THERAPY!" He screamed out to all the women in his life.

Noah's hand covered his face again to wipe away the stress, and when he laid back on the bed,

161

the phone rested on his chest, his mind rested on his wife and children, and tears his rested in his eyes.

Chapter Thirteen

- Like and Unlike Has Smile Speaks

Still using her hands to help her whispers carry into the room, Julian tried to inform them, "History demonstrates that eighty to ninety percent of all rapes go unreported for one reason or another, and we know the killer had to start with a first victim. NOT the victims we know about, but perhaps in their childhood, early adulthood, history of animal abuse, luring victims into his bed, etc... This man had to begin with someone and something-kindness and seduction, and developed into a methodical Rapist and consequently, the Killer out burying bodies. He raped, but did not murder at the beginning. He kept the one's he enjoyed, the longest. Who was he raping in in college?" Stopping her hands from talking, she gently cleared her throat, "Killers are born ladies and gentlemen but..." She added emphasis on her words,"...most are made by society, medications, stress, family, abuse, and the minds interpretation of everyone and everythang around them becomes infected and multiplies. Cancer is a bad cell that multiplies, and grows." The crowd just kept chatting amongst each other, and ignoring her work.

Karen was a Psychiatrist, and she nodded slowly in agreement as her highly educated mind went into its work zone. Jordan stopped to wait for a few more officers to find some seats as they came in and stole the time to flex her sore pelvic muscles. Her vulva was still proud-purple under her tight,

163

manly Texas Ranger jeans, and tight, pullover shirt with long sleeves.

She started again, and tried to remind herself to hold the flexing muscles, each time she spoke. "Our Killer started somewhere, somehow, and with someone, and we need to find out where. Old rapes? Recent rapes? Unreported rapes? Attempted rapes? We need a check of local offenders again, prison inmates who want to deal information, your Pastor, your husband, your Girlfriends, as well as the person standin' next to you at Wal-Mart. This Killer has a path of victims, and we need to cross it. Like Noah Taylor always says, 'It's easier to chop an arrow in flight from the side than it is from the front.'" Spencer raised his hand to ask a question. Jordan nodded her head and gestured him to go ahead.

♫ *Text Alert on Julian's Phone*

Jordan was getting aggravated with her phone alerts attached to her hip. So she turned down the volume a little to listen to Spencer.

"Judging by the evidence, a gay White male, so do we have any evidence that the Killer is a Giver or Receiver?" The entire room turned and looked at him, and started mumbling and smiling. Some even laughed a little, until Jordan stepped up to speak.

♫ *Text Alert on Julian's Phone*

"Quiet down. I know everyone...that sounds very funny to most of you out there, and admittedly, it sounds funny as a metaphor, there is a difference...and it is not just the position. The 'Giver,' also called 'Pitcher,' has more male or

164

testosterone driven tendencies to be dominant and defensive while maintainin' an aggressive attitude, as if they were one of you boys. Alpha." The groups didn't seem too interested in her words, or just missed Rachael giving the presentations. She was better at Public Speeches. Most just shared their phones with the other person, and bounced around the internet. SANICS Team was paying attention- which only included, Spencer and Karen.

"The other male is usually passive-aggressive, like a women or Soft-male. Beta Males." Jordan glanced over at Karen, before speaking again.

"Today's market, it is becoming more common for two Beta-males in a relationship." She looked around at everyone, and found herself getting pissed off.

"Now that we have established that, tomorrow mornin', when many of you boys are shavin' in the mirror, you will see a 'Giver.' And you ladies, you will see a 'Receiver'...uh providin' you're not shavin' your face either." The phones were just too distracting as the laughter, and the feet shuffling got louder. It was frustrating her even more, since she had to whisper.

Jordan stepped up her voice though, to interrupt the phone sharing, and Karen felt they were just rude.

"Which one is your husband?" Someone yelled out to Jordan.

She snapped around and looked at Bodi with a smirk, and he explained the masculine insinuation at her Femininity.

"Not everyone has a husband who cross-dresses as a male prostitute in an undercover operation, Taylor." Bodi yelled to her with a laugh.

Karen took notice of most of the officers playing on their phones, laughing and asked Jordan, with her eyes, "What did you get me into?"

♫ *Text Alert on Julian's Phone*

Jordan stopped to address the question with frustration as the room got louder.

"I mean with him being the UC, Jordan. You know." Jordan smiled and took a big sigh, missing her loud voice. The other officers in the front row, saw her frustration and chuckled as their phones alerted. It was a constant laugh of barking, giggling, texting, and very unprofessional. Jeff didn't smile nor laugh, and he was the first one to give Jordan the 'Do something' look.

♫ *Text Alert on Julian's Phone*

Pounding her fist on the table, she managed a to tone it down a little. Jordan went on, attempting to forget the innuendo about her cross-dressing, and beauty queen looks.

"Like we said, this Killer has a path in his past and we need to cross it to find the trail, and dust it off. Only ten percent of rapes are reported, and typically, in women they are ages sixteen to twenty-four. Our calculations tell us the-" The room was so loud now, and so distracted, Karen read Jordan's frustrations and stood up to speak.

"SHUT THE HELL UP PEOPLE! PUT YOUR DAMN PHONES AWAY AND PAY ATTENTION HERE! YOU GOT THAT? ALL OF YOU, PUT YOUR STUPID PHONES DOWN AND PLAY ON YOUR OWN DAMN TIME! I WANT TO HEAR THE REST OF THIS CASE AND YOU SHOULD CARE ENOUGH TO HEAR IT AS

WELL! THAT IS WHAT YOU ARE PAID TO DO!" She waited for the silence to arrive. Blonde and mighty she was, at six feet tall in three inch heels, she put the crowd to their knees.

"OFFICER JORDAN, PLEASE CONTINUE!" The room was dead silent. Only the soft whispers of music played on a few phones that had been placed down with their video still playing, could be heard.

"Thank you Special Agent Karen Ritzman, of SANICS Division." Jordan said, before continuing with a proud smile. "Our calculations tell us the Killer is between twenty-five and thirty-five years of age. Most assailants who rape women are between twenty-five and forty-four years of age. We determine this is not the case, due to political correctness that has swept the nation for more than a thirty years now. Making gay awareness and acceptance a little easier for society, is common. Therefore, I thank..." she turned and looked at Karen, "...We thank, the Killer is part of the younger crowd."

Karen nodded her head in agreement with her assessment. "The Killer does not know his victims. At least not on a personal level. The computer at the National Crime Data Laboratory have found no patterns in abductions or disposal. Therefore, they are as random as random can get....Excuse me officer Brody, is there somethang you would like to add to this important information that I am standin' up here tryin' to tell you, so you can save lives?"

Officer Brody was sitting in the middle of the room and stared back, quietly putting his phone down. This would be an opportune time to hinder the rooms internet addiction, and Jordan took it, and a little on the personal side.

♫ *Text Alert on Julian's Phone*

"I tell you what, why don't you, Officer Brody, tell us what it is that is so important on your phone, and we can all have a little smile, and then go back to work. Is everyone here needing that 'like' button for their dopamine rush? What is so important, Officer Brody, on Social Media that is just changin' your view of the world or people around you?" Not one person said a word. They only smiled or looked away, shamefully. Brody felt the bruise grow on his ego, and stared at her with wanting to press 'unlike' on his social media.

But, Brody just sat there, smiling and getting angry for being called out. Finally, rest of the crowd regained their composure, and turned around and faced her appropriately, and leaving their phones on the table.

"Now then, where was I?" She fumbled a second or two, "Where was I?" Panicking, she looked in SANICS direction, "Karen, where was I?" She rubbed her headache and listened. Spencer stepped up his game and whispered to her. She quickly stepped back to her proper side of the board, and wrote on the white board. "RAPE IS VIOLENCE."

♫ *Text Alert on Julian's Phone*

Before speaking, she ripped her phone off her hip, muted it, and slammed it onto the table. She walked right into speaking as if it never happened, "Rape is violence ladies and gentleman. It is not just about sex, and not just about male violators and women victims. But, let me tell you more...anyone ever heard of discrimination?" She paused for a few

168

seconds while everyone's eyes changed, expressing the unrecognized correlation between them.

"Individuals who face discrimination are at a higher risk of being a victim of sexual assault...would you like me to repeat that for you." She gestured to Karen for her loud bark. She gingerly stood up and barked it for her.

"THOSE WHO FACE DISCRIMINATION ARE AT A HIGHER RATE FOR BEING VICTIMS OF SEXUAL ASSAULT!" Jordan thanked her and waved for her to come up to the front with her. Karen was not prepared for that, but followed orders from her new boss.

"Those who face discrimination are at a higher rate of bein' a victim of sexual assault. For example, Gays and Lesbians, face discrimination every day in America, and looky here, we are discussing the death of several gay men." Jordan stopped to take a deep breath, and Karen came up, Jordan pointed to her speech list on the side table, and she took it. Karen offered her a drink of her cocoa, and she refused, and grabbing her own, she sipped fast. It was her usual fake sugar-free, non-cup-of-joe, and sat it down rubbing her head to sooth the ache.

Karen didn't understand why the others were not as motivated about catching this guy, but deep in her heart she felt, they really didn't care. Jordan started with a louder, raspy voice as she faced the crowd from her seat. The whisper bounced off the table, and helped her to be heard.

"On the street, I want each and every one of you keepin' your eyes and ears open for anything to do with male erectile dysfunction medicine. Our killer needs erectile-dysfunction medications. Not only does he feed it to his victims, which makes us believe he is a 'Receiver,' but because we believe he takes it himself. So any snitches or dealers on the street that you know, I want you to shake them up without stitches. Find out what you can about large buyers of Viagra, Cialis, Sildenafil-anythang that enables sexual capabilities." Jordan nervously sat back coughing and buried her face into her inner elbow, and Karen quickly cut in. Jordan's other hand, reacted to the pain in her head, and held her forehead.

"Do you have anything you would like to add, Officers?" Karen nodded her head, and stared at each officer in the room to give them an opportunity to apply themselves. She wanted her point across, and she wanted some action on the street to show her worth, to the unit.

"Okay, was that quick enough? And don't forget your damn phones. Dismissed. "

Jordan spoke up from her chair, rubbing her throat painfully, "Jeff, can we talk to you after everyone has cleared out?" Jeff slumped back down with the Mayor's snitch, and sighed.

The crowd was noisy and talkative as they left, with many of them smiling, and even glowing at Jordan; welcoming her return. This chatter was usually a positive sign, and meant they are actually listening, and discussing things but, their faces were all buried back into their phones with big smiles. Jeff just laid back into his chair, and waited to hear Jordan's excuses.

Chapter 14

-Shafting a Feeling of Safe Position

Noah crawled out of bed for the doorbell...again. His erection was napping with him, and he was already sleeping with his boots on, as demanded by his Texas wife.

Samira was standing at the door in tears with her hair roped into her mouth. He looked up at the wall clock. She had been gone for almost an hour. He waved her in, as he stood there, nude. She had seen it before, there was no sense in hiding it. A second visit, did not afford chivalrous accommodations, especially after being called an Abusive Husband and Rapist.

After she stepped in, she immediately began apologizing to him, and crying her heart out.

"Noah, you scared me with...with...with your kindness." She fumbled her words because of her crying, "You took power from me. I'm so sorry I called you names. You don't understand. I didn't understand what I was feeling. P...P...Pl...please? Please? Let me explain something to you." She did not give him time to answer as she feared being asked to leave, so she rushed her sentences.

"I...I...I...I had to leave to figure out me so you wouldn't see me weak. Please? I am remembering what Julian has told me about you, and it's helped me. I tried texting her but, she isn't responding."

Noah gestured for her to follow him and she did, admiring his rather strong looking nude ass. She smiled but, still filled herself with trepidations. He led her to the bedroom where he fell on his face on the bed. She quickly rushed over to the other side to talk to him. She was familiar with that side, and her subconscious put her over there, again. She noted his lack of emotional concern being offered, and told herself, this was a man whose feelings were hurt. Often, in a Woman's world, we ignore men's feelings easily. But to her, everyone's feelings mattered.

"Noah please, listen. That orgasm showed me I am submissive to you...and...and...and...I have never felt that way before-even with Women, and being with a man and not understanding. I th...th...th...think I felt afraid and my only defense was to argue and leave. Rachael told me you were abusive and a rapist. I'm sorry." She stopped to read him, and he just laid there on his chest, facing her with his eyes closed, and hopefully his ears open.

"It scared me. Rachael scared me telling me that. I'm so...s...so...so sorry. I have never done anything with a man...and thought since you are Julian's husband, and I should trust yo...yo...yo...you. BUT, I fear you. Are you listening to me, Noah?" Her inflection toned toward anger, in her question.

He nodded his head for both. "YOU ARE MARRIED!" She took another deep breath leaving her tears behind, and continued with what she had discovered, as it came back to her.

"I can't believe the how much fear I felt. I'm a strong woman, Noah. My defense mechanisms drove me to a...a...a...to run. All the anger we-women have toward men, I felt it-after the orgasm. I felt it because I felt your power was over mine but...but...I can't believe I AM SAYING THIS! Noah, I enjoyed it. I enjoyed feeling powerless to you. I loved the fear it gave me." She looked up across the room, checking her feelings again, to make sure it was actually true, and her subconscious nodded for her.

"I was angry at myself, and I shouldn't be angry at myself that my body enjoyed letting you touch me...letting my guard down to you...let...let...letting myself feel submissive to you. All the shit I have heard my whole life about standing up to men is so not right for me in bed." She looked up again, and her subconscious nodded again.

"I just felt and learned my role in this...this...this...in bed with a man, and I wasn't ready for it because I never knew I would ever feel like I wanted to be...well not in control of you." She took a big breath and spoke loudly, "I DOMINATE WOMEN IN BED! I DOMINATE! NEVER DId I think I would desire a submissive role to a man. A MAN! OF ALL THE PEOPLE ON EARTH, A MAN, NOAH! Plea...plea...plea...plea...please roll over and look at me. MAN!"

Noah slowly rolled over on his back and opened his brown eyes to her, and looked very tired, she said to herself. "Noah please, I felt my place with you. I didn't feel oppressed but, that was all I kept thinking it was. I fe...fe...fe...felt impassioned and desired and felt submissive. I don't ever feel submissive with a Woman, and I have never been with a man." She stopped speaking with her flailing arms, since she had his eyes on her.

"It felt so good to feel that way. It felt so knew and undiscovered." Her tone and speech got lower as her emotions evened out, "I gave myself to you and wo...wo...women have always told me that was wrong. My female friends. Noah, it was like a scary battle of emotions inside, Noey. I'm so sorry.

173

My heart wanted it, and my mind fought my heart. I
want to feel submissive to you-JUST YOU! I can't
believe I am saying this. I dominate in bed, and
only have been with a few Women. I know I was not
made to be submissive to Women. They are my
Bitches. I now that sounds bad but, Julian is my
Bitch."

She quickly pulled her tissues from her purse
to help the returning tears of honesty, running down
her face. He heard her voice giving sincere feelings,
and was really listening but, punishing her by not
answering her.

Why...why...why...is that wrong to me? It
really turned me on. OH Noey. I understand now
why Julian is so submissive to you. I...I...I thought
she was...like....I'm sorry I'm crying. I thought you
beating her made her that way. I see her bruised
vagina, and she told me she makes you do it. I
really thought she was lying to hide the abuse. She
was submissive with me, instantly. She is
submissive to everyone and I think I am only
submissive to men. I have only dated a couple men
and they were submissive...very liberal men. I didn't
understand the roles or the differences in men.
Noey please." She kept dabbing her tears and
leaning more and more towards him, without
touching the bed. Her subconscious was not
entering his territory, without a gesture from him,
even if it was from his subconscious.

"She...she...she Julian, gave herself that role
by chemistry, and I gave it to you only I never felt it
before. It felt right in my heart yet, and scared the
hell out of me. I feel the chemistry with you, and I
was not expecting anything like that."

Her tears stopped as her mind opened up to
the sexual world expanding, and it silenced her. She

looked around to see more of it, as she took in this new place, this new time, this new world. Instead of stuttering, she stammered at the room, to her eye opening acknowledgment of growth.

Suddenly, her Woman abilities read him instantly, when she looked back at his eyes, after seeing her world expand. Her voice changed instantly, and was no longer emotional or submissive or intentionally confrontational. For the first time, she felt she didn't have to put up resistance to a man. She felt safe, and not in need of control at the moment.

Her knew, stronger, more equal tone spoke to him. "OMG! Noah. I am so sorry. It really was me, and years of hearing how men just use Wo...Wo...Wo... Women, and use Women and lie and shit on them. I looked into your eyes Noey, and I saw the same thing in Julian's. You can't be a rapist. I think Rachael just doesn't like...that it...Julian said she was very controlling, very Progressive and hated that Julian desired submission to you. Until you just barely touched me and then my HUGE orgasm, I think I would have thought the same thing." She kept wiping her eyes with her tissue, even though, tears were not coming down. With her feelings changed by her experience from an hour ago, she began to speak, really fast, to get it out the emotions, as they came in.

"You were so sweet and generous and gentle and loving and kind and traditional somewhat." She started crying again, and it stopped the fast compliments from emotions as her roller-coaster turned. "I am so sorry I called you a rapist and stormed out. The entire image of men that has been taught to me, just collided with the kindness, and touch that my natural desires want, and both gave

175

me fear. My body didn't stop you, and my mind was screaming to stop you, and I did all of that to myself because my heart wanted to offer myself to you and when I stopped thinking about it, nature did the rest." She gasped for air, and wiped her eyes. "I...I...I am so sorry I called you names."

Noah offered her an understanding smile, and reached up to her and she took his hand, still holding her tissues, her other hand held her purse and tissue pack. She began shaking her head, as her body fell back into her own spell of attraction, "Everything I am learning about men is just not what everyone has told me. I know, as I...I...I...I as a strong Woman, I need to be strong and..." She shook her head faster, "...feeling vulnerable turned me on so much." She looked up with another thought, "This is what all my friends are angry about during sex. I get it now. Feeling fear."

Noah pulled her down to the bed, and she sat on it and got more comfortable, and he twined his fingers with hers. She gasped, and with a few tears caused by her enlightenment to things that had always been in front of her but, she let other people interpret for her. She gave him her heartfelt confession that she had never done with anyone, and the vulnerability from truth, made her feel good.

"Friends, they want men, hate men, and get men, and then complain about men. How I felt after the orgasm was nothing I had felt before. I was so emotionally guilty, and felt wrong because of what I thought I knew, but my body and heart felt what was really right. It is the after effect of not having control, and for someone like me Noey, con...con...con...con ...controlling, that is scary, and I rushed back into power in fear of feeling ashamed

176

as a Woman." She smiled as he smiled back, and let her keep waking up to the world, "I felt like I needed someone more than myself after the orgasm. So I ran to the safety of my female friends, not like literary, but, that is where I always felt safe, until this happened."

He finally spoke up, "The feeling after intimacy, is called The Vulnerability Stage, and it is very strong and can be detrimental, to Angels. This is what Julian has taught me, Samira."

"OHHHH I felt it, Noey. That feeling after sex is the most important thing, and I have never felt it like that. You feel vulnerable and in need of safety, and that in itself builds the trust-when you are...let yourself be vulnerable and let someone else be the safety. Mother Nature is a genius, Noey." He was nodding with his smile of appreciation that she was aware of what had happened, helping her understand it.

She finally looked at him without glancing. She smiled a little to him as he caressed her arm. He could read that she had said enough to get control of her fears again, and would still think about it for a lifetime. He pulled her, and she immediately dropped everything to the floor, climbed on top of him, and kissed him, and chased the fear, for the first time.

She kept her tongue in his mouth offering him her saliva over and over as he swallowed, and came back for more. She could not believe how wonderful Vulnerability felt. She had thoughts that she was Bi-sexual but, being with a man who gave her fear, and gave her safety with her fear, she was going to confirm her desires. This was scary territory for the heart of a good woman. She sat up on him, and ripped her blouse off, and held her breasts in her

177

hands for him, and let a few tears fall on them. They both glowed at each other. His smile offered her protection, and she wanted to take the chance to experience it, again.

Chapter Fifteen

-OCD of a UC with a Blue Pill

"Jordan, did Noah say anything about making it in today for the briefing?" Jordan responded first by shaking her headache.

"He was on Surveillance until early this morning. He was snoring when I left home."

Jordan got up to speak, with Karen next to her, beaming at Jeff, "We really need to push the pharmaceutical leads. We may come across somethang or someone of interest...maybe someone who knows someone of interest." Jeff just smiled and acted as if he understood or cared.

Karen was being a bit un-sociable with him, and did not offer any opinions or judgements. She wasn't avoiding the job but, she was avoiding verbal communication, until she had grasped everything about the case. But, she wanted him to see her stance was with Jordan.

"Karen and I think this guy, this Rapist and Killer, has a fear of failure, and granted that could be anythang, but along with erectile dysfunction usually comes a fear of failure, be it sexually, or be it in life. So I am getting the feelin' this guy is a tad eremitic. Not in the religious sense, but more along the lines of hyper-anxiety issues, utter paranoia, and apprehension toward establishment. He is not one for the stage-"

Jeff raised his hand to speak, "Killers usually don't hit the stage, Officer Taylor."

"Well yes, I know that, but life itself is a stage, and each of us plays a part-" she turned to see Spencer smiling and nervous. "What is so funny, Spence?" she asked him, stalling.

♫ *Text Alert on Julian's Phone*

"You sound like Elvis now." Spencer cracked up, and Jeff starting smiling really big. Jordan, did not get it at all, and just nodded with a smile, and leaned back toward Jeff in his seat.

"-The stage, this person goes unnoticed to society and the establishment, so either they are poor and live in a rundown house with Momma or Grandma who thinks they can do no wrong, because of the Arrested Development, or they are extremely wealthy and usually, if they are wealthy, they need entertained and compulsively eccentric." Jordan finally took a breath.

"Drama kings and queens, Jordan." Karen added as she pushed herself into the discussion. Jordan smiled at her knowing it was like the pig calling the cow fat.

"This is all very interesting Ladies, however, it is not really bringing us closer to the catching this guy. Or is it, and I just don't see it?" Jeff smiled at the Mayor's snitch, as she smiled back.

"It is helpin' us to Behavioral Profile this guy, and it helps build the case for the DA, and all of this is necessary with CSI-if CSI had Crime Scenes that were not washed away So bodies and Circumstantial Evidence is all we can produce. Other than that, the DA has nothing else." Jordan reminded him.

"You know Jeff..." Karen finally looked at him..."Our Killer could suffer from Sexual Pain

180

Disorder." Jordan immediately turned to look at her shockingly. She hadn't thought of that one.

♫ Text Alert on Julian's Phone

"Yeah, that's right, Dyspareunia, it is found in men, and men of urges use an enhancement to challenge the pain to force themselves into sex. Chronic mostly, and some men fear an orgasm because of the pain, and women also, so they practice celibacy, until natural urges are too great, and they pop a blue one and go hunting." Jordan was gazing off as she finished her sentence.

"I have an idea Jeff..." Karen suggested, "...why don't we let the UC get into the cars of the men that come by and solicit." Jordan was already responding with her eyes wide, and shaking her entire body back and forth. "Yeah, Jordan, we can pull them over, right down the street. This way...yes Jordan...this way, we...he will still be in sight of the surveillance team at all times. YES! Jordan." Karen continued to watch Jordan as she said 'no' in every way imaginable, without actually saying it.

"Come on Jay, it is not like the UC is in any more danger. The Uniforms are right there on his tail...along with his customer." She felt bad for saying it, and Snitch and Jeff, both laughed. Jordan fought back her smile but, it came out ever so slightly, as everything else about her read 'NO.'

♫ Text Alert on Julian's Phone

"There is no way in heck, I am lettin' an Under-Cover get in the car with this Killer. NO! No way, it is not goin' to happen Jeff." She continued to look at the both of them, and shake her head. "I

181

have seen this Killer's work. He uses electric prods and stun guns. The UC will drop instantly to a powerful shock to the neck, and then what. Hope we catch him...in this city of orange barrel mazes? No." She shook her head again to restate her opinion.

"Jeff, what do you think?" Karen asked.

"You know, it is not a bad idea." What is your name again, Karen?

"Ritzman. Karen Ritzman- GS13."

"Welcome about Karen. You are getting right down to it. I like that...A lot." He smiled warmly, waving his and her options in front of everyone, just like he did Rachael. Only, Rachael took his bait and switched.

"Jordan rolled her eyes, and wondered if Rachael was still sleeping with him and or his wife. She would warn Karen after the meeting of his position against the team.

Jeff continued after throwing himself at her, by speaking directly to the new Woman with long blonde hair, instead of her supervisor with long black hair. "The UC is only getting second hand info from the street, so why not actually make him a street member instead of just a walker....I like it...and with the 'information' coming out of the Mayor's office...which by the way...he will be here in a few days." He finally looked at Jordan.

Then he gave a warm, nacho cheese smile to the Mayor's Snitch sitting just feet away, "I haven't got the details yet...but this way, Noah and the UC can look and judge the person and interrogate them or be arrested...I like it Karen, make it happen." Jordan was shocked he gave direction to Karen, and not her-the Lead. She immediately knew, he was one of Rachael's goons. Jeff got up to go to back to his office and smiled at Karen, after obviously

182

admiring her long blonde hair. He straightened out his tie as if he made an Executive Decision, and proudly left them to bicker. Snitch followed right behind him carrying her notes.

"I cannot believe you want to let a UC get into those cars. I don't want him or her screwin' around with some pervert tryin' to get a victim Karen....I can't believe you suggested that?"

"Jordan, stop letting your emotions get in the way of your job. S.O.P. Jordan. Standard Operating Procedure calls for it. What's gotten' into you anyway? Last week you were flat on your back crashed in a car, and then having the time of your life resting three hots and a couch remote. Did you get soft or something? You know it is S.O.P. Right?"

"Yes I know, Karen. You are right. I know." She was flustered and disappointed, and showed it. "I just can't get this headache out of my mind. Now, I have to worry about the UC getting snatched. Part of the job." She agreed, rolling her neck around to pop it in every direction.

" You are on Medical Leave anyway. You don't even need to follow the case this closely. And when did you get an accent?" Jordan stopped putting her papers into her file, and slowly looked up at her. "Yes, you always look, forgive me with respect, 'Texas Cowboy style,' but, I don't remember your accent. Are you alright?" Jordan just nodded in frustration as she went back to gather her file.

"Jordan, if you remember, I counseled you about stress management and OCD several years ago. Annual checkup I think it was, and you talked about risk assessment differentiations to work and baiting. The case file says Noah is the UC back up now, instead of the UC. If you are comfortable with a UC that is proven more skilled in self-defense, weigh the risks and see if Noah is a better fit...again."

"Karen-" Karen put her hand up to shut Jordan up.

"Before we start arguing, we will discuss it, and with Noah, before YOU, make a final decision."

"Oh-your damn right we will. I will talk to my husband tonight for sure....ALONE!" They started walking toward Jordan's office down the hall.

♫ *Text Alert on Julian's Phone*

"Karen—" Karen quickly turned her head and stared without doubt of her S.O.P. procedure and recommendation to use Noah instead of Swisher, as the UC.

"Okay, okay...we will all talk about it later. I'm sorry." Jordan relented.

"Good. Now let's get this finished so I can get these eyes into the Matrix Formula."

"Let's take lunch up to my office, and work on this. Okay? Jordan pleaded rubbing her tense neck muscles in the back, and imagining her untouched brownie and breakfast burrito. She had jitters, and just knew her sugar was too low.

"Jordan, I bet thirty million men take something for erectile dysfunction, and that is the reported numbers. I'm sure with the internet and street sales, it is five times that. Even in this younger, generation today, who think everything has to give you instant gratification...I bet they are taking it, and don't need it. The same Generation thinks 'happiness,' comes in a pill." They both sat down at Jordan's desk, and Jordan flipped her hair to not sit on it, as she eyed her brownie. Karen nodded as she started writing in her workbook and chewing on part of her breakfast-lunch burrito.

"I bet the numbers for women are at least fifty percent of the male numbers." Jordan sat back to think for a minute before speaking.

"Karen, have you ever taken Viagra?" Karen immediately stopped writing, but she didn't look up. "Oh my Gosh, you have...haven't you? Oh my Gosh Karen, I'm sorry. I didn't mean for personal reasons. I'm asking because it is pertant...pertatent...OH MY GOSH, SAVANNAH!" Jordan stopped or hushed herself by taking a bite of her breakfast burrito with a grunt. She chomped like a cowboy at a campfire, to get her frustration worked out. Karen watched, and waited, seeing her friend was not feeling her best.

"PERTINENT to this case. I don't have any experience with that...maybe yet. As an MD, I only know what the website would say. I don't prescribe it to any patience.

♬ *Text Alert on Julian's Phone*

Karen slowly looked back up at her, and looked around. "Headache? Concussion Julian?" Julian waved her off shaking her head, and Karen threatened her. "Don't you dare tell Noah I told you this...You got that younger, Southern Lady?" Jordan's eyes were focused, as she nodded, and her world came to a quick and sudden halt, to listen.

Leaning in, Karen whispered to her, "Okay. Okay. Patrick and I tried it one night...like a year or so ago. Clinical trials of generics. I took it. Our office still gets samples of everything. I reported extra sensations some external and mostly internal. I didn't find it necessary, is the proper word for me,

185

but when he took it, I took a mental health day the next day. Jordan sat back in her chair, and twisted a rope of her hair and put it in her lips to think. She squared her shoulders like a Texas Ranger listening to a confession on a wiretap. She never thought about dosing herself with it.

♫ *Text Alert on Julian's Phone*

Karen busted up laughing at the hair in her mouth. She had forgotten Jordan did that. She politely pointed, and gave a friendly chuckle.

Karen looked around again, and sat back up to whisper, "It was different. Inside it was different. Pressure on the insides increased due to increased blood flow. Understandably, shrinking the canal by increased vagina fullness, meeting the increased cervix fullness." Karen was more clinical than Jordan who was now making plans to use it. She still had some stashed from what she used on Noah.

Jordan's eyes were wide open, and her forehead creases between her eyebrows grew from the concentration. She sucked her hair in more and more, until it pacified her imagination, and didn't bother to look around either, this was excellent insider info.

"It didn't really feel different with increased sensations levels on the clitoris as patients have reported but, inside was a totally enhanced sensation that I could see women enjoying. I could see why the male participants pre-ejaculated due to increased resistance." She nodded her head at Jordan, smiling. "An increase in deep sensations was reported. I was exhausted." She smirked after the secret, and both women enjoyed a quiet moment to think. Jordan was the first to speak.

"Labia majora and minora changes? Any effect?" Jordan asked curiously, and for good reason.

"I would say fuller. Not unusual or unmanageable. Just fuller-a little enlarged." Karen added trying to remember the nights.

"Noticeably fuller?" Jordan asked very gently.

"I can say noticeably, nor did I look. They felt fuller. For hours. I can say." Karen was sliding her lips together to the side to remember.

"Increase or decrease in lubrication flow." Jordan asked.

"Yes. Lubrication increased. I remember that." Karen said looking into her memory again. "Big increase."

Jordan rubbed her face, and stopped to hold her chin in her hand.

"Any increase in blood flow elsewhere that you can remember?" Jordan asked very curiously.

"Not that I recall reporting.

Chapter 16

-White & Black Meets Pink Vulnerability

Samira pressed her bare breasts into Noah's smooth, hairless pectorals, and kissed him again with fever. She could not give him enough of her DNA. Gasping, she told him, "I want to Witness you now, and see you rush back into power like I had to. I need to see the-YOU Vulnerable, Noah. Please. I will hold you afterwards. Let me watch you...NO let me give you an orgasm under my control. Please." She was glowing with excitement to the risk she wanted.

"This was not the same as me let...let...let.." He kissed her. "Thank you, Noey. "Not the same as an orgasm from another woman. This is so different. So much more fear-GOOD fear, Noey. Good Vulnerability fear."

She rushed back to kissing, and grinding herself against his erection under her. Hearing excitement and enticement in her voice, he listened. "This position feels right for me, Noey. I want to be on top of you. On top of a man. Yes, Noey." She answered, but to questions her mind was asking in the moment. "It does give me enough control so my fears don't win." Still rushing, she got off of him and wiggled her sexy, and very cut, muscular, round, black hips at him, as she slid her jeans, and thong off, and climbed back on him.

Samira was leaking all over his thick junk, and he was enjoying it. He reached under her, and held his own cock sticking out the backside, between her perfect dark Black, butt cheeks, and she was rubbing him against them, but not touching her back door. The terrorizing sensations kept her dripping, and experimenting with each touch. He soaked his fingers, and then sucked them clean as she blushed grinding against him slowly. She was learning her rhythm and control.

His fingers slipped back under, and when he put the tips of his fingers into her dark and pink Goddess, she fluttered, and he licked his fingers clean watching her eyes. Both of them were all smiles of approvals.

The front door of the house, slowly opened, and little footsteps made their way in. When Rachael got to the split stairs, she smiled to the voices coming from the bedroom, and pulled out her 9mm handgun.

Noah finally, pulled his penis forward, and she sat back down to capture it between her dark labia, and he kept it from going inside her with his fist around the shaft, just below the head. She was somewhat dismayed until she slid forward, and it stuck out through the center of her labia. She looked at him in question, as he slowly let go of it.

"You are a truly sexy woman, Samira. Your big breasts are beautiful, your mind is beautiful, your beautiful pussy drips, making me crazy, and most importantly, your heart and soul is untainted with hatred. What you felt today, is what is divine. Love and intimacy, is a gift from God, Sammy." She listened and made small smirks occasionally, as he interrupted her riding pleasure, and he felt the tempting wait of her vagina lips sucking on his thick shaft, and he gently leaked some for her.

189

Rachael's eyes got huge when she heard the name "Samira," and she covered her mouth laughing at the notion that Noah, was cheating on Julian. This was perfect.

"I can kill both of them while having sex, and he would be the Cheating...NO WAIT!" She said it so loud to herself, she stopped to see if they heard her. When they kept on in bed, she finished her verbal thought.

"I can make it look like he was raping her, and killed her first, then himself, after he puts his seed in her. OR..." She had another thought. "I can use his chalice of cum from the fridge, and put it in her." A long evil grin took her expression, and the zombie look in her eyes, grew even more evil.

Noah told Samira to look at the tip of his hare cock, and she did. He thrusted her a little bit rolling her eyes back, and more leaked out. She scooped his semen with her finger, and he told her to rub it on her clitoris only, and to make sure it didn't get on her labia putting it in.

She stared at him nervously, and fingered it onto her clit, and pushed back onto his warm, hard shaft, and didn't move. He stared, edging her on with his eyes, as she began to feel her body's natural chemical reaction to semen.

Her clit began to grow harder in pulses, and her eyes got wider and wider. "It burns, Noey. Why?" She said, in shock as a wonderful, first time sensation overtook her body against her conscious mind. She felt warm rising all over her skin.

Rachael crawled on her hands and knees down the hallway with her gun in hand, and listened outside the open door. At floor level, she delicately peeked around the corner, and saw a large round Black rear-end riding a pair of White male legs dangling at the end of the bed in Cowboy boots.

"It's burning, Noah. Why is that?" He smiled letting her enjoy the memory for her entire life.

"That is your soul, yearning for natural seed. Your mind doesn't even know it's happening. Your vagina knows what it is, and how to naturally respond to it. Your conscious mind has nothing to do with it. When you crave a certain food that is your unconscious mind making your body desire something it needs in that food. Your very beautiful pussy, is the same way.

Rachael listened as her wetness lubricated her labia. She actually felt some jealousy but, ignored it. She enjoyed fucking him more than she wanted to admit. Quietly, she got up, and crept to the kitchen and looked in the fridge for his chalice. It was missing.

Then she reached up and got Julian's Diddy Meds, and taking them with her, she crept down to the basement and looked around. There was something down there she wanted, but with all the Cowgirl Boot boxes, she was not sure which one it was.

Finally, she made her way out the sliding glass door, and turned and shut it, without locking it. She got a small tube of superglue out, and squeezed it into the key hole of the lock in the unlocked position, and tossed it in the corner under the deck. Bitching under her breath with jealousy, she walked away through the side gate, and back down the street. Frustrated.

191

"Do it again, Noey. Please." She was sitting up, staring at the headboard, while feeling the sensations take effect on her clitoris. Rolling her eyes back as they crossed, he worked the head of his cock against her clitoris, and leaked on it. She instantly burned, and scoffed a smile.

"It's burning so well." She said, enjoying it.

"That is your clit swelling to absorb it as fast as possible. It heats up fast. It feels like a burn. Use your mind to tell it to stop, and she will ignore you. Your vagina knows what to do with seed. It is natural to have it. Natural to desire it. It is necessary for your mental health, and for procreation. I will never waste your seed, Sammy, and you can never waste mine. Julian has taught me all of this. I never knew it."

Samira leaned down rubbing herself harder against the underside of his cock as it pushed up between her labia toward her stomach. His huge urethra ground up against her swollen red-pink clit, and she moaned as she got down on her elbows, and her thick puffy nipples buried into his chest. She kissed him slowly, and he pulled her hair over to his face, rubbed it on his lips, and stuck in his mouth. She smiled really big, and teared up as her natural desires started gliding her up and down the bulging urethra of his shaft. The Vulnerability was creeping in on her, and offering her a reward, to get his seed.

She kissed him forcing her tongue in with her hair, and enjoying it as she gently ground her clit with his wonderful, warm man organ jarring her burning nerve endings. She loved how hard and delicate it felt, and he flexed it for her. She instantly moaned into his mouth, and sucked his saliva and tongue into hers. She leaned up panting from the sensations below.

192

"Is spit Seed, too? And Noah nodded. "That is very romantic that you two worship each other's seed. Is the hair a seed? She asked, putting her own hair in her mouth.

"No, it's a gesture to Love and Ownership, and..." He chuckled, "...an acceptance of Julian's disorders and anxieties. We can't have a legal marriage so, she wants to exchange everything as a pseudo to the ring. It helps her cope with what she can't have. It is a very religious symbol for her. The crown is your hair, and a very romantic, and very loving offering, to the one you love. It is from her Bible, and it is sacred to Julian and Texas." Samira hoped she took it all in as her orgasm started getting close.

"Do you like me sucking on your crown, Samira?" She nodded looking down at him as her eyes crossed, and rolled back.

"Yes." Came her delayed, and very quiet answer. He kept thrusting with her.

"Do you like me sucking on your beautiful breasts? She nodded, focused on her first ever, sensations by cock. He pulsed his dick for her three times as it shoved her labia apart, like a hotdog, and a warm bun. She nodded, with a very vulnerable smile.

"That beautiful ass of your needs kisses, too? She nodded with a little more effort that time. Your feet? She nodded. Anything else you would like me to worship, my beautiful Goddess of a woman?"

With her eyes closed in serious concentration, she leaned into him again grinding herself hard and fast, and confessing to him with her moans. Getting herself close to orgasm on top of him, she finally told him through her moaning, "My Seed." And she burst into orgasm squealing her Vulnerability to him, and leaking all over his shaft and balls, as she rushed onto his chest for safe keeping. He quickly put his arms around her, and made her feel it. She buried her right cheek into his neck and shoulder, and moaned away from him as he thrusted her through her orgasm. Slowly, her moans turned to a soft cry, and she couldn't let him see that...yet. He kissed her head over and over, with his snuggle, and reassured her by his gentle petting.

He continued to thrust for her harder, and she tore into another orgasmic scream, and he held her tighter as it over-whelmed her. He could hear her snorting and feel her tears on his shoulder. He grinded her again drawing her soaking wet orgasm out of her, and she couldn't control her tears, and gave up fighting her desires and fears. He lifted her hips up while she was in her Vulnerability stage, and held her there, as he slid every inch of his leaking manhood inside her.

She gasped in pain, and laid on him, shivering and held onto him tightly. He wiggled his cock spreading his seed all over her cervix, and she broke into a long-cooing cry with short breaths to an exhale, to deal with emotional toll of a real violation. This was not one of her secret dildos that did not share real chemistry. She could not hide it any longer, but she could not show him her face. It was too much of a surrender for her proud feminine ways, during the first time.

"Is this your first time having it inside, Sammy?" She nodded with the right side of her face down on his chest, and her left hand curled against her mouth shaking. Her breathing was slowing down, and she couldn't face him with her tears. She slowly, slid her knees down the sides of his thighs, and took in every painful inch of his warm, hard,

194

leaking cock. Her eyes closed as it invaded her wet, canal, and made her feel in a way, she had never felt. Like a real woman. He felt himself pulse a little, inside her. Even his penis was eager to seed her.

He listened to her heart race, and rubbed her smooth back and rear, and put her hair back into his mouth. He pulsated his cock slowly for her, as she whined her weeps out to him. She squeezed his cock squealing little gestures of the painful satisfaction, and her face curled to the emotions as they came through her tears. She was being violated by a man, and she was letting him. He grabbed her hair, and pulled it firmly. Her face came up with it, and she revealed her pain to him with her tears falling down her cheeks. She was still shaking, and the most Vulnerable she had every felt. Her left fingers curled, and shook near her mouth, as she let him take her virginity, willfully.

He whispered to her. "Will you protect me after I come inside you?" She nodded, and her crying increased as she let herself finally look into his eyes. She wanted so bad to speak, and just wasn't ready. No longer holding her head up by her hair, he slowly rubbed her tears away, she felt his cock twitch, and burst his seed inside her, and she watched the pain on his face grow for her, stimulating her fears as he weakened before her eyes.

He closed his eyes with her sense of duty to protect him, and she rushed her arms around his sides and held him tightly, and watched his amazing expressions of the fulfilling pain. His squirts shot deep onto her uterus and cervix, and he moaned at her in pain with each squirt. She held him tighter for safety, letting her tears fall down her face. She recognized the empowerment over a man she longed for, as he needed her more than ever now. She held his gifting soul, as his body spit seed into her, and felt the pulses of her clitoris reaching for him. With each throb of his penis, her eyes shed another tear to him, and for his Vulnerability that seemed to wreck him. Her body absorbed his seed as fast as it could, as her heart absorbed his. Her body knew more than she did, and she let nature do its work.

Samira squeezed her cervix muscles on him and whispered with a scared voice, "You're safe Noah. Did you just cum inside me?" Her body was shivering, as aftershocks gently jerked them both from his painful elation. She was starting to feel like a Goddess atop him, taking his seed from him, defeating him, and protecting his Vulnerability, afterwards. Instantly, she recognized her place with a man, and endeared it. Her tears stopped as her eyes widened to this fact, and she reclaimed her empowerment.

He whispered, sucking on her hair as he held his face to hers, cringing from a pain that satisfies every man. When she heard him, she started rocking the last of juices into her vagina to make herself more powerful, and keep him in Vulnerability to her, and in need of her protection. Unfortunately, her body didn't see it as her mind did, and she found herself needing to speak.

"I...I...I." Without warning, she burst into orgasm again, and held on to him letting her moans turn to small bursts of her painful pleasure scream. He held her tightly as he tried to thrust into her with his limping, sticky cock. Their Vulnerabilities blended their seeds inside her, as she wept for his protection again. She shivered on him making herself remain still so her Vulnerability would last

196

for him, and their seed rolled down his shaft together, for the first time.

Quietly, she whispered to him, another desire, "Pull my hair."

Chapter Seventeen

-Humiliation is a Pleasure & a Pain

Karen didn't think Jordan's eyes could get any bigger but, they were. So she continued with the rest of the envious Viagra experience. "I was told it was better, and I couldn't tell the difference other than feeling more-full. Oh, and it got really warm inside, and a good fullness, and a good warm. Jordan just sat there staring. Karen could tell her eyes were not seeing anything, and she waved her hand in front of her smiling. Jordan jerked back, and started laughing. She was trying to be funny.

"You should try it Jay, get a Clinical, you and Noah might find something that has been missing. Not that anything is missing. As a Doctor, you should find out."

♫ Text Alert on Julian's Phone

"Oh no, we don't need anythang like that, I mean, Noah isn't like some huge...porno star or somethang...buuut..." she paused as her libido knocked on her very sore Venus mound, "...I thank I could get him a couple of them?" She finished quite shyly.

"HIM, Jordan? Two of them, for HIM, YOU?" Karen giggled suspicion of her friend's intentional misdirection, and held up two fingers to make sure she got her questions across.

"Yeah, a couple of them for Noah, not me I could never do that. I'm a Doctor." They both laughed at their lies. Jordan put a fresh, dry rope in her mouth, and started speaking, "I wonder what the side effects are?" Jordan put her fingers to her chin to think.

"Ours was a prescription for Sildenafil, so it shouldn't be a problem to find a couple." Jordan gave her a mischievous look. Any pain? Jordan was busy picturing the wonderful moment when sex could get even better, if it added a little pain bonus. And all this time, she thought only ten handsome Chippendale Dancers at the same time or Hillary Klugg, could make sex better, for her.

"Huh?" she thought to herself, *I will still hold on to those fantasies, just in case.*

"I guess side effects would include, hit the emergency room if it is longer than four hours." Karen laughed after she said it. "...Those commercials, you know."

"I'm not talking about in men Karen, side effects in us women."

They both smiled at each other knowingly, and maybe Jordan blushed a whole lot with guilt.

"I don't know, I guess many of the same things in men, only, if my Noah...you know...needs to get lanced, he isn't goin' anywhere for the first four hours...maybe a few more." They both laughed and got back to discussing the reports on the Stiff'em Killer.

♫ Text Alert on Julian's Phone

"Oh and tomorrow night, or Wednesday, I will take you on surveillance-YOU PICK! Bring your folders, notes, etc...you remember how boring they are." Karen nodded as she went back to reviewing the Matrix Formula.

Julian grabbed her phone to text Noah and Samira, and see how their meeting went. Julian saw she fourteen messages and assumed they were everyone welcoming her back or wanting meetings. As she read them, more came in,

Text from Brother-in-Law Samuel: Dog toy? Freak! Loved it! Thanks.

Text from Neighbor Christina: Loved it. I'm alone tonight. I have wine???

Text from Samira: Please call me. I called Noah names and rushed out. I'm sorry and I'm not sure what I am feeling.

Text from Bodi: Very Nice. Thank you. Sharing.

Text from Rach-The Emily Fat Girl Wiggle. Right Emily?

Text from Coroner Jack: Very Brave, and thank you VERY MUCH!

Text from Nurse Sheila: Yummy! Kisses. Dating?

Text from Officer Conner: HELL YES! THANK YOU GIRL! OMG!

Text from Officer Stillman: WOW! Very sexy Jordan. Thank you.

Text from Jeff: OK? My wife and I would like a Dinner with you???

Text from Rachael: I miss you Emily. Call me so we can get together. I have the men ready for us. Call me now.

Text from Tisha: Sexy Body Positive! Love it! Sharing. GO VIRAL Beautiful.

Text from Neighbor Chuck: Texas Cowgirls. Love you Cowgirls.#goviral

Text from Momma: Get dem clothes on Daughter. Texas gonna be hangin' ya Angel.

Text from her Counselor: Be yourself and be happy. Body Positive. Big Smiles. My help-sharing.

Text from Officer Williams: Sharing. Great from every angle. Anytime you want.

Text from Samira: NOAH HAS VENUSIAN DIMPLES? Never knew men could have them. All three of us have them. Very Sexy GF. Thank you for making me do this. Many kisses for you.

Text from Baxter: Love my Texas Cowgirl. Texas and I still waiting on you. Dump husbands body in Ohio. LOL

Text from Steph'an: Show off! Where do I tip? PROUD OF YOU! Sharing.

Text from Camry: IT IS HUGE JULIAN. HUGE! LOVE IT! Go Viral. KISSES

Text from Samira: Noah is amazing. I know why you married him. Thank you Julian. I will be good to you and him. I promise. I so want to hug you right now. Thank you for opening up my world. I want to be his Witness every day. Kisses my Girlfriend

Text from Frisco: What? NO Tobey Keith? You are all beauty. Both sides. That ass is amazing. Texas amazing.

Jordan was whiter than pale, when she looked up from her phone and into the recent past. Slowly, she spoke to herself, "No wonder everyone in the meetin' was playin' on their phones...my dance video."

"Oh Dear Jesus. No!" Her mind immediately went to Noah, and her fingers to her phones keyboard, as she told him he could have all the nude photos of her he wanted. She never imagined, he would share it with everyone she knew.

Text to Noah from Jordan: YOU WILL DIE TONIGHT NOAH JAMES!

Text to Jordan from Noah: I love you too Cowgirl.

Text from Jordan to Noah: YOU SENT JULIAN'S NUDE DANCING VIDEO TO EVERYONE? WTF IS WRONG WITH YOU? YOU WANT A DIVORCE OR A FUNERAL OR BOTH? FUNERAL SOLVES IT!

Text to Jordan from Noah: What are you talking about? The one you made the other day?

Text to Noah from Jordan: I WILL KILL YOU NOAH! EVERYONE AT WORK HAS IT ON THEIR PHONES! YOU SON OF A BITCH! MOMMA WILL BURY YOU ON THE PRAIRIE TONIGHT!

Text to Julian from Noah: HELLO Tomboy, you haven't sent it to me yet. Send it now so Sammy and I can Witness you. Take finger off trigger, Rodeo Queen

Text from Gabriella: Back in College? DAMN YOU ARE HOT! White Girls are so easy. 😏♥☺

Text from Sharon: You need to pray this goes viral. LET IT OUT GIRL! Sharing

As more fear and anxiety crashed into Jordan. She slowly looked up to God, waiting. "Strike me down now. I am gonna throw up," and her phone continued to alert at her.

"Julian done sent it to EVERYBODY?" Jordan said to herself. Quickly remembering Karen was sitting across from her, she looked up at her to see Karen staring at her, and looking at her phone. Her lips moved slowly without sound, "Emily?"

Chapter 18

-Angry Pleasures Deliver Cuckqueans

Rachael was laying back on the couch as Theresa shaved her skinny pussy for her. Rachael had her pinchers with small weights hanging from her nipples, as she talked. After years of pleasing Julian by stretching her nipples, she had gotten to the point where she enjoyed heavy weights on them. *Anything was better than being flat chested,* she kept to herself.

She muted the TV as the commercial came on, and went right back into the same old rant she did daily. "We are Modern Women, Treese, and that is how our relationship will be. Julian fucked me over so much stringing me along and promising she would leave him for me. She never did. She used me. I don't use people, and I don't like to feel used. I did everything for her. I kissed her fat butt. I never even told Noah that his kids were not even his. I brought her guys to get her pregnant because he couldn't do it. Julian just let herself fall victim to the fear of being an independent woman, and cages Emily. Emily is her real name. Julian is her psychosis personality from after her SO-CALLED RAPE!" Her frustration and anger, seemed to always end with a scream of the final words, and Theresa appreciated that. To her, this shaving was supposed to be romantic, and lead to better things.

Rachael started up again, as the commercial went to another one. "I love that you are living for yourself, Theresa. I really do. You are not letting the

204

Patriarchy choose your life for you. I mean, who wants to be a stay out home fat COWGIRL MOMMY WITH MENTAL DISORDERS? Wanting to be a Mother is a Patriarchy trick for oppression, and a Mental Disorder."

Rachael toyed with a cut rope of long black hair, rubber-banded together at both ends, and nearly a foot long. Over and over she put it to her nose to smell, and occasionally taste. It either stirred her frustrations or soothed them, or both.

After her close shave around the bottom of her perineum, Theresa laid a warm towel over Rachael's pretty vulva, smiling at her with her bright blue eyes, and double chin. She was a pretty girl, chubby, dirty blonde hair passed her shoulders, thick size twenty-two maybe, and square-figured like Rachael.

"That feels really good Treese. You really do that well. I knew you were special the moment you moaned at my touch in the hospital." Rachael smiled afterwards, still fumbling with the rope of hair.

Theresa spoke up, thanking her. "My last Girlfriend shaved her entire body except her head and eyebrows. I often had to shave her. I like doing it for you. You are the most beautiful Woman I have dated, Rachael. You are very sexy and strong." Rachael enjoyed the patronizing.

"Don't bring a stupid Bible in my house. Ever! Please! I had enough of that with Julian, and her raping husband." She burst out again and stopped herself from yelling, YOU SAW...what...he did to my Cuckquean, Emily, and she ran right back to him. He raped her several times and I fought to get her away from him. For years, he threatened to abuse her if I didn't sleep with him. Well I refused. Emily wanted to be under a fake name in the hospital to hide from him. That is why she used the name Julian and Jordan there." She took a breath as Theresa got up and got her another glass of wine.

"Fucking Stockholm syndrome! Men use it against weak Women for the patriarchy. I started sleeping with him regularly and when he got abusive on her, I got out of there. Julian said she didn't care that he raped me THREE TIMES while she was in the hospital." She sat up, and Theresa handed her a glass of wine, and sat on the floor between her legs listening to her, and snuggling one of her legs as she watched her sip.

"Battered Woman Syndrome, Treese. You saw it in the hospital. Na' mean. I will never let that happen to you. You are wonderful and smart and beautiful and not fooled by men. That is how men keep women oppressed. Abuse and fear of abuse. Rape. Every man is a rapist just waiting for his next victim." She took a sip, and smiled at Theresa warmly. "Feminism is going to change the world my Cuckquean, and we will be together when it happens." She held up her glass, and tapped Theresa's glass to celebrate and cheer.

After another sip, she told her, "By the way, we will be going to New York in a couple months to join the Pride Parade. I am excited. I want to show off my new Girl." Theresa felt warm inside. She was excited to finally have someone she felt things could really work out with. Someone, who helped her find her place in the right relationship.

"How long were you, and Emily together before he raped her in college?" Theresa asked curiously.

"Almost five years and Noah raped her and stabbed her breasts with a knife and she stayed with him out of fear. She refused to press charges and lives in fear. Makes up stories like, another guy did it, and she likes fear. He keeps a knife to put to her throat when they have sex, and she cries the entire time. He loves it-" Theresa interrupted her.

"Really. Oh my God. That is terrible. Aren't they both Police Officers? Can't she just shoot him with her gun or something?" Rachael picked up her phone off the sofa and texted Emily, hoping to catch Emily, instead of Julian.

Text to Julian from Rachael: I miss you Emily. Call me so we can get together. I have the men ready for us. Call me now.

"She has shot him. She shot him when he was trying to rape her once before. I think he threatened to kill the kids or something...maybe her family if she left him again." Rachael explained to her.

Theresa spoke up feeling the fear, "Jesus Christ. What the fuck is wrong with people? I'm sorry he raped you, and tried to brainwash you, Rach. I saw her using you in the hospital, and I hated it. I saw it." She got up beat in her inflection, "She constantly rejected you." Theresa had to defend her partner with what she knew. "Now I understand why you fought with her so much in the hospital, and tried to convince her, and you were screaming for her to 'Wake Up' during the fight."

"Yes. You are so right. Local Police won't charge one of their officers if a man beats and rapes a Woman Officer because of the publicity. Well now, I have him. I have his DNA and working my investigation. I will arrest him. He will get Life in prison and I will make sure Men rape him. I will destroy that Bitches life-" She stopped for a big drink, and looked back at Theresa to finish, "-when he goes to prison she will come crawling back to me." Theresa looked up in shock. "Don't you worry, I won't take her back, and don't let her cry to me on the phone either." She started mimicking Julian's voice, "Help me, help me. I be so sorry Rach. I want our relationship." Smiling, Theresa got up and leaned over Rachael with her thick body, and climbed up on her, putting her skinny lover between her legs.

Passionately, Rachael accepted her warm touch into her mouth, and Rachael loved how light her hair felt, compared to Julian's long, heavy hair. Theresa held Rachael's face in her hands, letting the chemistry between them burn wild. "You are so beautiful Rachael. I could make love to you forever, and still feel like I didn't give you enough. I will never let her take what we are building, away from us. Let us grow together, and find our happy place." Rachael smiled really big at her, offering her warm wetness in her mouth, and embraced each other. Rachael held on to the rope of black hair, tightly.

Rachael pulled the towel off the couch between her legs smiling at Theresa, as Theresa got back down on the floor between them. She felt comfortable beneath Rachael, physically and mentally.

Staring into each other's eyes, Rachael started gently whipping her wet pussy with the rope of twisted hair in her hand, and smiled at her. "I love watching you touch yourself for me." Theresa said, lovingly as Rachael stopped to drink more wine.

"Even though Noah beats her with the Bible he makes her memorize it, and quote it to him on command as he beats her-just like my Dad. My father raped me for years and used the Bible as an excuse. I hate it. Our Lesbianism is natural and honest, even gully. We have the real chemistry that

208

Mother Nature intended for Real Women to have. It brings Women together and allows for smart love. Not the fake shit men pretend is love. No man can love anyone without abusing them." Rachael waited for her to nod, and Theresa quickly nodded and spoke up.

"Every man I have been with was abusive to me, and hated my Girlfriends. EVEN when he didn't know I was sleeping with them." Theresa added. "They always had me sleep with their friends, and treated me like shit while they cheated on me. I started dating Women, and am much happier with my life. I hate men anymore, Rachael!"

"Damn right." Rachael barked. "It is so nice to be with a Modern Woman. I'm tired of masturbating...DON'T GET ME STARTED ON MASTURBATING! Julian is not allowed to masturbate without his permission. Can you believe that shit? Her own pussy is hers and HE gets to control it. HE IS A FASCIST! She isn't even allowed to braid her hair without the Fascist's permission. And that fat Bitch bows to him whenever she walks away from him. Freaking stupid Hillbilly. Are you a Hillbilly?"

"I was born in Cleveland. Is that Hillbilly?" Theresa said it smiling, and trying to quietly get Rachael's attention on her. Rachael just slapped her pussy gently with the long black hair, and stared at her, undecided.

"Fat fucking Bitch-Hillbilly Bitch, chews tobacco. Like what the fuck? I hope she sucks his dick and gives it cancer. And the Bitch needs rape to get off because he has raped her so much. Worst off, rape by a White Fascist MALE! I don't put out to men unless I use my tools for my gain. YOU...will not fuck any men unless I offer you to them. Agreed Theresa?" Theresa nodded at her excitement of future orgies on her mind. "I like some Dark Dick every now and then and you can watch."

"I want to be with you, Rachael. I am fine with you sleeping with men as long as I am your only, Girlfriend. I promise I will ask first." She started rubbing Rachael's inner thigh but, Rachael continued to bitch about the Bitch.

"I had to get men to fuck Julian. She is such a fat ass and her tits are...just nasty I had to cover her face with a bag and beg guys to fuck her. Truthfully. I am not fibbing to you. I was a good friend and Master to her. Her tits are so ugly. She has these thick...dark..." She offered Theresa a disgusting look on her face as she described them. "...brown...callus nipple area the size of dinner plates. They are this big." Rachael put her hands up and showed a diameter the side of a basketball. Theresa offered a gross expression to enhance it as she spoke.

"I saw them in the hospital. Yours are cute. Mine are ugly."

Rachael went on, "I would help...no I like yours Treese. I can suck your entire breasts in my mouth. It's nice to have a Girlfriend with normal breasts. I taught Emily how to dress sexy instead of like men, and taught her how to get men to hit on her. HELL! I even got men to rape her for her. That is what she wanted to prove she wasn't really an Angel of God, to me. As her Master, I had to pimp Julian to get her laid. SERIOUSLY! She slutted herself to everyone because when she got naked people cringed and wanted me instead. I am a good Master to my Cuckqueans. Just ask Emily. You will see that I like to satisfy my Bitches and get them satisfied. OH! And I love Transgender as well. Bring me Transgender and any Big Black Cock, Theresa."

Theresa was trying to keep up with the rant directions.

"Those are my favorite-Transgender Women with dicks. The more real African, the better. That is all you are allowed to fuck if we are going to be together. And you can never say 'no' to my wishes, if you want our relationship to grow together." Theresa quickly nodded, and rubbed Rachael's thigh closer to her busy spot.

"That is mostly who I sleep with now. I love Black men. They never stop asking for sex. And, men are disposable, so there is no need to keep them." Theresa quickly spoke up.

"Just find another Brother." She grinned, as Rachael got into her familiar territory, and moved her face closer to Rachael pussy, and asking permission by waiting for a nod. She added to the Rachael's sexual list.

"I love Black guys." Rachael slid down until her ass was off the couch, and Theresa started licking her Master's pussy.

"I had to fuck Emily with my double-dildo toy like, every week behind his back. He didn't even know it. She starts fighting with her voices and..and...and I FUCKING HATE HIM! His white dick is so small. I guess she can't feel it with her COW PUSSY!"

Taking a long deep breath to the pleasure sensations beginning to come in, she at least, stopped yelling about it.

"His dick is so small, he makes her suck it and drink his pee because he thinks he is an Angel. I medicated her over and over to help her and she just lays down for him. She was a drug addict and I rescued her in college. God did not intervene on his fat tramp Angel. That is how I got back at God for

211

letting my Daddy rape me over and over. I helped his Angel get raped over and over. She is such a fat cunt Whore, I had to prescribe her Ketamine every day to keep her from going crazy and fighting with her stupid hair voices."

Rachael leaned back, and closed her eyes as she got closer. "Lick it Treese. Lick my clit hard. I told you I like it rough. You know that already. Drink every drop. That is important to me. You must drink all my seed, every day. All of it. Every time. Put your finger in my Emily hole...just below my clit. Finger it when you eat me. You're the only I will let do this to me-YES! YES! Like that. OH YES! TREESE I'M CUMMING! FINGER EMILY! LICK-"

Rachael jerked back moaning, and grabbed Theresa's head, jamming it into her burning wetness mess. Theresa's finger slid deep in her urethra, and the pain was enormous with her orgasm. Theresa shoved her chin to Rachael's clitoral hood, and rubbed it into her clitoris, as Rachael screamed her name. Theresa sucked up the sweet, nectar of her tough lover with her lips, before it dripped on the floor below.

Panting, she screamed as Theresa slid her finger out of her Lover's urethra. "OHHH! That was good! Good!" Her chest was rising and falling as fast as her heart could race.

"I liked how you fucked my clit with your chin. Keep fingering my Emily hole." Rachael pushed Theresa's head forward, toward her Love Choices, as she started working two fingers in and out, one in each of her lovers front holes. She watched her face closely to learn her pleasure well.

"Lick your fingers clean each time. Eat my wetness EVERY TIME! I want you to worship my wetness." Rachael took a few short breaths to let the anger go, and focus on her new, beautiful, woman.

"You are my Cuckquean Theresa. My Pleaser and only my Pleaser and I am your Pleaser." Theresa smiled as she worked her wetness, and tasted the opportunity to have someone out of her league. This was something Rachael desired, because she would always be the boss.

"Theresa I was so good to Emily. I lied about her mental illnesses on every annual report for her. She is OCD with Dissociative Identity Disorder and hides it with a Multiple IDentifY program we designed in college and Med School to control her fatty ass. Her fat mother has it, too. They think they are God's Articulating Angels with Multiple Personalities. Noah even slept with her mother occasionally because Julian said she was an Angel and needed Noah's dick in her. Fucking sick Hillbillies. Mentally ill Theresa. I can handle some shit but fuck her mentally ill-sicko-manipulative-always lying-Hillbilly-Cheating-Bitch-fat cow ass." Theresa licked her harder to change the mood but, orgasm seemed it was a while away.

"Noah is cheating on here with some Black woman with a huge fat ass. I didn't see her fat face. I think it is the same woman I saw going into their house. I should get a picture of her and Noah fucking and send it to Julian's fat midget, cow butt." Rachael reached down and pulled hard on her nipple weights, and moaned in pleasure as they stretched, but when she let go, she went right back to complaining.

"Noah, uses her Mental Illness against her. 'Hides the Meds that I prescribed her, so she has nervous breakdowns and clings to her Daddy Master. That is how he got her away from me. I know it. He abuses her so much and scares her with rape and drugs her and steals her medication. He is an Animal. Our Feminism is the foundation for freedom for victims like her and she is too mentally stupid to understand her slavery. Feminism will rescue the oppressed Women like her from Rapists and she will have to thank us. I gave her a way out of-"

Theresa slid all four fingers into Rachael wetness, and her angry words turned to moans of pleasure. As Rachael pushed against her nearly shaking, Theresa lovingly slid her entire hand inside her stretching canal. Rachael jerked in pain as her eyes rolled back, and her lungs held her breaths prisoner.

Immediately, she grabbed the weights on her nipples, and stretched them downward, wincing from the rush of pain pushing her pleasure signals along. Each inch she stretched them, the wetness poured faster, and the higher her moaning pitch took, giving Theresa a boost of self-confidence.

Rachael dropped the left weight on her chest, and somewhat dropped the twisted rope of black hair, onto her Pleaser's wrist.

"Put this in my pussy when you make love to me." Theresa looked at it, and smelled it as Rachael through her head back exhausted from the fist working its way in and out of her most clustered nerve endings. It was then she realized Rachael was wearing an engagement ring. *She was not wearing it last night,* she thought.

Forcing the hair inside her, she asked, "Were you ever married? I see your ring?"

"NO! The fat Bitch gave it to me to drag me along while lying to me about us getting married-again. She lied to me so I am keeping it." Rachael leaned back, and enjoyed feeling her vagina feeling full, and her vulva getting stimulated, as Theresa put her hand back inside her, and made a fist around Emily's missing hair. Slowly, she worked her fist out until the hair stopped it, and back in as far as she could get it. Each time, Rachael burst out her exhale and quickly took another.

Rachael jerked back, scrunching her eyes closed, and slowly started to cry from the painful pleasures of her rushing hormones, and something else. Theresa slowly worked it almost out, and deep inside, and watched Rachael sob to her.

"Do you want me to stop?" Theresa asked with real concern. She recognized this opportunity to keep Rachael, and went for it. She laid her head down on Rachael's flat stomach, and put her arm around her lower back, and snuggled her, and fisted her slowly and painfully. Rachael immediately embraced her head with both her hands and cried. "I loved her so much, Theresa. She was my best friend." Rachael snuggled her even more, as she sped up her fisting to help her.

Rachael drew silent as the hormones defeated her tears. She thrusted her hips into Theresa's fist repeatedly, killing the emotional pain, and punishing herself, as her orgasm exploded up her spine and finally, jerked her into the scream.

Rachael motioned for her to pull out, and Theresa tried to turn the hair around to retrieve it but, couldn't. She pulled out and told her Master, "I need to get a hold of the hair rope. Lingering in oxytocin-recovery, Rachael leaned over sideways, and enjoyed the chemicals still invading her reward system. Her cries were chased away for the moment.

Theresa rubbed the wetness all over her underdeveloped, tubular boobs, and fingered her own wetness, and tasting it over and over.

"You can do that to me every night, Theresa. That was great. You really fist very good." Rachael sat up and un-pinched her nipple weights. "Put these on your nipples every day, when you are cleaning my house."

Appreciating the compliment, "I love getting fisted. It is better than a cock any day." And she pinched the weights onto her very short, barely protruding nipples. Finished, she smiled and got up wiping her wetness, and then rubbing it on Rachael's breasts. Rachael quickly grabbed her hand and stopped her with an angry stare. Theresa immediately felt as if she had done something wrong, and waited to be corrected. Gently, Rachael pulled Theresa's hand up, and licked her fingers passionately, making Theresa warm all over.

But, her words got stern. "You will never waste a drop of my wetness or your wetness. You will taste it and rub it on your breasts and face." Looking down at Theresa's thick bush, she told her while nodding to it, "Shave it completely, and keep it that way. Not one hair is allowed anywhere below your neck, Cuckquean."

Her Cuckquean quickly responded with nods and simpleton words, "Anything for you, Rachael. I want to make you happy. If you are happy, I will be happy." She was very nervous when she spoke back to her, and Rachael patted the seat next to her, and after she sat down, Rachael snuggled up to her between her legs and breasts. "Hold me, Mommy." Rachael said, as she told her about their immediate future.

"My new assignment starts next week. I want you to move your stuff in here this coming weekend. I have to meet with Julian soon about her case files, and I will have to stay at the safe house on my assignment...undercover teenage girl for internet bait."

Theresa hugged her more as she snuggled her Baby, and asked, "Can I come see you at the safe house place?"

"You are my Cuckquean, and I will take you everywhere I go. I don't know about the safe house yet. We will see. I'm sure we can have sex there a few times at least. Maybe with a few friends. From now on I want you to curtsy for me whenever you leave my presence and hold me every night like this. I like that a lot. I miss it with Emily but I want to share it with you. Tomorrow Treese, I want you to start growing your hair long and die it black. I love your blue eyes so I want you to always wear eyeliner and mascara. Make it extra dark for me. I think your eyes could be so beautiful."

"You don't like my blonde hair, Rachael? I colored it. Is Rachael your first name or middle name?" Theresa pulled on her own hair, and stretched it out in from of her to say goodbye to the blonde she loved.

"I told you last week on our date, my full name is Rachael Marie Briggs, Theresa May Daley. I like my woman looking good and long black hair and blue eyes and naked at all times in our house. All times. I don't care if we have guests you will be naked at all times for me to show your love for me and show them your love for me as your Master. Being naked for me in front of everyone shows me you are devoted to making our new relationship work. You will not masturbate EVER, unless I give

217

you permission, and you will not put anything in your pussy without my permission. Cuckqueany. We talked about this at the bar. I want us to be happy and those things make me feel happy."

"What about my tampons, Rach?"

"Yes. But, you cannot masturbate without my permission, EVER! Text me if you need to rub it out." Rachael reached down and pulled Emily's hair out of her pussy, and put it in her mouth to suck. When Theresa saw her suck on it, she reached out to try it, and Rachael pushed her hand away.

"Suck on your own hair from now on when I am with you."

Chapter Nineteen

-Chase the Facts, Fear the Truths, Enjoy her Mind

"I picked her up from school Noah, and she was in tears. She said the boys keep pullin' her hair and teasin' her about the length. So when I dropped her off this mornin', she gets out of the car, walks to a group of boys, and hands each one of them some of her hair, and they all walked away together with the boys carrying it for her." Julian paced back and forth in the bedroom. "You cannot let her skip her Diddy meds. Girls must have them to deal with boys." Noah, looked down at the carpet with a smile, and admired the smooth pattern she had worn in it over the last two years, while giving her self-talks to work out the bugs.

"I don't know how my mother ever survived my teenage years. I wanted to purge pain from every cowboy and girl in Texas. I am not goin' to be able to handle Ally gettin' into Angelic Responsibilities. My mother has already given her the talk, and the Song. She plays it constantly when I check her headphones. Over and over like I used to do."

Noah watched her go back and forth and back and forth, sucking on her hair. It isn't as if he has not heard this speech before. Usually twice a year. He laid back on the bed to repeat it word for word, and Julian snapped her fingers at him, and he sat back up to watch her pace. She needed him to feel what she was feeling.

Noah, snapped his fingers back, and pointed to the floor between his knees at the foot of the bed. Wearing her Shyanne Floral Festival Western Boots with Texas Jewelry, and his white long and large muscle shirt with her red yoga shorts, she curtsied him, and sat down looking for stress relief. She knew her place. This was another of her rituals, and always ended in her place sitting between Noah's legs, and getting her neck and shoulders rubbed.

"Are you taking your medications, Love?" He asked her kindly.

"Not yet. Where did you put them? Bathroom?" She asked.

"Baby, I don't move your medicine. They are always on the fridge. I can get them for you. Pleasssssse stay on your medicines." She leaned forward, and Noah headed out of the room, and buried her hands in her face from her over-active anxieties.

He came back carrying a beer, but that was it for medicine.

"If you didn't move my meds, Noah. Someone did. Did you change the key code on the door like I asked, Noey?" She asked him curtly.

"I already called in new prescriptions but, you have to pick them up tomorrow. They are in your name. Same old routine. I'm trying something different." She informed him.

"Julz, do you think Rachael?" He asked, and being a bit nervous of the idea.

"Well, maybe Ally, or Momma. Samira is a nurse and likely to look at them. She has her own door code but, I can't see her movin' them." They looked at each other in conclusion. "We need new codes for the key pads on BOTH doors, and the garage." Noah nodded in agreement.

"I haven't found anythang else missin'...yet."
She added. "Change the codes today. Please?"

She handed him the coconut oil as she took
control of her hair, and jerked it repeatedly from the
front. He handed her the horse brush to stop her
jerking, and sat down behind her, as she pulled his
shirt off, and got control of her hair again.

Noah worked the oil into her shoulders as she
occupied her concerns by brushing her hair. After
his first long squeeze of them, and her moans of
relief, he let go, and she exhaled about twenty
points off her blood pressure.

"Cowgirl, you have such toned muscles." He
tried to be silly, "Do you work out?"

"YES. Two kids and on my back for you every
day. That is a workout." She put him in her place.
Yes, her place.

"Momma will pick the kids up soon. She be
taking them to the Gahanna Stables to brush the
horses, and claim the kids be hers, so she can tell
everyone she is only thirty-five." She exhaled the
stress as she began to feel better. In a thought, she
leaned her head back, and looked up at him with
her beauty.

"I laid in the car with Samira half the night the
other night, Noah. I am so mad at you." She winked
at him to let him know, he was not really in trouble,
and her blue eyes jumped out of her very dark eye
make-up. He leaned down and kissed her nose, as
she spoke.

"You thank you Angel men could keep your
dick in your pants just long enough to help an
Angel? She cried the entire time with you, and she
cried just lyin' in the car, Mister. She said she has
been cryin' at work. She can't believe how she feels
since you did your bad boy Angel impression on her

too early. Noah smiled and repeated the topic she had ignored for days. "Emily."

"She says she is not sad at all but, is so happy, she is cryin'. Damn it Noah, I have said it before with Seshi, NEVER SEED AN ANGEL UNTIL SHE LEARNS TO MANAGE VULNERABILITY! Chickens under the porch know that. Poor Girl was a virgin, Noah." She slapped his leg next to her as he rubbed her shoulders. "You gave her the pure emotions, and seed at the same time. You can't do that to us women Angels in the beginnin'. We have to build tolerance to both, SEPARATELY or you get the mess Samira is now." He was grinning without her seeing him.

"NOAH JAMES!" She turned to look at him, you didn't tell her she was an Angel, DID YOU? NOAH? PLEEEEEEASE tell me you didn't." Noah shook his head, and she sighed in relief. "That is my job. I know when to tell her." She said, turning back to brush her hair again.

"Is that Emily's job or Julian's job, Emily?" He tossed at her, and felt her neck and shoulders tighten.

♫ *Text Alert on Julian's Phone*

"Sam took to my scars, Noah. She immediately tried drawin' my pain out from them. Acrotomophilia is what it is called, and it is the guaranteed sign of an Angel. I have never experienced that from anyone, but you. You constantly rub your cum on them makin' them feel loved, even though I denied them to you. She is going to be a strong angel, like you. I felt it. I got on my knees for her because I felt my position with her, like I do you. I tried to be dominant, and it was

222

her natural role, and my natural role submitted to her. Both times, her first touch was on my scars."

Julian looked up into thought before she spoke. "She was naturally dominant with me when we made love, and submissive to you when you made love. Yet, she needed to be above you for the pure emotions. Most Angels want bottom because they fear the purity, and don't understand the Vulnerability for Purgin' the pain yet, and she insisted on bein' on top durin' Vulnerability. I will have to work on that mystery in Bible study tomorrow."

He spoke up again, nudging the topic again. "Did you make love to her as Emily or Julian?" He was not letting her avoid it this time.

"You have to seed her again soon or it will only get worse. Noey. Work up her tolerance. I know you are seein' her for lunch tomorrow. Seed her for her sake. You have to build her up to it, Baby. Bring her here every day, and do not let her swallow it. Seed her. Give her your biggest loads. Take one from me if you have to. Isn't there a chalice for me in the fridge?"

He answered quickly, "I put two in there for you yesterday, did you drink them?" She was mean about her drinkin' seed. It was her romantic drug of choice.

"Yes, my love. I see yers' and I gobble them up." She grinned at her own remark, as she brushed and asked.

"Go get mine, will you? I feel depressed. And my Copenhagen. Please? I worship you, Angel." He got up, and she admired his boots as he walked away. "CHECK ON ALLY!" She yelled, as he got into the hallway.

She grabbed her phone to check the message.

223

Text to Julian from Anonymous Number:
Image of Woman with a pillow case over her
face and two men fucking her. 'I miss you Emily.
Call me so we can get together. I have the men
ready for us. Call me now.'

Sitting her phone down, she wiped the developing tears from her eyes and started talking to herself.

"I'm sure her body absorbed his seed like it was takin' its last breath." Julian looked down at her drooping breasts and rubbed her belly and vulva. It was not as sore as she liked it to be. "Why hath you forsaken me, Kitty? I pray. I let you have everythang you want. Why can't you give me another Angel or five of them? Please Kitty, one more at least." Julian smiled at her vulva in her palm as she squeezed the mound for pain, "OR I WILL GET YOU FIXED, BITCH!" Julian thought that would do the trick. Noah, was standing in the doorway smiling with her gifts, when she noticed him.

"Emily. I will pour this seed out, and waste my own for your sins." He tossed her an IDentifY mirror, and waited.

Growling at him and herself, she picked it up and looked in it. She was nervous with him watching, as she stared at herself without saying anything.

"Noah, I am havin' problems with IDentifY. I'm sorry I haven't shared that with you. I love you and I'm sorry." She put the mirror behind her on the bed and lowered her head. "I'm fragmenting and bleeding, Baby." When she looked up at him he

224

had moved a little closer, but kept his distance. He stood square like a Cowboy on a horizon.

"I have been workin' on it with patches. I thank I need Rachael to help me." When she looked up, she was teared up but, not crying. I can't let Andrea help me. Can I?"

"No, Julz, Rachael wants to crash you to destroy your memories of her drugging you and abusing you with her friends, and just so she could feel coddled by you. That was a heavy price for you to pay for her to feel unconditional love, Emily." He looked down and watched her stuff her hair into her mouth frustrated.

"Angel, how long has Emily been fragmenting into you?" Noah still held her Chalice hostage before her.

♫ *Text Alert on Julian's Phone*

"Stop callin' me Emily." She sighed after trying to be strong about it, and brushing her hair helped. "Two years...three, I guess." She looked up at him with those beautiful baby blues to make herself seem honest with him. Honest in her deception. "Emily never stopped showin' up after Simon. It got really bad after Ally was born, and...patches held for a while. You have seen her a few times since Zachary was born." She looked down to the ground, and picked up her hair, and rubbed it on her face, and looked up again, making sure he believed her.

"I thank Rachael has learned to trigger her with pokes to motivate her so she can get her back in bed. She is just an IDentifY Cover. Honest." Again, she looked back up at him. "It worked. Please punish me for her sins, Noah. Please." Noah was silent, as he led her eyes to her phone, to read her message.

"Could be Momma. Is she here now?"

Text Alert to Julian from Anonymous Number: Noah loved that picture. He got so turned on he raped me three times that day. I have been riding him since you married him.

After reading it, Julian through it into the hallway so she wouldn't answer it again.

"Julian, I will no longer punish you for the sins of your Alibis." She immediately got up on her knees reaching for his thighs. She felt instant and major anxiety.

"Noey. Please don't quit me. I can do better. I'm tryin' to fix it. Dear God, please don't take my punishment away, Baby. Please don't-" Noah shoved her back on her big Texas ass, and she stared up at him, having been put back in her place.

"Did Emily let men gang rape her with a pillow case on her head?" He crossed his arms as his signal.

"Alibis don't have restrictions, Noah. The Alibi Clause allows Emily freedom to be with others. But she doesn't. I try not to let that happen." She nervously looked up at him lacking confidence in her answer, and subconsciously glanced at her phone, then his phone lying on the bed.

"When was the last time you let men do that to you, Emily."

Julian leaned against the bed, crossed her arms and pouted, looking only at the bureau beside her, as she sat back in the same spot as before.

"I..." she just sat there, not finishing what she was going to say. The long silence was to his advantage. She was cornered.

Finally, she looked up at him letting him in on another secret, "I don't know. And I don't know if it ever really happened, Noah. I thank...I don't know. I'm having memory trouble with my Alibis from fragmentin'. You understand that, right? You have that now, with Jon gone."

"Emily, I saw a picture of you. It was happening. I saw your longhorn tramp-stamp in the picture. A man fucking your ass flexing his muscles in the air. Pulling your hair."

"Noah, I struggled through school with a many thangs. My miscarriage, problems with learnin' thangs and rememberin' thangs, Simon. Other thangs like Rachael and misplacin' thangs. I'm not makin' excuses to you. I just can't honestly say I did those thangs. It happened a couple times I'm sure-EVERY GIRL explores her desires. I was young and learnin' who I was, and angry, and strugglin' with God. Please stop throwin' it in my face, Noah. I'm a slut for you and Samira, and neither of you are complainin' when you're gettin' your way, so why shame me over my past IF I was bad for someone else. Please don't hurt me like that. Please."

"I won't shame you, Emily. I only need to know how dangerous this IDentifY is to you and I. Until we can Crash them away for good, and the Bitch is going away. Trust me. I will bury that Alibi."

Pleading her way through the argument, she was being heartfelt. "Stop callin' me, Emily. I'm your Julzie." She briefed a very small smile after saying it. It was interfering with her strength. "I am lookin' at Crash options to clean the slate, and she will go away."

♫ Text Alert on Noah's Phone

Instantly, Julian began to worry where his words were going, and who sent him a text. "I never get to see your other Alibis enough to get to know them, Julzie. I agree with Rachael, Jordan and Emily are crashing. You are accenting through their speech. Jordan never had an accent, and I don't know Emily. No accent went along with Jordan's professionalism, Julz. Even Emily, the other day, had your accent. The Crap System is just failing." She heard in his voice, the anger building behind it, and after ten years of marriage, felt it coming.

He started up again, and she felt it. "We are trying to work through this together. It is hard to help, when so many things are not spoken or intentionally kept from me, because of your guilt, and your secret Slut IDentifY Emily, THAT YOU USE TO HAVE AFFAIRS BEHIND MY BACK! I WANT HER CRASHED! AND NO MORE SIGNATURES OF YOUR LOVER ON YOUR ASS TO THROW IN MY FACE!" He tossed the one chalice still in his hand, against the wall to his left. She lowered her face into her hands, and jerked her hair over and over. His seed was her responsibility in her mind, and now, it was wasted.

Mildly nodding in agreement, she reached down and rubbed her sore vulva, and cupped one of her breasts, as she nodded in agreement to his belief about Emily. Her lies were just coming back to get her, and the cost was getting too much to pay. She squeezed her nipple, hoping milk would come out.

"Notre amour livrera nos circonstances ensemble," Noah whispered to her softly.

She quickly looked up at him as tears came down her cheeks, "Notre amour livrera nos circonstances ensemble, Baby." She gave back, feeling his love. She wasn't sure how her lies were going to work anymore.

"Julzie, what do I need to know about Emily. I need to hear it from you, Baby. Please tell me." Noah grabbed his manhood, and adjusted it in his panties. Even after he was done, she stared at his bulge, grinning-appreciating. She asked him to wear her panties for her fetish, and after so many years, he still commits to her desires and needs. She knew he loved her more than himself.

When he reached for his phone, Julian panicked, and wiggled her way up in her boots. He thumbed through it, seeing who it was from, and quickly deleted it. Julian could not see what he was doing but, she rushed to do anything.

Rushing to tell her truth, she spit it out as fast as it would come, starring him in the eyes, only, she had to get the delivery just right, to not face consequences. "Emily is an IDentifY who sleeps with Rachael. She...She...She offers herself to her. She is stupid-Superficial, Girl. She has the maturity of about sixteen years old with all the sexual power and freedom of...of..." She could not find a word, so she went with honesty, "...me. Me Noah."

She paused to decipher his reaction, and compounded it. "This damn headache! Fuckin' little tramp Girl Emily, and very manipulative, Noah. Never sleep with her if she shows up. Get me to bed immediately, and reset me." She watched him holding his phone. "And please don't give her Diddy Meds. Please Noey. She is Rachael's Bitch." She reached out and held his forearm with both hands, and catered to him. "Please God Noey, don't let Emily have my Ditty Meds." She overwhelmed him a bit, and he stepped back, and she held onto his arm.

Leaning away from her, he asked with a little fear, "Have I ever slept with her?"

"I could never know that, Noey. I'm havin' problems with Jordan, too," Her words grew more and more desperate as they got slower, as intuition kicked in on her. "Noey-All the time, I just...uh...you know...play with IDentifY sometimes, and let you please whoever I can get. You please women so well, Angel." Her search for words got too slow in her last sentence that he picked up on it. She was not speaking the truth.

He jerked his arm away from her and snapped his fingers pointing her back to her seat on the floor, where she was. Without contest, she sat back down on her Texas labia and butt, and waited. She lifted her knees and lowered her head back down hiding her facial responses to the skeletons. He just watched her in silence, and trepidation.

Her voice returned to a raspy whisper as she spoke facing her knees. "I'm fragmentin', Noey, and I did it to myself out of stupid fears and maybe..." she wiped the tears from her face keeping control of herself. "...maybe...needs I am..." she tossed her head back and rested on the mattress edge behind her so he could see her cry. "IDentifY desires or fetishes...or fantasies are bleeding into my own desires. I guess." She let out a huge sigh of relief telling him, and when the tension left her, she looked up at him, standing there, knowing her plight. He saw the weight on her shoulders finally lift, and knew that was honesty.

"Jordan is crackin' up-she fisted me in the basement that night, and I'm not sure who crashed the car into one of your prostitution customers." She exhaled again, this time, insecure about her windows, she looked back to her boots with her head down on her knees. "I got stuck in a hiccup IDentifY at work arguin' with Jon months ago. Jordan and Julian was hyperventilatin' and mumblin' "IDentifY. IDentifY. IDentifY, because Emily was comin'." With a long fresh breath of strength, she went on with the bones. "I have been hidin' other problems like that, and can't manage it. I need you, and I don't know how to fix it. My Diddy meds should be fixin' it, and they ain't workin' or I'm gettin' tolerant." He finally sat down on the edge of the bed, with his legs hanging next to her, and she leaned her head over on one.

"Rachael rescued me, recognizin' the problem. Told me I would have to Crash then, and she had an idea about Crashin' individual Alibis, and not all of them. We tried it. I was desperate for my career, Noah. Our future. Desperate for big secret. It just made my fragment worse. I have been hidin it from everyone...includin' myself. Now, I don't even see some of them in the mirror anymore. And Emily keeps showin' up, and I don't know it." She looked over and up at him, sighing her empty breath. He was taken aback by it. He had never seen her this confused about her Psychological Program, and she added. "I can't lose Jordan. I want...I just need Emily to go away."

"I was there Julian. You were arguing with Jon."

She got a confused look on her face, until he spoke again and distracting her.

"Dakota?"

231

She whispered quietly for some strange reason, "I still have her and others. I can't say for how long, though. I feel their needs comin' on me." She was trying not to disturb the Alibis. "I can't just Crash. I have Multiples in my brain, so it is a much bigger process than what Rachael did to you...and I'm sorry I wasn't there to protect you, Noey."

"What needs are you talking about? Does Emily give you to everyone or something? Is that what has been going on, Julian." He was getting uncomfortable now.

"No. I have slept with no one. Only you, Sam, and Rachael, and Rachael has total control of Emily. Thank you for sharin' me, Noah...with the Alibis. It really helps me realize my responsibilities to God. I just wish..." She didn't finish. Thoughts or Alibis had got her.

"Then what needs...desires are you feeling that we can't work with? We work everything out, Angel."

Julian looked down at her NOT pregnant body, "I'm really no Angel, Noah. Angels can't be this fucked up, and not gettin' pregnant."

She slowly shook her head as if she wasn't intentionally doing it. A reaction to her situation. "Noah, if there is ever a time for you to not want to know somethang Baby, it is now. Don't ask me again about Emily's needs." Enter the silence. A long silence.

"Every time we make love, Noey, you satisfy Emily's need enough in certain ways through me, to help me fight her back. Thank you for not judgin' me in our bedroom. I love you so much for that. I don't want her desires. I want my own. I never wanted her desire, and I have it. I'm infected with it. But...I can never let somethang' that terrible become somethang' I get over and over. It is only self-destructive." She shook her head again as if she was remindin' herself not to say it. Please don't ever change how we make love. I need your restrictions, Noah, and yer' punishments."

Rubbing her hands over her face, she palmed her fat mound, and felt all the wetness she was getting, just talking about Emily's desires, and how it has infected her now.

With real concern, she turned and looked at him on her knees, and put her chin on his thigh to look up at him to speak. "If I ever ask you to rape me again, please say no. Test my faith not with the cucumber but, of my bad Emily desires. No matter how much I beg. Give me the strange pleasures I need, and we will never have to do what we did, ever again. Do you understand?" Her words to him were very somber and honest. This was the closest she would get to her dirty confession. The bones had been swept under the bed this time.

Noah was a little spooked, and even more curious as to the desires he was or wasn't satisfying. He had ideas, but men tend to be a little slow linking the dots.

♫ *Text Alert on Noah's Phone*

She still stared at him making sure he understood the importance of her request. When he nodded, she felt some relief that she had finally opened up about her struggle, and that he understood the parts she wanted him to understand. She looked at his phone with less worry, and back to him. Following her lead, he picked it up.

Text Alert to Noah from Anonymous Number: Image of a positive Pregnancy Test next to a flat chest with long, bent nipples.

He rolled his eyes at the message and deleted it very quickly. He went right back to her, "Can I sleep with Emily just once, knowing it is her? So I can read her and understand. I never sleep with Jordan, Julian. I miss Dakota punishing me." Julian intentionally shook her head. "Why did Rachael get to sleep with your Alibis, but your husband doesn't?"

Julian looked up at him without any emotions, and he read the candid gloom in her eyes, "To keep Julian from sleepin' with her. To honor our Accord. It was the best I could do to control the person who controls Emily."

Noah, instantly felt a lack of being analytical, and apologized.

"I have to Crash to wipe them all out...and maybe Emily will go away too or damaged." Her whisper rose with her, as she crawled up between his legs, and rested her face on his wonderful eight-pack abs. "You are a wonderful man, Noah James. You always let me have my way, and protect me the entire time from my...issues. You are the Angel, not me." She heard him growl a little during his huge exhale of disapproval, and she smiled.

"I thank Emily was the one responsible for Jordan's askin' you to rape me, and Jordan rapin' in the basement. I don't really know. There have been other bad thangs over time I can't explain. Missin' time. Pains I don't remember you givin' me. I have to Crash them very soon."

"Rachael showed me a picture of you using the cucumber to rodeo in the hospital. I guess you lost that test of faith." Noah watched her arms and shoulders give up.

"Well, the skeletons just keep on coming, she said in an exhale.

"She also said her dad took her out of Texas since he couldn't get to you." His hands rubbed her Bright, white backside, and he took some of her hair, and put it in her lips.

"Maybe it was Emily in the picture, and I told you, Noey, Rachael is not Jenna. Jenna never left Texas. And a reminder since you keep forgettin' thangs, she was my first real love, and I made love to her. A lot." Julian's eyes rolled, and she didn't let him see it.

"PCP-Angel dust?" Julian jerked her head up at him in question. It was clear that did not ring a bell with her. "Rachael said you drugged me with it, and hard-on meds, like your other men."

"WHAT?" She screamed, and grabbed her throat in pain. "Noah James, I did NOT drug you. I would never. Prescription meds, of course, but not street drugs. NEVER!" She made sure she looked into his eyes. "She really got some cow-pies burnin' in that head of hers." She leaned in and kissed his tight, tan stomach, and put her chin back on his thigh, and her arms around his rear, and struggled with her headache.

"She said she drugged Simon with your blue water, and it had PCP in it, and that..." he paused for a moment..."She got Simon to rape you for your fantasies." She didn't look up at him, and he sat there reading her, as her chest started to shake, then her shoulders, and finally, she broke. She covered her face with both hands, and let it fall into the mattress beside him. He listened to her cry without a word or touch.

Crying through her hands, she tried to explain. "Noeyyyyy, I don't know everythang Emily did. I am beginnin' to see Rachael is much smarter than me, and I have been blinded by kindness and love and carin' for the wrong person. No good deed, goes unpunished." She snorted trying to stop everything from leaking. But, she was too humiliated to enjoy it, and kept her face hidden.

As her crying tried to hinder her words, she asked him. "Anythang else you remember she said about Emily? I CAN'T TAKE MORE OF THIS SHIT!" He kept staring at her, desperate for reading information and cues. She finally pulled her hands away with her head on the end of the sheet, fighting her runny nose.

"Julian, Rachael said she has been documenting my sexual abuse of you with photos, and drugged or programmed you to shoot me...and the only thing that saved me was my bullet proof vest." Julian jerked back, sitting on her boots, and glanced at him before racing her memory to connect the dots of clues. Crying would have to wait for this big one.

She slowly nodded subconsciously, and tilted her head as she concentrated, and moved on to the next file, then the next file, then the next string that attached the next memory with the emotions. She had to rush over, and remember the emotions she attached to each memory to re-evaluate what it was, and why she felt that way at the time, and recorded it in her memory. She was quick in her crowded mind, and her changing expression read to him like a mystery novel. She was a wreck in his eyes.

When she bit down on her lip to hold a memory, while she searched other memories, he

236

knew she was holding onto something she found...something important. The other side of her mouth bit down, and she shifted to holding the inside of her bottom lip with the whole front row of her teeth as she evaluated the emotions attached to each file memory. Her eyes never focused, they merely looked forward and fell downward slowly. Her head jerked back a little, as her re-evaluation of past events were swept, analyzed, and connected with logic and fact. She found her answer.

Delicately, her head turned, and looked up to him. Her eyeliner and mascara had run down her beautiful, pale face that only had trace amounts of bruising left on it. Her eyes were blue, and pure like her soul. They bared the truth to him, and to Julian. His prodding, prodding, prodding, had finally paid off.

She looked away into her memory again without moving her face away from his direction, and compared what she knew then, to how Rachael openly acted now. The tilt of her face, told him she was crossing the brain barrier faster than another Genius. As her lower jaw squared, she slowly nodded her head on the tilt, and squared her eyes with his to finish nodding.

He remained quiet out of courtesy, and respect; she was brilliant Woman, and filing all those memories into very important boxes, reminded him how small or slow, his male-brain really was. In her best moments, she intimidated him, and he couldn't be man enough to admit it. But, for Julian, years of guilt, and self-torment were being washed away from her files, by re-evaluating Rachael's role in his shooting.

She looked at him, and nodded her head to say she was finding what she needed. The feelings of inferiority had shifted back to him since, she found solace in realizing, she did not consciously shoot her Angel back then.

"Rachael said she drugged you in college and every day since then, to prove you were not an Angel, and a stupid hillbilly whore, and men paid her to let them have sex with you. Could this be true? And, I don't think she meant for me to remember anything."

Julian immediately went back to memory, and bounced around. This time, it was not with lightning speed. In fact, her mind was exhausted from the first big search that didn't put files back as neatly with a headache she had fought for weeks now. But she dove in, and he watched her face slowly reset, and her subconscious fade as her body fell to her relaxed, default position. She didn't move once she defaulted. Her mind drained her body for the energy she needed, as he admired her sagging breasts, and hoped she would want to fool around afterwards.

Chapter 20

-Subconscious Battering Pleasures

Leak

From her second favorite position, on her knees, the elation was coming in as she realized, she was not completely responsible for shooting the man she loved. Escaping her deep thoughts with a sighing smile of relief, and reassured him.

"A Woman who speaks the truth, has nothin' to fear, Noah. We will get through this, and I will give you another Angel. If I can't do it, we will ask Samira do it with us. She is an Angel. And by the way, she wasn't on birth control, when you seeded her."

She sat back down between his legs, and laid her head back against his shoulder, as he leaned over to hug her. His hands cupped her large, round, breasts, and she giggled as she exhaled her emotional exhaustion. Taking another long breath, she let the rest of her anxieties escape, and felt some strength in their conversation. She bumped her head back to hit his and, smiled warmly as her finger, touched her own wetness below, in secret.

"Thank you for tellin' me everythang' I didn't want to hear, and...thank you for forcin' that damn open communication we push to have. I'm sorry I shot you, Noah. I know I can't say that enough, and...thank you for lovin' me and staying with us after."

She kissed him on the cheek, and told him. "I want more tattoos, Noah, and like the last time, I need...want you to make me get some more tattoos." As if he didn't remember, she reminded him. "God forbids me unless you order me to do it. I want more. I be wantin' barb wire around my waist, and on my big ass and under my saggin' milkers. One big long barbed wire that wraps around my ass, up to my scars, and down to the most precious thang you own, Kitty. I be wantin' it on my huge, fat, bruised mound." Her tone got serious now, "I be needin' your name on her. I want to feel owned, and show people I am owned. I can't see Noah's Ark on my ass but, I love knowin' it is there and owned. I want people to know that be your ass. I want somethang I can see to make me feel owned. I want your name on my pussy, and I want my name on your pretty cock. I just need you to make me do it, Dominion. It would make me feel good, Noey."

She sounded like Julian, acted like Julian, but her aura was not as fluctuated. It was the best he could read. "Julian Michelle, thy MILF, when I take you to get tattoos. I demand that you obey me, and get all the tattoos you so desire because I demand it of you." Her wish of being owned was granted, and she smiled.

"Husband, creator of my wetness, father of our future babies, I own you. I be commandin' you to get my name tattooed on your body above your very pretty cock, that I love to worship...and maybe a little one on your ass for me." She smiled at him and he smiled back nodding. "'Property of Julian' right above your cock."

They could always work things out. The tension was saying goodbye for the moment now that the unspoken had finally filled the room. "And I want nice piercings on our bag down there too. I will pick pretty, girly ones for you. I be wantin' the belly button piercin's for you bag."

Noah got up, bringing her with him by her hair, and on her knees, he walked her by her leash, until she faced the side of the bed, and she sat down on her ankles. Keeping her hair wrapped around her hand, he got down on his knees behind her, and snuggled over her body, like they do when she prays. His head slid down next to hers, and his hard cock slid between her labia as it sagged to the floor between her ankles.

Feeling her arousal building, she reached down, and pushed his erection up into her mound, and he slid it in, and rested the large head of his well-groomed cock, into the pocket he had created between her mound and pelvic bone. The wetness just flowed for the secret meeting.

He had an idea, "How about I get a tattoo on my ass that says, 'I CRASHED HER' and one on your ass that says, "I CRASHED HIM." She smiled and put a twist of rope in her mouth as his warm cock pushed against her centerfold. He wasn't thrusting, but she was hopeful. He gazed at her from the side, knowing she was the most wonderfully complicated, and beautiful Angel, in the world.

He kissed her on the neck, under her left ear, as she tried to grind on his manhood, and his right hand bumped into her face on the other side as he gathered her hair, and pulled it tight behind her.

In her pretend childlike voice, "Baby, I'm scared about Crashin'. Will you love me if I am another IDentifY, permanently?"

He shushed her as he kissed behind her ear, and down her neck. His warm breath followed his gently kisses. "Always Angel. Zachary is asleep and Ally is outside playing with Tammy's kids." He loved her 'Damsel in distress' voice, and she knew it.

"That Dance video is the cause of my local stress, Daddy. I be thankin' Julian started recording it, and Emily took over somewhere. Tramp doesn't care about me, Daddy." She exhaled really big to tell him what she was honestly confused about, and used her normal raspy whisper.

"I thank Emily put it on the internet on purpose-OR RACHAEL! I am not trying to avoid-" She jerked her head up with a huge piece of the puzzle, solved.

"NOAH! EMILY! EMILY SENT IT TO RACHAEL AND RACHAEL SENT it to everyone! HOLY FUCK!" She said aloud as he tried to get her to put out.

"Is you be hearin' me, Noah James Taylor."

He nibbled on her ear, and her eyes slowly closed to his touch. She inhaled, his Stetson cologne and his pheromones. Unable to shut up, she started talking technical data again.

"Fragmentin', my Alibis means IDentifY can switch and or blend on me, without a mirror. Emily…" and she whispered, "…maybe Arizona shared it. I'm sure it is viral on social media by now. DAMN PHONES! I'm blamin' them. Not myself." She said playfully, realizing she may have hit the wrong buttons for 'Live,' when she recorded it. "Ally wants a phone. All her friends have one, Daddy."

His hands came up and rubbed her shoulders as he lifted her hair so he could lick the back of her neck. "Nope." Daddy put his foot down.

"But she be yer' Princess, Daddy." Momma purred to him sarcastically wanting her spoiled treatment spread to her little Angel. He squeezed her neck, and thrusted his cock under her mound. She licked her lips and concentrated on the burn rushing her loins. He hoped this would get her mood going.

"200,000 likes Daddy, and from every platform online. Everyone knows I'm a slutty Bad Girl, now. I deleted it. But like you said, it was shared and shared and shared, and will never go away. I don't know what else to do."

He signed on the back of her neck, and answered. "Honey, you are a Slut, and a Girl, and sometimes Bad, be thankful you ain't a Bad Slutty, Girl." He shook her as she tried to work her hips to shake his favorite ass at him, but she was sitting on it.

"Stoooooop it, Bad, Slutty Girl." He said teasing.

Still with her little girl voice she pleaded her guilt. "But Daddy, I'm a Slutty, Bad Girl."

"I will fuck you hard." He told her in her ear.

"I hope so." She countered. He thrusted into her mound stretching it, and her mouth fell open as her eyes closed. More burn.

"Yes." She whispered to the sensations.

Making sure he didn't alter his tone, he asked permission, "Can I beat you really bad tonight? I miss your Black eyes." He whispered as her head slowly fell back onto his shoulder.

"Yes, Baby. Beat me." She moaned as he worked his dick against her clit, and fucked her under her fat, Venus mound.

He kept his voice soft and seductive, "Do you think you have Battered Woman Syndrome?"

She reached down to her breast, and took his hand, and put it on the front of her neck, and squeezed his hand.

"Batter me, Daddy. Please batter me." She kept her head back on his shoulder, with her eyes closed, as his dick throbbed between her wet, warm labia, and under her mound. He did not squeeze her neck but, she squeezed her neck with his hand.

"You gag me with your cock, Daddy, so why not choke me? He squeezed a little as he watched her face light up with fear, and his dick got much wetter. The fire was lit in both of them, and the pieces of the puzzle fit well together, down below.

"Choke me...Pussy. See if I-" Noah's grip scared her as his palm pushed her windpipe in a little, and his fingers buried into the side of her neck. She dropped her hands down and worked them around her back. She found her hair, as he pulled his front back to give her room, and she wrapped her hair around her wrist and laid her hands flat on her back. Noah leaned back in and pinned them. As he did it, she moaned from the instant stimulation. She could not move, and his hand grew tighter, and his dick grew harder.

She tried to whisper, and he listened to her. "Fuck me, Daddy. Fuck me." He squeezed her neck harder.

As her air forced its way out of her spitting lips, he slowly fucked her. She fought her natural reactions to accept it, and leaned into him for a better grip on her. He inhaled her Dolce & Gabbana Light Blue perfume. Her mind focused on the pressure inside her head as the blood flow slowed, and he could see her face turning pink, and he fucked her wet, dangling pussy, like a rental.

She started bursting air and grunts, out of her closed mouth again, this time, repeatedly, and she let him, teach her, to be a Submissive, Slutty, Bad Girl. He held her until her face was as red as her eyes used to be, and she did not tap out.

Her sounds were awful, and her eyelids flickered up and down as her face muscled twitched. Her chest shook, and her arms jerked as she fought to keep them pinned, and the seconds clicked, and his dick got its money's worth. She was going to orgasm.

When the digital clock changed, he slowly disengaged, and she gasped viciously, and he started fucking her harder. She didn't try to get away, and just laid her upper chest to the bed, and let him have his fuck. When she got enough oxygen, she pushed him away, and rolled onto her side, holding her painful mound. Noah watched her, to make sure she was okay, and she pointed to the floor where she was.

He looked down and sure enough, she had leaked a spot nearly twelve inches across the carpet. He looked up at her, and she was wiping it off her ankles and pussy, and rubbing it on her nipples with a very daring look on her face. "I didn't pee like I worried...that is happy Kitty juice." She was happy with the results, but he wasn't.

He did it so easily, and she let him do it, and he liked it, and she liked it, and all that scared him. Her large labia left wet trails on the carpet as she dragged herself away to view it. She was right, he really was a pussy.

Rubbing her neck, she stood over the wet-trails smiling at them, and him. In her excited whisper she told him. "I liked that more than I thought I would, Noey. I wish we could have sex,

Noey...I'm sorry she can't take you yet. But, you can really put the fear in me sometimes." She pointed to the seed she covered the floor with.

"Now I be knowin' why you own me for real. I shot you once, and you could kill me now, and probably get away with it. Oh my Gosh, I am so turned on. Did you like it?" She hacked and coughed a few times, as she waited for his answer. She was panting a little from the arousal effect, and wiped her soaking wet vagina, and rubbed it on his face from the arousal burn, not getting abused.

He jerked away, and wasn't smiling at her with his glare. She looked at him confused.

Quickly, and shortly shaking her head, "What?" she asked with her palms up.

"What? I liked it. Don't be upset, Noey." She rushed to hug him, and almost dazed, he slowly put his arms around her. Men do take a little longer to analyze the feelings they try to hide from. Woman Rule.

Chapter Twenty-One

-Bonding Comes with Flavor, Not Inhibitions

He sat back on the bed, still analyzing the magnitude of what he had done, and how he felt about it. Julian on the other hand, climbed up on him and put him on his back to sort out his emotions, now.

With a giggle and a kiss, and a slip of his erection back into her sore mound, "I can't get pregnant, so maybe I deserve to be battered." She said with a small laugh afterwards.

"I like us to be battered, Noey, BUT I'm not a Battered Woman, Noey. You know that. I control the flow of punishments, Noah-by the word of the Bible. If I say stop, you stop. If I want more, you give me more. THAT my Angel, is the difference between bein' battered and bein' a Battered Woman."

He came out of his little tis, and kissed her as he reached down, and got some wetness on his finger, and sucked it. "Did it get rid of your headaches?"

"NOPE!" She said being silly. "I can't stop my headaches. I have jitters sometimes, and bein' scared I got a disease in the hospital. 'Like...like...like...like a heroin addict havin' withdrawals." She chuckled and shook her boobs to hit his big pectoral muscles.

Her tone got a little more serious as she filled him in. "Doctor Pratt said the MRI doesn't show any issues, and he could find no reason for my headache, and suggested PTSD from the accident.

My BP was up just a little but, normal." Her tone switched to sad for the next talk.

"I'm going to lose my job, from Rachael's reports. I'm a Doctor, and I can't figure it out. Maybe, I could find another male Angel to give me seed?" She just happened to throw that long awaited thought in there, and avoided looking at him, and hurried to fill the air with words.

"I find thangs moved around, and sometimes don't remember why I did somethang. That scares me and makes me sad."

Noah growled at her remark. It is not like he hasn't heard it before from her in her pregnancy challenges. "Maybe you need to get fucked in Texas, instead of Ohio. Tramp." He was brave enough to say it, only he made it sound like he was joking. He reached over to get the other chalice off the nightstand, and she climbed off of him to get it.

Being cautious she climbed back on him, and this time, he slid his cock back into her mound pussy. "Thank you, Baby. My pussy still hurts inside, and we have to wait a little longer to make me a Momma."

Slowly, she took a sip and another sip, and looked down at it, and her eyes closed, and opened directly at him. "I taste semen..your semen..." She sipped again and worked it around her tongue, "...thin like mine...Is it Samira, too?" Noah smiled really big at her, and she thrusted him a few times with a smile.

"That is wonderful. Thank you Noey, my Angel. I shall sit here on the...thangy of my man and sip the wine of those I love." She took another sip and relished it with smiles. "That is wonderful tastin'. Kitty is burrrrrrnin'. I love datin' Samira. She is so fun to shop with."

She turned seductive with her crave, "Noeyyyy, if I put this in my mouth, will you share it in a kiss. All of it." She put the begging eyes on her man, and blinked fast about five times with her smile.

"NO! Stop asking me that Julz. I can't. Isn't there some rule in the Bible that I can't do that? Please tell me there is a rule." She smiled at him with love, and sipped again shaking her head.

"Come on." He said, disappointed.

"Daddy, I will let you punish me...in public." She warmly offered increasing the flow from the burn beneath her. "Batter me...in public. Pull my hair...in public. Call me your Slut...in public...in front of other Woman."

He was already shaking his head. "Drink it and let's talk about things, Baby" he said, ruining her chances. "I need you to promise me you are keeping up on your Diddy medication."

"I am. At least have a sip and try it, Noey. Please? For me? I won't tell anyone. Just us." Noah shook his head. This was one time he was glad his ruling always overtook hers. Slowly, she poured it onto his chest, and fingered every drop out of the chalice and licked it, keeping it in her mouth.

Keeping their eyes locked on his, she leaned down and licked it off his muscular, tan chest, and savored it to him. Working it into a pile with her tongue, she made sure he watched as she sucked the thick, white semen up over her lips. He was kind, and started fucking her mound to keep her down there, and she made her move.

Noah tossed her into the air and rolled away as she landed on the other side of the bed, holding her hand over her mouth laughing. She had to swallow to stop from spitting it out and collapsed onto the bed with her big butt in the air.

Noah had dashed for the door and escaped. He could hear her deep laugh, and peaked back in the room.

Julian was laying on her side now, holding her stomach, and laughing so hard, she was crying. She curled into the fetal position, and kept on laughing.

"You big PUSSY COWBOY! Afraid of a little seed, Noey? COWBOY IN MY HANDSOME SEXY PINK PANTIES-COWBOY PANTIES! YOU BE A PUSSY IN PANTIES!" She busted up again holding her stomach in a fetal position, and trying to hide her face from being judged. Her body was shaking, and kicking as her funny bone tickled itself over and over. Noah crept back to the bed smiling. The insults would not put any man's seed into his mouth, not even his own, mixed with his new Black Woman.

He slapped her on the ass, and another wave of laughter came out of her.

"Kiss my big Texas ass PUSSY IN PANTIES! You love it so much." He slapped her again, leaving his red signatures, and the sting corrupted her laughter with more laughter. He slapped her on the Noah's Ark cheek, and she came rushing over on him putting him on his back. She was not laughing now.

She landed right on him licking his lips, and forcing her way into his mouth, and when his Girly scream escaped, she could only cave to her laughter again, as she tried to call him a 'Pussy in Panties'. It was just too hard to speak.

She came back into his face, licking and spitting, as he jerked away girly-screaming his panic, and she dropped her weight on him to trap the 'Pussy in Panties'. He jerked his face back and

250

forth as she spread it laughing. Both sets of hands were locked, and fighting each other as she was losing, and she began spitting on his face to win. His pleas were louder than her conjugal screams, and he tried to get away again, and she chased his face with her tongue laughing hysterically at him.

Finally, he kissed her, and she spit into his mouth everything she had left, which was mostly her saliva. She had soaked his belly with her seed below, and he rolled her over, and slid between her legs, and held her, as they melted each other hearts, and he put the saliva back into her mouth. Slowly, they pulled one another into her arms, as their chest pressed together.

She immediately soaked her fingers, and spread it all over his face and hers. Again, with her seed, she forced her fingers into their mouths, as they passionately gave one other their devotion, and love.

She finally cursed him, face to face, "You cheated Noah James. I only had saliva left and a little bit of seed. I want to kiss you when it is still hot and steamin' in my mouth. That doesn't count 'Pussy in Panties'. I want your cum in our mouths from now on, accept when I am ovulatin'."

He sat up laughing that he got away with it. He didn't taste anything he wasn't used to tasting from his woman's mouth.

"I really liked tastin' her seed with yours, Noey. Can I go down on her after you seed her? Both would be warm and rich, and ohhhh so lovely. Oh please, Noey? You have to be lettin' me go down on her after you seed her." Noah nodded to her still laughing a bit, and as he rolled off of her, she punched his dick for getting away with it.

251

He rolled over faking his level of pain, and she pounced on him, bouncing up and down with him between her legs, like breaking a horse, and yelling,

"I LOVE YOU NOAH JAMES! GIVE ME TEN MORE BABIES OR I WILL SHOOT YOU AGAIN!" Despite protecting his rising cock for dear life, and a five foot tall, one hundred and seventy-five pounds of Texas sexiness on him pouncing her dripping vagina all over him, he just kept laughing as she kicked his ass with her love.

She pulled her hair around, and began whipping him across the face with it, and yelling the best she could.

"I WILL HAVE YOUR NEPHILIM BABIES NOAH IF IT KILLS ME BOY! I WILL BE PREGNANT EVERY DAY FOR THE NEXT TEN YEARS ANGEL BOY! NOW GET ME AN EXERCISE TOY FOR FAT KITTY! THAT SEED HAS GOT ME RIDING WILD, NOEY JAMES!" She busted out laughing and collapsed onto him. Holding on to his dick, together they slid off the side of the bed laughing, and held each other for the fall. Her hair watched from the bed, as she started wrestling to get back on top of him.

Using his girly-scream, Julian mocked him and tried not to laugh when she did it, "YER' BATTERIN' ME! STOP BATTERIN' ME NOAH JAMES! HELP! NOAH IS BATTERIN ME!"

Laughing from embarrassment, happiness, love, and her extreme Texas sexiness smothering him, he really was her 'Pussy in Panties', and enjoyed it.

Both their heads jerked up above the bed, when they heard Zachary cry. He was awake now, and their playtime was over.

Chapter 22

-Weight Loss Ain't a Tragedy, Big Fish

When Julian and Karen pulled in behind Ellie and Bodi, they could see their faces were stuck together. Julian got a little angry, and Karen reminded her it was their night off, and agreed to come over until they got there.

"Okay, tell them to go ahead and go." Karen got out on the passenger side while Julian kept standing the car, so she could move up when they left. She climbed up, and out the window to yell at her friend as she got to their door,

"Tell them to be gettin' a room." Julian ordered.

Karen stepped back from the car and let them pull away. When they did, Julian pulled up and put it in park. As she climbed back in, Julian was getting a fix on Derence's location with the binoculars. Derence was nowhere to be found.

"Call Bodi. Use my phone please, and inquire as to whom the UC is tonight. I don't see Derence."

Looking closer, Julian finally saw him. "OH I see...he is wavin'...That is not Derence, Karen. That is Rachael Briggs. OH MY GOSH!" Julian said, feeling her anxieties bouncing around her head. "What is she doin' here? I have a meetin' with her in just a few days about the Matrix Formula. I can't believe this." She looked over at Karen angry but, calm. "She got re-assigned as a UC for online Sex Traffickin', why is she here on my case again?"

Karen began chuckling, and Julian waited her out. To her, this was not funny. "You know Julian, I

253

never knew how short you were, until I saw you driving. You can barely see over the steering wheel. How do you drive those big trucks you, and Noah have? How tall are you now?"

"I'm five feet and one eighth of an inch tall, and I only wear three inch boots" she said with immense Texas pride, glancing back at Rachael, and growling under her breath.

"So you have grown a heavy accent, cut your hair off the ground, since we worked together, and a second child, and married to one former Cross-Dressing UC?" Karen smiled being facetious.

"Well, I round up, and EMT's cut my hair, and Zachary was born." She put the binoculars back to her face but, it didn't hide her frustration with Rachael.

"No Julian, when you round up, it is to the next number, not the next few numbers."

"Shut up, okay. So I'm short, at least I have huge boo...BALANCE to go with my huge rear. Besides, how tall are you?"

"My last measurement was five feet nine inches. Thankfully, because my Marine is about six foot two inches."

"Without your three-inch heels on, Karen?" That is barefoot, Jordan-Julian. "Why did you ask me to start calling you Julian, instead of Jordan?" Julian stopped judging Rachael for a brief moment, and looked at her.

"It is my first name, and Jordan is my middle name. I am just tryin' to be more...well you are my friend, and my co-worker." Julian went back to the binoculars talking.

"Rachael is a gay woman, dressed as a gay man, tryin' to look like a gay male prostitute. I don't know how she got this assign-JEFF!" She looked over at Karen to explain clearly. "She is sleepin' with Jeff and his wife, I do know. But, well, she passes as a man easily."

"Can I ask you something Julian? And if you don't want to tell me that is fine but...how much does Noah weigh?" Julian dropped the binoculars slowly, and looked at her.

"Where are you goin' with this Karen?" Julian was not offended, just caught off guard.

"How much does Noah weigh? It is a simple-"

"About two hundred-fifty pounds, maaaaybe two-fifty. Why?" she demanded.

"How tall is he?" Julian looked over at Rachael across the street, and back to Karen. By the look on her face, she was very suspicious.

"Six feet four inches tall. Why?" she demanded again.

When Karen started to speak Julian immediately cut her off. "Don't you dare compare my weight to his height, please?"

Karen tried to be delicate. "So does your weight bother you, AND YOU ARE NOT FAT AT ALL! But, is there a reason you're looking to lose some pounds? Is your back starting to hurt from your...?" Karen gestured her hands out in front of her chest to symbolize voluptuousness. Julian glanced up to her pretentiously, but she didn't say anything...yet.

"I'm asking because I saw your diet plan book in your desk, and well, I have the same one. I peeked at it...you know...to compare meals. Does Noah know how much you weigh?" She asked with a very friendly tone, and realized what she asked. "NO! NO! I mean how little you weigh?" Julian looked at her, and didn't appreciate the topic. "I'm asking because...well Patrick gives me a hard time about my weight. I hate it. He guilt's me about having this little birthing tummy that I can't shake, but it shakes." Julian turned back to her with her mouth open, and her eyes even wider.

"Gosh no Karen, Noah thanks I weigh seventy-five pounds or somethang. My chest weighs that much! My butt weighs even more. He is strong enough that he doesn't notice I guess...HE better not notice, or he will be wearing an eye-patch for life, only to see half my size. He better never thank I'm fat, or he will lose the best thang ever...ME!" Julian got a little more into the topic, and asked, "Why all of the sudden do you be needin' to know my weight? How much do you weigh, Karen?"

"One hundred and eighty-five." She quickly announced, and steadfast with silence. Julian looked at her then up and down her body, and Karen waited her out.

"Same as me. Really." Julian smiled feeling a little more at ease with the topic. "Just ten pounds of give or take or more likely give." Julian took to her phone to check her messages, and decided to send one with a smile.

Texting Samira, she purposely sent it to Noah and not Samira: 'You are right. Noah loves thick women. I will help you learn to dominate him in time. You can sexually punish him and gain power over his SUPER SEED BIG COCK I WORSHIP! Seeing him get emasculated by a Black woman will make me so wet for you. He wants to be humiliated by my beautiful Black Woman with her beautiful White Woman watching. I can't wait to taste you again Beautiful. Touch it for me. Send me dirty pictures. Love and Kisses, your Submissive Pale Tomboy. Did Noah do his Girly-scream for you yet?'

256

Smiling her crooked smile, she realized Karen had been talking while she text, and missed it. She just blurted what general comment she could muster.

"...Yeah, we sure are different sizes. I'm a sixteen. And that reminds me, tell Jack Teasle, the Coroner, he ain't weighing me after I die." Julian was actually being honest, but it sounded funny. She went back to admiring her former lover cross-dressed and a woman, who wished she was a man, and taking medication to become a man, even though she was assigned Woman at birth. She hoped she would not leak through her blue yoga pants. She was mad at her but, they had a very long sexual history that included many satisfying moments and satisfying secrets.

"Noah works out, and jogs occasionally. God did not intend for me to jog, so he jogs for me." Being professional, she looked down at her chest, instead of saying it. "It's good to own a man you can make do those important thangs for ya." Julian laughed as she finished, and Karen joined her in the humor that carried a validity of truth.

"I work out but, I can't get rid of the baby fat belly." Karen was sneaking peaks at Julian's thickness and appreciating, herself a little more for being gifted with her height. "Was Noah in the service, at all?"

Julian sat back in her seat and dug out a can of Copenhagen from her rear pocket and packed it. "Noah wasn't in the service. I wish he had been in the Marine Corps. Marines look so good in their uniforms. The Dress Blue uniforms. I can admire that all day long."

Karen watched her in shock as Julian pinched a hit from her tobacco chew snuff, and stuffed it back in her tight pants. Julian dusted off her hands, and her clothes and noticed Karen's repugnant stare.

"What? I'm gonna' quit. Don't judge me, please?" Chuckling, Karen burst into laughing at her, and tossed her files up on the dashboard.

"Are you kidding me, Jordan-Julian? You chew snuff? I have seen it all now my friend. A Princess that chews tobacco." Karen burst into laughter again and Julian almost laughed. She was judged. "You really are Texas born and bred."

Julian reached for her empty soda bottle, and spit in it very quietly, and Karen cracked up even more. Julian smiled but, was not enjoying being laughed at, and feeling a bit condescended.

"Julian, I have to say it, you are the most vulgar Woman I have ever met. You are repulsive in your ways, yet so Southern Charmed refined, and Country. Your tobacco chew just proves it. Only a Hick from the Sticks, would chew snuff. You are disgusting to me."   Julian stopped smiling as Karen's judgement crashed into her, and Karen began laughing like the enemy and bounced back and forth in the seat, pointing at Julian's shocked expression. Karen cracked-up again, and called her a 'Brown spitting Hick-Chick.'

Struggling with her hurt feelings, Julian looked around for anyone to rescue her, and as she started to get Hick with her Night Stick, and Karen was holding up her own can of Copenhagen.

"YOU CHEW TOO?" Julian screamed at her in relief. "OH THANK GOSH! OH MY LORD! I thought our friendship was over." Julian said, as her blood cooled. Karen was nodding and bouncing back into the seat laughing, and Julian got tears of joy in her eyes, as she burst out laughing with her. Together, they had the car rocking back and forth as the worked up irony, flourished, and the laughter became repeatedly contagion.

The Women kept showing each other their can, in a flashy, quick presentation to mock Karen's presentation, and sparking the laughing fits over and over again. Julian finally spoke up trying to stop because of a cramping ribs the laughter was giving her. Her laughing muscles had a big workout with Noah, just days before.

"Noah was born with a chew in his mouth, and a roll of Copenhagen, and I started when I was a teenager. I don't chew all the time. Mostly in spring and summer. I used to try to sniff Daddy's snuff powder, and one day he gave me a can of Skoal, and showed me how to chew in my lip. I guess he got tired of rushin' me to the kitchen sink screamin', and me cryin' from snortin' the powder snuff. It was not pretty. He had to spray my eyes and nostrils to stop the burn, and it didn't work that well. Don't be knowin' how Momma does it?" She was laughing again as she packed it.

Text to Noah from Anonymous number: Look at all these rape pictures your wife sent me yesterday Danny, to help prosecute you. I know about the murders in Florida. Emily predated a Rape kit and got the evidence from you after sex. Her plan is to put you in jail soon for rape. Arrest is pending, boy. I warned you in the hospital when you were raping me. GET OUT OF HER LIFE NOW! Guess who your wife is spending the evening in the arms of right now. She missed me.

Noah slumped down on the couch, holding Zachary, and exhaled to minimize his stress, and looked over at Ally playing a video game with him. He tossed the phone to the other end of the couch, and sighed. He loved the children, and his life.

"Noah James, brangin' der' Angels to wash. Chow time. Takes'em to wash der' hands." Momma yelled from the kitchen. "Momma made your favorite lasagna with buffalo."

"Come on Kiddos. Let's go wash up for supper. Momma made the good stuff." He clicked pause on his gaming console, and Ally gave him a dirty look, just like Julian.

Karen joined in packing her can of chew, and was barely able to hold it, and flip it, to pack and smack the lid with her finger like Julian. It was a learned art that took years, and practice.

"Patrick has chewed for twenty five years, and when I gave up smoking, I started doing it with him occasionally, and now, I only really do it out of the office. Especially, on a surveillance."

Karen put a dip in her lip, and Julian watched, validating their Sisterhood. She really liked Karen, and one reason was, she didn't poke and nag for entertainment. Julian offered her the empty water bottle, and Karen pulled one out of her leather bag. Julian watched as she haggardly struggling, spit in it her bottle gracefully, and spoke.

"My sincerest compliments to the new you Julian. Your accent, your smile, even a fresh glow about you. I love your perfume by the way." Karen said, enjoying a hint of the fragrance. I just can't recall seeing you so down to earth.

"Well thank you for noticin'. I guess sheddin' a hundred pounds can do that to a Cowgirl, and make her feel better? It's called Cowgirl Dream's. Amazon.com"

260

Karen's eyes lit up as she looked Julian's figure up and down with shock, "YOU LOST A HUNDRED POUNDS? I don't remember you bein' fat?"

With crickets chirping around the parking lot, Julian's finger slowly raised up to point to Rachael, as she looked at Karen.

"OHhhhhh! Thaaaaat hundred pounds. I get it." Karen said it smiling, and agreeing with the weight loss.

"Julian, do you want to tell me what happened between you and Rachael. If not, I completely understand. We have plenty of case material to review. I am offering my services, as a Counselor." Karen reached for her spit bottle, and worked it a little better. Julian watched and chuckled, as she tried to spit out the window, and it didn't pass the outside of the car door, before rolling down the outside of the door. She was just too short.

"Well Karen, confidential agreement?" She asked, as she rubbed the headache she had had, for closer to two weeks.

"Always." Karen invoked it.

"Is Rachael under your umbrella in any way, Counselor?"

"She is not, Counselor." Karen said it, reaching for the spit bottle, again.

"I know you know, Rachael and I were...involved. But, when I tried to end thangs, she got ugly about it. Started playin' games, makin' threats. It has been ugly. Much uglier than I expected. I am tryin' to work with my husband so we can provide a wonderful home for our children and maybe...God willin', give me a hundred more Babies. I want to get back to basics, and Honor my

Religion." Julian gave a painful grin hoping it satisfied her curiosities.

"Everyone knew about your involvement with Rachael, and it effected your career in Pittsburgh, and I respect that you relocated. Rachael told everyone you two were secretly married, and that Noah dragged you to Ohio to get you away from her. Everyone that he was abusive, thanks to her stories. The day you left Pittsburgh, she filed for a transfer. Did you try and split with her back then?"

Julian nodded. "I was tryin' to let go of the burden our relationship was becomin' on me."

Julian's Counselor went on, "I think time will heal the wounds, and I would not recommend you work with Rachael again. And to be serious about it, do not depend on friends to stop her from following you via re-assignment, instead, file a restraining order toward-" Karen gestured toward Rachael across the street. "You would be best to get reassigned...Texas or Oklahoma has field openings for Behavioral Profilers."

Nodding, Julian spoke up, "I didn't know she would be here. I was told she would be removed from the case, but clearly, since she is sexually involved with Jeff and his wife, she has some pull. Noah and I are plannin' to return to Texas with my family." Julian spit into the bottle, and rested it between her legs.

"I think it sounds wonderful. Pat and I are already planning our retirement, and we are going to travel." Karen smiled at her. *It was nice not to be poked over and over,* Julian thought.

"You have done well in the Bureau, Karen. I hope your plans include Hawaii. I would love to go to Hawaii...but Texas is the best."

262

"Most certainly we are. We have been there six times now...since the kids are all grown up, we enjoy our month of vacation on the beaches in Waikiki. Nothing like the view of muscular brown men surfing." They both nodded in appreciation.

Julian turned the conversation to productivity with goals. "I want you us to come up with substance to finish the Matrix. Somethang! 'Because when Jeff and the Mayor comes knockin', I want SANICS to have somethang to put up a fight with...it may just be our last chance. We keep gettin' threats to pull fundin' by the Mayor. Don't sweat it if he does. Plan B lives."

Julian pulled some of the files from her leather bag on the floor, and handed them over to Karen to open. "This is the profile process model that identifies characteristics of behavior and personality of the individual...uh...from it, you know...we determined the general idea of the sex, traits, habits, lifestyle, social atmosphere, and mating habits and disorders of the Killer to find circumstantial evidence and predictive behaviors. It is the profile that identifies the type of individual for our Officers and UC over there..." She pulled out another file, and put it on the dashboard,"...to look for and question, as well as used to predict the Killer's intent." Sitting the bag on the floor between them, she picked up the binoculars and checked on Rachael.

Text Alert to Julian and Noah from Samira: A nude selfie, taken from above and from the side, keeping her face out of it, Samira made sure to include the curves of her front and rear, and covered her breasts with her arm.

Text to Julian and Noah from Samira: I'm off Thur Fri, Sun this week. ☺♥☻♥☺

"Jeff complained to me today about SANICS techniques, after nearly drooling on my heels." Julian rolled her eyes when she heard her.

"I don't recall seeing this listed under the list of capabilities for SANICS in Jeff's investigative report to the Mayor, Julian. In fact, Jeff reported to the Mayor's now FULL-TIME Snitch, your detail investigation merely showing SANICS as capable of asking questions, and not providing behavior patterns of Investigative Value, Julian." Julian looked at her, deciding.

"Karen, Clearance Code?

"Alpha Gulf Inchon Fife Two Bravo Niner Echo." Karen responded.

Speaking frankly and at a smooth pace, Julian warmed up to her. "We expect Jeff is goin' to recommend a thorough investigation of the case to tip off leads, before lettin' us truly investigate. I expect he will say it is a way to determine the effectiveness of SANICS. 'Prior to makin' decisions that generate a re-organization of his officers and staff." It is the same in every corrupted Government Locality." She was reassuring her that Plan B was in place, already, and with previous successes.

She went on to explain it, "So recognize that RICO Investigations have Plan B's." Karen looked at her, almost alarmingly before she spoke.

"RICO Statutes. So it is larger than Locality?" Julian nodded at her, tightening her lips. "Racketeer Influenced and Corrupt Organizations." Sounding excited, Karen said, "Thank you for inviting me onto the investigation. This just got so much bigger. Thank you." Karen reached over and tapped Julian on the hand, and offered an un-conditioned high-five.

"You are a good friend. We can do this. We thank Jeff is holdin' information back on the Stiff'em Killer, to look good without us, and help the Mayor shut us down. We will be shut down when he gets nervous. It's expected. Stiff'em is part of Human Traffickin' and Sex Trafficin'."

"NSA with the FBI has tracked the launderin' of election funds to different accounts. We thank Mayor's Fish Jr., is alive and well here in Columbus, and bein' financially supported-likely with the help of Big Fish, and Jeff, as his right hand man. We are still waitin' on Court hearin's to clear so we can subpoena direct information to the layers of false information on the accounts. A simple ATM photo of a 'fictitious person' using the card ID Number will give us a positive ID. Waitin' for the paperwork to clear...you know how that rolls." Karen's mouth watered as she finished listening and processed the hunt. She looked at Julian, holding back her excitement, but not enough, and nodded with a smile.

"You are the Profile Process Model Officer, Karen. You are helpin us catch the Raping Killer, and research and read him or her. Let's just hope we are not wrong on the lead on the Mayor's deceased son, Carlo-Fish Jr." Julian added.

"But the report says it is likely, a woman rapist." Karen inquired holding some files up to support her findings.

Julian lurched the words at her to get them to her faster, "That is classified!" And she waited for Karen to acknowledge it." After they shared a nod, Julian continued to explain what others should not know, "Let's keep it that way for now. There is a connection somewhere between Carlo and the Female Rapist Killer." Julian added. "This is why I am stalling the Matrix Formula from Jeff. I kept sabotagin' Data in it because Rachael started sleepin' with him."

Karen took a deep breath and started speaking from her review of the report as it stood. "Our Raping Killer grew up to become a paranoid Woman of medium organizational skills with high areas of common sense. Her rape probably carried on throughout her childhood and into her teens. Therefore she started as a victim of it all, and forced into promiscuity by her fears, and nightmares, and a parental figure, and maybe her multiple lovers. Uh...uh...she lives with symptoms of anxiety, unipolar depression, ADHD, PTSD, suicidal tendencies non-necrophilliac even though she was the victim of one..." At the same time they both said the same name, 'Carlo.' "...Killer is an exhibitionists sexually, but not fetish tempted..." Julian nodded as she read it, glancing at Rachael, and watching to read Karen's intuitions.

Karen broke it down into simpler words to make sure word innuendos against definitions, were not shuttered. "She was likely just a little girl when someone did this to her." Karen looked up at Julian. "Sex trafficking slave who grew up?" Julian nodded that she had the same thoughts, and twisted a rope of her hair to put in her lips. Karen went on, "She is Arrested Developmentally, and driven by her need for escape, mentally-but, not physically. All stemming from her repeated childhood trauma that may have stalled her into adulthood."

This time, Julian opened the door to spit. Karen followed her lead and spit out her own door.

"She has frotteurism but, non-transvestive but, cross gendered with dominance by disassociation...which means she had no one to love her, and care for her during this or after it all, and lived in a substantially balanced forum with an owner, which means, it was happening, and she never told a soul."

Karen fell silent, Julian was watching Rachael across the street through her binoculars, and holding her hair in her lips. "...Probably to this day, She-our Raping Killer, has never spoken of it and doesn't know it is wrong. She was probably taken from her home early, like a runaway child with fear, and forced into sexual slavery." Karen had added her own simple explanations, as she took ownership of her assessments.

Not looking at her file, she spoke in the night, as Julian took it all in. Though her eyes were on Rachael, her mind was listening closely. "By addiction, this Killer was...is drawn into sadism and masochism, even burning herself, and her victims without really knowing that pain is not associated with desire for what it is she is looking for, Mental Escape. She was forced to have pain by a man...most likely for his pleasure, and now she is confused by it, only needing it again and again. Confused in the sense that she gets adrenaline rushes...endorphins by pain or pleasure...sense of duty or security...only she can no longer tell the difference of why she gets them or needs them as she became addicted to the punishment and pain. They are necessary for normalcy, to her-the poor Girl." Karen nodded in agreement, as she spoke, and occasionally followed the markers in her file, and nodded in agreement.

"She has horrible personality disorders like schizoid and schizotypal, and...I added something Jord-Julian, dyspareunia-the sex pain disorder and not natural, it has been inflicted on her, and probably now likely practiced and dependent on it."

Julian spoke up, "Oh. I agree. I didn't generate that one. Good, and the poor child never met the opportunity of life. Her development arrested at a young age. Preteen likely or ten to fourteen, without social markers for that age." Karen took a deep breath nodding, and Julian glanced at her to read her answer.

Chapter Twenty-Three

-Tears and Fears and Closet Doors

Samira typed in her key code, and entered Julian and Noah's house, and heard a lot of nothing. Julian's big pickup truck was in the driveway, so Samira walked in smiling, and carried her bag of groceries to the kitchen, and unpacked a few things while sucking on her hair. Rachael however, didn't use her key code, and quietly slid the glass door shut in the basement.

Rachael stopped when she saw Julian's saddle, and rolled her eyes. She imitated putting her finger in her throat to vomit, and crept through the basement, and looking over every boot box...dozens of Julian's Cowgirl Boot boxes.

From the kitchen, Samira yelled out to her Girlfriend, "JULIAN? JULIAN COWGIRL? WHERE IS MY MANLY GIRLFRIEND, JULIAN?" After putting the wine for her and Julian, beer for Noah, and Julian ONLY bakery brownies away, she grabbed the can of Copenhagen she bought for her Tomboy Woman, a glass of wine, a beer, and headed up stairs. She glanced in the kids bedrooms, and finally in Noah and Julian's bedroom, and paused to listen to the rest of the house.

Three dresser drawers had been emptied on the bed, and tossed to the floor. She sat her gifts down, and glanced across the room at the many pairs of Julian's Cowgirl boots in the wall boot rack, made just for Julian. She was curious things were a mess, and maybe Julian couldn't find what she was looking for. After looking around, she eyed the racks

269

of boots, knocked over, uneven, and missing. She could not see them lying on the floor, because of the bed.

She walked out of the room, and peaked into the spare room, and the kids rooms. None of them were messes, so she stood in the hall, curious. Finally, putting her hands on her hips, she yelled one last time, JULIAN, ARE YOU HOME?"

When she didn't hear a response, she figured Noah rushed her to the store for something, and headed into the bedroom.

Pulling one of Noah's old t-shirts, now claimed by Julian, from the bureau, she claimed it, and slipped off her blouse and bra. After putting on the ragged, see through and ripped in multiple places, shirt, she slipped off her heals, and jeans into her pink thong. She thought she heard faint crying, and nervously crept over to the closet door with her eyes wide, and opened it.

Jerking back fast, she screamed and held her chest, she found Julian. She was sitting in the dark crying, alone. Her Secret Cowgirl box sat between her legs. She was completely nude, not even in her boots. Her dark eye makeup stained down her face, as tears rolled down. "Julian, are you alright? What's wrong?"

Samira stepped over to her, and got down on her knees, and pushed the rope of hair back in her own lips. Julian was shaking wildly with exhausting sobs. Her box was full of odd items Samira thought, as she looked over them delicately, not to seem intrusive.

In her real caring voice, she spoke to her. "Tomboy, what is wrong? Did something happen to Noah? The kids?" Samira slowly reached out to

270

touch her, and Julian finally looked up at her startled.

Samira's head jerked back as she made eye-contact with her. Julian, was broken, and Samira could see it.

Julian burst into sobbing at her, as she tried to tell her, "Help me please. I need Noey. I...I..I thank he left me." Her lips were quivering, and Samira scooted closer, on her knees. The Nurse looked into her eyes, and tried to see if she was intoxicated or worse.

"Julz, I spoke to Noah just a little bit ago, and he was taking the kids to your Mother's home after Ally's soccer game. Is th...th...that what you mean? Did something happen? Did you have a fight?" Samira reached out and touched her hair, and pulled on it a little. She realized Julian had stuffed all of it down under her front, and chose not to pull it out, but to hold it instead.

"FUCKIN' STOP ARGUIN ME!" Julian screamed well above her whisper shaking madly, scarying Samria back. She began fighting with her hair jerking it, and thrashing her body around as she screamed at it. She jerked it so hard Samira could see her scalp pulling across her skull, and rushed to grab her head, and stop her.

"JULIAN STOP! STOP IT! PLEASE! PLEASE TALK TO ME! When Samira held it, Julian stopped, and looked up at her in tears. Her lips and eyebrows were shaking viciously in fear.

"Julian, do you take any special medications that I should know about?" Julian didn't answer her. "Tomboy, answer me NOW!" Samira grabbed her face and shook her with authority, as she looked down into her eyes for prescription intoxication.

271

Trying to speak through her tears, she gave everything she could to explain. "I...I need Rachael. I need Diddy meds." Julian reared back screaming, and pulling her hair as hard as she could, and jerked her head backwards over an over to pull the hair she held in her hands, and clenched her teeth as hard as she could.

"STOP ARGUIN' ME! EMILY GO AWAY! PLEASE GO AWAY!" she cried out. Rushed with emotions, Samira grabbed her head, and pulled her into her chest, and subdued her from hurting herself. She instantly began her own tears.

"What the hell is wrong with you?" Samira said as Julian's screams faded into her sobbing fears.

"I can't have any more Angels. Noah will leave me for breedin' Angel. It is his purpose on earth. He must breed the Angels. My hair is arguin'. I need Rachaeeeel!" Julian began to panic again, and pulling on Samira to save her. "DON'T LET EMILY GET ME! EMILY SHOT NOAH! NOT ME! NO! NO! EMILY! GOD PLEASE HELP ME!" Julian held on to Samira with everything she had. Both of them crying. Samira's eyes got really big.

"NOAH HAS BEEN SHOT?" Samira screamed out to her.

"EMILY SHOT HIM!"

"TODAY JULIAN? TODAY?"

"NO! EMILY SHOT HIM! DON'T LET EMILY GET HIM!" Julian cried to her.

Samira peeked into the box and recognized her Bible, used pregnancy tests, diaries, and big yellow envelopes with names. Oddly, Julian grabbed a hand mirror from the box, and held it to her face, and cried for Jordan.

"EMILY IS COMIN'! EMILY IS COMIN! HELP ME! OH MY GOD SHE GETTIN' ME! HELP ME SAMMY! HELP ME! DON'T LET EMILY GET MEEEE!" Exhausted, she tried to pull Samira on her to hide, and Samira just held her harder, keeping out of the closet. Claustrophobia was creeping on her.

Unsure of what to do, other than to hug her, she scooted next to Julian but, on the outside of the closet, and kept hold of her. She put Julian's hair in her own mouth, and reached down putting her arm in hers, and held her hand. "Is Jordan your mother's name? Is it Rachael's other name? No wait! You used the name Jordan in the hospital, right?"

Sobbing and nodding, she begged Samira, "Don't let Emily shoot Noey! Please help meeeee. NOEYYYYYYY! DON'T SHOOT MY NOEY EMILYYYYY!"

Julian just sobbed into her for help. "Julian, I...LISTEN! LISTEN TO ME! I should ask you something. I'm your Girlfriend." Samira squeezed her hand to remind her. "Will you tell me what is going on? Who is Emily?" Julian held her mirror up again, and cried for Jordan again, and handed it to Samira.

"I can't find Jordan. I can't find Jordan. She is gone. She gone fragmentin' away. She stops Emily from hurtin' Noey!" Julian took the mirror again, and tried IDentifY Jordan, and cried harder as she threw it in the box. Samira was getting anxious, and unsure of how to console what she didn't understand. She felt she was missing something.

Rachael sat under the room, listening and smiling as her plan continued to unfold. She opened another box, looking for Julian's diaries, and looked in another box.

273

"Fat Bitch always keeps them down here so Noah doesn't find them." She lifted the last box and knew, it was empty, and looked around for other places she may have hidden them from the world.

Samira picked up the mirror and looked at it, and held it for Julian unsure of what she was doing. "If you look in the mirror Julian, I see Jordan. I met you at the hospital. You are Police Woman, Jordan?" Julian shook her head and her tears, and pulled her hair down with her free hand and rocked her head back as far a she could, with her teeth clenched. Samira quickly, petted her, and began to jerk her hair gently, for her. "Yo...yo...yo...you're beautiful, Julian. Please stop. Please. Your making me cry!"

"Jordan is my other me. She hides me from Emily." She murmured through her grimaced tears, shaking in fear.

Samira looked up to the room shocked, searching for an understanding, and looked around the room, and glanced back at Julian. *Noah's manly stuff is still there. Obviously, he would have taken his boots. Several pair still sit in front of the closet,* she assessed to herself. *Noah did not leave her.* Samira carefully looked at her, and scooted as close as she could get, to the open door.

"Julian, I need to ask you something very personal, and I need to know the truth, or I am leaving. Do you have Multiple Personalities or Schizophrenia? Are you hearing voices?" Julian nodded to her in fear of answering, and broke down harder.

"OH MY!" Escaped from Samira's mouth before she could stop it. "Emily. Emily argues my hair to me. I can't get her to stop arguin' my hair to me. I need Jordan and Rachael to go her away."

She whispered to her, letting her tears crawl down her cheeks. "My Diddy meds."

Samira let go of her hand to the instant fear she now felt. "Diddy meds?" Samira repeated to herself. Samira looked up to the left as she took to her Nursing skills. When she found what she was looking for, she looked at Julian with her eyes wide open. "Diddy meds? Dissociative Identity Disorder Medication? Multiple Personality Disorder Medication?" She instantly got up in fear, and reached for her phone on the bureau, and texted Noah. As she stood up, the fear really hit her, and she stepped away from the closet to protect herself from something that wasn't contagious, but just in case.

Julian started pleading with her, "You can't tell Noey. Please. Noey will leave me. Noey can't know Emily. Emily shooted Noey. Men can't know about Emilys. Momma said so. Emily shot Noey." She murmured. "Pleeeease don't tell Noeyyyyy. PLEEEEASE EMILY GO AWAY!" Tears rushed down her pale face again, carrying the mascara as she tried to lock her eyes to hers. Samira looked at the bedroom door, contemplating her choices.

Text to Noah from Samira: 911 at your house. Julian crying in closet. Missing Jordan? WTF? Why didn't you tell me about Emily? Please hurry. Do I call 911?

"Do you want me to call you Jordan, Julian, Emily or another name or personality? How many personalities do you have, Jordan?" Julian looked at her pathetically, and shrugged her left shoulder and shaking her head, unsure at the moment. Samira spoke very delicately to her, and took a deep breath deciding her own fate for them both. She looked over at the exit again, and then her heels, and back to Julian's sad blue eyes, and sat back down next to her accepting the responsibility, like Rachael did once.

Gently, she took Julian's hand and kissed it. "I am here for you, Girl. Why is Emily going to shoot Noah?" Julian glanced at her and sobbed nodding in fear that everything was getting out of her control. Samira could see she had some real fear happening as she felt how cold her hands really were. "Where is your Diddy medication, Julian?"

"I don't understand my Daddy's song. I don't hear God. What is wrong with me, Sammy?"

Sternly, Samira spoke up, "Where is your Diddy medication, Julian?"

"On the fridge. We take it." She was a mess of fear and defeat.

"Did you take it today, Julian?" Julian looked up at her showing her the truth.

"I don't know. I am not here today. I don't know if it was me, or Emily. I need Rachael. Rachael knows me." Julian poured into sobbing as she could no longer lie around the truths.

"If you come out of the closet Julian, I can hold you in the bed and we can talk. I will keep you safe."

"I can't. I don't know if I am Emily or Julian anymore." Julian cried. "I need Momma. Momma knows who I am."

Samira started to speak, "Noah will be-" She heard the front door slam shut, and his boots running up the stairs. She immediately stood up to greet him. When Noah ran into the room, both of them lit up, and Samira curtsied to him without knowing she did it. Samira did not let go of Julian's hand, for all the right reasons. Perhaps her curtsy was for Julian.

Noah watched Julian as he walked over to her kneeling beside her, and reaching out for her hand with his softest voice, "Are you alright, Angel? Did something happen at work with Karen? Did you run into Rachael? Can you IDentifY for me?" Julian shook her head to all of them crying harder now that he was there. Samira immediately thought Noah called her the personality name, Angel, and stepped out of the crowded closet entrance.

"Are you Emily, now?" Tears began to stream down Samira's face as she watched Julian shake harder to the name. Julian shook her head as slobber fell from the corner of her mouth onto the box she was snuggled up to. Noah reached over and got the IDentifY mirror, and held it up to her, and she just cried and turned away.

"Don't hide Jordan, Noey. Don't hide her." Julian mumbled.

"Are you another IDentifY I do not know about, Angel?" Julian pulled her hand away, and tapped herself and spoke clearer.

"I can't find Jordan any more. She is gone. I lost my Jordan, Noah. I am unable to find my Alibis. What am I gonna' do? I'm an argue in my hair. I need Rachael." Samira started wiping her own tears away, and watched Noah coach her.

♫ Text Alert on Julian's Phone

"I need my Diddy meds." She mumbled looking for help. "Angel, we can't find Jordan in the-" Julian cut him off.

"Will you marry me, Noey? Please marry me. Don't leave me." She spoke faster with a lot of urgency. "I am not an Angel. I...I can't make you babies." Her pleading fear got louder, "PLEASE

277

MARRY ME, NOEY! Please, Noey, marry me. Please marry me. I need Rachael, Noey. I need to marry you. GO AWAY EMILYYYYY!" She started thrashing and pulling her hair as her face clenched, and shook with all her neck and face muscles locked. It almost looked like a seizure.

Noah reached down and punched her in the vagina, and she immediately stopped, and seemed to regain control of herself, but she still cried and nodded to him. Samira stepped away, not appreciating his tactic.

Her screams began low and carried out as loud as her broken voice could get, and she began begging again. "PLEASE DON'T LEAVE ME! OH MY GOD NOEY! PLEASE DON'T LEAVE ME! I'M DIDDY SICK! I'M SORRY! SAVE ME NOEY! PLEASE GOD HELP ME! SHUT THE VOICES NOEY! PLEASE GOD! PLEASE DON'T LEAVE ME AGAIN NOEY! GO AWAY EMILYYYYYY! NOEYYYY! SHE IS GETTING' MEEEEEEE! NOEY STOP HER!!!! NOEEYYYYYYY! GOD HELP ME!"

Noah shoved her backwards, and began beating her mound repeatedly with his fist, and subduing her fear. In her screams she was reaching for him with both arms, and he quickly stood up, and ripped the closet door off the wall hinges, and tossed it into the hall, and rushed onto his knees in the closet on top of her and held her. She could no longer speak because of crying so hard. Samira began balling, and climbed into the closet to hug them both. 'PLEASE GOD HELP ME NOEY! ARGUE ME HAIR! PLEASE HELP ME! OH MY GOD NOEY! I LOVE YOU DON'T LEAVE ME ALONE NOEY! EMILY IS GETTIN' ME! EMILY IS GETTIN' ME! EMILY IS GETTIN'! ME NOEY!" She started thrashing under him and he tried to hug her and keep her safe.

"PLEASE DON'T LEAVE ME ALONE! I NEED MOMMA! TELL GOD I WILL HAVE MORE BABIES NOEY! PLEASE GOD TELL HIM! DON'T LEAVE ME NOEY! I CAN STILL HAVE YOUR BABIES NOEY! PLEASE DON'T LEAVE MEEEEE!" She was finally out of breath and lost to her cries. As Samira kept her arms around Noah and Julian, she could see Noah sobbing over her shoulder, and it burst her into crying speechless. She had never seen real love before. The moment would have to last until Julian could come out of her fear induced paralysis.

Noah held her down with his hand on her neck, and his head on her chest, and began beating her vulva with his fist. She instantly stopped fighting him, and screaming and relaxed under him as reward became his tool, instead of a weapon. He continued to punch her vulva, as she fell into an incognizant state. Samira watched, growing her fear of his abusive side, only to watch as Julian benefited from it. When he stopped and looked at her, he broke down crying, and hugged her with his tears. Samira immediately started balling and hugged him from the back.

When he regained his composure, Julian was just midly crying, and flat on her back, and he kissed her several times, and got up on his knees, and hugged Samira.

"She's okay now. She's okay. Come on Angel." He said, and getting her up. "Let's try to lay down together, the three of us, and find Jordan together. I will marry my Texas Cowgirl in the bed, Baby." He sniffled from his crying, and didn't try to hide his feelings. Samira got up, and both of them pulled Julian out of the closet. Oddly, Noah pulled her up by her hair, and Samira did not like that but, Julian did not complain. Each one wrapped their arms

279

around her, and hugged her as they walked her to the bed. Julian stopped before getting on the bed, and pulled her arm away from Noah. He watched her as she let Samira gently wrap her arms around her chest from behind hugging her, or keeping her from getting away.   Julian curtsied to him, and laid down on the bed still crying a little. Noah, instinctively pulled his shirt off, as she climbed up the bed with Samira getting to the other side. When his jeans came down, Samira saw his pretty silk panties, and instantly sat up in shock at his odd fetish.

With a repulsed expression she asked him, "Noey, are you wearing women's panties?" Her spare hand went to her chest to help her get her breath, as her bottom jaw dangled to him. He nodded at her with a smile, and after he pulled them off, he tossed them to her. Her eyes and mouth were wide open as she reached for them still holding her breath. She delicately picked them up and rubbed them on her cheek, as she smelled his familiar scent on the front. She held them in her hand, and laid back down still dealing with her body's chemical reaction to his cross-dressing, even if the moment was bad timing.

Samira snuggled up to Julian with her arms around her, and whispered to herself, and to the back of Julian's neck, "Noey wears women's panties?"

Julian was still shivering and weeping softly as Noah snuggled his chest up to her face, burying her, and she reached for his penis and held it with both hands, while snuggling into him. He petted her head softly, and shushed her to calm down. Her grip was painful but, he didn't complain about her need to grab on to something of his.

Samira sat up, and removed the ragged shirt, and pushed her breasts against Julian's back, and felt how cold she was. The three of them snuggled each other for the moment. Samira snuggled the panties to her face, still dumbstruck by his macho scent on pink silk. The image of his bulge was not far from her thoughts. She was thinking she needed a picture of that.

Softly, Samira kissed her back and neck, inhaling her sexy, familiar scent, and her fear, and petted Julian's long hair as she covered the three of them with it.

"Noah, I have never met or been involved with someone with this...this...this...disorder. Is this normal for Angel to hide in the closet? Is she off her medication? Noah had his arm around Julian's head and Samira, and jerked Julian's long hair. Noah, handed Samira a curry horse brush, and she brushed Julian's long hair down the side of her body, gently.

"Nooooo." He sighed, "She has been having problems since the hospital. Even before the hospital I'm finding out. Problems inside her mind, and so much stress on herself about things. She has never been so pushy about me leaving her, either. This is new. I think she has some undefined fears or problems going on she is not telling me about. Having all this time off from work, she has plenty of time to think and get her lasso in knots." He hugged both of them, and Samira saw him struggling not to cry.

"She is so smart, so strong willed..." He was crying into Julian's head, "She is working them herself and won't ask me for help." He kissed her head. "Something is going on that she is not telling me about. I just can't figure it out-and maybe she

281

can't explain them until she figures them out. She is so afraid of not being able to have any more babies. We have been trying since Zachary was born, and it's not happening." HE exhaled into her hair, and kissed her again.

"Her work is very stressful, and she is stressed out, and we think having some withdrawals from someone, and some medications someone she trusted was giving her, without her knowing." He got control of his tears, and exhaled them gracefully as Samira wiped away hers.

"Her and Rachael broke up, and she is making threats to her and me, and arrest us for what I did for Julian that night. I don't know think I know all of it." He wiped his tears again, and sniffled, "Her religious responsibilities are weighing down on her. So much is going on, and she is trying to manage it. Her nude video accidently got seen by everyone at work." He rubbed his face to relieve the tension. "I don't know."

"We have Emily, another Alibi, I just recently learned about, to thank for that. Emily sent Rachael the video, and she sent it to everyone at work. I am doing all I can for her but, she is a tough Short-stuff who insist on being in charge of herself. Emily seems be her troublemaker."

"How many pers...pers...personalities does she have?"

"I know of three or four. Rachael was her counselor, IDentifY Architect Partner, and doctor, and likely knows. She controlled her meds and psychotherapy and...and..." he spoke the term as if he wasn't sure it was the right term, "...Artificial Memories." I just make sure she takes her meds. Angel, did you take your meds today?" Julian nodded, and put her arm behind her to hold

Samira's hand. When she got it, she pulled it around front, and curled it up under her chin, held it, and kissed it repeatedly. Slowly, she let her grip relax on his penis.

Samira looked at Noah with concern, and he went on to explain things the best he was allowed too. The boss was laying between them at the moment, so word choices had to be delicate.

"She controls her Alibis with her mirror and medication, and things have been falling apart lately. She is dealing with migraines lasting days at a time, and has been to the doctor, and tests. This is the worst I have ever seen her." He leaned down and kissed her on the head. She wasn't crying anymore, but still had the shakes. "She is my, Angel."

Samira leaned in kissing Julian behind the ear and whispering to her. "I will be here for you, Julian. I...I...I...will." Julian turned over on her back, and pulled Samira down, and kissed her. She shared her breath with her, and gently kissed her again as she held her hand tightly. Samira felt better inside, and her fear seemed to pass as Julian seemed to regain her real self. The Women stared each other in their eyes, and Samira mildly smiled at her, and kissed her again. Julian reached up, and pulled Samira's hair into her mouth, and sucked on it. Samira pulled up some of Julian's hair, and gave it to Noah to suck on, and then she roped some for herself, and sucked on it smiling at Julian.

The Woman kissed again, and Julian turned and kissed Noah, and Noah leaned over Julian, and kissed Samira. Both of them snuggled down to Julian's breasts, and petted her body. She held both their hands, and quietly cried it out with nervous shakes now and then.

"I don't know," Samira said prepositioning her suggestion, "But, would it help to cut her hair if Emily is 'arguing her hair,' whatever that means? Julian immediately shook her head without talking about it. She made sure it was vigorous.

"Julian said you were leaving her, Noah. Is this true?

"NO! I will not leave her. She is getting paranoid about not having more children. It is her Alibis talking to her, and her Momma putting stupid ideas into her head. She is hard on herself sometimes. A little overboard. I'm not going anywhere, Samira."

"I thought you two were married...already. She asked you to marry her. Did she forget you are married to her?" Samira asked with severe eye contact with Noah.

"We have common law marriage. An Accord. Julian said we are not allowed to marry. Our religion. Mathewwwww something." Samira's expression had a lot of doubt in it.

Julian whispered to them, "Mathew 22:30. For in the resurrection they neither marry nor are given marriage, but are like Angels in heaven. I hate it."

"Are you two related somehow? Is...is...is that why?" Samira jumped at the conclusion. Her knowledge of Christianity was clashing with their story.

"NO! We are not related, only by our Accord." He rubbed his hand down her center-chest, to her very purple mound, and back up, as Samira rubbed her breasts.

Julian spoke up, "Noey, I got the Toxicology reports from the hospital this mornin'. I had Ketamine in my system, in the hospital and Adderall. I don't take either of those. I pulled my records from file goin' back five years, and Ketamine has been in my system for every blood test. I think Rachael WAS druggin' me like you said, she said."

"Ketamine? What is that? What does it do for you?" Noah asked.

Samira spoke up, it is a sedation medication. Popular on the street as Special K. It sedates pe…pe…pe…pe…students people. Anxieties. Maybe you were prescribed it, Julian. Wasn't see your Doctor?"

Julian shook her head as she stared at the ceiling fan. "In the hospital, I caught Rachael recommendin' it to the Doctor, and we got into an argument." She paused for a thought, and an 'Oh No' moment hit her.

"Back in college, Andrea and Rachael made smoothies for me, and she called them Special K's. She lived on Adderall in college, and Med School and probably still takes it."

"Maybe she meant the breakfast cereal, Julian." Samira suggested. "Do you think she is the kind of person who would drug you? Isn't she a Doctor?"

Noah and Julian both said, "Yes." At the same time. Both their experiences had proven it.

Noah spoke up, letting his investigation skills take over, "Let me ask you somethang Julian, without too much detail here. Did you get smoothies and then…you know…Emily show up, and men show up." Noah watched her eyes as she searched her memories. She smiled at one memory, as she linked the dots. Slowly, she nodded her head.

"I think so, Noey. I can only go by my diaries, and what I remember. I was faithful in my journals, and I can tell when Emily…" She looked at Samira, to make sure she understood, Noah couldn't know the truth about Emily. When Samira slightly nodded, she finished speaking. "IDentifY Emily never wrote in my diaries. Only myself."

Julian continued from memory, "Rachael said it was party night vitamins so we could stay up late. Special K Smoothies." Her voice faded toward the end as she delved into related information she had stored. Samira and Noah watched her think.

"Noey. I pilled your blue water with Sildenafil, but your blood test says you had PCP in your blood. You said, that Rachael said, she used to give it to...men in school. I would never do that. I thank she slipped it in your blue water that night. Rachael was playin' with the bottle before I brought it to you."

She looked up at him to tell him something that had drastic effect on his guilt, "Baby, that would explain why you were so brutal to me durin' the...that Therapy." Julian kept moving her lips as if she was searching for something to say. Samira was looking at Noah, judging him, as she saw the result of his abuse in the hospital.

"Julian, if that is true, than Rachael would spike your Smoothies, then and now. Are you taking Ketamine now, Baby?" Julian shook her head at them.

"I've never taken it."

"Noah." Samira said looking directly, "Did you rape her? Really rape her? Rachael told me it was rape, but you two said it was a car accident." Samira had stirred about these feelings every time they had been together, and could not find a way to bring it up. It weighed heavily on the back of her mind, until Julian stepped in.

286

"Yes Samira, Noah raped me. He did to me what we...I'm sorry I did this, Noey. We threatened to leave him, if he didn't do it...Rape Therapy. It was Rachael druggin' him with PCP that made it get so violent. All I did was give him a little extra power in the penis...it's a long story. He did what I manipulated him to do to me. Right or wrong. Please do not blame him for my desires." Julian stared at her waiting for a response, and Samira finally looked at her, instead of Noah, and nodded her head. Julian reared up a little, and they kissed to settle it. Samira leaned over her, and offered a warm kiss to Noah, and he smiled and kissed her back, then kissed Julian, and thanked her.

Rachael slid out the basement sliding door quietly, and ran to her car on the next street again, carrying one of Julian's boot boxes.

Chapter 24

-Dominion of Panties & Acquiescent Seshi's Angel

Waking up hours after her Nervous Breakdown, and feeling safe from Emily, Julian spoke up, "Noey and Samira. Wake up. I want to watch you two." Samira lifted her head up, and looked at her with her eyes wide open, and Julian looked back at her, then back to Noah. Only Samira shared a nervous look of question, and still holding Noah's panties in her fist.

"Really Sam. I thank I would feel better seein' you two make love. My va-ja-ja ain't lettin' me- NOAH get what he wants, and I am askin' you to do it for me, Sam. I can't take him inside me right now because his stupid big dick doesn't like my internal healing." She grabbed it, and shook it to be silly, and stirring Noah James.

"I love you both, and be thankin' I would feel better if you both were there to help each other, with me. And I be liken' the idea of watchin'. But, please share his seed with me." Noah stretched and faked a yawn, hoping Samira would say no, so he could go back to sleep.

Samira spoke up, you...you...you this...maybe...if you join us." Samira looked over at Noah for agreement, and Julian watched Samira work Noah. Samira smiled at him, and offered two short nods.

"Please Sam. I want to hold you while Noah makes love to you. Please? You and I have been practicin' you bein' on bottom with me on top of you. Your claustrophobia is gettin' tamer."

"I wouldn't mind." Samira whispered, feeling uncomfortably excited. She got off the bed and pulled her thong off, and tossed it at Julian nervously aroused. Noah was growing already, and poking into Julian's knee, as he took in Samira's firm, thick, Black curves. Holding the thong to her nose, Julian smelled her woman's fresh scent and rolling her eyes back. "I will do anything he asks, IF...IF...he is wearing Women's panties."

Samira leaned in, and began kissing Julian, and fingering her thick, Black to Pale labia. "I'm glad you're feeling better, Julian. You sound better." Samira whispered between kisses.

"Me too. Thank you and I'm sorry." Julian kissed her delicately, and offered her body to her with her wet kiss. Noah rubbed his hands over, Julian's breasts, and let her feel the warmth of his cock as it grew. Julian whispered to Noah, "Venus, please." Samira continued to kiss Julian, and Julian slowly pushed Samira back to speak to her.

"Spit in my mouth, Muslimah." Noah pushed Samira's hands out of Julian's labia, and palmed her large bruised mound, and she moaned in quick sensations burning in her vulva.

Samira looked up at Noah, and nodded to her, and he leaned over and put his spit on the tips of his lips, and let it fall into Julian's mouth. He squeezed her mound again, sending pain signals that stimulated her body with impending promises of pleasure. Samira felt her wetness grow from the dirty excitement of seeing saliva drip into Julian's mouth, and repeated it with her. Julian slowly opened her mouth as the seed from Samira's tongue strung down, and Julian pulled her closer with her mouth barely parted, and captured, before kissing Samira with it.

Noah slowly rubbed her breasts, and spread her leaking mound all over them, as Samira fingered Julian's leaking wetness from her sweet spot below. All three heard the sounds of Julian's wonderful wet essence, and each stirred in their own special spots.

Noah slipped his hand down again, squeezing her until she moaned in the pain, and held the squeeze as her mountain creek of wet desires flowed between his fingers. Slowly, he slid all his fingers deep under her mound, and held the mound fat in his hand. He owned it. A few jerks, and she was moaning into Samira's mouth as her entire body felt the warmth of her entire vulva shake with stimulation. The sound of the wetness increased intensely, and he lifted her mound several times to pain her.

Samira slid down, and began licking her labia one by one, as Julian lifted her knees back to her stomach, putting her boots in the air. Samira sucked each side into her mouth suckling them, and tasting her thicker pussy juice. Noah kissed his Angel, and slid his hand back down to her mound, and with his strong fingers split her labia apart at the top, and Samira immediately shoved her face deep, and licked Julian's aching clitoris. As Julian's head and eyes rolled back, her hands made it to the headboard bars, and she pinned them down, so she could not fight off her lovers.

Julian flinched back moaning as her clitoris hardened from the licks, and Samira reached over and felt Noah's cock, and squeezed him as she licked Julian. Samira could feel the heat from both of their primed organs, and her labia swelled to meet her urgent needs. After squeezing her breasts,

Noah slid his right hand onto her neck, and Julian lifted her chin in desperate submission.

Gently, he tightened his grip, as Samira's head bobbed up and down on her clitoris. Noah let go of her neck, and grabbed a handful of Samira's hair, and she submitted to his will, and pushed her face deeper into Julian's wet, and yearning, vulva.

With his other hand, Noah grabbed Julian's hair, and put it in her mouth like her favorite horse snaffle bit. The rope was thick, and crossed over her entire mouth to gag her like a horse. Letting go of Samira's hair, he tossed the rest down to Samira. Stopping only seconds, she fingered it into Julian's pussy, nearly a foot of it, and thumbed her clitoris behind it, as it divided her thickening curtains.

Julian felt forced to let them take what they wanted, thus making her feel safe from guilt, and offered herself to prayer, as her Cucks, let her submit to them. Both her eyes closed, and Noah choked her again but, just enough. She was restrained, and held against her will. The fear she loved, and prayed for rescue, but only AFTER the orgasms.

"Luke 6:38, give me pain, and I shall be given unto you. Mark 10:8 and 9, God has made us one flesh, shan't we separate our love. Proverbs 5:18 and 19, let our fountains of essence be blessed and rejoice in the wives of our, Dominion. Let our breasts fill each other at all times with delight, be intoxicated always in our love, my Dominion...and Samira's Dominion. Be thou ravished always with our love."

Julian slowly lifted her chin, and intentionally holding her breath to be suffocated, Noah tightened his grip on her throat, to really stimulate her need for prayer.

Samira had palmed both of Julian large, gifted labia apart, and held one in each hand. With all her fingers squeezing, and curling her labia against her palms, she was pulling on both heavy, thick labia as both thumbs pressure-rubbed each side of her little clit. Julian was now, forced to take what they were giving her. With Noah's forceful hold, she choked into her first orgasm, and when he held her down, and Samira kept forcing the pleasure through her Vulnerability stage, Julian shed a few tears from the corner of her eyes to the emotions, she was attaching to this memory. Samira pulled harder on the labia for leverage as Julian's face got redder and redder.

Her Venus mound poured down a warm flow, and Noah jerked his choking hand against her windpipe over and over, as she tried to force air out. Samira pulled Julian's soaked hair out of her wet canal, and put some of it into her mouth, as she licked up the large amount of wetness escaping. Slurping, she finally ground her face into her pussy, to feel owned.

The excitement began to overtake Samira's courtesies, and she reached down and fingered her own clitoris to put her fire out. Slowly releasing Julian's neck, Noah reached for a chalice from the end table, and handed it to Samira. She licked Julian toward another euphoric shake, forcing her to finally make herself breathe, and held it under her enticing flow of wetness as Julian squirmed, panted, and moaned through her earth quaking orgasm.

Noah unhooked Julian's locked wrist, and she reached down with both hands, and grabbed her breasts squeezing, and pulled on her nipples lifting her large breasts up to the shape of cones, and squeezing her nipples until it hurt, and then stretching them farther than they should go. Struggling for her breath to catch up, she stretched her nipples as hard as she could moaning to the pain, and held them.

Noah snapped his fingers at Samira for the chalice, and she rushed it to his hand, and he poured it into Julian's mouth as her moans skipped. Noah leaned down, and kissed her, sharing the rich lure of his wife's inner wetness, as his hand rested on her neck, and her arms dropped her breasts, and she embraced him for the long, succulent passion, they wanted to share with Samira.

After the kiss that required close eye contact communication afterwards, she whispered to Samira, "You two are killin' me down there. Thank you. Thank you Texas. Many times." And she motioned for Samira to come up on her.

Julian welcomed her on top, giving her exclusive rights to be between her legs, and pushed Noah to the side. She had seen him in her panties for years, so he would have to wait. Her Woman was the prize. Slowly, Samira began rubbing her mound against Julian's huge, sore mound, and Julian moaned to the wonderful rushing pain. Samira worked it harder, and Julian began panting out her breaths and finally, screaming from the pain with each gyrate that shook and stretched her mound, vulva, and clitoris root. She pulled Samira's seed covered face to her, and kissed and licked her, as she forced her moaning pleasures sounds into her Black skin.

Noah reached over and lifted Samira's hand off the bed, and placed it on Julian's wrist beside her, pinning it to the bed. Samira looked up at him after he did it, and he nodded for her to do the other one, and she did. Julian smiled as her puffs of severe pain jarred her with intense stimulation, humiliation, and now, fear. Samira saw her arousal level rise when she held her down, and smiled at Noah for sharing the trick. She worked harder now to beat Julian's large, fat mound, and her own.

Julian began calling Noah's name and he smiled, only she was trying to command her Cuckold.

"Noah! Noah! Noah! Proverbs me! Proverbs!" Samira reached up and stuffed Julian's mouth full of her own hair since she had lost most of her snaffle bit to pleasures. Noah knew what she wanted. It was one of Seshi's favorite Bible quotes to her Cuckquean, only Seshi, was back in Florida, and her former Cuckquean was under Samira getting tribbed. Huge Venus mound to not so huge, Venus mound.

The Cuckold, stood back stroking his cock to them, as he recited Seshi's Proverb. "Hand in hand, the wicked shall not be unpunished, but the seed of righteous shall be delivered."

Both women were moaning at each other as each one pitched higher, the other felt and heard the incredible acoustical stimulation, and seemed to tier higher against each other. Samira was the first gasp for breath and hold it, as Julian moaned out her Master's bedroom name over and over. "Muslimah. Muslimah. Muslimah."

Both their mounds trembled as their breasts shook violently, their seeds blended for each other, all over their Venus mounds and engorged vulvas. Finally, Julian gasped her breath and shook harder into their orgasms pushed to the mind with pain. Samira tossed her head to the hard left as the sensations from her vulva burned her, until she began shaking in a tight tense. Her bright white

294

teeth clenched as her senses burned, and Julian jerked her arms repeatedly to increase her fear, and forced to take the violation against her will, and the reward.

Samira collapsed breasts to breasts on her and both women struggled to give the other more seed in their roaring passionate, panting with moans, kissing. Noah stood back and smiled at the growing love his wife had for someone who really seemed to care for her. He stroked his cock in anticipation of his naked Black Beauty, and the idea that his wife, would get wetter, watching him seed her.

As Samira's Cuckquean, continued slowly tribbing with her Master Samira, Julian's Cuckold Dominion, got behind her Master, and she got up on her knees for him, and laid her breasts down on Julian, keeping her face, on her right cheek, between her shaking, White breasts that tried to hang over the sides of her chest.

Julian snapped her fingers at Noah, with a mean look on her face. His expression was confused, after all, he was a man with an erection, which meant, no brain function at that time. Samira's Cuckquean snapped her fingers again, and pointed to Samira's ass.

"You kiss her ass like you do mine, Noey. Always kiss our asses." He searched for a thought but, was incapable of one, so he could not debate it.

Noah, with his aching erection, got down on his knees, and kissed Samira's ass cheek and slowly rolled his tongue around it. Samira smiled with clear embarrassment and real empowerment, until his warm, wet tongue began working its way to the top of her Venusian dimples, and she got nervous.

Julian watched her face closely as Noah worshipped her, and looked for the cues of anxiety to see her conscience at heart. As he pushed seed out of his mouth, into her rear crack, it began sliding downward slowly, and his tongue chased it.

Julian scooted down, snuggling Samira under her chin as she attempted to hide her shame, and grabbed her hair on the back of her head, and jerked her face up to stare at her reward cues. Samira didn't even notice Julian because her mind was following Noah's tongue.

As it inched closer to her dark desire, her face began to curl in fear, shame, anxiety, pleasure, intense stimulation, empowerment and empowerment risk, and doubt, as Julian gripped her arm around the back of her neck tighter, to keep her from escaping.

As his warm, wet teaser slid to her anus and began swirling, Samira broke, and tears slowly streamed down her face, as she offered a small cry. Julian was hoping to see that. Another cue she needed to confirm. She read every cue about divine Venusian Dimples through experience, and recognized her Angelic qualities by the response to mild Purging. Noah continued to swirl her darkness, and her moans began to scream in short bursts with tears, and Julian let go of her hair, and embraced her virgin Angel during her next to last, confirmation.

When one of Samira legs jerked out behind her and him, he reached under and felt her drip into his hand, and wiped it on her ass cheeks as he licked her ass into orgasm. Julian's clit burned as Samira moaned, and shook on top of her, and begged for her turn, in her mind. Vulnerability had arrived for Samira.

When the aftershocks reverberated through Samira's body, he leaned in to her exposed pussy hole, and slurped and sucked her warm seed into his mouth like he owned it. Julian recognized the sound of wetness, and grinned at Samira's painful, licking reward that shook her into Vulnerability so fast.

Samira's muscles tightened down her back as her spine felt like it was curling in every side direction possible, as he lapped her up. Even if it gave her sharp, stimulating pains of satisfying pleasure, Samira's smile of a Woman feeling worship and empowerment, was self-incriminating. All thanks to the snap of her Cuckquean's finger.

Noah stood up and looked down her ass and back to Julian, who winked at her Cuckold with approval and a big smile. Her woman was satisfied externally, but her insides needed a beating; Julian style. It would not be gentle.

He leaned down with his palm up and slapped Samira's dripping, yearning pussy lips, really hard, and she screamed out in fearful pleasure to the beating. She was being introduced to pain, not realizing yet, how much she liked it. He hit her again, and she squealed into Julian's arms for mercy, as Julian watched her rear poised up in the air. She could see her Venusian dimples. Noah hit her wetness again, and her sounds shifted to gratifying, and Julian's watched her lower ass for more. Julian smiled more than Samira. He struck her again hard enough to lift her knees off the bed, and her scream was fearful and painful, and she wiggled hips to open her chubby, Black pussy up to his abuse. Like Julian had suspected, masochism was a big part of Samira's pleasure, only, she didn't know it.

With plenty of wetness to spare, Noah palmed it all from her chubby pussy, and licked it all off his hand, and spit it in the crack of her ass. Slowly, he worked the head of his cock into her wetness, and beat her clit repeatedly with his meatus. Her mild jerks calmed as he beat it harder and harder, and her reward system in her mind, made her offers, she couldn't refuse.

Julian spoke up as she snuggled Samira through her pain and pleasure, and captured her in her arms. With both her arms around the back of Samira's neck, she trapped her, and forced her down into her. Her tone changed to instant Dominance.

"Beg him Samira. Beg your Dominion for his seed. Beg him for your punishments, and he will reward you with his seed. BEG HIM NOW SLUT!"

Samira's fears rushed her as claustrophobia bit her hard, and panicked into a scream and struggle. Noah reached down and grabbed her wrists and pulled on them to control her arms.

Samira screamed as the tears ran from her eyes, and Julian slowly loosened her grip. They were teasing her fears, and it worked like a charm.

Her voice was shaky with fear, as she submitted to them, "Fuck me Noey." She said, feeling herself get more turned-on by the humiliation.

Julian smothered her again, and barked her commanding tone, "Beg him to punish you. Never ask for pleasure Slut. Ask for your punishment Sammy. BEG HIM FOR PUNISHMENT SO YOU WON'T BE A SLUT! And he might reward you with his seed." Julian jerked her as she held her down. "Never ask for pleasure, like a Slut."

Samira did not hesitate, as her wetness soaked her expectations. "Please fuck me and punish me Noey. Fuck me hard." Samira said it, feeling her power being taken away but, her desires stir so much more. When Julian started to speak again, Samira spoke up for herself, loudly.

"CUM IN ME NOEY! PLEASE CUM INSIDE MY PUSSY! PUNISH MY PRETTY BLACK PUSSY!" Julian smiled proudly, and kissed her as she used her biceps to push her breasts closer to Samira's face, and make her feel trapped.

The tip of his long, thick cock divided her wetness and without kindness, she slammed it into her making every inch give her satisfaction with pain. She immediately squirmed and squealed as the pain shot up through her stomach, and she pulled away to relieve it, only to have Julian hold her down.

Noah kept her by her wrists as her arms stretched behind her to him, and forced it back inside and fucked her with the pain. She squirmed and squealed to him, as she squirmed chest to chest with Julian for rescue. It was a good response for Julian, as she set the parameters of Stockholm Syndrome into Samira's subconscious mind. Noah gave the pain, and Julian controlled her pain, thus, be extra good to Julian. The effects are instant, and follows SANICS motto of using disorder against disorder; phobia against phobia.

"Noey. It's too much. 'Too much for her. Take it easy on her." Julian's raspy whisper said, and he pulled back silencing Samira's painful pleads. Samira wiggled to get deeper into Julian's arms for safety, and Julian grinned at the cue marker. Samira had no clue, this was real love.

299

"I can't take all of it, Julian." Samira said to her. I'm sorry. It hurts too much." Noah slammed it back into her for a last squeal and pulled out completely as she sought refuge in Julian's arms. Her seed dripped off the underside of his cock, as he smacked her clit with it. Pain can make the body do wonderful things.

As Julian coached her back up on her knees as Noah pulled her by her arms, she was cautious as he slid it back inside, and raised her head when it was the perfect length, and one by one, he let her breasts rest on Julian's chest when he let go of her arms. She immediately put her hands under Julian's backside seeking safety with Julian, and unknowingly, give Julian complete control of her.

Noah used his hand to space between her ass and his abdomen to give her the right length. Girth was just a given.

Samira nodded when he got the right length deep in her, and he began working her nerve endings. Samira had a shallow vagina compared to Julian, and Noah liked it.

Noah needed relief more than she did, and got up to speed with is thrusting, and finally, slid his hand out and watched his cock glide in and out of her, and glistening in the wetness she was offering him. He kept a tight eye on the distance, and worked to satisfy his new Angel, and find his pain. It would not take long for her, to find her wet and, oh so satisfying, reward.

She jerked as her orgasm shattered her will to escape, and Noah grabbed her long bushy hair, and jerked her like a Slutty wife from Texas, giving her necessary abuse, as she gasped into her scream of oxytocin pleasures...again. She slobbered all over Julian's neck and shoulder as Vulnerability raped her inhibitions. The orgasm felt beyond wonderful with pain.

She had in fact, taken all of his big cock, only this time, the painful timing was perfect. The severe pain signals, followed the pleasure signals to the brain, and jumped in the pleasure center pool, together.

He began to crackle as his reward took on his signals, and Julian watched his face, while holding her breath. Eager for her only man, Samira flexed her cervix for him and gave back what he needed, as his pain level broke his will to escape, and raped his inhibitions. Julian's pussy always leaked when a man gave up his seed. Now, her man was giving it to someone she wanted them to desire, together.

"CUM IN HER! SEED HER! SEED YER' BLACK ANGEL! CUM IN HER PUSSY! SHE ORDERED YOU! I'M ORDERIN' YOU NOEY! YOU CUM IN HER PUSSY EVERY TIME SHE BE TELLIN' YOU!"

Samira kept wincing and shaking, and letting herself get used for his pain now. He was putting all of it in her, for his pleasure, and out came his girly-scream. Instantly, both women smiled as their pussies got a rush from it, and their empowerment came back. THEY, took HIS seed.

Julian's chest shook as she chuckled at his emasculation through pleasure. It was a big price that her Cowboy loved to pay, and it made her want to get fucked by a train, when she watched him in pain reward. She giggled even more as Samira wiggled up moaning, stopping her shoulder under Julian's chin. Noah was still planting the seeds, and bursting his girly-scream to the moment.

When Noah's squirts finally settled down, he respired to catch his breath, and Julian barked at her Cuckold.

301

"Stay in her. Stay in her. I'm comin' down."
Julian began lifting Samira up, who was still
intoxicated by the chemistry, and very satisfied.
Julian on the other hand, seemed to be in a panic to
get there.

Noah reached down to Samira's hair, and
jerked her up like the used Slut she just was, and
lifted up her entire body. She didn't even moan as
she got owned, and Julian wiggled through her wet
sheets, and slid down to taste her lovers seed
cocktail, again.

Samira slightly put her hands in front of her
and held herself, but Noah kept her by her hair, as
his cock softened up inside her with gentle pulses of
warm seed. When Julian got between his legs, and
her face under her Woman's used and abused
pussy, she grabbed his balls, and pushed him back
slowly.

His cum soaked cock slid out, and she reared
up, and took it into her mouth as her hand rushed
to cover his heart. Soft, he was hanging at about six
inches, and that was six inches covered with seed,
she couldn't let be wasted. Semen, was her candy.

She sucked him like she worshipped his cock,
and waited for his Vulnerability to end. She watched
his face to judge when his mind rebooted
completely, and spit him out, clean. She got back to
Samira, and he slowly let her hair go, as Julian
licked the dripping warmth from her labia that had
stretched from engorging, for is seed donation.

Noah spoke up to her in a very caring tone.
"Sammy. Baby, flex your pussy. Flex it slowly."
Samira didn't show any sign of acknowledgment,
except her back door pinched tighter, and shifted
toward her wet canal, and slowly, his seed dribbled

out, and the more she flexed, the more warm cocktail, came dribbling.

Julian lapped it up as fast as she could as Samira began moaning again from the licks that spread warm, male proteins onto her clit, which fired up instantly to absorb it. She recognized that burn.

Flexing more, Julian drank her, and scooted back up the bed, under Samira, and both rushed to kiss each other. The passion was stimulating as their kindness and concern blended into each other's hearts, as well as both their big sets of breasts. Neither of them felt afraid as the safety of their passion embraced them.

Their tongues shared both of Julian's lover's cocktail mix, and Samira was just as eager. She rolled onto her back, and pulled Julian with her, as their mouths still forced the seeds back and forth.

Julian, as a symbol of her willingness to share power over Noah, slowly worked all the seed together in her mouth, and gave it to Samira to own. Noah crept down on the bed, and snuggled the two Woman, as they rested in each other's arms. When he put his arms around Julian, they both looked at him and commanded their Cuckhold Noah.

"GET AWAY!"

Chapter Twenty-Five

-Panties for him, Semen for her, Emily?

Noah kept his sunglasses and hat on, and kept his head down in the Panties Section at Clothing store. The Women however, enjoyed themselves shopping for his panties. Samira just could not wait any longer after he and Julian sexually dominated her days ago. So after working at the hospital, Samira and Julian, snapped their fingers at Noah, to take them shopping. A simple ploy to get him into the store.

No amount of IDentifY could get him out of the humiliation he was feeling at this moment, and having to hold two purses while all the other shoppers stared at him.

"I love these Julian. Do you like these?" Samira was holding up a very sleek, and sexy pair of bright pink mesh panties, just for Noah, as she sucked on a rope of hair. As Samira walked over to him, and held them around his waist, he cringed from every direction blushing. Samira was laughing so loudly, half the store could hear her. Getting to dress her man for her now known, secret fetish, was the truest intoxication. Emasculation with intense arousal, as she explained it to Julian on the phone.

Samira had a Fetish for Men and Women who cross-dressed, and had masturbated to it since she was a teenager. She didn't know why, and didn't care now that she had two lovers, who accepted it, and practiced it. She wanted her man, cross-dressing in her panties, and her Woman, dressed manly.

Julian giggled her approval for the very emasculating pair, and picked out others to see if Samira liked them. After all, this was about Samira having some emasculation power over Noah, which had not happened. Julian blamed Noah for screwing it up on their first attempt at Witness. Julian could see she had more will, and more into the emasculation for humiliation, when she leads.

Julian gave her a very sexy rainbow pair with the words, 'Bi-Girls' written on the front. Sucking on her hair, she jumped up and down to show Samira.

"I want to get these for you. For me." Julian said with her excited tone. Samira was smiling really big as she looked at them nodding. Only, her smiles seemed different. More natural would describe it. She was feeling the public display of being out of the closet, and liking it. Poor Noah, stepped away to dodge the flamboyant celebration of his mandatory sexual humiliation, by finding a tall rack to separate himself from the moment.

Samira saw him, and power walked over to hold them in front of his waist, he looked around, as he moved around to avoid her yet, smiling playfully. His five o'clock shadow failed to hide his blushing tan cheeks. Samira looked around, and made sure Julian couldn't hear her whispers. She grabbed his package through his jeans, when she spoke. "I told you, If you wear my panties, I wo...wo...won't say 'No' to anything you want to do to me. She winked at him with a smile as she blushed, "Anything, Noah." She reiterated.

He barely shied away from her with his arms crossed as she palmed his cock that rested into his left thigh-brow. And bribed him to be emasculated for the hormones it released in her.

He hoped the Security cameras were not following him, but with two beautiful, thick, sexy, and loud BBWs surrounding him with panties, he knew someone was staring.

"Julian, are you nervous about tomorrow." Samira looked up at Julian. She started nodding her head.

"What's tomorrow about, Noey?" Samira asked him letting go of her Boy-toy, and Julian spoke up. Obviously, she could hear them.

"I'm meeting Rachael for lunch to get my files and debriefing, Sammy. Let's make him try them on." Julian said it laughing and sticking her tongue out at Noah. Looking through the panties, she roped her hair into her lips in a flash, and right back to picking panties. Noah was winning Samira over for a Submissive Position to him; one that Julian already had, and wasn't planning on sharing, full time.

She walked over to Samira, and pulled her over to Noah. From his back pocket, she pulled his small spit bottle out, and Julian looked at Samira when she spit in it. Samira blushed at her manly behavior with a big smile, and Samira slapped her on her big butt.

"I love you using that manly stuff. I will try it one of these days with you, Julian." With a serious look on his face, he was still shaking his head to the original statement. Backing away, Noah did not need to try them on.

"Noey, you will try them on here, and Sammy and I will watch." He kept shaking his head and backed away further.

Julian spoke up to bait his guilt, "Noey James, you don't love us anymore? You are never romantic with us anymore. We don't ask for a lot Noey.

Maybe a couple times a day." His expression demonstrated her false declarations.

"Maybe we should get him in a negligee," Julian added. Samira stopped breathing as her eyes lit up the world and her clitoris starting kicking and screaming.

With her entire world stonned, she tried to breath. "REALLY? I would love that... ver...ver...very much, Noey." She just stood there in her fantasy world, holding another pair of panties for her Boyfriend. "OH PLEASE NOEY? I would beg you." Out of nowhere, she curtsied to him.

"Please?" Samira asked, begging. "I have never enjoyed this before, and you can model them for us. Please, Noey? OH PLEASE FOR US? PLEASE DO THIS?"

"NO!" He said with a few steps away from them. "I am required to wear panties under my jeans. I am not required to show them off in public. No. Hell NO! And no nighties, either." He walked away at a very fast pace. His owners though, decided to console their strategy.

After a few minutes of throwing sad and coy expressions at him from afar, they decided he needed another approach.

When they walked over to him, five fresh, new, sexy pair of Women's panties in Samira's hands, they made their stand. Noah kept his arms crossed ready for an argument, in the Men's Dept.

"After very careful considerations, Noey, we have decided you were right. Completely right. However..." Julian looked over at Samira to make sure she was ready. Together, they finished their sentence, "...we have the vaginas, we make the rules." Noah stood his ground smiling at their threat, knowing he was going to lose this battle because, they could easily play with each other's vaginas, and leave him stroking himself in the corner, like a true Cuckold.

Moving his lips around as he hid behind his sunglasses, he stared at both of them and Samira's cleavage. Back and forth. Forth and back. He was trying to find which one was weaker in the moment so he could plead to her...another form of emasculation that turned on both women. He knew, he needed to get them separated.

Julian had different angles to push his buttons, and she knew how to play. Looking around, she pulled the front of her red yoga shorts up, and made sure her large labia jumped out at him, and gently rubbed the contours of her very fat vulva, as she spoke.

"Noey, my Kitty needs some pain. She needs more bruises, and your huge cowboy needs her. She needs him so bad, Baby." She was tossing that seductive tone at him with a bucket. "Let me touch myself for you, right here in public." Samira blushed but didn't run, she was not that public yet. But she blushed while Noah rolled his eyes behind his glasses. Taking glances at Julian's crotch, Samira was thankful Julian wore yoga shorts. Just seeing her bulging labia through them, made her tingle.

Noah must be dying inside, Samira thought, because it would work on her.

Samira spoke up with her inexperience's, "Anything light colored, and her Cowgirl va-jay-jay would be much more noticeable." Subtly, she pulled out her vagina wedge to hide her precious contours.

Samira looked around again as the two stood-off, and all their mouths watering at her public display. Samira offered something, "If you try them on, I will need some of that rough loving, Noey.

Maybe my Venus Mound needs a bruise." Noah quickly looked at her, but Julian looked at her faster.

The bait was delicious, as he nibbled on it, and Samira offered a condiment to his meal, "Be the sexy man that wears Women's panties for us..." Her voice got real low, and meek as she loosened her empowerment for him, "...and owns our pleasures." Samira looked around and stopped herself from begging. It was beneath her, unless he was beneath her, in bed. She was actually thinking of flashing her vagina at him. After a quick second-thought, she was right. She couldn't do it.

Noah shifted his weight shaking his head, and stood fast with a growing erection taking the blood from his noggin. Julian could read him much faster, and as she stepped up to him, she quickly tossed her hair over his shoulder, and leaned up on her Corral Red Birds & Flowers Embroidery Western Cowgirl boots tips, and kissed him, and made an offer in a her raspy seductive whisper. "Samira will suck your cock...like I do. HERE!"

He busted into a huge smile, and his lips shook as he tried to fight back his excitement. Samira jumped in when she heard her offer, "NO I WON'T! I am not do...do...doing that here. Julian, I don...don....I CAN'T DO THAT- " Julian cut her off.

"You told me you the other day you wanted to learn to suck cock the way I do it for him. I'm tryin' to help ya here, Girlfriend." Julian quickly kissed her and shoved her back. "Command him, remember?" Julian turned and stared at him with her short-stuff big boobs puffed out in front of her to keep the stand-off active.

Samira was shaking her head at Julian. "I CAN'T DO THAT! I'VE NEVER sucked one

before...not...not...not a real one. NOT IN PUBLIC!
Samira was looking in every direction, as fast as she
could and giggling from her nerves. She was game
for play, but not sucking him off in public.

The brave wife reached down into her shorts
fingering herself, and both wet fingers came out and
she went slowly to make sure he saw her wetness,
and tasted it, seductively. Samira covered her face,
and peaked. Without looking around, she fingered
herself again, and offered it to Samira who looked
around before licking her fingers as fast as possible,
and covering her face again.

As a woman with a cart strolled by, Samira
put her hand over her heart as it raced, and tried to
look the other way, as if nothing was going on.
Julian's public seed, was making her tingler burn, as
Julian fingered herself again without concern for
publicity, and tasted herself again.

"What is with you Cowfolk? Always a battle."

"Noah James. I will hold Samira down for you
in the truck, and you can do whatever to her. If you
try them on for us in the dressin' room."

"WHAT? HELL NO JULIAN! HELL NO!" Samira
crossed her arms and shuffled her legs, humming,
"HUH UH! NOT GOING TO HAPPEN!"

Julian could read that he was getting looser,
and she glanced at Samira to see if she was reading
it. She was still crossing arms and reassuring herself
it wasn't going to happen."

"You make out with me in the truck Samira,
why not Noah?" As her smile crossed her face with
her blushing, Samira rolled her head away to keep
Noah from judging her, and stuffed her hair into her
own mouth and sucked on it.

Before he made his offer, he looked around
rubbing his face in avowal, and pulled Samira closer

by her blouse that matched his wife' shirt, "I want to both of you, in a public place, with people watching us...and..." He looked at Samira..."We get to video tape it." Samira immediately lost her power, by tossing her head back and her arms into the air, and stomping the floor as she marched in a circle a couple times. The stomping didn't have much effect, other than letting out her sexual frustration from feeling her empowerment get pawned.

"Deal." His wife said as she sold Samira out. Quickly, she adjusted her labia sticking to her inner thighs, and smiled at Samira boldly. "Command him in public, Girlfriend. You have that right."

"JULIAN? I can't do that. I...I....I..I-" Samira's Girlfriend reached up and yanked her down by her hair, and kissed her on the lips. Samira stormed away blushing, aroused, excited, but not wanting anyone to know. Especially, Noah. She was not the type of girl those words stuck to...but them sticking to her, was something different.

Samira and Noah followed the wife back to the back of the store holding hands. Both of them watched Julian's Texas size ass with a perfect shape, and perfect shake. Each cheek held firm as the other quickly dropped, and then they switched.

"That shake...That Texas ass...that gigantic, perfect wiggling ass, the size of Texas ass, whips me silly." He said to Samira, as she clung to his hands, since fear had frozen her extremities.

"So you're an ass man?" Samira said to him, and owning it, he nodded to her with a smile.

"So am I, Noah." He looked down at her. He was not expecting that, and she smiled really big at Julian's shaking butt.

311

"That big Texas ass is mine, Noah." She looked up at him, and he was not comfortable in the ass sharing. "I have a big ass, Noey." She learned, she practiced, and she just baited her man.

"I love your ass, Samira. Big and dark and purrrrrfect."

"Good." She said, "Because you're going to be kissing it, to get some of that savoring Texas ass from now on." He immediately stopped and turned her to face him, and she smiled with a wink. Slowly, he began to smile.

"I hope so Samira. I hope so." As they locked their fingers together holding hands, as they worked to catch Julian.

An Associate was waiting to count the pieces and offer her assistance. "Sam." Noah whispered to her, and she refused to answer him.

"SAM!" And Samira just ignored him.

Noah reached over and grabbed Samira, and turned her to him. "Can I kiss it now? The sign says Women's Dressing Room." He nudged her, and gave a big smile, knowing he was getting out of the modeling gig, and his anxieties floated away as his smile drew wider. He was elated as he stood holding her hand and waiting.

Samira watched Julian rock back and forth, as she chewed on her nails, and it was a little different. Samira smiled as the manly behavior enticed her. She knew Julian was doing it just to arouse her. Samira whispered to Julian as she bounced back and forth on her boots. Julian leaned over and spit brown Copenhagen Tobacco juice into the trash can in front of the counter, and waited for the Associate to finish.

Samira rolled her eyes and smiled as Julian manned up for her. This behavior was extreme

Tomboy, and Samira loved how it made her feel, like the Feminine Woman in their relationship.

"No enter. No enter. No men allowed." Noah was saying under his breath.

Samira whispered back at him, "Shut up. We have to try this for Julian. She is insecure about her breasts scars, and told me she needed to show them in public to build up her confidence, again." Samira watched the Associate, from behind Julian.

"Sir, you can't go in there. These are for Women only." He stopped, smiling really big with appreciation at Samira, and Julian turned to glance at him his smile.

"Of course. I'm sorry." He said thankfully.

His wife spoke up with a raspy, deep voice, "I'm his...his...his owner, and he ain't hangin' out...out...out here with you sk...skin...skinny Bitches." She looked at Noah seriously, and then looked at Samira next to him with an unsure glance, and back to the Associate.

The Associate smiled nervously, and didn't really buy into it, and Samira spoke up, "He...he...he...he is trying out his Transgender Identity, and chose to shop he...he...here as a Woman. Are you telling me he is allowed in the women's bathroom, and not...not..." she pointed at the dressing room, "...not the women's dressing rooms? Obama made it a law for a reason." Rolling her eyes, the Associate politely opened the door, and let them in with a smile.

Julian, led them to the stall farthest from the door and was already pulling her shirt off before she got to it. Noah was smiling excitedly, and Samira was already making an exit strategy, and trying to hide her nervous induced giggles.

When they walked into it, the Julian stepped up on the bench, and immediately began kissing Noah and aggressively unbuckling his rodeo belt. She was only about two-inches shorter than him now. He put his around her waist to keep her from falling, and Samira continued to look around as she stood at the stall door...guarding, even though the stalls only came up to her shoulders. He mind was set. Her clothes were not coming off.

Julian, jerked Noah over to her by his redneck, and was giggling as he smacked her face playfully, as she kissed him. In the middle of the kiss, she slapped him back as her hands fondled his package.

Julian dropped to her knees on the floor, and tugged on his boots, he lifted his foot, and Samira pushed on his back to keep him from getting on her. She was laughing, but not participating. Quickly, she crossed her chest to hide her hands under her arm pits.

Julian spun him around facing Samira, and he lifted his other boot for her to remove. His smile was alarming to Samira who kept dodging it, until she saw his pretty red cotton panties, had a bulge in the front, and Julian pulled his jeans down. The bulge seemed to be calling Samira, and when her mouth watered, she knew she had to have just a little taste. Just to tell no one about it.

Keeping on her knees, Julian kicked his boots under the bench, and opened her mouth as she turned him around, tore down his panties, and sucked his cock like a champion. Samira looked around, and peaked around to watch, as her hand felt his rock hard, ass.

"This is stupid. We are going to jail. I am going to jail. My mother is going to kill me. AND

314

FOR A WHITE GUY!" Samira said in protest, as she felt left out. Glancing about, she reached around, and stroked Noah's cock as Julian sucked on it. Her pussy instantly started to think for her, as the desires got stronger than her fears. She stepped up to his rear, and began humping him. Her senses exploded on her as she went through the motions, and let go of his cock for his hips, and she thrusted him with her imaginary strap-on. She couldn't stop the fantasy that began burning her clitoris like warm, creamy cum on it. She had never pegged a man before, but plenty of women had moaned her name during her pegging fetish.

His women worked him rough until his penis stood at attention for their needs, and his wife rushed up to her feet on the bench, and finished undressing, and kicking her boots off. Samira looked up at him anxiously while thrusted her hips into his rear. She knew Julian wore boots every time they made love, and wanted to see if it shocked him.

Julian tugged at Samira's blouse as she bobbed on Noah's stiff cock, and Samira bent over let her pull it off. Her arms rushed to cover her boobs, and backed away from Noah, as Julian reached for them but, got a hold of her yoga waist-band instead. When she tried to pull her yoga pants down, Samira stopped her laughing and pleading.

With manly force, Julian jerked Samira to her and buried her face in her camel toe, and trying to bite it. Samira jerked back laughing, still covering her breasts with her arm, and stumbling into the mirror. Julian did not lay in haste, as Noah grabbed Samira, Julian pulled them down to expose her pretty, and extremely wet, dark pussy.

Samira began yelling without trying to yell as she choked on her laughter. Julian licked into her

315

wetness on her knees as she palmed both of Samira's Black butt cheeks. Noah reached around and shoved Julian's head into Samira's crotch as Samira accidently pushed her hips forward and spread her legs apart. Samira reached around and palmed Noah's ass, and enjoyed what she wished she could do to him. Still covering her boobs with her arm, she succumb to the pleasures of semi-public sex, and grabbed Noah by his thick, hard cock, and stroked him beside her.

"OH! OH! YES! EAT ME JULIAN! EAT ME!" Samira moaned out as Noah put his hand around the front of her throat and held her, and his other hand palmed her ass. Slowly, her chin lifted, and everyone could hear the wetness of her arousal splashing across Julian soaked face. As the sensations got near the point of no return, Samira dropped his cock, and grabbed Julian's head, and fucked her face.

As hard and fast as Julian licked her throbbing clit, it didn't take long for Samira to moan her body into Noah for support. His hand slid down her chest, and stopped in the center as her pleasure raced toward orgasm, and Vulnerability. Julian did not let up as she pugnaciously licked her clitoris, paying close attention as Samira began to shake. As Samira's knees gave way, his wife jerked her head away, and stopped her orgasm, as she wiped Samira's seed along her arm. Oddly, Samira liked seeing that but, hated being denied.

"Get my ha...ha...ha...hairbrush out of m...m...m...my purse." Looking around, Samira rushed to get it before another Woman or a Man, Identifying as a Woman, came in to try on an outfit. Julian sucked on his cock until she got the brush from Samira. "Lay...lay...lay on the floor, now. I'm gonna' bust your Phoenix."

He smiled really big, as he picked up on her terminology, and didn't argue, and being the space was tight, the Women stepped aside and gave room. Julian pushed him down impatiently after he got on his knees. Samira immediately pulled her thong, and pants back up, and looked at the door to make a decision. But the Wife, waved to her to come down to Noah's dick, and sucked him up and down a few times, until Samira pushed her out of the way, and slid the head deep in her throat. She finally did it, in a semi-public place. The first ever real cock in her mouth, and she went for broke.

"Hurry up. We got to b...b...bust his Phoenix." Julian said, slapping herself in the face with it as she got it back in her mouth.

Waiting her turn, Samira tried to listen over Noah's moans, and shushed him, and slapped his inner thigh. Julian slammed her hand into his ball sack, and abused it.

Samira's eyes widened as she saw her, physically-sexually abusing him, for the first time. Julian grabbed the brush from Samira, and with the flat backside, quickly smacked his balls with it making him jerked, and moan instantly.

Samira's eyes got really big at the intense abuse response he offered sounding just like pleasure. Her expression was excitement as she watched his face in pain, but she was certainly shocked, and realizing everything she knew about pleasing men, might be lacking some details.

Julian grabbed his sack without mercy, and pulled it up his long shaft as far as at could go. His balls pushed through his sack at the bottom, which was now stretching upward towards the ceiling.

317

Samira watched as Julian smiled at her with a hint of evil in her blue eyes, as she touched each one gently with the back of the brush. Julian leaned down and licked each testicle, leaving them wet. Samira then tried to suck his cock, and Noah pushed her away.

With all the empowerment she needed, she slapped his nuts with it, and then pointed out he was leaking semen already. Samira rushed to lick his dick, and stole Julian's seed. She felt obligated to Julian, and wanted to maintain her Onan rule. Smiling at Samira, she offered a kiss, and Julian kissed her.

"Beat his balls until he...he...he...he can't stand it, and keep beating them for him. You are beat him when you please him." Samira nodded gleefully watching and listening. This was good, secret man stuff.

"Hold his dick back on his belly don't st...st...st...str...stroke him at all. Never stroke him when you beat his balls. Pun...pun...punish him. Beat his balls with the back of the brush as hard as you can. He loves the pain. Men n...n...need the pain." Julian gestured toward Noah, and told her. "Get up on him, and use your knees to hold his arms down watch me."

She smacked his balls at a slow pace to stop his mind from reacting to Samira getting on top of him. Each smack he seeped out of the tip of his cock. When she got him pinned, she felt the wetness on her thong, and smiled at Julian as she held him down.

Bending his cock back, Julian began spanking his protruding balls, and Samira watched his dick as it pulsated and flexed. The tingles turned to burn as she felt the amazing rush of arousal striking her wet

318

loins. His sounds were certainly the sounds of pleasure and severe pain.

"Work up the pace, do not go too fa...fa...fast or he'll just cum a small amount. Pace it and torture him longer, and find his Phoenix." Samira was nodding with a big smile on her face. With each pounding, his face slammed into her ass making her laugh with stimulation.

"Slowly beat your men for at least ten...ten...ten minutes before you fly his Phoenix. Black guys are the same way. Punish him for being a man by taking yo...yo...your time, and make sure to spank them really hard. When he gets close, punish his balls by hitting harder but, slower. It will drag out his pain to give the Phoenix. If he comes early on you, beat them as hard as you can and fast."

Julian handed her the brush, and got up to switch places. Samira got on his legs, and Julian tossed her leg over his face, and pulled her labia apart, and delicately lowered herself onto his nose and mouth. He tried to use his hands, and she put them under her knees. His breathing was now dependent on her pussy's generosity.

"Eat me, Taylor Boy. I loves it." Julian said, looking up at Samira, she was sucking his dick all by herself, for the first time. The Wife smiled, feeling proud of her. She went back to grinding her wetness into Noah's face, and making sure he smothered, and heard the brush smack, and Noah jerked his face up into her labia, soaking it more, and pleasing Julian.

"Who wears the panties, Taylor? Who wears them now?" She smiled rapaciously, and pulled her hair around so it would sit between her ass cheeks, and smother him more.

Samira beat his nuts as she held his dick back on his belly. She struggled not to masturbate. This was a huge turn-on that she didn't know about. Abusing her man, was only going to get better. Julian slid her feet out under the stall door, and buried her soaked, pulsing, vulva on his face.

"Eat it, Taylor Boy. Who wears the panties now?" She started laughing as he struggled to breath, and Samira beat his balls with the brush.

I have never heard Julian call him that, she thought, as she began beating his balls with the brush.

Julian got louder and meaner, as she tried barking, "DON'T TOUCH ME! I don't want to feel your hands on me, TAYLOR!" She jerked her weight down on his face to get her point across and grabbed his wrist, and pinned them to the floor. Noah willfully submitted again, and desperately tried to make her cum before he suffocated or drown. Samira nervously went back to holding his bag up on his shaft, and with each spanking, he jerked, and screamed his face into Julian's mean pussy.

Samira quickly stopped, and had to finger her clitoris through her pants. Her clit hurt as bad as Noah's balls. Julian leaped forward, letting him panic-breath, and avoided the string of his cum, dangling off the head of his dick.

Rachael slid the glass door open, smiling, and slammed it shut. The trucks were not in the driveway, so she felt safe to creep. Slowly, she worked her way upstairs listening for sounds of anyone and making sure her backpack, on her chest, didn't rub against anything. Getting to the top of the stairs, she pulled out her 9mm pistol. She crept through the kitchen and pulled out Julian's medicine bottles from her backpack, and walked over to the fridge. She took out Julian's new medicine bottles, and opened each one as she poured the older, and different, prescription into them.

She kept listening for anyone, and only heard the central air blowing. Smiling, she poured the last of the old pills on top of the new ones in the last bottle, and put them back on the fridge. Her devilish smile glowed with her success. When she opened the fridge, she saw a chalice of Noah seed, and offered it a disgusting look.

"She is one OCD, mentally ill, Bitch." She whispered, as she left her a bakery paper bag with her favorite brownie in it, in front of the chalice, and a grin to go with it.

She took her backpack with her as she walked to the stairs to listen, before tiptoeing up to the bedroom. Seeing that it was not occupied by her former lover and her personal rapist, she grinned as she moseyed into the room doing her victory walk, and dropped her backpack on the bed, and listened for anyone, again before tossing herself onto the bed.

Noah was bucking from suffocation as Samira beat his balls. She wondered if the ten minutes were up, and if cameras were enjoying the scene before they were arrested. Julian jerked forward letting him have the lifesaving oxygen he needed. Listening to him struggle, she laughed at his demise.

"How's it ta...tas....tasting back there? We want your Phoenix? Lick my ass hole, Taylor, and you might give it up real quick?"

His murdered brain cells were busy gasping, as he gasped over and over without complaining.

She looked back to monitor the real fear level in his eyes. It was wonderfully exciting to her.

"Next time you can fly your Phoenix faster. Don't tease me...me...me. EAT MY PUSSY AND LICK THAT ASS BOY!" Noah was really struggling and Samira, being so inexperienced, just kept up to holding his dick and abusing his balls at that slow beating pace. Each spank was loud and painful, and thick semen strung from the tip of his penis onto is stomach. Each time she glanced at it, it took her breath away.

Julian was still laughing, using every pound of her one hundred and seventy-five, to smother him. His hands came roaring up, and she fought them outward, as she laughed harder. His face was red as his eyes flickered in panic, and wiggled on his face, and he heaved her off of him into Samira. Julian busted up laughing as she knocked Samira backwards onto her ass, and as he huffed to breathe. In severe pain, rolled himself in the fetal positon holding his nuts, and heaving.

Samira rushed to his cock, and used her fingers to pick of his string of seed, and held it up for Julian to suck. Julian's response was not what it should have been. Her disgusted look on her face grew as she shook her head.

"Don't put that shit on me." Julian said.

Samira quickly stood up in confusion, as her clitoris decided kept knocking.

"Julian, this is his seed. You need it." She gestured toward her with it, and Julian raised her eyebrows and frowned at it.

"I don't ne...ne...ne...need it. I like popping guys off" Shaking her head at Samira, "I ain't drinking them." Samira's eyes just got bigger, and

322

she looked at the semen on her fingers, and down to Noah still in immense pain.

"OH NO!" She looked at Julian, and slowly sucked the seed off of her fingers, as Julian demonstrated her disgust for it. If anything, she was covering for her, in the moment of confusion.

As the warm, and very sweet cum scent lifted to the roof of her mouth, her tongue tingled, and surprised her. As the tingling spread, she inhaled the fragrance and felt herself tingle without fear, again. It clung to the roof of her mouth, and she wallowed her tongue around in it slowly, amazed at the thickness and purity that it felt inside her mouth. With regret, her saliva pulled it to the back of her throat, and she swallowed him.

"OH MY! THAT WAS PURE!" She said to Julian.

Rachael laid on Julian's bed and smelled her pillow, and looked over at the dirty laundry basket. She quickly got up, and pulled her blouse off, and dug through them finding a pair of Julian's dirty jeans. As she sat back on the bed, she smelled the crotch, and smiled as she rolled her head backwards letting her eyes flutter, and sharing a smile. It was the pheromones she longed for.

She rested on the bed, and hugged the jeans against her bare chest, and began rubbing herself under her loose jeans. She started to cry moaning out for Emily, as she pleasured herself for the woman she controlled, and loved. "I love you, Emily." She said it as four fingers pushed her clitoris in circles.

Samira looked down at Noah, as he struggled to jerk himself off. She smiled at him to laugh until she saw the amount of real pain on his face. He looked injured. Looking back at Julian, she squatted down and rolled him over. He was in tears as he clumsily stroked himself.

"Stop jerking off, Noey. Relax." She said chuckling at him and feeling the emasculation of saying it.

Struggling to speak, he told her. "I can't. It's backed up inside. I'm blocked. Help me." He grunted as he barely got himself stroked.

Samira looked back up to Julian for help, and Julian told her. "I don't drink that shit."

Samira looked back at his face, as he struggled to unclog his pipe, and Samira took charge of her man. She pushed his hand away, and stroked him hard, as he winced repeatedly. She looked back up at Julian watching her lay back on the bench and began masturbating herself. The Julian problem was occupied for the moment.

Noah began moaning as he finally spoke. Both his hands held his testicle as she jerked him.

"OH FUCK! OH FUCK! HARDER! HARDER!"

In her shaking voice, "Are you cumming Noey?" He was pounding his head up and down as he winced in severe pain.

Samira rushed to her knees, and put her mouth on his cock, just as he screamed his load into her mouth. She rushed up and down on his cock with her mouth and hand, as each full load shot to the roof of her mouth, and deep into her throat. To keep from gagging, she kept stopping to swallow, and kept listing to his awful girly-scream.

He shot more and more into her mouth lighting fire all the way through her labia, and heard Julian moaning her orgasm, as she slid on the bench, and fingered herself her wet, hole to happiness.

After about the fifteenth load into her mouth, she watched him fade into Vulnerability, and quickly put her hand over his heart, as his dick still pulsated with small squirts.

She reached over and grabbed Julian's left tit as she shook into her orgasm, and kept her hand on Noah's heart, and his dick in her mouth. She needed to masturbate now. Julian rolled her head around in Vulnerability, and finally looked at Samira.

Samira glanced back at Noah, and got up swallowing the last of his Vitamins.

"What the hell Jul-" She stopped herself, as Noah's male brain took longer to reboot.

With a serioius look in her eyes, she stared at Julian and asked her, "Who the hell are you, Emily?"

She was breathing off her reward when she shook her head, and spoke.

"No. My na...na...na...name is..."

In the next Book:

Submission is Natural, When Desires Burn

When Julian, Jordan, Emily, Arizona, Andrea,

Rachael, Noah, Samira, and Theresa, Meet

Lady Savannah, Samuel, Chadley, Momma &

Emily, Mr. Beauchamp, and Saddle

Comanchero.

Chasing Her Fetishes

Submission is Natural, when Desires Burn

From the Life of

K.K. Foster

Buy it today at Amazon.com